TRUER

BEAUTY

by

Jean Jegel

Published by Emery Press at CreateSpace

ISBN: 978-1732411906

Discover other titles by Jean Jegel at jeanjegel.com

This book is a work of fiction. Any references to historical events, real people, or real places are used fictitiously. Other names, characters, places and events are products of the author's imagination, and any resemblance to actual events or places or persons, living or dead, is entirely coincidental.

Scripture taken from the New King James Version®. Copyright ©1982 by Thomas Nelson, Inc. Used by permission. All rights reserved.

Cover by Dave Simmons

To Carl
For letting me be me

Chapter One

"Move!"

Hannah opened her eyes to find her older sister, Lucy, climbing into the back seat of Hollis Rumsford's used, black, 1929 Model A Ford, four-door sedan. Clutching her knapsack tightly to her chest, Hannah slid across the seat. Since she could no longer avoid sight of her childhood home by closing her eyes, Hannah turned her gaze to the side window.

She stared between trees down the hill at Placerville, the only home she ever knew. The small mining town lay at an important crossroads. Only ten miles south of Sutter's Mill where the gold rush began, it was home to the first California state highway. The road ensured Placerville was unlikely to become a ghost town even in the current depression. It was the main route over the Sierras through South Lake Tahoe and all points east. Hannah deeply inhaled crisp, pine-scented air as if it were her last breath.

"Why'd you come out here so fast?" demanded Lucy. "It's freezing."

"I'm ready to leave, that's all." Hannah stole a

glance at her sister, who was furiously rubbing her hands together in an effort to stay warm. Lucy was the firstborn child, a worldly girl disinterested in the academia that fascinated Hannah. With her raven hair and gray eyes, Lucy always garnered the attention due a true beauty. "You didn't come out here to sit with me. Why don't you go back inside?" Hannah asked.

"Aren't we cheeky this morning. What's got into you, Miss Mousey?"

Hannah cringed at Lucy's criticism of her personality. Even Father called Hannah his little mouse but she considered that a term of endearment. In truth, Hannah often felt lost in their family—not pretty like Lucy, not fun-loving like her brothers, not as needy as the two youngest Granvilles.

Hannah caught her reflection in the window. Big green eyes, probably her best feature, pooled with tears. Her curly, light brown hair escaped beneath a green knit beret. She cut her hair at shoulder length, secured the top with bobby pins and allowed the bottom to curl naturally. Unruly hair caused countless hours of distress until current hairstyles became popular.

"You aren't going to cry, are you?" Lucy asked. "You're 18. Don't act like a baby!"

Hannah heaved a sigh, wondering how she failed to hide her feelings this time. Mustering her composure, Hannah turned to face Lucy and evenly replied, "Go back in the house if you're cold."

"No, I'm not going to do that. I'll sit here and freeze with you. It's better than watching Rumsfords issue dramatic farewells. Those people make me sick. I can't wait to get out of this Podunk town. I'd tell you this was all your fault, and it is; but I've been trying to find a way to leave. Now, I'm going. So, thank you, Miss Mousey."

Believing her sister's behavior was a primary reason they were being shipped out of town, Hannah asked, "How is this my fault?"

Lucy rolled her eyes. "You're the only one who could have stopped Father and you didn't do a damn thing about it. We're all in this mess because of you."

It was true, Hannah was the last person to see him alive. Not a day went by that Hannah failed to condemn herself, wondering if she missed some clue of his intentions. Father did not seem tense or upset.

She would always remember how the sunlight from the window backlit his head, making the silver in his hair gleam. His warm brown eyes were no less merry; his smile no less earnest.

It was the stock market crash of 1929 that caused Father's suicide. Knowing his in-laws refused further funding, he made careful investments only to have the market crash days later. Unable to face his wife's wrath, Father pulled a gun from the drawer and fired a bullet under his chin as he sat at his desk. Headlines from the newspaper sprawled across the desktop served as the final punctuation of Aloysius Granville's life.

This unfortunate turn of events devastated the Granville family. Mother, overcome with problems, monetary and otherwise, was bustled off to a wealthy aunt's house in Chicago after the funeral. Younger Granville children were placed with various relatives across the country. Having nowhere to go, Lucy and Hannah ended up at the Rumsfords, their next-door neighbors. It seemed a lifetime since Hannah had her own home and family. At this moment, she wanted nothing more than to avoid Lucy's scrutiny.

"I imagined you'd sit in front with your suitors," Hannah suggested in an attempt to coerce her sister from the back seat.

"That's what I'd prefer. Aunt Bitsy is getting her marching orders so I don't expect to enjoy our journey."

Hannah could not imagine what Bitsy might do to rein in her sister's errant behavior. Lucy played the Rumsford brothers against each other much like a cat tormented a mouse. The two smitten boys did not seem to care. Bitsy, though only slightly older than her nephews, was afforded the respect due an aunt. Lucy held no such respect.

"Where *are* they?" Lucy was clearly short on patience.

"How can you be in a hurry to leave? Aren't you concerned about what will become of us? At least we had a place to live here."

"Working in a boarding house is not my idea of living. I know you were happy but I was always more ambitious than you."

"That's funny. I can't remember you ever putting in a day's work. I wouldn't call that ambition," noted Hannah.

"Were you planning on working your way to fame and fortune living in the Rumsford attic? All you'd ever get is room and board and time to read your precious books. I was not cut out for menial labor."

"So, you left the work to me while you flirted your way through every man in Placerville."

"What's gotten into you today?"

As was her custom, Hannah backed down. "Nothing," she replied. As time went on, Hannah's initial melancholy over Father's death evaporated into a quiet anger. Her family was gone, never to be reunited. Her dreams of higher education dissolved. Her undeniable crush on Hollis Rumsford, who only had eyes for Lucy, served to intensify the hostility Hannah harbored for her elder sibling.

"Did you remember to thank Mrs. Rumsford before you left?" asked Hannah, knowing the next-door neighbors were not the cream of society Mother and Lucy sought to cultivate.

"Thank her for what? Kicking me out?"

"For giving you a home. What would we have done without them?"

"Something else. Who cares? I'm about to get my chance if those people would say goodbye and get on with it."

"We owe a debt to the Rumsfords," assured Hannah.

"Piddle. Mrs. Rumsford got plenty for her lousy attic space—help with housekeeping, cooking and laundry. You'll never learn, Hannah. You'll end up living in someone else's attic, mark my words. The Rumsfords are not the type of people we need to be concerned with."

"What is that supposed to mean?"

"Mr. Rumsford sells farm equipment. He's gone more than he's home. When all but Hollis and Dock moved on, Mrs. Rumsford turned that lovely home into a boarding house, of all things. You'd never see Mother do something like that. They're very common people."

"That didn't stop you from chasing after Hollis and Dock."

"I never chased after them. I can't help it if they find me charming."

"Not charming enough to marry you. I seem to recall there were no proposals when the bank foreclosed on our house. Wasn't that your plan all along—marry some innocent rube who could support you in the manner you imagine you deserve?"

"You're wrong. There were plenty of proposals."

"Then how did you end up in the Rumsford's attic

with me?"

Lucy looked on her sister as an ignorant and innocent girl, basically a thorn in her side and too inexperienced to be taken seriously. "A girl has to use discretion when selecting a husband. There are financial aspects to marriage I doubt you understand. I'm not going to wind up like mother—with a houseful of children, begging money from relatives."

"Especially since you haven't any relatives to beg from," sniped Hannah. "Maybe you're too headstrong and opinionated to ever catch a husband." Hannah found her sister's ideas about men both fascinating and appalling. Lucy took up with any man who could pay her way—no small feat in these desperate times.

"You're simply jealous because I'm pretty and you're not." Certain she'd struck a nerve, Lucy displayed a smug smile.

The discussion came to an abrupt conclusion as Aunt Bitsy, playing chaperone, climbed into the back seat. The two Rumsford brothers settled in front.

Hannah was on her way to an uncertain future. Suddenly desperate to fix the picture of her childhood home in her memory, she turned in her seat to watch the blue and yellow Victorian house fade into the distance and disappear from sight.

Imagining this could be the adventure of a lifetime, Hannah tried to put a good face on her journey. But when the familiar Sierras gave way to flat and barren terrain, a severe case of homesickness overwhelmed her.

* * *

As Hollis' Model A bumped along the highway, Hannah considered the events that resulted in her current exodus from Placerville.

After dinner last week, Mrs. Rumsford asked to meet Hannah at the kitchen table. They often discussed household projects over a cup of tea. But when she entered, Hannah was amazed to find the Rumsford brothers and Aunt Bitsy already seated around the large table. Hannah quietly took a chair. Before she could inquire about the nature of the meeting, Lucy entered and took her own seat.

Hannah noted the Rumsford brothers' expressions. They might be surprised to be invited to this impromptu meeting but they were no less appreciative of Lucy's presence. Hannah imagined the boys might actually drool, they appeared so idiotic in their admiration.

Her heart gave a flutter as she observed the youthful Mr. Rumsford, the ideal of all Hannah's girlish dreams. He was tall, fit from working in the mines, with dark hair and friendly brown eyes. No movie star held the appeal of the flesh-and-blood, 22-year-old Hollis Rumsford seated across the table.

Although Dock was as tall as his older brother, having the same dark hair and brown eyes, his features didn't align in a pleasing manner. Perhaps his nose was too hawkish, his brows too thick or his chin too weak. Hannah knew Dock—they attended school together. He was the obnoxious older boy who pulled the girls' braids, never failing to harass them.

It was Dock who broke the silence.

"So, Lucy, how about you and me snuggle up tonight? It's plenty cold. Let me sweet-talk you into a little smooch."

"We'll have none of that," commented a serious Mrs. Rumsford, having overheard Dock's comment as she entered the kitchen. "I'll box your ears, Dock Rumsford, if I hear so much as another word out of you."

"Yes, ma'am." Dock's proper response was laced with a lascivious grin in Lucy's direction. Lucy returned

Dock's comment with her practiced, coy smile.

Mrs. Rumsford's sense of humor was what kept Hannah going through the dark days of the past two years but this novel meeting held no trace of comedy.

"I called you here to address several family issues that also concern Lucy and Hannah," began Mrs. Rumsford.

"We're sorry, Ma. We won't fight at dinner again," offered a repentant Hollis.

"You most certainly will not. Of all the harebrained things you could do in front of our boarders."

The boys came to physical blows at the dinner table that night, jealous competitors for Lucy's favor. Although the bowl of mashed potatoes was right in front of Lucy's plate, she smiled demurely at the brothers and asked if they might pass the dish.

Too eagerly, Hollis and Dock reached for the bowl, upending it. Dock grabbed Hollis by the shirt collar. Hollis slapped Dock's shoulder to gain release. Soon, the boys fell backward in their chairs, each intent to clobber the other as they rolled about the dining room floor. Naturally, every last resident of the boarding house was in attendance.

Interrupting Hannah's reverie, Mrs. Rumsford continued, "I believe I have a solution that will keep you out of trouble, at least in Placerville. Aunt Bitsy is moving to Santa Barbara for her wedding next month. I'm tired of listening to her fret about the train ride. It's a safe way to travel, Bitsy. I don't understand why it bothers you so.

"I'm weary of badgering you boys to get another job. After all, your grandfather died from black lung disease. I want you out of the mines." Mrs. Rumsford removed a teabag from her cup.

"Last, but not least, the large Cropton family is

about to be turned out of their home by the bank, Mr. Cropton having lost his job. Mrs. Cropton is my dearest friend on earth. I am dedicated to helping that family any way I can.

"I've come to realize this complex series of events provides the answer to my prayers." Mrs. Rumsford paused for dramatic affect. Even Lucy seemed to be paying attention.

"I am putting my problems in a car and sending them to the coast. It's time my sons left the nest. You boys will deliver your Aunt Bitsy to her in-laws by way of Hollis' automobile while easing my own anxiety. There are job opportunities in Santa Barbara. You can find work above ground. If you choose to fight at a dinner table, it will no longer be mine. Your room will be let out for additional income. After all, your father and I are not getting any younger. We need to make the most of the opportunity our large home provides.

"Aunt Bitsy's room has been promised to a gentleman currently staying at a hotel on Main Street. Lodging, albeit cramped, for the Croptons and their 12 children will be found in our attic.

"A change of venue will open a whole new field of admirers for you, Lucy. I never believed you had any real interest in either of my sons. I'm certain they provided you with a distraction but I imagine you'll find new beaus in Santa Barbara."

Hannah almost laughed at the boys' incredulous expressions, stupefied at their mother's accurate deductions. Lucy remained silent; her reaction was hard to read but Hannah knew she would jump at any chance to leave Placerville.

Mrs. Rumsford reached over to pat Hannah's hand and continued, "Of course, that also means Hannah must go. Don't look so broken-hearted, dear. I believe this is best. There is more to life than working in a boarding house without a future. Life is waiting for you, Hannah: friends and adventures. A fresh start is exactly what you need. I will miss you terribly. You've been such a help. I can only hope Mrs. Cropton will be half the worker you have been." Hannah was singled out for her praiseworthy efforts, a deliberate slight to Lucy's meager contributions. But Lucy only thought her sister stupid and easily manipulated.

There were two people who made living in the Rumsford home bearable for Hannah. Proximity to Hollis Rumsford, her ideal man, served to fuel Hannah's imagination. In her daydreams, Hollis pursued her relentlessly, much as he pursued Lucy in reality. Something as mundane as pinning his shirt to the clothesline set her pulse racing.

Mrs. Rumsford took Hannah under her wing from the day she moved in. She gently guided Hannah through her chores and was always appreciative of her efforts. But it was Mrs. Rumsford's oft-repeated and humorous tales of family members, historic and present-day, that brought delight to Hannah's day.

She suddenly recalled the first story, which seemed appropriate to current circumstances. Hannah stood at the kitchen sink, washing lunch dishes, fighting back tears, when Mrs. Rumsford walked beside her and took up a tea towel.

"You don't have to do that. I'll dry the dishes. Lucy isn't feeling well." It would soon become obvious, Lucy was seldom well enough to perform chores. Thinking back, Hannah believed Mrs. Rumsford always knew Lucy would fail to benefit the household.

"Oh, nonsense. Once these are done, you can settle in. I won't need you until around 4. I heard you like to read."

"Yes, that's my favorite pastime."

"You can help yourself to any books in our library. We keep those for boarders. Books come and go, so if there's something you like, best grab it when you see it.

"My brother, Bart, was a bookworm. That boy always had his nose in a book. One day, he was walking in the woods reading, strode clean into the New Weber Ditch and hit his head. Thank goodness, he was near the road. A teamster on his way to Folsom saw him, pulled him out before he could manage to drown and took Bart along. The boy couldn't remember his name or where he lived.

"By nightfall, Mom was in a panic. Nobody knew Bart in Folsom, but the child found a book to read in the sheriff's office and was happy as a clam. They gave him food and he slept on an empty cot. They figured someone would make a claim to him eventually.

"It was three weeks before a neighbor told Mom they saw a notice in the Folsom *Telegraph* about a boy living in the sheriff's office. Mom bustled right over there and flew through the sheriff's door to find Bart sitting on a stool reading.

"'Bartholomew?' she says, about ready to faint. She was certain sure the boy was dead. 'Hi, Mom,' says Bart, as if he left that morning. His memory came back just like that." Mrs. Rumsford snapped her fingers. "Mom was so relieved she didn't even whoop him.

"Funny thing is, Bart had an affinity for Folsom after that. He never strayed from home before, but every time he turned up missing, that's where we found him. Mom got sick of hauling him back, so when he disappeared at 18, she determined not to fetch him again.

"Dad got fed up after nearly a year of listening to her complain so he went to Folsom only to find Bart married with a baby! Dad said he guessed Bart finally found something to do besides read! I guess when a body finds their place in life, that's where they need to be, no matter how they get there."

Hannah hoped she was on the way to find her own place in life.

Chapter Two

The Rumsford expedition was headed for Fresno. This farming community marked the midpoint of their journey. Mr. Rumsford, who was visiting farmers in an effort to drum up business, planned to meet the Placerville exiles for dinner.

The depression had a devastating effect, even in the golden state of California. Businesses and banks were failing. Farm income fell steadily. Customers for new farm equipment were few and far between. Everyone was trying to make do until times got better.

California was a destination for displaced workers and their families from across the country. Hannah noticed makeshift encampments off the road as Hollis drove ever further from home. Whole families were living in cars and tents. There were poor families in Placerville but Hannah never witnessed poverty of this extreme. She appreciated what a blessing it was to have neighbors you could depend on.

Hollis stopped for gasoline at noon. Aunt Bitsy laid out their picnic under the only tree in sight. She wasted no time taking control of Lucy, who was suddenly fascinated with gassing up an automobile. Hannah understood this was a ploy to avoid helping with lunch but she was surprised Aunt Bitsy was savvy to Lucy's tricks.

"Lucy, come and help."

"I'm learning about automobiles, Aunt Bitsy. Hannah will be glad to help."

"I need you over here, right now."

Lucy's animated expression turned to a deep frown as she ambled toward the picnic site. Hollis and Dock did not attempt to hide their admiration for Lucy's retreating figure.

Hollis had never shown Hannah the slightest interest and her sensible nature told her he never would. Although Hollis' attention was clearly focused on Lucy, Hannah dreamed of a day when he might look adoringly at her. Hannah also helped with lunch while imagining how it would feel to be held in Hollis' arms.

Aunt Bitsy's soon-to-be in-laws were providing initial accommodations in Santa Barbara. Hannah planned to get a job as quickly as possible. Her intent was to part ways with Lucy first chance she got. It seemed likely each of the passengers would go off on their own once they settled in Santa Barbara, except the brothers. A practical Hannah doubted she would ever lay eyes on Hollis again.

Once the boys finished their chore, Lucy hurried to serve their plates. Hannah watched Aunt Bitsy grab Lucy by the ear when she tried to take a seat between the brothers.

"Owww!"

"No, you don't. You will sit here with Hannah and me. I will have none of the goings on you are used to on our current journey."

"I don't know what you're talking about," Lucy proclaimed, all innocence.

"Yes, you do. There will be no flirting, no provocation and no fighting under my watch. This will be the most uneventful journey in the history of our state. I am responsible and we are all getting to Santa Barbara in one piece, if it's the last thing I do. I have a lot at stake and intend to live long enough to see my wedding day." Aunt Bitsy slapped Lucy's arm with her fan and proceeded to wave it in the air as if it were a rapier.

She turned toward her nephews and continued, "Do you both understand?" then opened the fan to cool her face. Although it was winter, the increased temperature in the flatlands was apparently more than Bitsy could tolerate.

"Yes, ma'am," came the joint reply.

"I want to be able to report to your father you have been gentlemen on our journey. Do not disappoint me."

"Yes, ma'am."

Hannah took a quick bite of sandwich to hide her smile.

Their meal was, of necessity, rather quiet. All the young people were afraid to ruffle Aunt Bitsy's feathers. As Bitsy settled the picnic items back in the basket, Lucy excused herself to powder her nose before their journey commenced.

No sooner did she disappear than the man who ran the filling station walked over to his customers. He somehow recognized Aunt Bitsy was in charge.

"Excuse me, ma'am, but I wondered if I might get a picture of the young lady beside my gas pump? I collect photographs to advertise my business. If she's willing, I'd pay her—not much, but something."

Aunt Bitsy peered at an astonished Hannah. "Are

you willing?"

"No, no, ma'am. Not that young lady, the purty one."

"Oh, you mean our Lucy. You'll have to ask her yourself. I'll walk over with you." Apparently, Aunt Bitsy had little trust in Lucy or the gas station man and felt it unwise to leave them to their negotiations unsupervised.

Thankfully, Hannah was slow to answer Aunt Bitsy's question or she might have been embarrassed. She should have known the man didn't want a picture of her. Even so, she did not understand her sister's effect on men, which seemed to go beyond a natural attraction to her beauty.

Lucy agreed to the picture and walked toward the gas pump as the owner prepared his camera. Hannah heard the expression "a woman who drove men wild." Lucy raised her arm over her head and rested it on the pump, spreading her fingers to grasp the corner, then leaned seductively against the machine. She used her other arm to embrace it as if it were a lover. Hannah realized any nice girl would have simply stood next to the pump for a picture. Her observations were abruptly interrupted.

"Hot-damn, Hollis, I never wished I could be a gas pump before," Dock snickered.

Hollis chuckled. "Watch your language there, boy. You don't want Miss Hannah to rat you out to Aunt Bitsy, do you?"

At this comment, Hannah gazed in Hollis' direction. For perhaps the first time in her life, Hollis was actually looking at her, right at her. She felt an uncomfortable rush of blood to her face and was certain her cheeks were a brilliant crimson.

"Look there, Dock, you made the lady blush."

Hollis' gaze was fastened on Hannah, who quickly looked at her hands, folded daintily in her lap.

"Oh, Hannah, don't go bitching to Aunt Bitsy now," urged Dock. "I'm sorry. I forgot you was there."

Desperately wishing she could think up some memorable comment, Hannah simply shook her head and continued to stare helplessly at her hands. Her heart was beating so hard she was certain the two brothers could hear. Finally managing a demure bite of cookie, Hannah was quickly ignored by the young men, who continued their conversation as they headed toward the Model A.

"Do you think Pop will have any money for us tonight?"

"Ma said no. We need to find jobs as quick as we can," Hollis replied as he removed a handkerchief from his pocket. He carefully polished the hood of his beloved automobile, the pride and joy of his life. "Haven't you been saving your money?"

"Not much. You know me, I like to spend it on the ladies."

"You won't ever have enough money to settle down if you don't get serious, Dock. Ma's been threatening to throw us out for over a year. Didn't you believe her?"

"Nope. I thought you were going to ask if we could come back if there ain't no jobs. She always did like you best."

"Yeah, Dock, I'm real good at talking Ma into things. I couldn't even convince her you can't get black lung in a gold mine."

Dock laughed. "That's true enough. Her mind was set on that one for sure."

Hannah lost interest in the conversation. Quickly ignored as she sat quietly on the picnic blanket alone, she acknowledged the filling station owner insulted her. Dock thought her so insignificant, he forgot she was there. Yet, the memory of Hollis' warm brown eyes, locked on her face, brought a smile to her lips. At last, he noticed her.

* * *

Hannah stood when Aunt Bitsy gathered the picnic blanket.

"Let me help you fold that."

"You've always been so considerate, Hannah. My sister is going to miss you."

"I'll miss Mrs. Rumsford, too."

"You've hit some bumps in the road in your young life. How are you handling this latest turn of events?"

"I'll admit, I would have stayed in Placerville if I could."

"Maybe your mother would want you to live with her after all this time. Did you tell her about your move?"

"I'll write once we get settled. I don't believe Mother has recovered sufficiently to take any of us in. She and I were never close."

"I didn't know her well."

"She wasn't a neighborly person. I never wanted to be like her. She was the disciplinarian and source of unhappiness in our household. As I've grown up, I think I understand her better."

Bitsy raised her eyebrows. Mrs. Granville always appeared the epitome of a shrew. "Your father was a real gentleman—so distinguished and handsome."

A proud smile lit Hannah's face. "He always made me feel important. No matter how silly my juvenile distress, I could crawl on his lap knowing he would be sympathetic."

"I can't recall him being anything but cordial. The

man was a pillar of the community, someone whose advice was sought and put to use. You must miss him terribly." Bitsy stopped walking, intent to finish her conversation before they reached the Model A.

"But the truth is, Father was not much of a breadwinner. It might not have looked that way—Mother was intent to keep up appearances. His failures probably caused her vicious moods. She came from money, you see. It's only natural for her to crave the life she was accustomed to. Father was not a skilled man of business and couldn't hold a job. What can a woman do when her husband proves to be a poor provider?"

Hannah bit her lip to prevent further revelations, knowing it was Mother's family who supplied almost all financial support. Father may have been an affable and trustworthy friend to virtually everyone in their small town but when he described himself as "unlucky" in commerce, he was being as kind to himself as he was to others.

"I'm surprised you've taken your mother's side," admitted Bitsy.

"Lucy is the one who provided clarity on this issue. Mother and Lucy were always close. I know she resents our situation and blames Father—when she's not blaming me. But her comments caused me to reconsider Mother's problems."

"I'd be careful before taking advice or opinions from Lucy. I'm sorry. I know she's your sister but that one's out for herself. I have nothing but pity for anyone who stands in her way." Bitsy proceeded to the car, leaving an intrigued Hannah staring after her.

* * *

The remainder of the journey to Fresno was as quiet as the beginning, at least in the back seat. Lucy gave her sister a condescending smirk as she dropped her earnings in her dress pocket but the girls refrained from conversation, to Aunt Bitsy's delight.

Hannah noticed male relationships were different than women's. At school, it seemed the female sex tended to cling to perceived injustice—perhaps forgiving but never forgetting. She and Lucy were at odds what seemed forever but particularly since they moved into the Rumsford attic. Their relationship never wavered from acrimony. Always coming out on the losing end of any conversation with Lucy, Hannah learned to keep her feelings and opinions to herself at an early age. She could not recall a time in recent years when the sisters shared so much as a laugh or interesting tidbit of gossip.

Hollis and Dock proved an enigma to Hannah. The pair might come to blows at the drop of a hat but abandoned hostility as quickly. After the brothers' fisticuffs at the dinner table, Hannah spotted them clowning around in the backyard. They were obviously rivals for Lucy's attention but she was quickly forgotten once out of sight. As eager as each was to outshine the other, they did not hesitate to joke at every opportunity. In fact, the two brothers traded barbs the rest of the way to Fresno.

Mr. Rumsford was happy to see his sons. The man was a true gentleman, gracious to his sister-in-law and the Granville girls. They shared a quiet supper at the small hotel where Mr. Rumsford stayed. The boys slept on the floor of their father's room. The three ladies shared a simple but clean room—Aunt Bitsy took one bed. Lucy and Hannah took the other.

Apprehension over her circumstances made Hannah tense and the memory of Hollis Rumsford's gaze prohibited a state of relaxation sufficient to fall asleep. Acknowledging her wakeful state, Hannah headed to the kitchen for a glass of milk. To her surprise, Mrs. Simms, the hotelkeeper, was seated at the table doing bookwork.

"Do you mind if I help myself to some milk? I can't get to sleep."

"Oh, no problem, dearie. Help yourself. You was so quiet at dinner, I didn't know you could talk," teased Mrs. Simms.

Hannah poured a small glass and taking a sip, sat down at the table. "What are you doing?"

"My books for last month don't balance. Mathematics has always been the bane of my existence," Mrs. Simms added dramatically.

"I always liked mathematics," admitted Hannah. "Would you mind if I took a look?"

"Help yourself." Mrs. Simms pushed her ledger at Hannah, then paused to savor her cup of Sanka. "I do love coffee but it keeps me awake. Nothing else quite hits the spot, but instant coffee comes close and I can drink as much as I like. My brother always claims it tastes like the water that drains out of flowerpots but how would he know? Men!" Mrs. Simms shook her head in disgust. "Find anything?"

"I believe so. I think the mistake must be in this column. Give me a moment and I might be able to figure it out." The ledger sheet balanced perfectly in less than five minutes. "There you go!"

"Thank you, Miss. I might actually get a decent night's sleep thanks to you."

"My pleasure. You must like this work to give up sleep for it."

"Well, this is my business. It ain't all that much, I know well enough, but it's a living. My rooms are spare but they're clean. I try to help folks out, as much as I can."

"How do you manage that?"

"Poor families who relocate to California have a real hard time. Why, there was a lady with four children living in her car just down the road. Her husband went to buy groceries and never come back. That lady sold the tires right off her car to raise a little money. I felt real sorry for her and the children. I used to take them leftovers. Then one day, they were gone. I don't know where they went. I like to hope somebody took them in.

"When a feller has a chance at a job, it don't go so well if they don't look the part. I let them come in and get cleaned up as much as they're able. It helps sometimes. That's about all I have time for or can afford. I work at the soup kitchen at church a couple times a month.

"These are real hard times, I never seen the likes of it. Even folks who do manage to find work on the farms hereabouts have a rough go. A lot of farmers don't treat their people good. You'd be shocked at the way they have to live—women and children too." Mrs. Simms shook her head in disbelief. "Do you have people where you're going?"

"No. My people are spread all over the country, except for my sister. I intend to get a job and support myself. Have you any advice?"

"A sweet thing like you should have no trouble if someone will give you a chance. That's the thing, someone has to give you a chance. You got any experience working?"

"I helped at the boarding house where we lived. Mrs. Rumsford ran it. She gave me a letter of referral but I didn't make a wage there, only room and board."

"Well, you was lucky to have that. You'll do fine. You sure can do bookwork. A woman might make a real wage doing something like that."

"Maybe so, but I doubt anyone would make me a bookkeeper right off. I'll keep it in mind, though."

"I tell you something. One of my brothers manages a hotel in Santa Barbara, that's where you're headed, right?"

Hannah nodded enthusiastically.

"I'll write his name down here for you. If you have trouble finding work, call on him. I'll write about you in my next letter."

"Thank you, Mrs. Simms. I might do that. You must be anxious to retire. I'll be off to bed. Thanks again for the milk and the referral."

"No, thank you. I'd be at this for another hour if it were up to me. Sleep tight!"

Early next morning, the travelers prepared for the last leg of their journey. Lucy excused herself from the breakfast table before her meal was finished. As the boys packed the car, Hannah went to find her sister. She located Lucy in the bathroom, having been sick to her stomach.

"Are you ill? Do we need to stay here?"

"No. Mr. Rumsford can't afford to put us up another day. I can make it," Lucy assured.

"I'm not so sure. You look pale."

"I think the sausage didn't agree with me. Don't tell anyone I was sick."

"What if you're sick in the car?"

"Well, if my upset stomach lingers, they'll just have to stop so I can puke in the road. I'm all right, Hannah. Mind your own business."

Lucy seemed unusually considerate of Mr. Rumsford but her disposition did not match her empathy. Hannah shook her head as Lucy started for the car. Her sister was in an ugly mood.

* * *

Having never seen the ocean, Hannah was enthralled from the moment it came into view. She craned her neck every way possible in order to see.

"Sit still!" commanded Lucy.

"Don't you want to see the ocean?"

"I could care less about a bunch of water. I want out of this blasted car."

"Language!" warned Aunt Bitsy.

Sunlight shimmered on the vast, blue Pacific. Ignoring her sister, Hannah kneeled on the seat to have a better view.

"Look there," Dock pointed. "It's an island. I wonder what it is."

Lucy derisively glanced out the window. "It's Hawaii, of course."

Dock nodded thoughtfully. "I always wanted to go there. I didn't think it was so close."

Both Hollis and Bitsy attempted to stifle laughter as Hannah glared at her sister.

"What's funny?" Lucy asked.

"It's not Hawaii. How could you think such a thing?" Her sister's ignorance embarrassed Hannah.

"Hawaii is in the Pacific. What else could it be?"

"You can't see that far. That's one of the Channel Islands. Didn't you ever pay attention in school?"

"You need to respect your elders." It seemed a good idea for Lucy to change the subject. Hollis and Aunt Bitsy laughed for some reason. "Children should be seen and not heard."

Her comment served to quiet everyone in the car.

It was late by the time Hollis found the home of Aunt Bitsy's future in-laws. Her fiancé, Silas, waited anxiously on the porch. Mr. and Mrs. Oddgood proved caring hosts. A light supper was provided for the travelers, who were then free to settle in and relax.

The Oddgoods were generous people, but Mr. Oddgood was unemployed. He worked as an accountant in the thriving movie industry until it deserted Santa Barbara and headed south to Los Angeles. The older couple had difficulty making ends meet, having chosen to retire instead of gambling on a new business venture. The young people were carefully instructed to pull their own weight so as not to be a burden on Bitsy's future relations.

Intent on being an informative host, Mr. Oddgood explained Santa Barbara fell victim to a great earthquake in 1925. There was considerable debate about architectural reform before the catastrophe. Due to massive destruction, the city unified around a Spanish Colonial style for new building projects. This lent an undeniable charm to the beach city. He spoke at length about the Mediterranean revival architecture and lavish resorts, the agricultural influence and outstanding civic values.

"Why, Santa Barbara was voted the most beautiful residential environment in the nation in 1926. You'd be astounded at the posh villas and gardens, especially in Montecito. What started off as a winter resort for the retired rich has become a tourist destination year-round.

"Unlike other bay cities in California, Santa Barbara never courted the military. Our breakwater was privately funded and allows the yacht harbor you see today. Yachting, polo, riding and golf are abundant here—pastimes for the wealthy. Jobs are more plentiful in Santa Barbara than in most places, mainly due to the petroleum industry. Vast oil fields provide tax revenues for the city and employment in the private sector.

"I'll do my best to help you young people find work but I warn you, some folks can't make ends meet here. It is a city of, by and for the rich." Wedding plans soon became the paramount topic of conversation.

Aunt Bitsy took up residence in the guest room. Lucy and Hannah got the maid's room off the kitchen since there wasn't a maid. Hollis and Dock settled in a tiny apartment over the garage, the former home of the groundskeeper. All four guests were gently reminded their lodging was temporary.

Hannah awoke in the middle of the night to find Lucy missing, a frequent occurrence. She tried to stay awake until her sister returned but the long ride in the car proved tiring. Hannah fell into a fitful sleep until the sun shone through the bedroom window. By that time, Lucy was snoring softly in bed beside her. Hannah clenched her teeth. She would undoubtedly be the only job seeker from their family today.

* * *

With high expectations, Hannah felt well-prepared when she left her room. Having never attempted to find work before, she was surprised what a difficult day it proved to be as she dragged herself back to the Oddgood home.

Hannah's wardrobe was limited. She had a warm winter coat, which she doubted would ever be used again. It was January and Santa Barbara seemed like a summer day in Placerville. At breakfast, Silas Oddgood stopped paying attention to his fiancé long enough to warn not all days were so balmy.

Hannah owned a total of three dresses, two for housekeeping, one was her summer church frock. Additionally, she owned one suit—her winter church clothes. She considered the brown suit her most adult attire, perfect for a job search. Unfortunately, the wool suit proved incompatible with the warm beach day.

Her face turned a worrisome shade of red as Hannah tromped from business to business on State

Street. She wished she had a penny for every time someone told her they already hired for the winter tourist season; no further help was needed.

Haggard, dejected and hot, Hannah ignored an angry driver honking nearby. She was startled at the sound of Hollis Rumsford's voice.

"Hey, I'm honking at you. Can I give you a ride back?" Hannah's amazed expression appeared comical to Hollis, who laughed aloud. "Trust me, I don't bite."

"No, no, I didn't think you did. I would appreciate a ride. Thank you." Hannah climbed into the front passenger seat and quietly folded her hands in her lap. Having no idea what to say next, she wanted nothing more than to gaze adoringly at Hollis' handsome face. Instead, she stared out the front window, occasionally glancing furtively at her driver.

"You can talk. Your sister isn't here."

"What does that mean?"

"You're always so quiet and Lucy can be—I guess mean would be the word." Hollis spent years listening to Lucy's derogatory comments regarding her younger sister. Hannah always seemed a sweet, if shy girl, who did not deserve her sister's wrath. "I hope I'm not being offensive. That's not my intent. It's just—she isn't around. You can be yourself."

"Oh, I can hold my own," commented Hannah, but she could tell Hollis doubted her by the smirk on his face.

"How did you do on your job search?" asked Hollis.

"Not well, I'm afraid. This might be harder than I imagined."

"Well, it's only been one day."

"How did you do?" ventured Hannah.

"Swell. I got a job for me and Dock, but he doesn't

know it yet."

"How did you get him a job so fast? How did you get one? Do you think they would hire me?" Hollis laughed again. Hannah thought it the most wonderful sound in the world.

"I don't think a woman could get that sort of job. We have work as roustabouts."

"What's that?"

"It's dirty work. I got us jobs in the Ellwood Oil Fields in Goleta. We're starting on the bottom. Worms is what they call it; you can imagine why. It's not much—it's physically demanding but we're young. We can work our way up. You can make a good living once you have a start. I don't think it's any harder than the mining we were doing in Placerville and I don't mind driving that far. I'm going to ask the Oddgoods if we can pay rent and stay above their garage. They need the money and we need a place to stay."

"Congratulations." Hannah was truly envious. "But how did you find out about these jobs?" Curiosity and need quickly overshadowed her awe of Hollis Rumsford.

"It's like this. I was at an A&P trying anything I could think of to get hired. The manager told me the Chamber of Commerce sponsored a program, something about Emergency Unemployment Relief. Wealthy citizens felt it their civic duty to provide relief for household and resort workers who lost their jobs since the depression began. They started a fund to reemploy these people.

"I'll tell you something, Hannah. Santa Barbara might be civically inclined as Mr. Oddgood mentioned, but they are none too happy to have all these Okies in their city. You and I might be Californians but we're outsiders. You best give the Oddgood's address and forget to mention you're new to town when looking for a job. I didn't know that when I went looking for my own unemployment relief. I got lucky, though. One of the men at the Chamber told me to try looking for work on the oil rigs, which is pretty much what Mr. Oddgood mentioned. The Okies aren't usually fit for such hard labor. Since Dock and me are hale and hearty, they were eager to take us on.

"I sure hope the Oddgoods go for renting out that place we're in. My Pop thought we could stay at the Salvation Army Men's Center but all the charitable places are full of transients. Like I said, best to look as if you fit in." Hollis glanced up from driving long enough to notice Hannah's worried expression. She did not look the part of beach dweller in her wool suit. Hollis offered encouragement. "Maybe your search will go better tomorrow."

"Yes, I hope so." Hannah had no way of knowing her world, already in tatters, was about to come undone.

Chapter Three

Frantic to remove her itchy, hot, wool suit, Hannah was not surprised Lucy was gone. Aunt Bitsy evidently felt her job as chaperone ended once they arrived in Santa Barbara or she would have expressed concern. Lucy could come and go at will through the maid's private door to the outside world.

Hannah made excuses for her sister at dinner, offering stomachache as the reason for her absence. Conversation turned to congratulations for the Rumsford boys' successful job search, details of the rental of the apartment above the garage and expectedly, additional wedding particulars.

Hannah noted Dock's sullen mood, apparently triggered by his new job.

Mr. Oddgood played the piano while the ladies did the dishes, then helped Hannah make a list of businesses where she might find work.

"Since you haven't much experience, it's probably good to try for something similar to your work at the boarding house."

"You mean, cleaning, or cooking or laundry?"

"Yes. You have younger siblings. You might even find a job as a nanny for a wealthy family. You have to look at the ads in the paper for that."

Mr. Oddgood drew a map and directions for Hannah, offering to put in a good word wherever possible. The hour was late when their conversation ended.

"What about your sister?"

"I'll see if she wants something to eat."

"I know she's under the weather. Do you think she'll be able to look for a job tomorrow?"

"I'm not certain," Hannah admitted. In actuality, Hannah was only concerned about her own job search. She would not be surprised if Lucy extended her stay at the Oddgoods as long as possible, even until the kindly couple lost patience and threw her out. Hannah wanted nothing so much as to be free of her sister.

Opening the door quietly in case Lucy let herself in and fell asleep, Hannah managed to make out a still form in the bed they shared. She closed the door and attempted to find her way across the room in the dark.

"Hannah?" came a weak voice.

"Sorry, I didn't mean to wake you."

"Ohhh," moaned Lucy.

"Is something wrong? Are you sick, again?"

When no reply came, Hannah impatiently turned on the lamp beside the bed. An ashen-faced Lucy breathed heavily, sweat pouring down her face.

"You are sick!"

"No, no. I'll be fine."

But Hannah could tell something was terribly wrong. She put her hand on Lucy's forehead. On a hunch, she pulled back the covers. "Dear God! What happened?"

"Nothing. Leave me alone."

"No! I'm going to get help."

"You can't." Lucy grabbed her sister's arm with surprising strength. "No one can know."

"No one can know what? What happened to you? Why is there so much blood?"

"It's all right. It's normal."

"Normal? What's wrong; what have you done?" Hannah asked.

"I'm going to be fine now. Nothing will stand in my way."

"Stand in your way? What are you talking about?"

"You understand my plans, Hannah. Don't pretend innocence."

"What plans? What do plans have to do with this?"

Lucy glared at her younger sister. "You are so stupid. My plans to catch a rich husband."

Understanding took root in Hannah's mind, albeit a horrific understanding.

"You got rid of a baby, didn't you?"

Lucy grimaced. "It wasn't a baby. I was late, that's all. Now everything is taken care of."

Hannah's hand flew to her mouth. The horror of her sister's selfishness seemed incomprehensible to the impressionable girl. Babies were a cause for celebration and joy.

"Why couldn't you marry the father? This was your child, Lucy. How could you? Where is the father?"

"I wish I knew. No, really, I don't."

"It has to be someone back home."

Lucy stared at her sister. "I don't know who the father was."

As Hannah grasped the implications of that statement, she believed she knew the precise location of two likely candidates.

"I need to tell the Oddgoods. You need a doctor."

"You can't tell them, Hannah. Don't be a fool. They will kick us out, you as well as me."

But Hannah noted her sister's complexion turned a waxy yellow color. She had never seen so much blood in her life. Hannah knew her sister would die if left untreated and she knew exactly where to go for help.

* * *

Hollis and Dock sheepishly consumed their breakfast as Mrs. Oddgood commented, "Hannah is late. Perhaps I should knock on the door."

Thinking quickly, Hollis suggested, "Maybe Lucy is still sick. If Hannah cared for her during the night, she might be asleep. I don't think you should bother them."

"That might well be. I suppose I could save some breakfast for Hannah and—oh, there she is now."

Mrs. Oddgood failed to notice the Rumsford brothers' shocked expressions as they watched a disheveled Hannah approach the table.

"Sorry I'm late."

"Did you have a rough night, caring for Lucy? Is she better this morning?" Hollis improvised.

"She's doing much better, thank you," came Hannah's stern reply. "I'll grab a muffin and be on my way. Lucy's asleep. I've left some water and crackers for her. There's no need to bother her. I'll be back shortly." Hannah headed for the front door.

Hollis quickly rose from the table and pulling Dock's sleeve, explained, "She looks tired. We'll drop her off downtown on our way to Goleta.

"Hannah, hold on," Hollis yelled once he closed the front door. He was not surprised when Hannah ignored him and continued down the street.

"Get in the car," he commanded Dock as he hurried to detain the single-minded Miss Granville. Once Hollis grabbed Hannah's arm, he was surprised when she forcefully threw him off. "I just want to help."

"You've helped too much already."

"Tell me what happened after Dock and I left the hospital last night. Hannah! Don't ignore me."

Hannah halted in her tracks and stood staring down the street.

"Is she dead?" Hollis whispered.

"No. The doctor thought she would pull through."

"Thank God."

"Yes, thank God," responded Hannah. Undoubtedly both Hollis and Dock would think they were off the hook now. Feeling the need to be polite, she continued, coldly, "Thank you for taking us to the hospital and for disposing of the mattress."

"That was the least we could do. Hannah, why did you tell that lady at the hospital Lucy wasn't a charity case? The hospital will expect you to pay."

"We don't need charity."

"I have never seen anyone in my life more in need of charity than you and Lucy. You have no money; you have no job; you have no home. How are you going to pay a hospital bill? I don't think this is the time to play martyr."

Years of suppressed anger came welling up in the normally tranquil Hannah Granville. Her rage seethed below the surface since her father deserted their family, leaving them to their own devices. She served as Lucy's victim for as long as she could remember, always taking what was handed her, rarely responding. Hannah was more disgusted than she could ever express. Having long understood Lucy was shallow and selfish, the horror of last night was more than Hannah could tolerate. On the verge of independence, she was burdened with an invalid and bills. Hannah turned toward Hollis and exploded.

"Don't you dare tell me what to do. If I took anyone's advice, it certainly would not be yours or your worthless brother's."

"Look here, Hannah, we're just trying to help you out a little. There's no reason to be mad."

No response could have shocked Hannah so completely. Was this the true way of the world? Was it a place where the most intimate and binding act had no consequence? Where a father, or possible father, had no responsibility? As angry as she was at Lucy, Hollis was the one standing in front of her and he was the one to bear the brunt of her anger. Hannah wound up and slapped Hollis' face with all her might.

"How dare you!" she screamed, then turned and marched down the street, leaving an astounded Hollis in her wake.

Rubbing his cheek thoughtfully, Hollis watched the departing figure.

"For a little girl, she sure packs a wallop," he said aloud. Hollis smiled to himself as he climbed into his Model A. He didn't want to be late on his first day of work.

"What the hell was that all about?" asked Dock.

"Damned if I know, but there's a lot more to Hannah Granville than meets the eye."

"Yeah, she's probably about as crazy as her old man," was Dock's cogent observation.

* * *

Hannah sat on the beach, realizing she wasted most of the day. Her attempts to find a job proved disheartening. She forgot the list Mr. Oddgood made. Further, she knew it was her duty to visit her sister in the hospital but could not stomach the prospect of seeing Lucy. She hadn't slept in over 30 hours, having spent last night waiting for word of her sister's wellbeing after emergency surgery.

Disgust welled in her throat. Lucy did this to herself. Hannah felt no sympathy for her sister's grave condition, which was completely unwarranted—a choice Lucy made. Having snuck into the maid's room as Mrs. Oddgood started to serve breakfast, Hannah quickly changed into her wool suit to appear ready for the day. She felt guilty about lying to Aunt Bitsy's future in-laws. A voice in her head told her to leave the guilt to Lucy, Hollis and Dock, although Hannah would have to admit, none of them appeared to feel much shame.

As she watched the sun sink near the ocean, Hannah understood all her girlhood dreams about love and handsome men paying her court evaporated in a single night. No daydream would ever take the face of Hollis Rumsford again. She always believed the Rumsfords were a fine, upstanding family. How could the two youngest sons turn out to be complete wastrels? But then, how could Lucy do what she did? How could Father have committed suicide? Evidently, families were not all they appeared to outsiders. In fact, in under 24 hours, Hannah's naiveté went extinct.

Someone always told her how to act, what to do, where to be. For the first time in her life, she was on her own. It was best to put childhood behind her for good and all. Realizing her destiny was in her own hands, Hannah contemplated her future.

She intended to pay the hospital bill, knowing Lucy would ditch her responsibility in a heartbeat. Hannah was done taking ridicule and direction from her older sister. She was determined to stand on her own two feet.

Women were attaining success at business in unprecedented ways. Many prospered in male-dominated fields. They were becoming doctors, lawyers and professors. She read about the architect, Julia Morgan, who ran her own firm and produced incredible structural designs. Hannah did not have the advantage of education, no matter how well-read she was. All she needed was a start. She was certain she knew where to begin.

Hannah stood and brushed the sand from her clothing. At least this day was not as warm, so her suit wasn't a burden.

Across the street was the Vista Mar Monte Hotel, which Mrs. Simms' brother managed. Hannah was prepared to be assertive as never before in her life. Content to put her duty to Lucy off as long as possible, Hannah knew visiting hours would be over by the time she finished.

* * *

Hannah stared at the steps outside the groundskeeper's quarters in the Oddgood's backyard. Having little choice but to climb the stairs and speak to the two young men she so despised, Hannah considered events of the past week.

She managed to talk her way into a job at the Vista Mar Monte. Mrs. Simms' brother proved a downright grouchy adversary. Hannah was shocked when he relented to her earnest pleas and assurances of aptitude. True, it was only a maid's job but it was a start.

Hannah felt an incredible sense of accomplishment on her first payday. She managed to avoid the hospital and her sister for the entire week but knew Lucy must be due for release. Hannah appeared at the hospital today after work. She missed Lucy's departure by only an hour. The on-duty nurse assured her a tall, good looking young man with dark hair and brown eyes paid the hospital bill and took charge of her sister.

Fairly certain Lucy wasn't able to charm any

suitors during her brief stay in Santa Barbara, Hannah realized Lucy's savior must be none other than Hollis. Relieved to have Lucy off her hands, she wanted to confirm her help was no longer required. Hannah hoped Hollis acknowledged his obligations and stepped up.

The Oddgoods accepted Hannah's explanation— Lucy was at the hospital due to an "abdominal problem." They were sympathetic and offered to help care for Lucy when she was discharged. Apparently, Hollis made some other arrangement. It was Hannah's intention to discover her sister's whereabouts as she knocked softly on the door.

"Come on in Dock, this is your home too," Hollis yelled.

Hannah stepped quietly through the doorway, realizing Hollis was in another room. She walked toward what appeared to be the kitchen door, then stopped dead in her tracks. Posted on the wall were a variety of lewd and obscene pictures. Hannah's mouth was agape as she took in the shocking images.

Her attention was first drawn to a picture of a man standing beside a woman. A scarf barely covered her chest. The man's hand cupped her breast. Hannah's face burned hot as she gazed at the other photographs. Several featured women barely covered by a hand, fan or flimsy piece of fabric. By far, the most shocking was a frontal picture of a seated woman. Fringe lay across her knees. She wore a shawl off her shoulders and a hat, but not a single stitch of clothing.

Hollis came through the doorway to find Hannah staring at the wall, so absorbed, she didn't notice his approach.

"Uh-hum," he began, but Hannah didn't respond. An amused Hollis took her arm, physically tugging her away from the artistic display. "I can see you're enthralled by Dock's ode to the female body, but is there something I can do for you?"

"Wh-what is that?" asked Hannah.

"Mostly Ziegfeld girls."

Hannah was speechless. She had truly descended into a pit of immorality and forgot completely why she came.

Her shock was not lost on Hollis. He decided Hannah Granville was like a younger sister. Perhaps it was her short stature that made her appear vulnerable. Some unfamiliar protective instinct rose in him now as it had the night she came for help with Lucy.

Hannah was a quiet and demure member of their household for over two years, awkwardly sharing in holidays and celebrations much like some distantly-related family member. Lucy, on the other hand, was the epitome of every man's desire. Hollis never considered her a member of their family.

Knowing it was improper to have a young lady in his rooms, Hollis guided Hannah toward the door when she suddenly pulled her arm from his grasp.

"Don't touch me!" she warned.

"All right. Why don't you tell me why you've come?"

Hannah paused, struggling to remember the point of her visit. "I went to see Lucy this afternoon and was told she left. Did you take her? If not, I need to go to the police."

"Because you're such a devoted sister?"

Hannah blushed an even brighter red. "No, I wouldn't say that." Admittedly, she felt guilty about her intentional negligence. "But I would like to know where she is."

"I know you didn't go visit. Don't get me wrong, I think I understand."

"So, you made some arrangement for her?"

"Aunt Bitsy told me you found a job. I didn't think you had time to play nursemaid and Lucy is not well. One of the guys in my crew has a cousin who's a nun. She works at a facility that cares for the sick and indigent. There is no charge. Lucy will be well taken care of. Here, I have the address. You can take this." Hollis fished a business card from his pocket and handed it to Hannah.

"What about the hospital bill? If you think Lucy will pay you back, you are mistaken."

"I'm not concerned about the money. I'll be repaid. Don't worry about it."

"I will pay you back. I have my job now and can give you a little money each week."

"No, Hannah. I saved my money over the past couple of years. Now I have a good job. Living here above the garage is thrifty. I'm not a fan of Mrs. Oddgood's cooking and chose to save money on rent by providing my own meals. I'm not much of a cook, so I'll likely eat out more."

Hannah could not decide if Hollis felt responsible for his actions. She found no hint of guilt in his demeanor, although he accepted the obligation of the hospital bill.

Several young maids at the hotel rented a house near the beach—although nothing in Santa Barbara was far from the beach. One of the girls was recently married so there was need of a new roommate. More than anything, Hannah wanted to be out on her own This seemed the perfect opportunity, if not for Lucy.

Having momentarily forgotten the pictures, Hannah took a closer look at Hollis. He'd been fighting; his cheek was bruised and there was a gash above his eye.

"Where is Dock? Why did you think it was him at

the door?"

"Well, my brother and I had another falling out. I assumed he was returning, tail between his legs. Maybe it's just as well he stays out on his own a while. It might make a man out of him. He lost his job already."

"And you got in another fight?"

Hollis rubbed his bruised face. "Are you enthralled with my looks?" he joked, but nothing he said proved amusing to the young Miss Granville. "Actually, our fight was about something else."

Thinking the fight must have been about Lucy, she replied, "I'll be on my way, then." Hannah was eager to depart this den of iniquity. "If Lucy did not thank you, I thank you on her behalf."

"She's no concern of yours, Hannah. She's a big girl. She can take care of herself."

No doubt Hollis would see to her welfare now. That was his responsibility and for the best. Hannah felt light of heart as she made her way to the little room at the Oddgood's home. She planned to move out come Sunday, her only day off.

* * *

Avery Rowland considered himself a shrewd judge of character, which was why he refused to trust anyone to hire employees. True, he was only a manager but he was the sort of man who took his work to heart. His responsible nature forbade any idea the Vista Mar Monte was anything but his.

At 43 years of age, he had the look of a responsible businessman. His spectacles lent a scholarly symbol to his graying temples and recently acquired pot belly. He dressed immaculately and expected the same from his employees, even the underpaid ones.

Avery nervously tapped a pencil on his desk as he looked out his office window toward the shoreline. He was at a loss how to handle the curious case of Hannah Granville. She did not match his preconceived notions of a proper maid.

The girl seemed timid when she introduced herself. Yet, she was unusually persistent, even that first day. Further, there was a certain joie de vivre in her attitude, as if she were some prisoner recently released from incarceration. He decided early on to keep an eye on her.

His sister's letter followed by post shortly after he hired young Hannah and it was all the girl claimed it would be. Besides commentary on her bookkeeping skills, Deb included favorable comments garnered from an Aunt Bitsy, who assured Miss Granville was a sweet girl and easily manipulated. At least that was how Avery took his sister's message.

Much to her credit, Miss Granville was initially enthusiastic about her new position. It took only a short time before he caught her taking tea and visiting with fellow employees in the kitchen at the end of the day.

Avery personally inspected Hannah's work, finding it impeccable. Hard as he tried, he could find no fault and the frequent, favorable comments by patrons served to pique his curiosity. Customers, though quick to complain, rarely took the time to commend hotel staff. He remembered clearly their exchange when he called Hannah out for her lackadaisical behavior.

"Miss Granville, shouldn't you return to work? If you are on some kind of holiday, I refuse to pay for it."

"My work for today is complete," she calmly replied.

"Then I have clearly not given you enough to do."

"I assure you, I have as much work as any other maid. I've always been a fast worker. Once I caught on and thoroughly cleaned the rooms that are my responsibility, my work does not take as long as it did initially."

Avery clearly had no use for the pert new employee and determined to sack her that very day. Then the conversation took an odd turn.

"I pay you for a full day's work. I will see to it you are assigned extra rooms."

"I'll be glad to take on several more rooms but you will have to pay me for the extra work."

"I certainly will not," Avery responded.

"So, because I am quick and organized, I will be punished for my hard work, making less per room than any other maid?"

This impertinent girl certainly had her nerve. What kind of maid spoke this way to her superior? On the other hand, Avery always considered himself a fair employer and her comments cast him in a poor light. Further, he held a deep-seated fear of the Hotel Workers' Union. The last thing he desired was for some upstart female to squawk about unfair wages, which might serve to muster support for improved working conditions.

"When you finish your work tomorrow, please report to my office," he commanded before beating a hasty retreat. He needed to think on this dilemma.

Miss Granville appeared at the manager's office two hours before quitting time the next day. Avery was entrenched in an accounting difficulty and did not need to pretend absorption in his aggravating paperwork.

"Miss Granville, please explain why I should not fire you for impertinence and dereliction of responsibility?"

"It is surely your right to fire me at will but you will lose a fine employee. I do my work efficiently, I mind my own business and never interrupt other workers once my daily duties are complete. Any conversations you may have witnessed were started by others. I do more and better work than any of your other maids, who tend to dally during the day—no doubt so they won't be called on the carpet."

Hannah eyed Mr. Rowland's sheet of figures. She was suddenly reminded of Mrs. Simms' similar plight. Perhaps mathematical ability did not run in their family. She walked to the side of the desk in an attempt to get a better view of her employer's difficulty.

"What do you think you're doing?"

"Your sister must have written to you about the way I solved her accounting problem. Perhaps I could assist you in a similar manner."

Avery chuckled. Was there no end to this girl's conceit? "I highly doubt it."

"Show me your problem."

Mr. Rowland shoved the book of accounting at the soon-to-be unemployed maid. "Are you telling me you are some kind of accountant?"

"No, but I am good with figures," Hannah commented as she perused the numbers. "Did you add these columns?"

"What if I did?" Avery answered indignantly.

"Give me your pencil."

Only the memory of his sister's letter kept Avery's temper in check. He threw his pencil across the desk and watched Miss Granville erase several numbers and correct his work.

It took only a few minutes before she pushed the ledger book toward her boss and smiled. "I think you'll find the ledger balances perfectly. Perhaps I can be of further assistance with your accounts receivable?"

"Yes, you might be able to work a full day for a full day's wages in that manner."

"Mr. Rowland, I think I made myself perfectly

clear. I will be happy to take on additional responsibilities—for a fee."

"That's ridiculous. You are nothing but a maid."

"I am a maid who can do mathematics. But if you'd rather struggle on as you have been, I'll go back to the kitchen and have a cup of tea—my reward for a full day's work."

Avery believed the girl was pushing her luck. Her behavior certainly did not match his original perception of her personality or demeanor. Yet, the idea he could slough off this odious duty for what would likely be a pittance was appealing. This day proved to be the first in an ongoing series of negotiations between Mr. Rowland and Miss Granville.

Before Hannah left the office, she agreed to perform the accounts receivable bookwork, including making the daily deposit at the bank, for double her salary. Her accounting would begin when her duties as a maid were complete. Her hours were unspecified, dependent on the time it took to finish her work. It was a bargain Mr. Rowland would quickly regret.

Chapter Four

Having splurged on a new dress for Aunt Bitsy's wedding, Hannah intended to appear the successful young woman she recently invented. No one would think her job as a maid exceptional but she did not plan on discussing that part of her workday in any detail—or at all. It was her work as an accountant she intended to expound. As Hannah stared at her reflection in the mirror, she could see success evident in every detail of her appearance.

Never a fan of the sharply angled hats that were the rage, her own was a simple gray bucket hat. The side brim turned over a pink velvet rose. Her gray polka dot dress sported puffy, short sleeves and a gauzy overlay, meticulously pleated down the front of the bodice. Hannah's new pair of black-and-white spectator shoes had thick heels and straps. She wore the latest in makeup: mascara, eyeliner, rouge and the pinkest lipstick she could find. She felt the epitome of the modern woman as she grabbed her sweater, wedding gift and purse, and headed out the door.

It was quiet in the house on this last Saturday in February. All her roommates were at work. Hannah carefully considered her attendance at the wedding before she took the afternoon off. There was only the slightest chance Lucy was invited or would attend. She longed to see Mr. and Mrs. Rumsford but Hollis and Dock were also likely to be there. It was her intention to avoid those two boys as much as humanly possible. She was anxious to see the Oddgoods, as well.

Hannah knew she'd been cavalier about her job. She hadn't any clue as to her own behavior of late. Real freedom was never a possibility before. If not for her relocation to Santa Barbara, she might have lived forever in the Rumsford's attic, working steadily away, her nose buried in a book for the rest of her spinsterhood. Even now, she believed she was destined to die an old maid.

From the moment she talked her way into a job at the Vista Mar Monte, Hannah's outlook widened. Santa Barbara was a unique place. Businesses managed to thrive. Hannah didn't understand why, but she knew there was money in Santa Barbara and money meant opportunity. Her imagination ran wild.

Previously, she felt anxious about her life and the unknown. Her father's suicide lent a pall to every day. Lucy's constant criticism made Hannah defensive. Now she had her own life and her own income. The sky was the limit. Hannah meant to make the most of her opportunity as an accountant, which could prove the catalyst for a lucrative future.

This was America after all, a land where hard work and determination still made a difference. If Abraham Lincoln could fail at every single business he tried until he became a lawyer at 27, Hannah was willing to fail a few times before she found her way to success. After all, she came to Santa Barbara penniless. She could certainly survive starting over. Graciously, Hannah considered her father might have proven a success at some point if only he didn't give up. Her newfound dreams and outlook served as a catalyst to a bright and shiny new Hannah Granville, who was about to prove almost unrecognizable to those who knew her best.

* * *

"When your father stood in front of me and said, 'Look who I've found,' I truly could not figure out who was there beside him. I swear, Hollis, I did not recognize our little Hannah. It's darling the way she smiles all the time. I can't recall her ever looking like that when she lived with us. Hannah has been here such a short time but it's certainly made a difference. She seems level-headed and I'll tell you what. I think she would be a wonderful match for Dock, don't you?"

His mother was so intent, Hollis could not get a word in edgewise. "I don't think—"

"They are close enough in age. How old do you think Hannah is now? Dock will listen to you, he always admired you so and tried to emulate you."

"Maybe that was true when I was five and he was three."

"Nonsense. You have always been a good example. You simply need to point out he could use a steadying influence and Hannah might prove a valuable asset. Don't you think she would, Hollis?"

"Ma, I don't think Hannah has much use for me and none at all for Dock."

"Why is that?"

The last thing Hollis desired was for his mother and Hannah to have a heart-to-heart about the deficiencies of the Rumsford boys. "We never got along. Hannah was like an irritating little sister. Dock was always interested in Lucy. Besides, I thought you liked Hannah, why would you try to push Dock off on her?"

"Any girl would be fortunate to capture the heart of either of my precious boys. What are you saying? And you were interested in Lucy, as well. Do you think Bitsy invited her to the wedding?"

"I don't think there was any love lost between Bitsy and Lucy, so I doubt it."

"Doesn't Bitsy look radiant? For all that Hannah seems mature today, Bitsy appears light-hearted and young. She really is young but she's always been such a serious girl.

"I am reminded of my Aunt Sophie. Do you remember her, Hollis? She was always overburdened with family responsibilities and then she got the influenza in 1919. Everyone thought she would die but she somehow pulled through. She was so blissful when she recovered, enjoying the simple things in life and truly at peace. She looked like an entirely different woman. Then, she got hit by the milk wagon and that was the end of that. Do you suppose that's why Hannah looks so different today?"

"Because she's about to get hit by a milk wagon?" Hollis couldn't resist the facetious comment.

"Oh, heaven's no! Because she left her family problems behind, including that sister of hers. Perhaps her father's unfortunate demise has faded into the past. She's simply light of heart."

Hollis continued to play the part of captive audience. His mother was always busy working. This was the rare occasion when at least part of her family was reunited. She was thrilled her youngest sibling found wedded bliss. Hollis pretended to pay attention to the endless prattle as he watched Hannah Granville. There certainly was something different about her.

* * *

It was difficult to tell who was more shocked when Hollis and Hannah reached for the same plate of wedding cake. Hollis watched her smile disappear for the first time that day.

"You take this piece, I'll get another, but you know what this means don't you?"

In all seriousness, Hannah replied, "It doesn't mean a thing."

"Surely, you've heard that tradition—when you share a plate of wedding cake, you become lifelong friends."

"I have never heard such a thing," but then it occurred to Hannah she was being teased. Even so, her smile did not return.

"Look, Hannah, I don't know why you're so angry. Before you run off, I wanted to tell you, if you ever need anything, you know where I live."

"Why would I need anything from you?"

"Us Placervillians need to stick together. We're far from home. I promised my mother I'd keep an eye on you."

Anger snapped in Hannah's green eyes. "I assure you, Mr. Rumsford, I don't need anyone keeping an eye on me. I can take care of myself."

"I'm sure you can but if there is ever a need—" Before Hollis could finish, Hannah turned and headed toward Mrs. Oddgood, her smile in place.

Having made his best attempt at a polite overture, Hollis doubted he would ever see Miss Granville again.

* * *

Complaints plagued Mr. Rowland since the day he hired Miss Granville to do his books. Suddenly every employee felt the need to promote themselves and their various abilities. If the newest and youngest member of the staff could double her salary after only a few weeks of work, surely, they needed raises as well. His secretary's gossipy nature opened a can of worms and Avery was paying the price. He could always fire Miss Granville to solve his problems.

There was something about her, though. He came to enjoy her smiling face, her enthusiasm for work, even her friendly banter. Her attitude was appreciated at a time when he felt beleaguered.

The entire country was shocked at the kidnapping of the Lindbergh baby. Charles Lindbergh, the first pilot to fly non-stop across the Atlantic five years ago, was a national hero. Each new twist and turn in the investigation was carefully scrutinized in every corner of the Vista Mar Monte, be it by guests or staff. It was difficult to get a decent day's work out of anyone. Miss Granville seemed the only bright spot in Avery's day. He should not have been surprised at their next business negotiation.

His idea a maid would never be the object of robbery was simply ingenious. No one would suspect the young Miss Granville, in her work attire, could be trusted to carry large amounts of cash. This clever disguise was about to go the way of King Tut, however.

"I was wondering if you might look over the accounts payable today. It wouldn't hurt to have a backup should I ever be away on business," Mr. Rowland began.

"I'd be happy to," commented Hannah, ever on the watch to improve her station. She gave her boss an endearing smile.

Expecting some form of monetary negotiation, Avery suspiciously let that subject drop. "Are you not effected by the kidnapping? You seem so happy every day while the darkest of clouds hangs over the general populace."

"I can't imagine the horror the parents are going through. To think their baby was stolen right out of their house when everyone was home. If it were me, I could never stop blaming myself. It makes you think. Celebrity certainly has its drawbacks. I am thankful that burden is not mine to bear. I wish all the best for them but I have my own business to attend to."

In actuality, Hannah was upset to think a mother who, unlike Lucy, wanted and bore her child, was robbed of her precious gift of God. Hannah had been robbed of her own tiny niece or nephew, a fact that continued to disturb her. Unable to rationalize those upsetting circumstances, she buried herself in work and avoided the newspaper, radio and gossip.

Hannah began a preliminary investigation of the accounts payable. She quickly became appalled. Evidently, it was Mr. Rowland's custom to pay every bill in full, never bothering to check the accuracy of the statements received from vendors who serviced the hotel. That first evening, Hannah managed to uncover only a few of the discrepancies from the ice company invoice. She knew if all the accounts were in such a state of disarray, there could be hundreds if not thousands of dollars of savings to be found.

The next morning, instead of starting her day cleaning, Hannah made a trip to the manager's office.

"Mr. Rowland, I spent no little time last night going over one invoice."

"So, you understand my procedures?"

"I do and I find them completely unsatisfactory."

Avery was not about to be dressed down by this snippet of a girl. "I suggest you watch your tone, there, missy. You are addressing the manager of the hotel where you are employed." He watched in fascination as his normally happy and smiling associate began to lay into him.

"Mr. Rowland, you are missing every conceivable opportunity to keep your vendors in line. I found mistake after mistake that you simply pay. I'm quite certain every vendor in Santa Barbara must know you don't examine their billing and they are all, most probably, taking advantage of you."

"See here!"

"You need help, Mr. Rowland, and I am prepared to be that help."

Avery knew the girl was correct and although he would never admit it, he admired her spunk as much as he detested bookwork. "What are you suggesting?"

"I suggest I take on the accounts payable. It's a big job. I can only imagine the difficulty I will have trying to straighten out months, if not years of inflated invoices and downright errors."

"So, you would do receivables and payables?"

"I will. But this is too big a job for me to continue cleaning rooms," Hannah stated firmly.

"I see that might be the case. Fine. You will report here every morning as my new accountant. You guarantee you will save the hotel money?"

"I guarantee that, without doubt. Of course, my pay needs to increase accordingly."

"I didn't say anything about that."

"I think double my current wage will be sufficient."

"Now, see here."

"Surely, Mr. Rowland, you would agree an accountant should make more than a maid."

"You already make more than a maid."

"Actually, I make a maid's wage for cleaning rooms, and I make a maid's wage for the accounts receivable. I believe double what I'm making is fair—

for now. And I'll need an initial bonus."

"A bonus! Are you mad, woman?"

"I can hardly wear my maid's uniform for an office job. I need proper clothing and haven't sufficient funds to dress in a manner representative of my station at the hotel." Hannah understood appearance was one of Mr. Rowland's weaknesses. "Fifty dollars should suffice. And one other thing. When my work for the day is finished, I will be free to go."

At least on that point, Avery knew he held an advantage. Even the self-assured Miss Granville would not be able to sort out the billing anytime soon. In fact, she would likely be working extra-long hours for months to come. When Hannah left the office to shop and dress for her new duties, Avery Rowland chuckled to himself. That girl was bound to go far in life. He wanted a front row seat.

* * *

Hannah stood at the bottom of the staircase beside the Oddgood's garage in the waning daylight. Having decided on her current course of action, she was, nonetheless, reluctant to ascend the stairs. Taking the first tentative step, she considered the changes in her life since she last visited.

Although she was eager to don the plain black dress, starched white apron and lacy cap of her maid's uniform, she also abandoned it gleefully. Her experience of purchasing and wearing clothing of her choice for Aunt Bitsy's wedding proved life changing.

Hannah spent her childhood wearing Lucy's hand-me-downs, a normal enough occurrence in large families. The few clothes she wore in Placerville and brought to Santa Barbara were practical and durable, homemade as cheaply as possible. She never imagined wearing lovely clothing could prove so exhilarating. Her sudden business success enabled her to increase the size of her wardrobe considerably.

She continued to share rent with three girls who worked at the hotel, although Hannah's interests and goals could not have been more different. She was not interested in finding a boyfriend, which seemed to be the main goal of her roommates. The three girls spent endless hours gossiping and plotting, eager to display their attributes to anything in pants.

Hannah's sole focus was getting ahead in life. She read books on business, studied every aspect of practical accounting and spent every spare moment imagining ways to expand her business. She no longer considered herself an employee of the hotel. Hannah was an independent businesswoman, who spent her mornings completing her client's bookwork and her afternoons offering accounting acumen as a free trial to anyone who showed interest.

Hannah managed to anger Mr. Rowland to the point he fired her on two separate occasions. It took weeks of intensive work to straighten out the accounts payable. Hannah spent every waking moment—even taking bills home to review at night—to make sense of what was owed the hotel. She spent countless hours on the telephone talking to billing clerks and visited various businesses in an attempt to clarify payments to bewildered accountants.

Mr. Rowland initially congratulated Hannah on her devotion to work. He was thrilled at the money she saved and smug about the bonus he allowed that enabled Miss Granville to be fashionably attired on her appointments. His gratitude faded quickly the first day Hannah completed her work and left at three o'clock. Avery's initial reaction was to fire her for dereliction of duty, but try as he might, the manager could find no fault or incomplete work. Although he didn't approve of Hannah's short workdays, he agreed to this term of her employment and had no one to blame but himself.

His accountant was sacked the second time when he received a phone call from a friend who owned a haberdashery on State Street. Evidently, the ambitious Miss Granville spread her business cards all over the city in an attempt to start a company. She offered his name as a referral. Avery never agreed to share his employee and considered her double-dipping a gross violation of employment. Only the pile of invoices and deposits that accumulated over the next two days caused him to relent. He so hated paperwork. Miss Granville was rehired both times at a higher rate of pay.

Knowing her youth worked against her, Hannah adopted a severe hairstyle in an effort to appear older than her 18 years. French-braiding her hair near her hairline, Hannah used a large clip to secure the back.

When the Lindbergh baby's lifeless body was discovered near his home, Hannah developed a new business plan to soothe her anxiety. This was the reason for her visit to the Rumsford brothers' abode. After all, it was Hollis who told her to call if she ever needed anything and he was the only person she knew who could help.

Startled when Hollis threw open his door in response to her timid knock, Hannah believed he appeared equally startled to find her on his porch.

"Is something wrong?"

"No. You told me once if I needed anything to ask."

"But nothing is wrong?"

"No, no. Everything is fine."

Hollis seemed not to know what to do next. "Sit down on the step and tell me your problem, then."

"It's not a problem. I want to learn to drive. To be honest, I don't know anyone else who owns an automobile. I have no one else to ask."

"Yes, I'm sure you wouldn't ask if I weren't your last resort." Hollis could not seem to make the girl sit down, she insisted on standing. "Do you want to come inside?"

"I simply want to know if you would be willing to teach me."

"Why do you want to learn?"

"Is that any of your business?"

Hollis was astonished by her blunt reply. After all, she was the one asking for a favor. "Probably not, but I won't agree unless I know what you're up to."

"Very well. I have a business and I want to purchase a car."

"Why do you need a car?" Hollis could see his questions proved irritating and he rather enjoyed it.

"I have clients throughout the city and it will save time if I can drive. I also plan to add signage on the doors of my vehicle to advertise my business. A stylish automobile will lend an air of prosperity."

"Do you know anything about cars? How will you know what to buy? Do you know how to maintain a vehicle?"

"I thought there were mechanics for that."

"They will surely take advantage of an ignorant girl who knows nothing about cars. Same for any dealership. They will see you coming."

"Look, Mr. Rumsford—"

"It's Hollis."

"I only want to learn to drive for now. Will you help or not?"

Hollis rubbed his chin in consideration of the request, intent on giving Hannah as hard a time as possible. "You must be doing well to afford a car. How many clients do you have?"

"Two right now but I anticipate more shortly."

"Two paying customers?"

"Well, no. One is a paying customer but the other will be soon."

"I don't know. This sounds like a risky idea. I'm not certain I want to be a party to impending indebtedness."

"Will you help me or not?"

"What do I get out of it?"

This question took Hannah by surprise. "I—I don't know. What is it you want?" she asked as she pulled the collar of her blouse close around her neck, clearly not trusting the decadent Hollis Rumsford.

"Hmmm, let me see. I agree to teach you to drive on Sunday afternoon if you will agree to make a fried chicken dinner for me afterwards. I believe you know how to follow my mother's recipe?"

"Yes, she taught me how to fry chicken when I stayed at your house. I'm not certain that seems a favorable bargain, for you, that is."

"It's my birthday on Sunday and I feel rather homesick. My mother's chicken is all I could hope for. The deal is struck," and he held out his hand.

"Wait. I don't have a place to cook. Men are not allowed where I live and I can't simply commandeer the kitchen."

"That's all right. You can cook here."

"I don't think it would be proper."

"We can leave the door open for all the world to see. And I'll let Mrs. Oddgood know you're making me birthday dinner. Will that serve to legitimize our deal?"

Hannah shook hands on their bargain but hadn't felt so insecure in months.

* * *

"Why didn't we eat at the hotel?" asked Hannah.

"I thought you might enjoy the exquisite surroundings. El Paseo is the heart of Santa Barbara. The complex surrounding the restaurant served as the inspiration for the Spanish Colonial revival after the '25 earthquake. This dining patio is housed between some of the most historic buildings in the city."

Hannah gazed up at huge swaths of cloth hanging from adjoining rooftops. Potted plants and colorful bowls of florae hung in the courtyard arches. Roses floated in a tiled pool in the middle of the restaurant. Hannah turned her attention to Mr. Rowland.

"You come here often? Why did the maître d' think I was your daughter?"

"I come here quite often. I enjoy the food. Alberto made an assumption. I usually come alone." Avery could see suspicion written on his young companion's face. "Don't worry, I have no designs on you, Hannah. I wanted a place where we could have a private conversation away from the hotel."

"About what?"

"Look at your menu so you know what to order. Then I'll explain."

Once the waiter came to Mr. Rowland's special table and took their order, a curious Hannah continued, "So why are we here, exactly."

"I admire your work, Hannah. It's true, I fired you. It took me a while to trust in your honesty and responsibility, unusual in a girl your age. I appreciate your ambition. I always found your tactics entertaining. When I received inquiries from business people calling for references, I was disturbed by your pluck. Quite frankly, there is little in my life as fascinating as your antics."

"I can't tell if you are scolding or praising me," commented Hannah.

Avery laughed. "This may be a foolish notion but I consider you something of a business apprentice. I would like to help you."

"I think I do accounting better than you do. Perhaps you should take a turn at being my apprentice," Hannah slyly commented.

"Point taken. But this is exactly the area where you need guidance. I chose to praise your abilities whenever someone called for references. I have no doubts about your capacity to perform your work or your honesty. I even appreciate that cocky attitude you have, but not everyone understands. Your pride in work can read as arrogance. I don't believe you are an arrogant person. I do think you are confident in your abilities—at least as far as business. But even the hint of arrogance in a woman trying to promote herself in business can be lethal. Did you know Mr. Barney is an old friend of mine? He took my positive comments about you seriously. That's how you got his haberdashery account."

"Thank you, I think."

"I take it you're not getting along with Mr. Barney?"

"He phoned me the other day. He yelled at me because there was a mistake in his deposit. I looked over my bookwork, double, even triple-checking to try to find some error. I went to his shop to find out what he was talking about. I simply pointed out he was in error and there was no problem. He was offended, as if he could never make a mistake. Anyone can make a mistake."

"I see. I don't want you to take offense at what I'm going to tell you. Mr. Barney phoned me. I've known him for probably ten years or so. We see each other at

Chamber meetings and often have lunch afterward. I realize he can be a difficult customer.

"Santa Barbara is an unusual town. It's not only the location or the architecture. Although various industries helped develop this area, it is basically a resort town, one that caters to the wealthy. There are many people of lower classes who vacation here. But a significant proportion of the citizens of Santa Barbara are well off, to put it mildly. Many civic projects financed before the stock market crash also serve to pull the town through these rough times. Santa Barbara has been the recipient of generous public funding. The oil industry and its abundant tax revenues keep the city afloat." Avery paused as the waiter delivered their lunch.

"There was a grocery store in town, Diehl Grocery Company. I always admired their business savvy. They catered to rich households, especially those in Montecito. They ran their business on credit. Wealthy customers were never expected to pay cash, in fact, they were encouraged not to. What could be friendlier than signing for anything you need? What could be easier? What could encourage unlimited spending more effectively?

"My awe proved for naught, however, when Diehl went broke. You see, not all the rich here have remained so since the depression began. When a significant percentage of their clients defaulted on monthly invoices, they failed to meet expenses. Diehl effectively serviced the rich citizenry of Santa Barbara for many years. They catered to what could often be difficult and demanding customers and they did it well. It's astounding to me they failed so completely in the end. One bad business decision caused their downfall.

"Your little company provides a service to middle-class business owners. No matter how accurately and efficiently you perform your work, there is more to owning a business. Your customer is always right."

"But Mr. Barney was wrong."

"And I believe you pointed it out to him in a rather harsh manner."

"I don't know what he said to you but it probably wasn't accurate. I was quite clear when I showed him his error. I didn't have time to repeat myself endlessly until he caught on. It's all I can do to keep up most days, much less pay calls on prospective clients. I don't have time to provide accounting tutorials to customers who don't need to know anyway."

"The customer is always right, Hannah. You are young. I'm only trying to impress upon you that you need every customer, every favorable comment, every client on your side if you are to make a go of this. Mr. Barney could make or break you. I would also say, I put my own reputation at stake when I supported you. I assured him you would come by to apologize."

"Apologize? Why would I do that? I was right."

"You were right, what of it? Do you need clients to make a profit?"

"Yes, but—"

"Then I will help you construct an apology and you will make it." Avery could see Hannah digging in her heels. "I'm only trying to help. I am not put off by your impertinence. I once felt the same about my work. I can admit, now, many years later, being right never made me a success. The ability to engage customers and employees effectively is a more vital tool to success than being right will ever be. You do wish to keep Mr. Barney as a client, I assume?"

"I do."

"Then we will go over a few simple rules about how to charm your customers. I believe you could be extremely enchanting, especially where old, lonely men are concerned."

"Are you suggesting I flirt with Mr. Barney?" Hannah was flabbergasted.

"I certainly am not. You are much too young to flirt with Mr. Barney. I am suggesting you be a ray of sunshine in his mundane workday. Let me see your most engaging smile."

"Why?"

"Because, dear Hannah, you need to use every tool you can find if you are going to put Mr. Barney squarely in your corner. We will go over some business etiquette and exactly what you need to say when you visit the haberdashery this afternoon. I am intent on making you a professional businesswoman of the highest degree."

"Again, why?"

"My life has become tedious. I believe I need a challenge. I have no son on whom to impart my business acumen, so I am about to pick on you. Are you up for it?"

"I don't know what to say. Thank you?"

"I'd rather hear I'm sorry. Let's begin again. Show me that smile."

As Avery critiqued and coaxed Hannah over lunch, he was intrigued to find his apprentice exhibited few qualms about failure. This made her unnecessarily reckless—too eager to take risks and too willing to suffer consequences. He became convinced she needed something to ground her, something to work for if she were going to be serious about the future of her business.

Chapter Five

"Stop yelling at me!"

"You have to use the clutch, Hannah! Use the clutch!"

"Which one is that?" Hannah flinched as the driver behind them laid on his horn.

"Get out of the car and come around," yelled Hollis. "Put on the brake!"

Hannah took a moment to recall where the brake was while the horn of the car to the rear continued to blare. By the time she walked around the car and got in, Hollis crawled into the driver's seat, then headed his Model A toward the curb. He turned off the engine and swiveled in his seat to address his pupil eye-to-eye, wanting nothing more than to yell. Since Hannah appeared unnerved, charitably, at least he felt he was being extremely charitable, Hollis apologized.

"I'm sorry. I guess I didn't explain well enough."

"You certainly did not. There's so many levers and pedals, I can't keep them straight. How could you expect anyone to learn to drive a car that way?" Hannah did not mince words.

"Look, Hannah, we're not doing anything all that difficult here."

"Are you implying I am stupid?"

"It could be part of the problem, yes."

"I am *not* stupid. You take that back."

"I told you to use the clutch to change gears. I was extremely clear."

"You told me a lot of things, none of them made much sense."

"That's because you don't know anything about cars!"

"I admitted that. You're the one who's supposed to teach me. Besides, you scream like a girl."

"You have to watch out for pedestrians. You almost hit that man with the bicycle."

"You told me to turn right on State Street."

"But you have to watch for people in the crosswalk!"

Hollis took a deep breath, attempting to calm down. He told Mrs. Oddgood Hannah was like a sister to assure there was nothing risqué about her visit this afternoon. He thought she seemed an annoying little sister at the moment but anger was not going to get him any closer to chicken dinner. Hollis silently restarted the car.

"Where are you taking me? You promised to teach me to drive."

"Keep your pants on. I have an idea."

"Is that any way to talk to a lady?"

"If there were a lady in the car, I would have noticed." Hollis could not control his tongue. He drove a sullen Hannah out of town to an open field and stopped the car.

"This is what we're going to do. I'll demonstrate

how to drive the car from starting to parking. You will sit there, listening intently and watching. When I'm done, you can ask questions and we will review. Then you will try. Have I made this simple enough?"

Hollis looked at his passenger. All that was missing was steam coming out her ears. Her extreme disapproval was apparent.

"I will take your silence for consent," he added and began a laborious demonstration. "First, confirm the parking brake is pulled toward you. Turn on the gas. Next, you put the lever on the left of the steering column all the way up. That's how you retard the spark lever. Now you pull the throttle lever a third of the way down and turn the carburetor adjusting rod first to the right until it's closed, then one full turn to the left to open it. Put the gear shifter into neutral."

Hannah rolled her eyes. How was she supposed to remember every detail? Hollis hadn't moved the car a single inch and she was completely confused.

Despite his sincere intention to aggravate Hannah, Hollis enjoyed her enthusiasm once she caught on. When she competently drove back to the Oddgood's home, Hannah's radiant smile reflected her pride of accomplishment.

"Thank you, Hollis. You did much better on your second demonstration."

"I didn't realize this was supposed to be a learning experience for me," he drolly replied.

"Isn't life surprising?" she continued. "Just when we think we know it all, something comes along to prove us wrong."

Hollis was too anxious for chicken dinner to start a war. The meal was exactly what he would have eaten at home. Hannah served his favorite fried chicken, mashed potatoes, gravy and carrots and surprised the birthday boy with a batch of cupcakes. He was delighted from his first bite. The crispy coating crunched between his teeth as juices from the tender chicken escaped down his chin. Dinner conversation revolved around cars: how to tell if a used car is worth the asking price, the importance of clean oil, how to check tire pressure and gas up.

In the end, Hollis agreed to help Hannah buy a car and demonstrate maintenance in return for two additional Sunday dinners. Wishing to avoid time-consuming pleas for help, his intention was not so much helpfulness as catastrophe avoidance.

* * *

Hollis pulled in front of the house Hannah shared. He honked his horn impatiently. Soon, Hannah's boy-crazy roommates surrounded his car, flirting outrageously.

"Hannah, where have you been keeping your boyfriend?" asked the tall, shapely brunette named Rita.

"He is *not* my boyfriend," Hannah declared.

"Then he's fair game?" queried the plump redhead named Darla.

"He's all yours, ladies," was Hannah's generous reply, "as soon as he helps me today."

"Oh, are you coming back here, mister?" asked the redhead.

"Now that I see what beautiful women live in this house, wild horses couldn't keep me away!" declared a silly Hollis. "See you later, girls."

The roommates squealed with delight as Hannah closed her car door and Hollis sped away.

"You should have told me about your interesting roomies."

"They're shallow girls, only interested in marriage."

"Marriage is not such a silly thing. It's what makes the world go around. Doesn't it interest you?"

"I am interested in commerce, Mr. Rumsford. I thought I made that clear."

"We're back to Mr. Rumsford then?"

Hannah stared out her side of the car and fell silent.

By the end of the day, Hollis helped his young automotive protégé bargain successfully for a blue 1930 Model A coupe. It was the most impressive car Hannah could afford. She stared at more opulent vehicles with what Hollis interpreted as a good deal of lust. But the Model A was in fine shape from a mechanical standpoint, Hollis saw to that.

He was impressed when Hannah competently drove her new purchase to his rooms, where another negotiated dinner would be constructed.

Hollis read the paper while Hannah cooked, then eagerly enjoyed pot roast, potatoes, carrots and peas, and gravy. She served a chocolate cake she brought from home for dessert. Dinner conversation consisted of further automotive instruction, Hollis' insistence on clean windows and how to wash the Model A. He then allowed follow-up questions. Hannah thought her mentor arrogant and condescending and so, ventured a different topic.

"Why is Dock never here?"

"My brother and I had a serious falling out—a true rift we have not been able to repair." He could see the curiosity on Hannah's face but would not discuss family problems with an outsider.

"So, he doesn't live here? You're the only tenant and pay all the rent?"

"I never believed Dock would be an equal partner as far as paying our way but I hoped he'd settle in and take on some share of the burden. I think I mentioned to you before, he got fired from the job I found him. He shows up here on occasion to sleep and eat. Then he takes off again. I'm not certain how he gets by. Did you know my mother thought you would make a good wife for him?"

Hannah's already large eyes widened. "Why would she think that?"

"She hoped you could be a steadying influence. At least she was willing to admit Dock needed a good influence," Hollis conjectured, almost to himself.

"She surely did not tell him this?"

A broad grin lit Hollis' face. "I'm not certain. Why, you never know. He could show up on your doorstep ready to court you."

"Not seriously?"

Hollis felt undeniable pleasure at Hannah's alarm. "I thought that was every girl's desire, to be a wife and mother. Are you telling me you wouldn't accept my brother if he paid you court?"

"I certainly would not. As odious as I find you, I find your brother devoid of any redeeming characteristics. You Rumsford boys are a true disappointment. I have half a mind to write your mother and let her know exactly what kind of boys she raised."

"My, aren't we the self-appointed judge and jury. I never understood your disapproval, Hannah. Perhaps you could enlighten me?"

"You know very well why I dislike you and your brother." Hannah's cheeks turned a vivid red. "I'm surprised you would dare discuss this topic."

"Jealousy of your sister has evidently eaten away at your brain," commented Hollis.

"I am *not* jealous. I have my own life. I live in my own world now. I am happy," although she sounded anything but at the moment. Hannah rose from the table, her cake uneaten. "I should have known better than to ask you for anything. I'll do the dishes as part of my obligation but I don't think I require further help."

"Oh, but you do. You need to understand the mechanical aspects of your automobile or mechanics will cheat you out of all your money. You need to understand how to maintain your car." And I want one more dinner out of this, thought Hollis.

"Very well. I will put up with you for one more Sunday afternoon, and then I never want to lay eyes on you again, Hollis Rumsford!"

Hollis showed up to demonstrate the finer points of car ownership the following Sunday. A sullen Hannah watched carefully and took notes, then handed her adversary a basket of foodstuffs he could reheat on his stove, feeling this qualified as a homemade meal.

Hannah peeked out the front room curtain after she stormed into the house. She was not surprised when Hollis managed to make dates with two of her roommates before he drove away. Once a womanizer, always a womanizer, thought Hannah in disgust.

* * *

Things improved between Dock and Hollis. The fact Dock settled into a job at the chandlery in the harbor made a world of difference. He paid his share of rent; the brothers split all other costs. Although Dock was jealous of his older brother's rise through the ranks at the oil company, he kept it to himself. Months of living from hand to mouth had a humbling effect. For now, Dock was happy to have a place to sleep, food to eat and a little cash to spend on the ladies.

It was rare when anyone paid a call to the suite above the garage. A curious Dock answered a knock at the door and was astonished to find himself standing face-to-face with Hannah Granville. It was difficult to tell who appeared the more surprised. Dock thought it best to keep conversation to a minimum, considering

Hollis' hilarious accounts of their former neighbor's antics.

He left Hannah standing in the doorway and made a hasty retreat to the bedroom after yelling, "Hollis, it's for you."

Hollis appeared in the doorway, but his pleasant demeanor quickly turned to dread.

"Oh, lord, what have you done now? I told you to check the oil. You blew the engine in your car, didn't you? I told you Hannah—"

"My car is fine, but I need you to look at something."

"Is it parked downstairs?" Hollis inquired.

"Yes, but it's not about the car. I need to fix something and I need you to show me how."

"I'm done with this, Hannah. I dislike you and it's apparent the feeling is mutual."

"But I don't know who else to ask."

"Get a boyfriend."

"Please, Hollis. You know I'd never ask you if I had a choice."

Hollis glared at his visitor. "What is it?"

"Well, I bought a house."

Hollis frowned. "How could you afford to buy a house?"

"It's a long story, but I need someone to show me how to fix a pipe. It's not far. I could drive you—"

"Wait just a minute. First of all, I have a date tonight. Second, I wouldn't let you drive me anywhere, I've seen you drive."

Hannah took offense at this slur. "I am a good driver! And even if I weren't, it would be your fault."

"I refuse to take responsibility for the way you drive. I did the best I could for you and received not so much as a thank you for my efforts."

"I believe I did thank you but I will be happy to repeat. Thank you, Hollis, for helping me purchase my automobile and teaching me to drive. Now will you come and show me how to fix my pipe, please? I promise, I will never ask you for another thing for the rest of my life."

Hollis took a look at his wristwatch. "I only have half an hour. How far is this house?"

"Five minutes. I promise, you will be back in less than 30 minutes."

"I am driving. I'll drop you back here so you can get your car when I'm done." Hollis grabbed his jacket.

"Thank you." Hannah exhaled dramatically. Once the pair took off in Hollis' car, Hannah provided directions. "Turn left here."

"You must be lost. You could never afford a house in this neighborhood."

"I'm not lost."

"Tell me how you bought this house, then."

"I told you, it's a long story."

"You can begin while we ride."

"If I'm not going to see you again, you'll never know how my story turns out."

"I'll have to live with that."

"Well, the last time Mr. Rowland fired me—"

"What do you mean the *last* time?"

"He fires me all the time. Then he comes to his senses because he doesn't want to keep the hotel books and hires me back. I always get a raise and time off work, so it's not as if I mind. And he knows if he hired a male accountant, it would cost more than I charge."

"What did you do to get fired this time?"

"Well, Mr. Rowland lets the desk manager take an advance on his pay from time to time. For some reason, he did that four times last month. It became difficult to make the daily deposit. When he looked at the ledger page, Mr. Rowland came to the dramatic conclusion I must be stealing from the hotel, so he fired me. I left because I was tired and needed to do some shopping. Besides, I knew he'd figure out I was not to blame and then I'd get another raise."

Hollis' head was spinning. "What does any of this have to do with buying a house?"

"I'm getting to that part. You're the one who wanted to know why I got fired." Hannah returned to her narrative. "Anyway, Mr. Rowland called and asked if he could take me out to lunch the next day. I knew an apology was forthcoming and as I started to ask for a raise, he surprised me by saying, 'Miss Granville, I know what you're going to say, so let me save some time. My budget does not allow for another raise.' Now I know that's not true; I do the hotel books, after all. Anyway, he told me an interesting story. Turn left here.

"It seems he has an older brother who moved to Santa Barbara years ago and invested heavily in real estate. Property took a downturn after the 1925 earthquake, so Mr. Rowland decided to invest. He bought a lot of damaged property and one piece, in particular, was purchased out of spite. You see, Mr. Rowland's brother acquired pieces of property in this neighborhood to build large estates. Only one little house remained because the owner could not be located. Mr. Rowland found the owner and bought that house to vex his brother. It sat empty ever since. Here we are."

Hollis parked his car, unable to see any house. "Where is it?"

"It's right here, come on." Hannah made her way through heavy vegetation, obviously out of place in the upscale neighborhood. She pointed toward a tiny ramshackle building and announced, "This is my house.

Come inside."

Hollis was stunned. He walked across a porch buried in debris through a doorway left ajar. "Hannah, you can't possibly live here."

"Of course, I can."

He grabbed her arm. "This doesn't look safe. How much did you pay for this?"

"Oh, a dollar."

"What?"

"I paid a dollar. Mr. Rowland said he knew he could trust me and remembered some comments I made about wishing I could afford to buy a house. He didn't want to keep this property, feeling there could be some liability if squatters took up residence or there was a fire or something. So, he sold it to me for a dollar on the condition I would keep the house and live in it. This will serve to vex his brother for years to come and reward me for my hard work, not to mention what a generous apology he conveyed."

"But you can't possibly live here. You need to hire a fixer upper. Do you have money for that?"

"No," Hannah replied firmly. "I can make repairs myself. But I can't begin to clean if I can't use the kitchen sink. The bathroom sink is too small to fill a bucket and I can't turn the handle in the bathtub."

"You're surely not trying to stay here now, in this mess?"

"No, of course not, but I gave notice and only have a couple weeks to clean enough of the house so I can sleep here. We're running out of time. The kitchen is back here."

Hollis followed the new homeowner through a small living room and down a short hallway to a nicely sized kitchen. Every room looked to be a complete disaster.

"Here's the sink. See, if I turn on the water, it pours out below."

"Turn that off! I get the idea. I'm dressed for my date and I don't want to get dirty." Hollis took a superficial look beneath the sink. "The coupling needs to be tightened. I can't fix it now. I need tools."

"I have tools. They're out in the garden shed." Hannah flashed a short smile of delight. She hoped Hollis would fix the leak for her. He seemed willing to do so.

"Not gardening tools, I need a wrench, probably other things."

"I told you, I have tools. I know the difference between tools and gardening tools." She could see Hollis did not believe a word she said. "Come outside."

He followed through what once was a screened porch and into a small backyard. Vines covered fencing on the sides and rear of the property. A small shed sat in the corner. As Hannah promised, there was a stash of tools inside.

"Why do you have so many tarps in here? It's impossible to find anything."

"I didn't put them there. All I've done is look inside. Just pile them in the corner."

Hollis managed to select items he might need and returned to the kitchen. A small tarp served to ensure Hollis wouldn't soil his shirt when he crawled under the apron-front sink.

"Your tools need care," he warned. "You need to use mineral oil to remove the rust." As he tightened the coupling, it became obvious something was wrong. "Shit!"

"What is it?"

"This pipe is corroded. It needs to be replaced."

"How do you know?"

"It broke when I tightened the coupling."

"You broke my pipe?"

"I didn't break your pipe."

"Well, it wasn't broken when you got here, was it?"

Hannah stood well back as Hollis climbed from under the sink. Without further comment, he returned to the shed for more supplies. He located extra pipe, a pipe cutter, plumber's putty and a device Hannah soon understood would thread the pipe so it could be screwed in.

Hollis paused before crawling under the sink to request, "I need to use your telephone."

"I don't have a telephone yet. I only got the water and electricity turned on so far."

"But I need to call my date to let her know I won't be on time."

Having no remedy, Hannah offered, "You're already not on time."

"Then I need you to go pick up my date so I can finish here."

"You are not serious."

"I am perfectly serious, Hannah." Reluctantly, he added, "You can drive my car. Here's her address."

Hollis' tie, watch and jacket were abandoned on what he hoped was a clean chair. He took a note from his jacket pocket and handed it to Hannah.

"Her name is Mollie. She's very nice. Tell her what happened and bring her back here." Hannah's reluctance was obvious. "This is the least you can do. Otherwise you completely ruined my evening. The key is in the car."

"All right," Hannah hissed as she strode out the door to begin her mission.

* * *

An insecure Hannah stood on the front porch of the

strange house and rang the bell. She was hardly dressed to pay a call. A threadbare white apron covered the ugly pink dress she wore to clean the Rumsford boarding house. She looked more like an Okie begging for food than a respectable businesswoman. Why was it Hollis Rumsford always made her feel self-conscious? She jumped when the door opened.

"I'm so sorry to bother you, well, no I'm not," Hannah began. "You see, Mr. Rumsford is late because he helped me, and it took longer than he thought, and he asked me to come and explain he was going to be late. I could drive you back to my house and you could leave on your date from there. I mean, if that's all right with you—and your parents," Hannah threw in for good measure. "I'm sorry about the way I look, I was about to clean when the plumbing problem happened." She looked hopefully at the exquisitely attired brunette on the other side of the screen door.

Although surprised, Mollie seemed eager to go. She made a quick explanation to her father, who loomed in the background.

"I'll be sure to bring Hollis in when we return from our date, Daddy," she assured.

"Mr. Rumsford is a true gentleman or he wouldn't be fixing my pipe," Hannah assured, but cringed at the thought she was throwing this lovely girl into the arms of a lecher.

As the two ladies crawled into Hollis' Model A, introductions seemed in order. "My name is Hannah Granville."

"Nice to meet you. I'm Mollie Standish. Does Hollis let you drive his automobile often?"

"Well, no, but I have driven it before and this was sort of an emergency. Have you been dating long?"

"This is the first time. I'm certain my father is not

happy. He's old fashioned. My parents have been married forever, since way before prohibition or women's suffrage, even before the Great War. They don't understand modern customs. Thank you for putting in a good word for Hollis. I've looked forward to this evening. I'm glad he didn't have to cancel."

"My pleasure. I owe him a debt for his efforts tonight."

"Are you a relative?"

"No, not at all. My family lived next door to his back in Placerville and I worked in his mother's boarding house. Several of us came to Santa Barbara together and Hollis helped me out a few times. I suppose he thinks of me as a menace. You'll have to excuse the way my house looks. I just bought it and it needs a lot of work."

The two girls eagerly shared personal information. Hannah explained her business, the thrill of owning her own automobile and now, her house. Mollie was duly impressed. Older than Hannah, she shared news of her recent college graduation and hopes for the future. By the time they reached Hannah's house, the two were fast friends.

Hannah led the way to the kitchen in the dusky twilight of the summer evening to find Hollis climbing from under the sink.

"Is it fixed?" she asked eagerly.

"Seems to be," Hollis replied, then looked toward Mollie. Both girls laughed. "What's wrong?"

"Hollis, there's dirt on your face." Hannah noticed his shirt was dirty as he rolled down the sleeves. He looked ill prepared for a date. "Go in the bathroom and have a look in the mirror. That sink works." She handed him his jacket as he headed for the less-than-immaculate bathroom.

When he emerged, Hollis seemed surprisingly tidy and enthusiastically offered his arm to an eager Mollie Standish.

"Wait! You need to drop me off so I can get my car."

Hollis fumed as he drove home. Mollie and Hannah kept up a lively conversation, to which he was excluded.

"Have fun you two," offered Hannah. "Thank you, Hollis, for your help." Hollis glared at her over his shoulder as Hannah climbed from the backseat. "Nice to meet you, Mollie."

"Same here," offered Mollie. "I'll drop by and bring those books you want to borrow."

"Wonderful!" Hannah climbed into her own driver's seat with a grin. Her friends fell away after her father's suicide. Mollie could be the first of a new set of comrades. Thrilled to be a homeowner, Hannah hoped other happy changes were on the horizon. And her kitchen sink actually worked!

Chapter Six

No sooner did Hollis get home on Monday night than a caller knocked on his door. After pulling off his work boots, he padded across the living room floor and opened the door to find Hannah, dressed in a fashionably businesslike maroon suit.

"What do you want now? I thought you were never asking me for anything again? And shouldn't you be working on your hovel?"

Hannah inspected Hollis' filthy work shirt and dungarees. He had some nerve criticizing the state of her house.

"Nice to see you, too. I have something for you." Hannah held up her hand. Hollis' wristwatch dangled from her finger.

"I wondered where that went."

"You left it on the table in your haste to play the part of ardent beau."

"Thank you for returning it."

"My pleasure. And thank you again for your help. I took your advice about asking questions at the hardware store. They are eager to sell me everything I need and more than happy to provide instruction."

"I still think you should hire a fixer-upper."

"As always, you have every right to your opinion. I also wanted to ask if you would like to come for Sunday dinner. I wish to express my thanks with fried chicken in your honor."

"Exactly where are you asking me to eat?"

"In my new home, Sunday after next." Hollis was obviously uncomfortable with the hygienic aspects of her kitchen so she changed the subject. "How'd your date go?"

"Not well, thanks to you."

"What did I do?"

"You must have said something negative about me to Mollie."

"I certainly did not. In fact, I actually praised you, even to her father. I know that's difficult to believe but it's true. She won't go out again?"

"It doesn't look promising."

"You probably did that to yourself. You were not in the best of moods, as I recall."

"If I was in a bad mood, it was because of you and your endless problems. I was in a fine mood before you showed up on my doorstep."

"Well, I'll be getting off your doorstep, then," Hannah retorted as she started down the stairs. "See you in two weeks."

Hollis watched the retreating pest. Her cooking was probably her only asset, poor girl. He shook his head in disgust, considering the state of her kitchen. Only a fool would eat there. But, by the time two weeks elapsed, Hollis forgot his irritation. The lure of his mother's fried chicken proved irresistible.

* * *

"I can't tell you how much I appreciate your help," Hannah commented, inspecting the dresser to assure aqua paint covered every inch.

"To be honest, it's nice to get out of my house. I was independent while I was away at school. I find it suffocating to be under my parents' wings again," replied Mollie. It was as if the two young women were lifelong friends. Mollie admired Hannah's practical skills and accomplishments. Hannah longed for every detail of Mollie's college experiences and appreciated textbooks she shared.

"You shouldn't be hard on your parents. They love you and want what's best for you."

"Where are your parents? They must be very proud."

Hannah took a deep breath. The conversation took a turn into uncharted waters. "My father has been dead, it will be three years come October. My mother lives in Chicago with relatives. My siblings are spread all over the place. I recently received letters from everyone." Hannah tried to sound cheerful about this recent correspondence but the posts proved discouraging. She was not able to hide her disappointment from Mollie's sharp eye.

"Weren't the letters to your liking?"

"I guess they weren't. I've made a habit of writing everyone at Christmastime but since I moved to Santa Barbara in January and then again to my house, I sent letters with my new address. I'm afraid the replies were not the gladsome tidings I envisioned."

"Why?"

"First my mother told me not to write again until Christmas. My letters upset her and she accused me of deserting my older sister when she was ill.

"Our father's brother and his wife took in two of my younger brothers. They live in Montana. Samuel is 14 and David is 16 now. Although our uncle and his wife seemed anxious to give the boys a home, they were more in want of farmhands than relatives. My brothers' letters have been distressing for some time. It's a rough life. They begged Mother to let them come to Chicago and she said no.

"My little brother, Jonah, is nine. He can't write very well. One of my mother's cousins in Pennsylvania took him in. Her reply contained unhappy news. Her husband is not well and she's not certain how much longer Jonah can stay. She's on the verge of sending her own children to relatives and neighbors.

"My littlest brother and sister were taken in by another aunt. She wrote to tell me, although she will keep my address, she doesn't want me to write again. Turner and Jessica don't remember their real family. They consider my aunt and uncle their parents and my aunt believes it's for the best. My mother approves of this plan. At least they have a good home. My aunt never had children of her own.

"I'm sorry, this is an unpleasant topic for me. I never shared my family problems before. You won't mention it to Hollis? Promise me?"

"Oh, I would never. That is tragic, Hannah. I'm sorry."

"Maybe that's what drives me toward success. I don't have a family. I'm on my own. That's not a bad thing. I seem to have blossomed here in Santa Barbara."

Mollie listened intently and considered Hannah's life, aside from her accomplishments, heartbreaking. "There, I'm done with the drawers."

"Good. The paint can dry overnight. My bedroom may not be glamorous but it's almost clean, tidy and usable."

"You've been lucky to find sturdy furniture at rummage sales. The paint is so cheery."

"I have to admit, I'm getting tired of painting and I have a long way to go." Hannah looked through the window at the peeling paint outside.

"Well, you could spend time sewing up curtains on the new Singer you bought. It's a fine machine. I think you were right to splurge. It will come in handy for years to come."

"I haven't sewn in a while but I used to enjoy it. I think it will save money in the long run. It was such fun to buy fabric. Thanks for your suggestions."

Mollie took a deep breath.

"What's wrong? Why the long sigh?"

"I want to be out on my own. When Hollis asked me out, I was thrilled. He's good looking, so manly, and strong and tall. I couldn't help but wonder if he was the one. I hoped he might be."

Hannah recalled her own historic longings for Hollis Rumsford but she was a stupid girl then.

"Aren't you interested in Hollis?" asked Mollie.

"No."

"I thought you might be. I didn't want anything to interfere with our friendship."

"No worry there. I grew up next door to Hollis. He holds no fascination for me. How did you meet?"

"It was the strangest thing. I was mailing a letter and he came up to the post box. We started talking. He asked me out right then and there. Of course, it wasn't a proper introduction. That was the first strike against him, as far as my father was concerned. The fact he didn't come to get me on our first date was strike two.

"When Hollis asked me out again, I told him I would have to ask my father and then, I didn't want to lose you as a friend. We became such fast friends, it's as if it was meant to be. I'm happy you have no interest in Hollis. He's supposed to call tonight to see if our date is on for Friday."

"Do you mind my asking if you will accept? I feel some guilt for interrupting your date. I think I would feel truly guilty if that ruined things for you. Ruining things for Hollis wouldn't matter but you and I are friends now."

"I will accept. In fact, I'm thrilled to go out again. Maybe this time, he can impress my father. I can't tell you how much that would help."

The two girls spent every possible moment together since they met, scouring rummage sales and working on Hannah's wreck of a house. Both seemed satisfied Hollis Rumsford would not play a role in their friendship.

* * *

Sunday afternoon, Hollis hesitantly knocked on Hannah's door. Hannah showed him inside and escorted her guest through the living room, which Hollis noted showed little improvement. The rubble was cleared, the floor swept and a few boxes were piled against a wall. Other than that, he could see no difference. Once they walked down the short hallway, the kitchen showed unbelievable progress. Hollis stood in awe as he categorized the changes.

"What's wrong with you?" queried Hannah.

"I'm impressed. I was prepared not to be."

Hannah frowned. "Why do you always have such nasty things to say?"

"That isn't nasty. I'm complimenting you."

"No. You said you were prepared to be unimpressed. That is entirely derogatory."

"Did you put new tile in?" Hollis chose to ignore

his hostess's barbs.

"No. It was so dirty, you couldn't tell what was here. I took the minty green from the tile for the wall color. We painted the cupboards a nice clean white, inside and out, and I got new black handles that match the black tile trim. All I did was scrub the rest of the room, oh, and paint this table and chairs. Those were here already. They seem sturdy enough. I sewed and trimmed the curtains in green and black myself," she admitted, proud of her economical handiwork. But Hollis' attention was clearly elsewhere.

He considered the table, set for two. Mismatched china from a set of solid jade green and another from a floral pattern made up the place settings.

"Not enough money for a complete set?" Hollis asked.

Hannah glared.

"This looks nice though. The dishes go together." Hollis took a seat, ready to enjoy his fried chicken and certain nothing could diminish his fine mood. He looked forward to this dinner since Hannah invited him and was prepared to take it outdoors to eat, although this now appeared unnecessary. Hollis helped himself when Hannah placed the serving dishes on the table.

"How did your date go last night?"

"Who wants to know?" This was not a topic Hollis wished to discuss.

"I do. That's why I'm asking."

"You're not asking on behalf of your dear friend, Mollie, are you?"

"What an insulting thing to say." But then, Hannah was used to Hollis' insolent behavior.

"I don't think it went well," Hollis admitted as he savored a succulent bite of chicken.

"Why do you suppose so?"

"You are nosey. You should learn to mind your own business. But I will confess, I don't think Mollie and I have much in common."

"She seems a witty and pleasant companion to me. It must be your fault."

"I'm pretty sure it's not." Hollis rose to the bait. "All she talks about is college and *you*. You are not what I want to discuss on a date."

"Well, it's only natural for a person to talk about current activities and Mollie has been an enormous help to me these past two weeks. Isn't that what you talk about—what you've been doing?"

"No, not really."

"Oh, I see. You probably do nothing but talk about cars."

Hollis stopped eating and glared at his hostess. "Why, what did Mollie tell you?"

"Oh, she doesn't seem to think you have much in common either."

"What are you talking about? She is interested in cars."

"A-ha! Just as I supposed. You talked her to death about cars, I knew it!"

"I did not and besides, she is keen on cars."

"She probably said that to be polite."

"No, I'm certain she was fascinated. She wants me to teach her to drive."

"That simply won't work. You better tell her no if she asks again."

"I taught you to drive, I could teach her."

"You couldn't. She wouldn't last a minute. She's used to being treated with courtesy and respect. If you treat her anything like you did me, she will consider you an ogre."

"Where do you get these ideas? I taught you to

drive in a single afternoon."

"Any sensitive woman would have run for the hills the first time you lost your temper. What did that take, 30 seconds? You best not teach her to drive or it will be the end of your romance, I promise you."

"What do you know about romance, you've never been on a date, have you?"

Hannah took offense at this remark, true as it was. "I've been on dates."

"Now you're making stuff up. You have no idea what a date is like and absolutely no idea how to act on one."

"I have an imagination. I know for sure, I don't want any boyfriend of mine to think more of his car than he does of me. And I certainly know what makes a good date."

"Really? What makes a good date, Hannah?"

"Where did you go on your date?"

Hollis considered Hannah and Mollie might already have discussed last night's events so he answered honestly. "I took her to a movie and then to the soda fountain."

"Did you bring her flowers? Did you make amends to her father for your rudeness the last time?"

"I was not rude last time."

"You didn't have the opportunity to introduce yourself, the way a proper gentleman would."

"That was your fault. How can you condemn me for that? I was ready to go on my date, on time, before you appeared on my doorstep."

"You shouldn't have gone to the movies."

"There's nothing wrong with that."

"Perhaps, but it's not a good way to get to know someone, sitting there staring at a movie screen. You probably sat and talked of nothing but cars at the soda fountain. What an uninspired and boring date. You can't always skate by on your looks, Hollis. I wouldn't blame Mollie if she never went out with you again."

"Is that what she told you?" Hollis was ready to drop Mollie like a hot rock until this very minute. He suddenly wished to prove himself an adequate suitor.

"Not in so many words. I know you, Hollis. I know your habits and your weaknesses. Of course, there are so many of those, I don't think you will ever prove yourself a worthy beau."

"What do you care if Mollie and I go out or not, anyway?"

"She's my friend and I want her to be happy. I think you need my help if you intend to succeed."

The argument continued through dinner and dessert. As Hollis stuffed one last bite of chocolate pie in his mouth, he leaned back in the chair and considered his hostess.

"Well, go ahead and tell me what your idea of a perfect date is."

"You will listen and not interrupt?"

"You have my word."

"To display your generosity, you should bring flowers or some small gift next time. I'm certain your mother explained this to you. What is wrong with you, Hollis?

"Further, you need to make a serious overture to Mollie's father. Find out what he likes. If he is a pipe smoker, maybe you could get him a tin of tobacco or some such small token.

"Avoid the movie theater until you and Mollie get to know each other. You should take her for dinner and probably dancing. Even walking near the beach is better than the movies. And do not, under any circumstances, bring up the topic of cars."

"What am I supposed to talk about, then?"

"Current affairs, your job, what you liked about living in Placerville. And most important, ask Mollie about herself. There's nothing more flattering to a woman than someone who takes a real interest in her desires and opinions. A real interest, Hollis; you have to be sincere. I think you should practice in the mirror—several topics and questions—so they seem natural when you say them. You can practice on me, if nothing else."

"This means you're asking me back for dinner so I can practice?"

"No, I am not asking you back for dinner. You eat like a horse. Every spare dime I have is going into this house. I can't afford to feed you."

"What are you going to do in your living room?" Before dessert, Hollis made a trip to the lavatory, which proved as impressive as the kitchen. The black-and-white hexagonal tile floor gleamed. A fresh coat of white paint renewed the room and every inch was scrubbed.

"I don't have anything to put in the living room. All I'm going to do is scrub for now. I need to paint outside."

"Have your neighbors been by to offer assistance?"

"My house is considered the castaway of the neighborhood, which makes me a pariah. No matter how I fix this place up, it will never fit in, nor will I. But that's fine by me. I don't need a bunch of snooty neighbors who can't mind their own business."

"Have you ever been to Goleta?"

"No. It's too far away to have business interests there."

"And that's all you're interested in—business?"

"All I was interested in was my business. Now I'm interested in my house and my new friend."

"Your new friend is thanks to me." This drew a frown. "You should visit Goleta. It's an interesting place."

"Because you work there?" Hannah scoffed.

"Most assuredly. I am the highlight. There are abundant lemon groves. It's a favorite spot for aviators to land and take off. Did you know the oil we drill is under the ocean?"

"Then how do you get it out?"

"Oil rigs are spaced along the length of piers where I work. There's pier after pier of rigs. It's something to see."

Hannah gathered a last bite of dessert on her fork. It wavered in mid-air as she glared across the table at her dinner guest. "What are you doing?"

"I'm making small talk—practicing for my next date. You didn't think I could, did you?"

"Just get your mind off cars, Hollis, and you'll do fine. I have paperwork to do tonight, you need to go home."

"You're kicking me out?"

"It sounds like it to me. Are you hard of hearing?"

"I tell you what, Hannah. When you buy the paint for the outside of your house, I'll get some buddies from my crew and we'll come and paint for you."

"What's in it for you?"

"Oh, maybe a few Sunday dinners. We can arrange the details after we paint."

"I don't trust you to make details later."

"When can you buy the paint?"

Hannah bit her lip in consideration.

"How many clients do you have now?"

"Four."

"Four who pay?"

"Three pay. One will start paying in another couple

of weeks."

"How many more clients can you handle?"

"I thought I could do two more small businesses, but now I spend so much time on this house, I don't know if I want any more clients."

"Well, do the math, how long before you can afford paint?"

"Maybe two weeks if I don't spend money on anything else."

"All right. We'll plan for two weeks. You have a phone now?"

"Yes, do you need to make a call?"

"No, but you can call me if you don't have the paint by then." Hollis grabbed a notepad from the edge of the kitchen counter and wrote his number. "Don't lose this now."

Hannah was skeptical. This was the first time Hollis offered help of a specific nature. She escorted her tall guest to the front door and opening it, found another visitor.

"Well, well, isn't this interesting?" asked a well-dressed and coiffured Lucy Granville. "Have you taken up with one of my castoffs?"

"Good night, Hollis. It seems I have another guest."

Hollis raised his eyebrow, wondering if he should stay and act as referee.

Hannah caught the appreciative look Hollis gave her sister, just like a man. Lucy called him a castoff, yet, he was all agog at her beauty.

"Lucy," Hollis tipped his hat as he traded places at the door. Then he was on his way.

"What do you want?"

"Is that any way to greet your sister?" Lucy inspected her sibling's dwelling. "Whatever are you doing here?"

"This is my house," Hannah replied, defensively. "Where did you get my address?"

"From Mother, of course. I need you to do something for me."

"Don't hold your breath."

"My, my, Hannah. One would think you were the wronged sister. I went to great lengths to explain to Mother how you left me to those insipid little Sisters of Mercy or whatever they're called. Why, you never even came to visit in my hour of need. She is quite vexed with you. She assured me you would cooperate when I explained my need."

"I don't think you've noticed. Mother does not speak for me. I'm not a child any longer."

"Well, I think you can do this one simple thing for me. You see, I am recently engaged. There is a party to announce the engagement. My fiancé, Gregory, was under the impression I had no relations in California but then he showed me your business card. He picked it up from an associate of his near Stearn's Wharf. When I saw your name emblazoned across the card, I admitted you were my sister. If I was thinking properly, I would have said I didn't know you and life would be much easier.

"But it's too late, now. He wants you to come to the engagement party and I assured him I would ask. It's a formal affair. You must dress appropriately. Here's an invitation. I expect you there, Hannah. Mother expects the same. You are to appear a proper lady and behave accordingly."

"What's in it for me?"

"Are you serious?"

"Perfectly. If I have to buy a dress and spend my precious time on your behalf, I want something out of it."

"What is it you want? I can't believe you're asking me this. I'm your sister, after all. You owe me this much."

"I don't owe you a thing. You might be my sister, and I'm supposed to love you but I don't like you at all. I find your attitudes and actions reprehensible. How do you know I won't mention your escapades to your fiancé?"

"Are you threatening me?" Lucy was dumbfounded. Hannah was always so easily manipulated.

"No. But I will be compensated for my time."

"Very well." Lucy opened her purse and pulled out a ten-dollar bill. "Will this do?"

"No. I have to buy a dress. I don't have any formal wear. This will cost $30."

"That's absurd."

"Take it or leave it." Hannah noted Lucy's demeanor took a nasty turn as she handed over two additional ten-dollar bills.

"Be there on time," Lucy threatened as she headed out the door, primly holding her skirt away from the door frame.

Hannah watched the haughty, retreating figure of her older sister. Lucy evidently found a wealthy beau. Looking at the money in her hand, Hannah found ample funds to purchase paint. Whatever anxiety she felt about her commitment was pushed aside as visions of her freshly painted house surrounded by a lovely garden captured her imagination.

Chapter Seven

"I have the perfect solution!" Mollie's eyes grew wide. "My aunt sent me a dress for graduation. The trouble is, it's too tight. I can't send it back but you're slight of figure. I think it would fit you perfectly. I don't believe you made your sister pay to have you attend her party! Hannah, I can't believe she would actually pay you."

"If there's one thing Lucy understands, it's manipulation. As you can tell, we don't have a warm relationship."

"It's the most deliciously scandalous thing I've ever heard. Oh, how I wish I could go along to see what you're going to do!"

"What I'm going to do?"

"Certainly. Don't you have a plan?"

"I'm going to eat dinner, say as little as possible and make a hasty exit. I don't really know why I'm going. I don't even know why I asked for the money, except to see if she would actually pay me. I'm not going to think about it, that's how much I dread this. Maybe I should send the money back."

"No, no—you should go. I can't wait to hear all about it. Do you know how difficult it is to breach the fortress of Santa Barbara society? If nothing else, you'll have entree to the upper crust. It could help your business."

"My business?"

"Who knows, someone might be interested in your accounting business. There could be opportunities you won't get anyplace else."

"Let's go see the dress."

In less than 30 minutes, Hannah stood in front of a cheval mirror in Mollie's bedroom. The elegant black dress had a small collar, sheer pintuck bodice, short gathered sleeves and a floor-length full skirt. The revealing garment was form fitting from the bodice to the hip. Hannah was shocked at her own feminine figure reflected in the mirror.

"It fits you like a glove!"

"I can't possibly wear this."

"Not only can you wear it, it's yours to keep. It will never fit me. You are beautiful!"

Hannah thought Mollie's idea ridiculous. "I can't accept this."

"Yes, you can. I'll tell Mother you're staying for dinner and I'll explain about the dress."

It was clear Mollie took Hannah's predicament to heart and there would be no turning back.

* * *

If Hannah was apprehensive about her sister's engagement party, she gave the appearance of a confident, capable, and mature woman as she stepped through the doors of Mr. and Mrs. Edison's opulent home. Mollie's mother added her own touches to Hannah's ensemble—rhinestone combs to hold her curls in check and a fur-trimmed, black velvet cape.

Hannah nearly ruined her image when a sweet and innocent Lucy gave her a hug and gushed, "Oh, dearest, I am so happy you are here." Then she whispered so no one else could hear, "Give me a hug, stupid. I paid for this performance. You better make it good. I want my $30 worth."

As if on cue, Hannah returned the warm embrace and replied, "I'm so happy to be here!"

Little else was accomplished in the way of sisterly displays. Hannah stayed in the background, pretending to listen to others' conversations while munching canapes.

The party included a sit-down dinner. Hannah found herself seated between two young men, competitors for her attention. She retreated to comfortable silence and left the two men to their verbal combat, only commenting when necessary. The young man on her right, Randy, was rather intriguing, especially when he hit upon the one topic Hannah was eager to discuss—her work.

"Why have I never seen you with your sister?" Randy asked.

"I have my own business. I'm afraid it takes most of my time."

"You have a business? Aside from the fact you are thoroughly female, aren't you rather young to be in commerce?"

Lucy's fiancé admitted himself to the conversation. "No, she's telling the truth, Randy. An associate of mine gave me her business card. My future sister-in-law does accounting for businesses in our fair city. I might add her customers, at least the ones I know of, are complimentary of her work."

"That is ridiculous," offered Gregory's father. "Women are taking jobs from men who need them to support families. What is the world coming to?"

"I assure you, Mr. Edison," replied Hannah, "my business was my own invention. A man might be able to make a go of it but I doubt he would last." Hannah knew, only a few months ago, she would never have been so bold. She did not care about these people. If she promoted her business or found a new customer, there was nothing to lose.

"What do you mean, he wouldn't last? Do you actually think you do a better job than a man?" It was clear Mr. Edison was outraged at his youthful guest's audacity.

"Now Father," soothed Gregory. "Hannah is our new sister. We need to make her feel welcome, not castigated."

"That's all right, I'd like to answer." A thrill of delight overtook Hannah at Lucy's forbidding stare. "First of all, I have mathematical ability that enables me to excel at sums. Secondly, male accountants would not work for the low fees I charge. I've also found many men don't have the kind of persistence that enables me to expand my business." This last comment brought guffaws from a few men at the table.

"Hannah," began Lucy, "you mustn't exaggerate your abilities."

"I'm not, sister dear. You of all people should understand my drive to succeed. And I hope, if anyone is looking for an accountant, they will consider my services."

Lucy was alarmed at Hannah's shameless promotion. Before she could comment further, Gregory put his hand over hers. "Lucy, darling, I think your sister is a refreshing example of the modern woman. Why have you kept her hidden away from us?"

Lucy's smile seemed forced but Hannah was

probably the only one who knew her well enough to notice. "She is just the cutest little thing, isn't she?" agreed Lucy.

Conversation amongst the partygoers dissolved into private discussion. Hannah pretended to pay attention as Randy droned on about changing morals and the depression's effect on families. Once the dessert plates were cleared, the guests were invited to the music room, where a renowned pianist was set to perform.

Hannah thought this the ideal time to make her departure. She lingered at the table, then walked toward the front door, collecting her borrowed cape along the way.

"Hannah!" came a concerned shout. "You're not leaving already?"

"I'm afraid so. Lucy understands I have an early morning, so I must be on my way," Hannah lied. "It was a pleasure meeting you, Randy."

"The pleasure was all mine. Can I take you home? How did you get here?"

"I have my own automobile, thank you."

"My, you really are the epitome of the independent new woman. Might I walk you to your car?"

Hannah could think of no excuse to dissuade the obviously interested Randy. "Certainly." This was a new experience, to have a man pay attention.

Randy offered his arm and made small talk as Hannah pointed out her blue Model A.

"Well, that's a practical automobile to be sure," he commented kindly. Stopping beside the car, he bent forward to kiss Hannah on the lips. She pushed him away.

"I don't know what you mean by your admiration of modern women but I assure you, I am not that kind of girl. Please let go of my arm."

"Now Hannah, your sister filled me in on your habits after dessert."

"What habits?"

"She told me how you use men to get things you want. I couldn't believe you were so self-sufficient. She assured me, your success has not come from any mathematical or business abilities. I want to know what it would take for me to be the one to tuck you in tonight?"

At this, Hannah slapped Randy's face as hard as she could. He laughed in response.

"I always did like the feisty ones. Lucy knows me only too well. As she predicted, I am taken with you."

It seemed Randy's hands were everywhere. Hannah ignored him, intent on her own course of action. As quickly as she balanced herself, she slammed her knee into Randy's groin. His reaction was gratifying as he fell uselessly onto the lawn, drawn up in a ball as he struggled for breath.

"I hope that serves as a lesson to you. Modern women *are* completely self-reliant. And don't believe a thing my sister says. She is a deceitful bitch." At this, Hannah climbed into the driver's seat and sped away.

By the time she parked her car at home, the shock of Randy's behavior began to take a toll. Hannah hurried into the house as a steady rain started to fall. Her hands shook noticeably as she removed the cape and hung it up to dry. She walked into the bathroom to remove the combs from her hair, a difficult task while trembling.

Taking a deep, calming breath, Hannah noticed an odd noise coming from the hallway. She walked out of the bathroom and looked toward the ceiling, first in the hall, then in the kitchen and living room. Even her bedroom echoed a sound too intense to be caused by rain hitting the roof.

Hannah quickly went out the back door and around the side of the house where she had seen an old ladder. She brought it into the kitchen and set it beneath the crawl space to the attic. Gingerly crawling up the rungs, Hannah gave a push on the access door and slid it to the side, then used her flashlight to take a look.

Containers were scattered across the attic as if a forest of giant mushrooms sprouted from the floor. They'd evidently been placed by previous owners to catch the rain when it poured through the roof. As Hannah shown the light around the attic, it appeared to be raining inside at about the same intensity the rain fell outside.

* * *

Hollis was startled awake at the sound of furious knocking. Looking across the room at the empty bed, he first surmised it was Dock making the racket but remembered the door was unlocked. Hollis pulled on his trousers and headed for the door, swinging it wide to find a sopping wet Hannah. She shook visibly and seemed too upset to utter a word. Wet curls covered her head. She wore what must have been quite an elegant frock. It was black and clung to her skin so completely, Hollis could not help but stare.

"I'll get my coat," was his only comment.

"I'll drive," offered Hannah once they reached the bottom of the staircase.

"You certainly will not. You should not have driven over here when you were upset."

"Is that another of your rules? Thou shalt not drive while upset. Besides, I'm—not upset," Hannah proclaimed, trying not to cry.

"Get in my car. What's wrong with you?" This question got more of a reaction than Hollis intended.

Hannah began to sob in earnest. "My roof is

leaking! All my hard work was for nothing! All the money I spent on paint—all my time wasted. The rain is going to ruin everything."

"It can't be that bad."

Hannah nodded her head briskly. "Yes, it can. And that's not all. I went to Lucy's stupid party. I made her pay me and this is my punishment. I called her a bitch. She is a bitch but I shouldn't have said that. She told this man I was easy! Can you imagine?"

"No, I can't imagine anyone would believe such a thing," Hollis facetiously replied.

"He attacked me!"

"Are you hurt?" Hollis asked with more concern.

"No, I kneed him right in the groin as hard as I could. He was completely disabled."

"Why am I not surprised?"

"Can't you drive faster?"

"Did you plan on getting to your house in one piece?"

"I sold my soul for 30 pieces of silver, just like Judas."

"What are you talking about, Hannah? You aren't making any sense."

"Here we are. Park! Park!" Hannah flew from the car before Hollis managed to stop.

What was he in for now?

* * *

Hollis stood on the roof, afraid the whole thing would cave in at any moment as a flash of lightning lit the sky. He reassured himself by muttering his thoughts aloud.

"This is a fine time for a storm. I will probably die up here on Hannah's hovel, fall through her Swiss cheese roof or get struck by lightning. I cannot believe she got me up here in the pouring rain. Why do I keep helping her? She is the most obnoxious girl I ever met."

Hollis, despite the wind, managed to stretch canvas across the roof, nailing the edges as he picked his way along the perimeter. "Why couldn't that girl take my advice and hire a fixer-upper? He would have inspected the roof and told her it needed to be replaced. If I die, it's going to be on her head." Hollis stood upright to make his way toward the ladder as another lightning bolt lit the sky. "Holy shit! Hannah! Do you know what's behind your house?"

"What?" she shouted from the ground.

"Do you know what's behind your house?"

"Come down from there, Hollis, and stop playing the fool."

Hollis scrambled down the ladder and grabbed Hannah's arm. "There is a graveyard on the other side of the fence! I saw it from the roof."

"What a surprise. Are you finished?"

"Didn't you hear me? There is a graveyard right there."

"I'm going in the house. If you want to stand out here like a blithering idiot, be my guest."

Hannah turned and tromped through her back door, listening intently. Had Hollis managed to prevent the rain from pouring through her roof?

As Hollis brushed the water from his slicker, he could not keep his eyes from Hannah's figure, displayed in breathtaking detail beneath her rain-soaked dress. He quickly looked away when she turned to face him.

"What is the matter with you?" she inquired. Any trace of insecurity was mitigated by her anger at Hollis' every move.

"There are graves on the other side of your fence. I saw them from the roof."

"So?"

"What do you mean, so?"

"What difference does that make?"

"You knew about this?"

"Of course."

"Why didn't you tell me?"

"Why would I do that? It only provides you another opportunity to criticize my home."

"Then you do admit, it's rather shocking."

"No, it's not shocking at all. It's one of the many reasons Mr. Rowland sold the house to me. The graveyard is not exactly a selling point. The owners of the two estates on the sides of my property wanted to buy this land, knock down my house and plant heavily so no one would know the graveyard is back there. Trust me, those people have been dead for years, they don't get visitors."

"Why is it there?"

"Of all the stupid questions. How elementary do I have to get? When people die, they get buried."

"I'm losing patience, Hannah. Doesn't it bother you to live right next door? A girl, all by yourself?"

"It does not bother me. In fact, I have come to like it a great deal."

"You what?"

"I like it there. It's peaceful. I would take you and demonstrate if it weren't raining."

"You go there at night?"

"Sometimes. Why, does that scare you?"

"Yes, quite frankly. I find it disturbing you go at all."

"Don't be such a coward. I suppose you think all the horror movies are true and bats and monsters are my new neighbors. Oh, watch out Hollis, Dracula is standing behind you!"

Hollis jumped, involuntarily. "I am fed up, Hannah. I'm coming as I promised, to paint your house. I am going to fix your roof, then I want to be done with you forever!"

"That's fine by me."

"I'm going home now. If you want your car, you better come along because I'm not coming back until the day I paint. I don't care if you show up half-starved on my doorstep, you understand?"

The drive to Hollis' house was silent except for the sound of rain. Hannah believed her decision to plead her case in person was wise. Hollis would likely have hung up on her if she telephoned. Hannah managed a sullen, "Thank you," as she exited Hollis' vehicle.

* * *

After a hot bath, Hannah climbed into bed. The patter of rain hitting the tarp should have lulled her to sleep but this was an eventful evening. Thoughts swirled in Hannah's head. The face of Hollis Rumsford soon supplanted memories of Lucy's party, Randy's bold advances and even her leaky roof. He was so angry. She knew he would be, that's why she never told him. His reaction to the cemetery was exactly as she envisioned. He didn't understand. She recalled her initial visit the day Mr. Rowland sold her the house.

Her new home was an undeniable wreck, no less than she expected. But it was hers. Pride of ownership lightened her step as she walked out the back door. The sunlight was fading and she intended to investigate every detriment Mr. Rowland listed.

Knee-high, withered weeds covered the backyard. A shed with a broken window sat in the far corner. Honeysuckle spilled over the top of the shed and obscured fencing on all sides of the little yard. Finding the gate seemed more a chore than she imagined.

As she threaded her way toward the back, dry weeds crunched beneath her feet. No trace of a gate could be discerned when she looked across the wall of yellow flowers. Their heady scent saturated the yard.

It seemed a waste to walk the width of the property near the fence but she stepped on something hard near the corner opposite the shed. Tugging dried vegetation aside, she found a stepping stone, a possible marker for an opening.

Fortunately, the honeysuckle was easily pulled from the fence. Before long, she cleared enough of the vines to distinguish the edge of a wooden gate, badly in need of paint. She tugged the latch up, then realized the gate moved more away than toward her when she gave it a shake. She threw her full weight against the gate and it reluctantly gave way.

Hannah found herself standing in the small cemetery Mr. Rowland warned her about. If these dead people were her new neighbors, she needed to overcome any trepidation before moving in.

Perhaps as many as 80 stone and wooden markers arose from weed-covered soil. Crosses, rectangles and arches commemorated lives long forgotten. Only a few had toppled to the ground.

She picked her way between the monuments, glancing at now familiar names as she went: Prudence Witherby, born 1872, died 1891, May she rest in peace; Maria Elena Abril, aged 27 years, Beloved wife and mother; George Spindler, Lived to a ripe, good age, Died of small pox.

Several hardy rose bushes survived decades of neglect. A tangled yellow rose glowed in the final rays of daylight as the sun set behind her house. Tangled in honeysuckle, a deep red rose near the fence shot its flowers toward the sky. The fine scent of delicate, pink, damask roses filled Hannah's senses as she bent forward to read a small marker near the edge of the graveyard.

Eliza May Carpenter, born August 1, 1882, died September 20, 1882.

She sat down and leaned against a large marker. It was soon too dark to read headstones. A smile graced her face as an owl hooted in the distance. She took a deep breath and closed her eyes. Her neighbors were at peace. There was nothing to be afraid of.

As always, the memory served to soothe. Hannah drifted off to sleep.

* * *

Hollis seethed quietly as Mollie meticulously noted each detail of her best friend's tribulations. He managed to demonstrate every gentlemanly habit Hannah suggested, against his better judgement. But having accomplished such a titanic task, he was failing utterly to enjoy his date. Hollis wished they'd gone to the movies. At least he could have sat in silence for a while without the name "Hannah" being mentioned.

He took the time to discover Mollie's father enjoyed an occasional cigar and presented a few Cuban cigars as a peace offering. Hollis stopped to purchase a small bouquet of flowers when he properly called for Mollie and assured Mr. Standish of his gentlemanly intentions. He took Mollie to a nice restaurant, where the litany of tragedy commenced.

Honestly, he heard all this from the horse's mouth. Still blistered from her recent rude comments, the last thing he wished to discuss was the thankless Hannah Granville. When he proposed a different topic, his suggestion was met with an unusual level of hostility.

"Why? You and I are Hannah's only friends. We have a common interest in her."

"I am not interested in any way, shape, or form, in Hannah Granville. I don't know what she could possibly have told you to make you think such a thing. She is an irritating, self-centered and rude person. I frankly can't imagine what you see in her. Why don't you tell me what you like for dessert? Then we can settle on a different topic."

"I'm full."

It was clear, Mollie was devoted to his arch enemy. There seemed no middle ground. Hollis was not surprised at Mollie's next declaration.

"I have a headache. I want to thank you for the lovely evening, but I think it's best you take me home."

"My pleasure." Hollis grinned inappropriately. His torment was about to end. There were, after all, many fish in the sea.

* * *

Hannah was relieved to discover the storm was an oddity. She felt assured no further damage would be done before the roof was repaired.

Working at home after picking up her clients' paperwork enabled her to refurbish the house in daylight. Hannah often completed her real work in the small hours of the morning. Since Mr. Rowland ceased checking up on her, Hannah's time was her own to spend as she pleased, as long as she managed to keep up.

She continued to lunch with Mr. Rowland at least once a week, when he imparted business knowledge and urged Hannah to practice her communication skills. The information and training enabled her to charm her clients. Even Mr. Barney smiled at sight of her, although the haberdashery proved the most time-consuming stop along her route.

After a hurried trip through Santa Barbara on Monday morning, Hannah parked in front of her house. Gathering her work, she started for the door, only to find a young man standing on her porch. Something seemed oddly familiar as Hannah slowly approached. He held a mangled cap nervously in his hands. His overalls and shirt were filthy and torn. A trace of hopefulness sparkled in his eyes. Hannah's heart began to pound.

"David?"

"It's me, Hannah," replied David.

Hannah rushed to the porch. The boy grew incredibly in the three years since she had seen him. At 16, he towered over Hannah as she hugged him for dear life.

"What are you doing here? Where is Samuel?"

"We flipped a rattler and come here. Things was bad in Montana. There weren't enough food and we got blamed 'fer everything."

"You did what?"

"We hopped a boxcar and got out of Montana for good. We met a Boston bum who showed us how to get here."

"Is Samuel here?"

"Yeah, but he feels poorly. He played tear baby once we got to California. We ate high on the hog and it didn't settle good."

David pointed to the corner of the porch where Samuel sat against the wall, in equally bad shape as his older brother, only pale. Both boys were nothing but skin and bones. Their brown hair was dirty and dull. Their hazel eyes reflected dim expectation.

"Help me get him in the house." Hannah was stunned when 14-year-old Samuel proved taller than she.

"Howdy, Hannah," mumbled Samuel. "You'd be proud of us. We weren't no gummies. Things will be hunky-dory now, won't they be?"

Hannah was perplexed by the hobo jargon the boys picked up. The first order of business was to get her brothers fed and clean. Samuel was too weak to sit up, so after ushering him from the bathtub wearing only a towel, she put him in her bed and fed him there. David was so thin, he managed to wear his sister's robe.

Hannah urged the boys to eat slowly but they were ravenous. What was she to do? They had nothing but the clothes they came in. Those clothes were too threadbare to consider washing. Both boys were clearly exhausted.

David gave an account of their adventure, especially the cruel treatment they received from their Montana uncle and his wife. Practical matters began to weigh on Hannah's mind. She soon lost focus as David rattled on about the hard times the brothers suffered.

"David, tell me what size you and Samuel wear. I need to get you some clothes, underwear and pajamas, at least enough to see you through the next couple of days. I need to buy groceries."

"I seed your fine automobile, Hannah. Can I come too?"

"David, you don't have anything to wear to a store. You would look like an Okie, even if I managed to wash your clothes without shredding them. I'll take care of the shopping today. You stay here and keep an eye on Samuel. There will be plenty of time for car trips later. Tell me what your plans are."

"We don't got no plans, Hannah. Sam and me comed here to you 'cause that's the only place we could come. We won't be no trouble, I give you my word. Mother won't take us. There's nowhere else to go."

"No, I guess there isn't." Hannah gave her little brother a heartfelt smile. "I guess the Granville family is back in business!"

* * *

Hollis looked disgustedly toward his door. It was silly to think he could recognize a knock, yet he was as certain as could be, Hannah was standing on the other side.

Content to make her wait, he took a sip of coffee and finished the newspaper article before answering. He was not surprised to find Hannah on his doorstep, exactly where he told her not to come. Without a word, he started to shut the door in her face.

"Wait, Hollis. It's not for me and you don't have to leave your house."

He held the door slightly ajar. "Who, pray tell, would it be for?"

"My little brother."

What hogwash was Hannah peddling now? "You have exactly one minute and then I'm closing the door."

"My brothers ran away. They hopped a train and came here to find me. They're in desperate straits, Hollis—emaciated, destitute and distraught. I spent all the money I have to buy them clothes and food. You know I've been spending money on my house.

"But Samuel is sick, really truly sick. He has a high fever and needs a doctor. I don't have any money left. All I'm asking for is a small loan, maybe five dollars to tide me over until I get paid. I'll pay you back right away. Please, Hollis. I'm desperate or I wouldn't come to you."

"Why didn't you go to your new friend, Mollie?"

"I'm too ashamed to ask her for money. She's done so much for me already."

"And I haven't?"

"Yes, you have certainly helped, and I admire you for it. But you told me you were promoted at work, so I know you could afford five dollars."

"What about Lucy? Those are her brothers too."

"You know Lucy. She doesn't care about those boys and wouldn't be put out for them. They're in rough shape, Hollis. What manners and English they used to know have been forgotten. Lucy would not tolerate them."

"What will you do for me in return?"

This comment brought ugly memories of Randy on the night of Lucy's engagement party.

"What did you have in mind?"

"I intend to be repaid but I want four Sunday dinners, starting next Sunday, the day after we come and work on your house."

"Agreed." This seemed a simple request, in light of recent propositions.

"And you have to eat outside."

This condition drew a glare. "Agreed," was Hannah's reply, although she longed to tell Hollis Rumsford she didn't want to eat with him either.

After Hollis retrieved a five-dollar bill from his bedroom, he handed it through the crack in the door and watched as Hannah hurried down the stairs. If ever a girl needed a husband to keep her in line, it was Hannah Granville.

Chapter Eight

Hannah looked out the window as Hollis bade farewell to the five men he brought to repair her roof and paint her tiny house. He paid each one, shook their hands and thanked them for the day's work. Even though she toyed with the idea her ill-gotten paint might have some curse, the spring green color and stark white trim made her house look new. The wood shake roof appeared water tight. It was amazing how quickly the men transformed the exterior of her abode.

As Hannah pulled her curtain to the side, she watched Hollis pay Samuel and David for their help. The boys were used to hard labor but were in such poor shape, they did little but fetch and carry. It was thoughtful of Hollis to include them. The uncomfortable idea Hannah owed more to Hollis than she could ever repay preyed on her mind as the boys escorted their benefactor to the front door. Hollis tipped his hat at the doorway but did not enter.

"I'll be going then. What time is dinner tomorrow?"

"Four. How much money did you spend today?"

"Not much."

"That's not true. You paid for the roofing materials and I saw you pay those men. I want you to give me an accounting of what this cost. I need to pay you back."

"I agreed to do this. It's not necessary."

"Yes, it is. I won't be beholden to you."

Hollis glowered at his old neighbor. "I'll bring you a written accounting tomorrow."

"Thank you. And thank you for today." Hannah wished to express sincere gratitude but could not bring herself to say anything further. Perhaps she would make an extra effort for Sunday dinner. Hollis was bound to understand her thanks, even if she couldn't express her true appreciation.

The first of Hollis' Sunday dinners went off without a hitch. Dinner was perfection, including apple pie and vanilla ice cream for dessert. Hannah took her dinner on the back porch, all the while listening to Hollis entertain her brothers. She could not make out many words, but frequent laughter left no doubt the boys enjoyed Hollis' company.

She made an initial payment of three dollars on her debt, which had taken an alarming dip into the red. Hollis presented a tally of expenses. It seemed a staggering sum to Hannah, who suddenly faced financial concerns she could not have imagined two weeks ago.

Taking a deep breath, she watched Hollis depart. After all, there was much to be thankful for. Her brothers were here, safe and eventually, sound. Her house was water-tight and cozy, if incomplete. She felt blessed to have a dear friend and a good business. But Hannah wasn't one to dwell on satisfaction. The coming weeks would provide sufficient challenges to put Miss Granville on a tear.

* * *

"How was school?" inquired Hannah as the reunited family sat down to dinner.

"Not good," replied Samuel.

"Why not?"

"We ain't been to school in ever so long. It don't hold much appeal."

"You haven't been to school. Ain't is not a word. And it doesn't hold appeal. You boys have lost all proper grammar."

"We're right glad you agree with us, Hannah," offered a cheeky David.

"I'm not agreeing with you. I'm correcting your English. You can't hope to get ahead in life if you don't use proper English. And you won't find a good job if you don't have a proper education."

"You didn't get much of a education, Hannah, and you seem to be doing all right, 'specially for a girl."

"I may not have gone to school as long as some, but I did read as much as I could and I continue to learn as much as I have time for," which was no time at all at present. "My goal is to prepare you for manhood. You need a good job, a good education and good manners when the time comes for you to pay court to the girl of your dreams."

This drew a snicker from both boys.

"Don't laugh. That day will come before you know it."

Mollie picked this moment to enter the kitchen. She long since abandoned the formality of knocking when she arrived at her home away from home.

Knowing both her brothers were enamored of Mollie, Hannah completed her little lecture.

"Mollie would notice if you boys were more articulate. She went to college. She wouldn't consider any suitor who sounded ill-bred."

A timid, "Yes, ma'am," by David was the only comment either boy was willing to offer in Mollie's presence.

"I'm glad you're here, Mollie. Have some dessert. I have an announcement to make." Hannah attempted enthusiasm in her tone. "I received a telegram from cousin Aubrey. She put Jonah on the train and he'll be here tomorrow. It's one more part of our family reunited!" And one more mouth to feed, Hannah thought to herself.

"Why is he coming here?" asked Samuel.

"Aubrey's husband is ill. Her children have been sent to live with family and friends. She simply can't keep Jonah. She wrote to Mother the same as you boys did and got the same result."

"Where is he gonna sleep?"

"I'll have to buy another mattress for your room." Hannah took a deep breath and plastered a smile on her face. "I know it will be tight but we'll find a way to make this work, you'll see. The important thing is, so many of us are together."

Mollie sat quietly at the kitchen table. As difficult as life already seemed for her friend, this was bound to make everything worse, no matter how cheerful Hannah appeared.

* * *

Hollis was confused when a new and different boy opened the door on Sunday afternoon.

"Who are you?"

"I'm Jonah Granville," came the polite reply. "Won't you come in? You must be Hollis. My brothers told me you were coming. How do you do?"

Hollis shook the hand this small gentleman offered. "Very well, thank you."

"My sister has dinner prepared. Won't you come this way?"

Dinner was already on the table. David and Samuel quickly took their seats and offered Hollis his usual place near the wall.

"I'll get my sister," offered Jonah.

"Naw, she's not gonna eat with us, Jo. Set down there and help yourself," commanded David.

Jonah's lip quivered.

"Don't go bawlin' again now. We got company. Nobody's gonna bite you just cause your sissy ain't around," Samuel tormented.

As usual, David and Samuel were ravenous. Jonah picked at his food, too distraught to do it justice. An acrid odor hung in the kitchen.

"What's that smell?" inquired Hollis.

"Hannah burnt the spuds," explained David. "Don't worry, there's plenty enough for dinner."

"Where is your sister?"

"Aw, she has work to do. She's up in the attic."

Hollis understood Hannah gave her bedroom over to her brothers. Hannah seemed eager to take the attic as her room, claiming it was a quiet out-of-the-way spot where she could work in peace. The old ladder stood in the corner beneath the crawl space, a poor substitute for a staircase.

As had become his custom over the last weeks, Hollis engaged the boys in conversation about baseball, the beach and school. He attempted to draw Jonah into the discussion. Overcome at Hollis' questions about his appearance in Hannah's house, Jonah watched teary-eyed as his brothers explained.

"Hard times has hit the relations where Jonah lived. They sent him packin'. This was the only spot what would have him. He ain't none too happy to be here though," offered David.

"Yeah, he wants his mommy," Samuel added.

It was apparent the older boys had not warmed to their proper and well-dressed little brother.

"Hannah!" declared Jonah as his sister descended the ladder.

"I'll get your dessert."

Jonah leapt to his feet and hugged his sister. "Won't you come and eat with us?"

Before Hannah could respond, Hollis decreed, "Yes, why don't you sit down and have dessert?" It was obvious Jonah needed his sister's support and Hollis was willing to suspend hostilities for the boy's benefit.

Samuel and David shot curious looks across the table. Neither Hollis nor Hannah spoke ill of each other but it was apparent the two shared some deep-seated animosity. This was the first time everyone would be seated together at the table, if Hannah accepted.

"All right," agreed Hannah, who coaxed Jonah to serve wedges of butterscotch pie before she took a seat. Jonah quickly scrambled onto her lap.

Hollis took a look around the table as he savored a forkful of pie. David and Samuel seemed to be recovering from their ordeal in Montana. Their faces filled out considerably and their clothes, which originally hung loosely, fit better each time Hollis saw them. Hannah, on the other hand, was thinner than ever. Dark circles rimmed her eyes. Hannah nervously ran her hand along Jonah's arm as if to comfort him or perhaps it was to soothe herself. Hollis continued conversing with the older boys until the dessert plates were empty.

"Why don't you boys clear the table? I need a word with your sister."

"And then you need to get your homework out. I want to be certain you're prepared for school tomorrow," warned Hannah. Both older boys grumbled loudly at this suggestion. Only Jonah seemed eager to please his sister.

"Where can we talk?" asked a solemn Hollis.

"This way." Hannah led the way out the back door and through the yard.

"Where are you going?"

"The boys are all as terrified of the graveyard as you. They won't be able to hear us if we walk through there. Don't worry. I'll protect you," Hannah taunted as she held the cemetery gate.

"I'm *not* afraid of the graveyard."

Hannah rushed to explain, "Before you lecture me, I don't have any money for you. I'm working on it. I had to buy another mattress. I can't imagine when I'll be able to buy real beds. Samuel put a hole in the knee of his dungarees already. At least Jonah came with clothes. I don't know what I would have done otherwise.

"Jonah cries all the time and the other boys tease him mercilessly. They think he shouldn't cry at his age. He doesn't eat much, at least not so far. It's all I can do to buy food right now. It's true, David doesn't go to school every day but he'll get used to it.

"I'm sorry, you have to wait for your money a bit longer. I'll have something for you soon, maybe next week." Hannah seemed sincerely apologetic and more than a little frantic.

"Hannah, you are not a parent. What makes you think this is going to work? Those boys are bigger than you. You are barely older than they are. Why did you let them stay?"

"What else could I do?" asked an incredulous Hannah.

"Your mother needs to take responsibility for her own children. No matter how you try, you are not going to turn them into sophisticated gentlemen. Samuel and David led hard lives. Do you even listen to them when they talk? They don't want to go to school."

"School is free. Schools are closing all over the country but not here. I would have given anything to stay in school at David's age. It's a wonderful opportunity."

"Maybe for you but they want to work. They learn with much younger children. It's embarrassing. All they do is go to school and do chores. They are able and willing to make their own living. You need them to if you aren't going to send them to your mother. You can't provide for everybody."

"Yes, I can. I only need time to adjust."

"You should never have given those boys your bedroom."

"Why not?"

"They can come and go at will. You won't know what they're up to. You should have put them in the attic. Jonah obviously led a sheltered life. He shouldn't share a room with his brothers."

"Well, he usually comes to the attic to sleep. This will all resolve in time. Jonah likes school. He still misses cousin Aubrey's home and the room he shared with her son."

"He doesn't want to be here, does he?"

"Not now. He wants to go home, his home in Pennsylvania. He's nine now, not so small as when Mother packed him off to cousin Aubrey. He's a sweet little boy, just confused. He'll get used to being here."

"This is a recipe for disaster."

"It's none of your business, Hollis. This is not your family, it's mine. I'm sorry about your money but there's nothing I can do about it."

"I'm not talking about the money; I don't care

about the money."

"I don't understand. Why are you mad at me?"

"I'm not mad at you. I'm trying to explain, you are making foolish choices. This is not a good situation. Nothing good can come from it."

"And you're afraid I'll need help and come to you? You don't want to be bothered. You made that very clear. I won't come to you ever again. I owe you one more dinner and then you'll never have to see me. I give you my word."

But Hollis made a bond with David and Samuel. He was determined to help them chart their own course. Disgusted, Hollis walked back to the house.

Hannah stood rooted in place, not wanting to consider any of Hollis' arguments. She frowned at his comment when he entered the kitchen.

Hollis' rich voice drifted through the open window. "Who wants to go to the beach? We can have a game of volleyball."

"What's that?" inquired a suddenly enthusiastic Jonah.

"We'll teach you," explained Hollis.

"Aw, he's too little," noted Samuel.

"No, it's never too soon to learn the latest craze. You can be on my team, Jonah."

Hannah ambled across the backyard and seething, entered her empty house.

* * *

Having gotten off work early, Hollis stopped at the bank to cash his paycheck and went directly to the five and dime. He was determined the Granville brothers needed a little fun in their lives and he was prepared to provide it. After all, it was not so long since he was a boy. Hollis bought a baseball and bat, intent to take the boys to the beach and teach them to hit.

Hollis made his way to Hannah's house and parked in front. He understood she often worked at home and hoped to catch her there. His intention was to avoid further acrimony by explaining his plan to entertain her brothers. He was surprised to find David and Samuel laughing on the front porch. Laughter ceased when the boys spotted him coming up the walkway.

"Shouldn't you boys be in school?"

"No, no," mumbled David, "but we need to go to the grocery for Hannah. We best be on our way."

The boys bounded off the porch and made a beeline for the sidewalk.

"Is Hannah home?"

"No, she's at work," shouted David over his shoulder.

Something seemed not quite right to the once mischievous Mr. Rumsford. He tried the front door and found it unlocked. Quietly, he peered inside the bedroom door to find a mattress-strewn mess. The living room was empty, as always. He walked down the short hall, past the bathroom and into the empty kitchen. At first, he was relieved the boys were honest but then he heard a sob. Standing completely still, Hollis perceived someone crying in the attic. The ladder lay on the floor against the wall. Quietly, he stood the ladder in the crawl hole and climbed up to find Hannah sitting on her bed, weeping. She quickly wiped her eyes when his head appeared through the attic floor.

"Go away."

"If I go away, I'll take the ladder down," Hollis threatened.

"Fine."

True to his word, Hollis started down the ladder when Hannah reconsidered her reply.

"No, wait."

Hollis climbed back up to behold the lady of the house, still seated on her bed. "Would you like to come down?"

"Promise me, you won't say it."

"Say what?"

"I told you so."

"You have my solemn word. How long have you been up here?"

"All day," she admitted as she scurried toward the ladder.

"I see. So, this was some little joke of your brothers'?"

As Hannah stepped onto the kitchen floor, Hollis looked her over, waiting for a reply. His first real memory of Hannah was at her father's funeral. For a man who was revered in the entire community, few attended Mr. Granville's somber ceremony, not wishing to condone his loathsome act. Hannah stood solemn and dry-eyed, her arms around two of her little brothers.

The stigma of her father's suicide served to distance Hannah from former school chums. She led a solitary life, working in his parents' house or sticking her nose in a book. It was as if the girl did not exist until she came to Santa Barbara.

He never saw her cry until the day of the unfortunate storm. He was unnerved to find her crying alone in the attic today. To Hollis' surprise, Hannah somehow became a friend, albeit an infuriating one.

"They didn't want to go to school. They took the ladder when I was getting ready for work."

"What about Jonah?"

"I imagine he went to school. He's like me, he likes to learn."

"Did he know the older boys took the ladder?"

A tear slid down Hannah's cheek as she nodded in

reply.

"Hannah, there's more to life than work."

"What is that supposed to mean?"

"You want your family together, no matter how difficult it is. You have this fantastic notion of what life could be, if only those boys would follow your advice. But David and Samuel are more men than boys. They had to grow up in Montana. I'm certain they are grateful you've given them a home but you need to listen to them."

"Samuel is only 14."

"He knows his own mind. He's not the little boy you imagine him to be. Jonah, on the other hand, needs a mother. Are you ready to be his mother with all that entails? Are you even mature enough?"

"I am reliable and dependable."

"I won't argue. But you aren't any fun, Hannah, and those boys need to live in a happy household. How are you going to give them that? You told me you've never been on a date. Why do you think no one ever asked you out?"

"I'm not pretty. Boys never liked me."

Hollis grabbed her arm and pulled her to the front door. A small mirror hung beside it.

"Look in there. What do you see?"

"I need to go to work."

"Not yet, you don't. Tell me about this young woman. How does she look to you?"

Hannah seemed confounded.

"Is she ugly? Full of warts? What about her skin? Has she suffered from smallpox? Is her nose pointed? What about her chin?" An odd thought occurred to Hollis. Hannah was a pretty girl, simply overshadowed by her sister. He frowned.

"What are you getting at, Hollis?" Hannah was

clearly losing patience.

"My point is, not only have you no alarming characteristics, you are a lovely young woman."

Hannah's eyes grew wide at this impossibility.

"It's true. Lucy is a stunning beauty but that doesn't make you less attractive. Your beauty is not only on the surface, you are a splendid person inside. That shines through in a way your sister's beauty never will. And boys did like you but you scared them to death."

"That can't be right."

"Oh, it's true enough. Not only were you smart, you have always been serious and determined. Everyone thought you a snob. In short, you are scary and no fun. I'm certain you terrified any boy who ever dreamed of asking you out. There is more to life than books and learning, work and success. Your brothers will never understand your drive or determination. They already consider you something of an enemy. There is no way to keep them here unless you make a happy home for them.

"Mind you, I still think this is a horrible idea and I wish you would consider other options. But if you are determined in this, you need to think about what you can do to make the boys your friends and compatriots instead of bossing them around, ignoring their ideas and making their life miserable."

"But they need to be punished for what they did today."

"Maybe not."

"Surely, I can't condone such behavior. Things will get entirely out of control."

"I think you need to look at this a little differently instead of assuming the mantle of disciplinarian to recalcitrant children. The boys were probably playing a practical joke more than they were trying to be cruel. I think you need to play one back on them. Why don't you leave this to me? Wednesday is Halloween, isn't it?"

"Yes."

"That seems the perfect time to exact your revenge."

"But Hollis, this could escalate into a war between us. I don't think it's a good idea."

"Who do you think knows more about naughty boys, you or me?"

"I'm quite certain you have a wealth of experience."

"Then take a deep breath, go to work and act as if nothing is wrong when you come home. If you can't manage indifference, frosty silence will work just as well. I know you can manage that."

Although Hannah sincerely doubted Hollis' plan, she gave an adequate performance after work. The boys waited in mounting anxiety for her to mention their little prank and became increasingly unnerved as the evening progressed in silence. Only Jonah's quiet tears gave evidence of a guilty conscience.

Hannah didn't know all three boys received a stern lecture from Hollis, who tracked them down after Hannah left for work. He spread the guilt on thickly, not hesitating to mention how much they owed their sister, how she gave up her life to provide sustenance and a roof over their head—although he considered the roof his own since he had yet to be reimbursed. Hollis explained in detail why Hannah encouraged their studies and wanted nothing more than their success.

All three boys felt entirely miserable when they got home. Prepared to apologize once Hannah scolded them, her silence only served to fuel their guilt.

* * *

Only knowing she was to meet Hollis in the cemetery at

7, Hannah reluctantly adhered to his plans. Her brothers formed enough of a bond to ensure their Halloween night was festive. Samuel and Jonah dressed as hobos—not a stretch of the imagination, by any means. David refused to dress up but agreed to accompany his brothers for trick-or-treat, a custom that gained popularity in recent years.

Hannah made an effort to make the holiday fun, helping the boys construct costumes and providing pumpkins they carved to decorate the front porch. She bought candy for revelers who might happen down their street, not wishing to be the victim of any tricks. Since the front yard was overgrown, Hannah's newly rejuvenated house still gave a spooky appearance, lit only by the smiling faces of jack-o'-lanterns.

She switched off the kitchen light after grabbing a flashlight from the drawer. Leaving the back door open as instructed, Hannah headed for the cemetery. There was enough moonlight for the grave markers to cast shadows on the ground. It was certainly a pleasant evening but Hannah pulled an old shawl close around her body.

"Hollis, are you there?" she whispered.

"Over here," came his reply. Hannah picked her way to the farthest corner of the graveyard to find Hollis seated on a crooked tombstone.

"Hold my beer, I'll be right back."

Hannah had little choice but to comply. She sat against the same stone, gingerly holding the bottle Hollis shoved at her. He was back in no time; she could barely make out the smile on his face.

"What time did you tell the boys to be home?"

"No later than 7:30."

"Fine. All we need to do is wait."

"What are we waiting for?"

"Why, the witching hour, of course." Hollis stared at the tree above.

"What are you looking at?"

"I'm making certain my handiwork is secure. We'll have to pay attention to tell when your brothers come home. I took the fuses from your box. The boys will put up a hue and cry when you aren't in the house and there are no lights. I saw you left the door open."

"I wish I knew what you were up to."

"It will be more fun this way. You want a beer?"

"Is it legal?"

"I made it myself," lied Hollis. He watched his companion take a swig.

"That isn't very good."

"Aw, you never drank a beer before, did you?"

"Never beer, but I have had spirits."

"Yeah, I bet you did."

"No, really. My father gave us a sip of his wine on special occasions, holidays and such. I think the wine was better than your beer."

"It's an acquired taste. Have some more." He smiled as Hannah guzzled a decent amount of beer, then squished her face and shuddered. "You're right about this," Hollis admitted.

"About what?"

"It is peaceful here, even on Halloween. I confess I wanted to prove I wasn't afraid but I don't mind it at all."

"What are we doing?" Hannah asked as she downed more beer.

"We are drawing out the demons of Halloween," Hollis declared using the spookiest voice he could muster. "You said your brothers scared of the cemetery. I don't think they'll be playing any jokes on you after tonight." In an effort to pass the time, Hollis, who already consumed more than one beer, continued, "So Hannah, what are your plans for the future?"

"Why do you care?"

"You painted yourself into a corner as they say. You have ensured your lifelong status as an old maid. No man in his right mind would take you on, much less your houseful of brothers. By the time they're old enough to set up their own homes, you will be an old maid.

"To be honest, you don't strike me as the type of woman who would subjugate herself to a man. Of course, there are men who don't mind a bossy wife, even long for one. Somehow I don't think that type of husband would have enough ambition to suit you."

Hannah took another sip of beer. "I never knew you were a seer, able to read my mind and dreams for the future. You should probably set up shop as a fortune teller. I can see the sign now—have the amazing Rumsford tell your future. Money back guarantee—he will make a fool of himself in less than 30 seconds or your money back."

"All right, Hannah, what do you suppose my plan for the future might be?"

"I imagine your future will look much like your past, full of debauchery and irresponsible self-indulgence."

Hollis chuckled. "You don't know a thing about me. You will be surprised to learn, I want to start a family. Living here, away from Placerville, I have a desire to find a wife and have a houseful of children. That's the way I grew up. I'm ready to head up my own household."

"Well, you certainly haven't managed to capture the heart of any poor, ignorant woman to date. I'm only stating the obvious. Smarter ones catch on so quickly.

Mollie, for instance."

"There are many fish in the sea, Miss Granville. Your friend Mollie and I were not compatible. She was devoted to you and I certainly am not. I am actually seeing two other girls now."

"Two? One at a time isn't enough?"

"I'm considering narrowing the field but can't decide which girl stays and which one goes. Besides, who knows what lovely lady might be lurking in my tomorrow? I have to find the perfect one, after all. A lifetime of some headstrong, willful, annoying and needy nag is not my goal. Quiet! I think your brothers are back."

There seemed to be some commotion on the other side of the fence. Hollis stood on a grave marker long enough to catch a glimpse of Hannah's house.

"Scream," urged Hollis.

"What?"

"I need you to scream."

"Someone will hear."

"It's Halloween and your neighbors aren't close by. Come on, Hannah. Pretend you're a movie actress playing a part."

Hannah had an irresistible desire to giggle, no doubt due to the bottle of beer she polished off.

"Pretend I'm trying to kiss you, then."

Since there was no reaction, Hollis lunged at Hannah, who managed a respectable scream. She crouched behind the grave marker to see what would happen next. Her brothers were evidently in the backyard.

"Hannah!" yelled David. A few seconds later, Samuel followed suit.

"It came from the graveyard," a rattled David whispered, just loud enough for Hannah to hear in the still night air. Her heart melted at the sound of Jonah crying.

"There's nothing for it," uttered Samuel. "We have to go in there."

The two older boys stepped gingerly through the back gate. Neither said a word as they looked across the graveyard and started through the headstones.

"Hannah?" whispered a nervous David.

No sooner was the word out of his mouth than Hollis, standing behind the tree he recently inspected, pulled a rope. Hannah watched in amazement as a "ghost"—evidently a bedsheet, stuffed, tied and hung from the rope—dropped behind her brothers and flew across the little cemetery. The boys squealed like girls and ran for the safety of their gloomy house.

Hannah turned to look at Hollis as they both burst into laughter.

"Oh, Hollis, it wasn't right to scare poor Jonah so. He probably didn't have a thing to do with any of this."

"Don't be naïve. Whose idea do you think it was to take the ladder down?"

"Oh, he didn't," Hannah actually snorted in an attempt to refrain from further laughter. This only made her begin anew.

Hollis loved the sound of her glee. He tried to remember if Hannah ever gave him so much as a polite smile. He couldn't recall hearing her laugh.

"Shhh," Hollis put his finger over his mouth but could barely contain his own mirth. "We'll go alongside the house. I'll put the fuses back in the box and you can go to the front door. Pretend you've been out looking for the boys."

"Aren't you coming too?"

"No, Hannah, this is your revenge. But I want to know what happens."

At this, Hollis caught her hand to lead her through the graveyard. There was no sign of the boys in the kitchen as they walked across the yard. Hannah wondered if they were hiding in their beds with sheets pulled over their heads. This caused her to stop and snicker but it might have been the beer that made everything so silly.

She watched from her porch as Hollis walked down the street to where he left his car, then smiled and waved. As she grabbed the doorknob, Hannah found it odd that Hollis Rumsford was the first boy to hold her hand, and what a strong and manly hand it was. She shivered involuntarily as she turned the knob and walked through the front door.

"Boys, are you home?"

"We're here," came a shy answer. Jonah ran out of the bedroom and clung to his sister for dear life.

"Why are you here in the dark?"

"The lights are out," explained Samuel.

Hannah flipped the on-off switch near the door and the light came on.

"No, they seem to be working." It was difficult to keep a straight face in light of the terror-stricken expressions confronting Hannah. "I must have gone the wrong direction. I walked down the street to make sure you were on your way home. Is something amiss?" she innocently inquired as she headed for the kitchen. "You look as if you've seen a ghost."

Samuel and David turned to stare at each other.

"Hannah did that!" whispered David. "She got us back."

Chapter Nine

A new and curious respect came Hannah's way in the days that followed. The sight of her brothers caused Hannah to relive their girlish screams of alarm. She struggled to keep her amusement in check.

Significant changes occurred in the Granville household. Hollis frequently arrived for dinner. Hannah did not object since he always brought a bag of groceries. The items he selected did not often complement each other but he provided meat, fresh produce and a few canned or packaged goods. Hannah knew this was charity on his part, no matter how Hollis disguised his generosity as a desire to avoid his own cooking. His gifts were a godsend. Hannah simply did not make enough money to support her newly reunited family. She thought it odd this felt like charity; it never seemed so when she asked for Hollis' help.

The boys fell into a habit of completing their homework before dinner, except for problems requiring their sister's help. Hannah did not know if this new devotion to academia was inspired by fear of her next revenge or if her brothers suffered some sort of revenge or if her brothers suffered some sort of epiphany. Even their grammar was improving. Jonah's emotions quieted down.

The hours after dinner were given over to entertainment, such as they were able to afford. Hollis purchased a few jigsaw puzzles and a checkers game. But the Granvilles plus Hollis began to play the card game hearts regularly. As the weeks went by, even Jonah became expert. The fact everyone went gunning for Hollis did not squelch his joy in the game, even if he was the most frequent recipient of the queen of spades— the most lethal card. His resultant attempts to "run the deck" often proved successful. On Friday and Saturday nights, Hannah made popcorn, and fudge or cookies to complement the family fun.

Although there was an awkwardness the first time Mollie joined the group, Hollis was amiable and the two were cordial before the night was done. The boys invited school chums to play and Mollie's father, who loved cards, joined them on occasion. Hollis was even known to bring a date to the house for a few rounds of hearts.

The kitchen table became obsolete, so Hollis constructed a table in the living room made from two sawhorses and long boards. Seating was another issue, quickly solved when the boys found empty kegs in a vacant lot.

Hollis brought wood and enlisted the boys' help to build a narrow staircase from the kitchen to the attic, making it impossible to maroon Hannah in her bedroom. He made a primitive railing upstairs to ensure no one, meaning Hannah, would fall through the expanded opening in the attic floor.

Hannah rarely engaged her benefactor in conversation, while realizing fully her brothers idolized Hollis. The household came alive when he visited and

Hannah was content to let her brothers enjoy their hero until such time as he lost interest. Hollis often took the boys in his car to the beach to play ball or swim in the cold Pacific. There were random trips to a movie theatre. They went fishing and, on occasion, shooting. These interludes provided Hannah the opportunity to catch up on work, care for her home and tackle the endless mending the boys created.

Her brothers insisted Hannah ask Hollis for Thanksgiving dinner, even though Aunt Bitsy and her new husband already invited him and Dock to join them. Hannah's cooking won out in the end, to the boys' delight.

Life settled into a comfortable rhythm, albeit a hectic one for Hannah. She could see the difference a little fun made to her brothers but their frequent game nights meant she often stayed up most of the night working. As Christmas neared, she worried over her ability to afford a celebration for the boys.

As she counted out receipts at the Vista Mar Monte one Monday morning, Hannah was startled by Mr. Rowland, who generally kept to his own office.

"Miss Granville, I'm glad I caught you."

"Is something wrong?"

"No, no, of course not. Your work is as meticulous as ever. I have a business proposition for you."

"What kind of business proposition?"

"It seems Mr. Sugarman, the gentleman who traditionally took care of the payroll, is moving to Los Angeles. I have no desire to do bookwork. That is a constant in my life. I wondered if you would take this on for an increase in pay? If anyone understands your bargaining power, it's me. I'm surprised you haven't asked for a raise lately." Silas noted his young employee was not as eager as he assumed she would be. "Unless your business has expanded to the point you don't have time to take any more work?"

"We haven't talked in a while. I told you I've taken in some of my brothers. They aren't children, well, one is, but they take a lot of my time. I need the money, quite frankly. I appreciate your confidence in me. I will be happy to assume the payroll duties. Thank you for the opportunity."

Silas was alarmed. He was used to Miss Granville's traditional enthusiasm. "Are you all right, Hannah?"

"Just a little tired. I am thankful for your trust. I won't let you down. Is Mr. Sugarman still here? Will he be able to show me how he does the payroll?"

"Why don't you let me take you to lunch? I've missed our visits and Sugarman will be here when we get back. He can show you the ropes this afternoon." Silas offered his arm, then led Hannah toward the hotel restaurant. "How are things going at the house? I know what a big mess you took on. Are you settled in? I have to tell you; my brother is absolutely livid I didn't sell your property to him. Nothing could make me happier."

Hannah spent lunch recounting her efforts to make the house livable, gave a detailed history of her accumulation of brothers and even shared her tale of the mutual practical jokes. It was nice to have someone to talk to. By the time her plate was empty, Hannah felt as if a burden was lifted from her shoulders. Mollie was no longer her confidant. She took a job in Carpinteria, finally achieving her dream of independence.

* * *

Fran Norwood was quite tall and the most promising young woman Hollis found to date. They'd been going out for a while, long enough for Hollis to drop his other lady friends. He was determined to see if Miss Norwood might be "the one." She was smart with a healthy sense of humor, dark hair and blue eyes. Her one and only requirement in a male companion was that he stood taller than she, a feat Hollis lived up to easily. She was not at all childish, being the same age as Hollis, now 23. Tonight, his intention was to take Fran to the movie she longed to see, *A Farewell to Arms*, based on the Ernest Hemingway novel.

Hollis strictly adhered to the dating advice Hannah administered. It seemed to work well, although he would never admit it. The only reason they were headed for the movies was to fulfill Fran's ardent request. They dated long enough that Hollis believed the movie taboo no longer applied.

After he picked Fran up this lovely December evening, Hollis stopped by the Granville household. He lost the boys' baseball at the beach, having whacked it into the ocean. Since the weather was fair, he intended to drop off a replacement ball in case the boys needed it over the weekend.

"You don't mind, do you?" he thoughtfully inquired.

"Not at all. But I don't understand your relationship with these boys," admitted Fran.

"They were neighbors back in Placerville. They have no father and their mother doesn't want them. Their sister puts them up and I entertain them from time to time. The sister doesn't have a sense of fun."

As was his recent custom, Hollis first knocked on the Granville door, then let himself in, holding the door for his date. The Friday night card game was in full swing.

Almost before she knew what happened, Fran found herself seated at the large game table in the living room. Hollis introduced her to so many people, she couldn't keep them straight. As Fran scanned the table, it appeared likely the woman named Hannah was mistress of the house. She was the cookie baker and seemed to be in charge.

Several boys urged Hollis to play a hand or two. Always a gentleman, Hollis left the final decision to his date. Not wanting to disappoint the boys, Fran agreed after Hollis reassured they could catch a later show. One hand led to the next and it became obvious Hollis abandoned any idea of leaving. It was too late for a movie, once the game broke up.

After saying their goodbyes, Hollis drove Fran home and parked in front of her house.

"I'm sorry about the movie. I promise we'll go. What about Sunday? We could do a matinee."

"No, I don't think so."

"I've made you angry. I thought you were having fun playing cards. This is my fault. I tend to get carried away at hearts."

"I was having fun. But I can't see you again, Hollis."

Hollis was not used to being dumped. It was usually him who ended relationships. "I don't understand."

"You seemed too good to be true when you told me how much you wanted a family, how serious you were about finding the right girl. You are so perfectly tall!" Fran gave a sincere smile. "The trouble is, as I saw for myself tonight, you already have a family."

"You're joking, right?"

"No, I'm perfectly serious, unfortunately."

"Look, Fran, those boys mean a lot to me but they're not family."

"They seem to think you are. You seem devoted to them. But they're not the real problem."

"Then what are you trying to tell me?"

"It's Hannah. If the boys are your substitute sons, you and Hannah are as married as any couple I ever saw."

"You can't be serious. I don't even like her. She despises me. You misread the situation."

"No, I haven't. You two may snipe at each other, but there is deep affection. I watched you when Hannah mentioned she took on more work. You were livid. If you don't care for her, why does that matter? You're concerned for her welfare."

"No, you don't understand. She always gets herself in scrapes. If she doesn't take care of herself, I'm afraid she'll dump her brothers on me. Similar things happened in the past. I'm done helping her out."

"Funny, you don't seem to be avoiding her. And I heard something about you bringing groceries. If you don't want to help, what are you doing? Did you see Hannah's face when she dropped that last queen on you? She might enjoy getting under your skin, but it's your attention she craves and you were so eager to provide it.

"Making a marriage isn't about being madly in love. It's about the nuts and bolts of life, how you overcome adversity and how much you trust each other. I saw you with your family tonight, Hollis. There is no room for me. It's been fun dating you but I see you're already taken.

"Don't get out of the car, I'll let myself out." Fran reached over and kissed Hollis on the cheek. "You have my best wishes. I really hoped you were my one and only, but I need to keep looking. Thank you for a fun evening. I'm sorry it was so revealing, but better now than later."

Hollis sat stunned as Fran hurried to her parents' front porch. She misjudged his situation horribly. The ugly thought occurred to him, what if she hadn't?

* * *

Hollis drove home but found it impossible to go inside. Instead, he returned to the Granville house and parked in front. There he sat for over an hour, trying to decide what to do. He could see the light in the kitchen was on. Hannah was still up.

Hollis was stiff from sitting in the chill night air once he emerged from his Model A. It seemed inappropriate to knock and intrude as was his usual custom. He decided to go to the back door so as not to disturb the boys or frighten Hannah.

One final moment of indecision made him pause as he caught sight of her sitting at the kitchen table pouring over some undone work. Her chin rested in her hand as she tapped the eraser of her pencil on the table, then stopped to write in the ledger book.

Hollis realized he could walk away. In fact, he could walk away from this entire mess. Hannah, her brothers and her frequent dramatic problems were not worth the fried chicken dinners or any other meal Hollis claimed as his reward. Why did he keep coming back? He intended to find out and determined to complete his quest, for better or worse.

As he inched toward the window, a mewling kitten rubbed against his ankle. He used the side of his shoe to push the kitten away and tapped on the glass.

Hearing the noise, Hannah looked toward the window and seeing Hollis, waved him toward the back door and met him there.

"Did you forget something?"

No sooner were the words out of Hannah's mouth than the kitten came bounding into the bright kitchen. Hollis tried to push it outside with the toe of his shoe.

"Don't hurt it!" cried Hannah. "Oh, look! Isn't it the sweetest thing!" She bent down to catch the tiny creature and cuddled it in her arms. "Where did it come from?"

"How should I know? Put it outside, Hannah."

"What if it's hungry?" Hannah continued to hold the kitten while she poured a saucer of cream, then placed both on the floor. "Look, she's starving."

"The last thing you need is another mouth to feed. That kitten will find its mother if you don't interfere."

"But she's so skinny. She must be lost."

"That is the ugliest cat I ever saw."

"No, she's not. How can you be so mean? She is a cat of many colors. Look, all her little feet are white! I'm going to call her Boots."

"Hannah, I am serious. You can't feed a cat. You can't even feed yourself."

"I can't help it if you bring food. I didn't ask you to. Besides, you eat twice as much as anyone here. It's only right if you bring some of the food. I'm not asking you to feed my cat."

"Your cat?" Hollis bent to pick up the kitten, intending to put it out. Hannah protectively stood between Hollis and his victim.

"I asked if you left something. I didn't see anything in the living room."

"No, I didn't leave anything here."

"What about your lady friend? Did she leave something? Fran is nice. I like her. Will you bring her again?"

"She is nice and no, I won't bring her again."

"Why not? I thought she had a good time."

"We are finished, she and I."

"Oh, Hollis, what did you do now? I told you how to be a proper beau, what is wrong with you? I can imagine, don't tell me what you did. Something highly improper, I'm certain. At the rate you're going, you'll have to move to another city. You already dated most of the eligible women in Santa Barbara. Fran showed such promise, too."

"I didn't come here to talk about Fran."

"Why are you here? It's the middle of the night."

"Shut up and let me talk, then." Hollis took Hannah's glare as consent. "There's a little carnival on the beach tomorrow, some games and a few rides, nothing fantastic."

"The boys would enjoy that."

"I'm not asking the boys."

"Then why are you here? Really Hollis, it's too late to beat around the bush like this."

Hollis gave a snort of derision. "I'm asking you to go with me."

"You want me to come and bring the boys?"

"No. You aren't listening to me. I am asking you and only you."

Understanding dawned. "Why would you ask me to go?"

"It's a date. I'm asking you on a date."

The rolling pin lay on the sink. Hannah glanced at it and considered her guest likely required a strong rap on the head. He assuredly was not thinking clearly.

"What are you looking at?" Hollis attempted to follow Hannah's gaze.

"Nothing, nothing. I don't understand."

"There is nothing to understand. I want to pick you up tomorrow at five. We can have hot dogs on the beach and see what the carnival offers."

"Why would we do that? I don't even like you and I know you feel the same."

"Look, Hannah, you ask me for help all the time. I never ask you for anything. Why can't you do this one thing for me? It's not like I want you to bail me out of jail, or rob a bank or even stand on a roof in a lightning storm. I just want to go to the carnival with you. Since you've never been on a date before, I'd think you might be curious. Consider it a new life experience. Will you come?"

"All right, Hollis. I will go. One time, on the condition I never have to go again."

"Fine. I'll see you tomorrow at five. Now let me take that cat outside."

"No." Hannah scooped the kitten into her arms. "Boots stays here or I won't go tomorrow. You can hunt up some unfortunate, ignorant girl who isn't onto you."

"I thought I was going with an unfortunate, ignorant girl." Hollis eyed the kitten. "You are showing poor judgement once again."

"You better leave now. This is my house and if I want to keep a kitten in it, that is hardly your business."

Hollis pursed his lips. What was he doing? Why would he even consider taking this stubborn and irritating girl on a date? Rather than continue their antagonistic discussion, Hollis headed for the front door. "See you at five, then." He received no response.

Chapter Ten

Hollis could not recall feeling nervous over a date. He appeared at Hannah's front door promptly at five, dressed in his brown tweed suit, a bag of groceries cradled in his arm. Hollis knocked and waited for someone to answer, feeling this more appropriate than his customary entrance.

It was Jonah who appeared. "Why are you standing there?"

"I'm taking your sister on a date and I thought I should knock."

"Oh."

"Can I come in?"

"Sure, Hollis."

"Where's your sister?"

"She's in the kitchen."

Hollis walked down the hall.

"I brought some groceries and a roast for Sunday dinner. I'll put this away while you change."

Hannah was dressed in a white shirt. Long blousy sleeves buttoned at the cuffs. A large plaid bow hung loosely from her wide V-neck collar. She wore a pair of gray trousers. Hollis assumed she was working around the house and didn't have time to dress for their date.

"I'm ready to go," she asserted.

"Aren't you wearing a dress?"

"No. Is there some reason why I should?"

"This is a date, Hannah."

"It's not starting out like one. Where are my flowers and candy?"

"I brought you a roast."

"That's not the kind of thing you bring for a date. I've been over this with you before. Maybe you should make a list of the things you're supposed to do since you can't seem to remember."

"Girls are supposed to wear dresses on dates. The girls I take on dates most assuredly wear dresses."

"Well this girl is not wearing a dress. My trousers are warm on a chilly evening and more suited to rides and hot dogs than a dress. If you can't abide my decision, you'll have to go by yourself."

Hollis could see he was losing this round and acknowledged he viewed the evening more like a boxing match than a date.

"Just get in the car." As Hollis followed down the hallway, the annoying kitten scampered toward him and pawed at his shoe, yet another reminder of Hannah's lack of respect for his intelligent and logical advice.

Hannah grabbed a sweater and yelled, "I won't be late," so the boys could hear. She gave Hollis a smirk when he opened the front door.

The beach was not far. Hannah stared out the passenger side of the car, completely mute. She did not acknowledge Hollis' attempts at conversation. It didn't take long for his anger to boil over.

"Can you hear me? Have you gone deaf?"

"I can hear you."

"Then talk. I know you can talk."

"This is different."

"What are you saying?"

"I don't know what to say to you."

"You didn't have any trouble expressing yourself for almost a year. Why should tonight be different?"

"Because it is. I don't know what to say on a date."

"Oh, for heaven's sake. I never heard anything so ridiculous."

"It's not ridiculous. I can't think of anything to say to you."

Hollis braked for a stop sign and was promptly rear-ended. Hannah fell off the front seat. She looked up at Hollis, visible in the light from the street lamp. His beloved automobile was undoubtedly damaged and he was about to explode.

Almost as an afterthought, Hollis asked, "Are you all right?"

"I think so," replied Hannah as she attempted to pull herself off the floor. Help did not appear forthcoming. Hollis was out of the car in a flash, intent on confronting the negligent driver.

Once Hannah crawled onto the passenger seat, she folded her arms over her trembling hands in an effort to still them. As a police car approached, she turned to see what Hollis was up to.

Hollis was a powerfully built man who outweighed her by 80 pounds or more. She never feared him, no matter how angry he appeared. Hollis yanked the other driver out of his car and held him by the shoulders of his coat, giving him a good shake. Hannah believed if the older man was not so drunk, he would be scared to death.

"Can't you see? What the hell is wrong with you?"

yelled Hollis.

Hannah thought this a stupid question. Even she could see from a good 15 feet away, the man was inebriated.

"You ssstop't in 'da street for no reason!" explained the drunk.

"There's a stop sign there, you idiot!"

The police car pulled up alongside the damaged vehicles and two officers got out.

"What seems to be the problem?"

"This old sot ran into my car!"

"No, ocifer, th'as 'is fault."

"Mr. Henry, is that you?"

"Um-huh."

The taller policeman asked Mr. Henry for his wallet and proceeded to remove a few bills, handing Hollis the money.

"Look mister, this here's a relative of the mayor. He gets swacked and into scrapes all the time. That should pay for the damage to your vehicle plus a little extra. This ain't the first time this happened." He turned to Mr. Henry and continued, "We're gonna take you in again, Mr. Henry. You can sleep it off at the station. I gave this man some money so he can fix his car. That all right?"

"Tha' fella' cain't drive."

"He was stopped at the stop sign. You want me to call your wife instead?"

"No, no. Tha's fine. I'll go to the station. Don't call Mel'isa, now, you promise?"

"Okay, Mr. Henry. As you say."

"Did you give that feller enough money?" Mention of his wife seemed to have a sobering effect on Mr. Henry.

The policeman looked toward Hollis, who

responded, "It should be enough."

After pushing Mr. Henry's vehicle to the side of the road, the officers called for a tow truck. The front of his car was badly damaged. Steam escaped around the hood.

A devastated Hollis stood transfixed, staring at the damage to his car. He remained stock still until the police car drove away. Hannah thought it best to give him a moment to collect himself, then crawled from the car.

"Your car doesn't look so bad," she advised.

"What are you talking about? The lights are broken. Look at that dent." Hollis pulled his handkerchief from his pocket and began to polish the damaged fender, as if he could obliterate the destruction with a wave of his hand.

"Maybe you should take me home."

"What?"

"This is a poor start to the evening. It's better if we call it a night."

Hollis was not about to let her off the hook so easily. He imagined she would claim their bargain was fulfilled and refuse to go out again. "No, I'm all right. We'll go on ahead. I'll worry about the car tomorrow." But Hannah could see the automobile was on his mind.

The car started right up. Although it made an odd noise, Hollis didn't mention it. In fact, he was as silent as Hannah before the accident. He parked the car on palm-tree-lined Cabrillo Boulevard and opened the door for his date.

"I'm starving but we could do a ride before we eat. How about the Ferris wheel?" Hollis asked.

"I don't like heights."

"Well, it's not a big Ferris wheel. It's probably the best ride here."

"I've never ridden on a Ferris wheel. I don't like

heights," Hannah repeated.

Hollis was not pleased. "You're too scared to go on that little ride?"

"I'm not scared, exactly."

"It sounds to me like you are."

"It would be nice if we could do something we both enjoy," commented an uncharacteristically tactful Hannah.

"I guarantee, you will like this ride." Hollis was not about to relent and proceeded to the ticket window. He stopped to buy a box of Cracker Jacks along the way. "This will tide us over until we eat," he assured.

An unhappy Hannah found herself seated beside her date in short order. As their passenger car left the ground, Hollis gratuitously patted her arm. "Don't fret, Hannah. I'll take care of you."

"I wouldn't trust you to take care of my cat."

"That would be a wise decision on your part. That cat needs to go."

He received a nasty glare as they stopped for the next chair to load. Hollis opened the Cracker Jacks box and offered it to Hannah.

Reaching in, she pulled out the prize.

"Do you want this?" Hannah inquired.

"No, it's all yours."

No sooner were those words out of his mouth than Hannah reached to get a bite of caramel corn. Her hand hit the box, which sent it flying. Both riders watched silently as their sustenance floated to the ground. Hannah quietly opened her prize—a metal ring sporting a piece of glass for a stone.

"You might need this for your next date," she suggested as she dropped the toy into Hollis' breast pocket. He glowered at her. Their chair moved higher so another car could load.

"We'll go around without stopping once all the cars are full," Hollis explained. His stomach growled noisily.

But several moments went by and they didn't move. The car rocked as Hollis looked behind the chair to see what the holdup was. Hannah grasped his arm as the car continued to sway. The generator fell silent and the lights on the Ferris wheel dimmed.

One of the carnival workers yelled up at his customers, "Stay put folks, we'll have this going in no time." But as the minutes wore on, it became obvious his prediction was inaccurate.

Hollis could tell Hannah was becoming anxious. She let go of his arm once the car stopped swinging but gripped the handlebar so firmly, her knuckles were white. There was a boyish prankster inside Hollis who wanted to swing the car and terrify the staid Miss Granville. Instead, he tried to soothe her by drawing her into conversation.

"I'm planning on going home for Christmas. I wondered if you and your brothers might like to go. Several of my sisters and brothers and their families will be there. It's something of a family reunion. Dock can't get off work, so he's staying here." He could see this idea held some interest for Hannah. "It will be a quick trip. I plan to make it to Placerville in a single day and come back the same way. Sound interesting?"

Hannah bit her lip. "No, I can't leave my work. There's no one else to do it and everyone is busy because of the holidays. The deposits must be made. Christmas is on a Sunday, I would miss work on Saturday and Monday, at minimum. I can't do that to my clients. Besides, there's nothing in Placerville for me. My home belongs to other people. I would like to visit my father's grave but we would be a burden on your mother. Even my old attic space at your house belongs to someone else."

It was clear to Hollis thoughts of home were causing considerable melancholy. He watched as a ladder was propped up so the people beneath them could evacuate the ride. The ladder was not tall enough to reach their car. Hollis grew hungrier by the minute.

"If I held the car steady, you could crawl over the back of the seat. We're not up high and the arm holding our car is level to the ground. We could walk along the bar and shimmy down the perpendicular brace."

Hannah slugged him in the arm. "Have you lost your mind?"

"Oww! Well, you're the one who wore trousers. If you wore a dress, I would never consider that mode of escape. Once you crawl over the seat, all you have to do is hold on until I crawl over, then I'll help you."

"I am *not* crawling anywhere and you're not either. If you think you are leaving me here alone, you have another thing coming. *I* was not the one who wanted to come on this ride, remember?"

"Aren't you hungry?"

"I am, but I'm not willing to fall 50 feet for a hot dog."

"We're not up high. Twenty feet at most."

"I don't imagine falling 20 feet is much different than falling 50."

"You aren't going to fall." Hollis turned to see how far they would have to go before being able to grip the spoke above. "You could sit on the bar and scoot along for those first five feet. It's easy. I'll show you."

"I will scream, Hollis, if you try to crawl over the seat. And I will kill you once we get off this ride, mark my words."

"I just want to get dinner and get this over with."

"What do you want to get over with?"

Hollis let more slip than he intended. "The ride. I want to end the ride."

"No, you don't. What did you mean?"

Hollis drew a deep breath. He stuck his foot in it; he could not think of anything to say but the truth. "It seems you have a knack for breaking up my romances. I'm good enough at that on my own, I don't need help. First there was Mollie. To be honest, I don't think we were a good match. But now you have sent Fran packing and I believe we were well-suited."

"Hollis, you are insane. What could I possibly have done to break up any of your romances?"

"You made a friend of Mollie and all she wanted to talk about was you."

"And Fran became my friend in a single night and dumped you?"

"No! But she believes you and I have some attraction. I know, it makes no sense at all. It's too late to prove this to her, I'm afraid."

"But you needed to prove it to yourself. That's what tonight is about."

"You're right," Hollis confessed. "It wasn't my intention to be so blunt. I'm sorry. You didn't want to go out for obvious reasons. I didn't really want to do this either. But my curiosity got the best of me."

"Well, Hollis, you needn't be concerned. I find you no less reprehensible than I did that night—never mind."

"What night?"

"It's not important. I loathe you and I understand the feeling is mutual. I hope your curiosity is laid to rest. And if any of your future sweethearts have similar delusions, feel free to direct them to me. I will be happy to straighten them out." Hannah gasped as the Ferris wheel lurched upward.

"Oh, good. We can eat now," mused Hollis.

"Why would we do that? Why can't we go home? I see no reason to continue your experiment."

"We should see it through. Besides, I imagine you won't cook me dinner and I'm starving."

"I certainly will not cook dinner."

"That settles it. But I need something more substantial than a hot dog. We can go to a restaurant and get a real supper before I drop you home." And, he wanted to make Hannah pay for wearing trousers.

When they reached the ground, the ride operator gave them a choice of continuing around or getting off.

"I'm getting off," replied Hannah.

"Don't you want to go around without stopping?" urged Hollis. "We might as well get our money's worth."

"No! Let me out," she commanded.

Hannah pushed against Hollis' chest and climbed over him in her haste to exit the ride. He had to hurry after her; she wasted no time heading for the car.

As they approached the street, a woman ahead screamed, "Stop that man, he stole my purse!"

Hannah stuck her foot out and tripped the man before he could run past. Hollis, still several paces behind, saw the man fall almost at his feet. The woman's purse landed on the opposite side of the pathway. As Hollis attempted to apprehend the thief, another man running along the path barreled into him and sent Hollis sprawling on the ground. Both strangers sprang to their feet and ran off.

Hannah walked nonchalantly to her prone date and offered her hand to help him up.

"Nice try. Remind me never to nominate you for chief of police."

Hollis picked up the woman's purse and handed it to her when she approached.

"Oh, thank you, sir. I can't tell you how grateful I am!"

Hollis grinned at Hannah as he basked in the praise. Evidently the woman didn't see Hannah's part in the little drama. Hollis did not intend to share his glory.

"No problem at all. I'm happy I could be of assistance."

"I simply must give you a reward for your bravery! I haven't much but—"

"No, no. Your gratitude is more than enough."

Hannah noted her date could be charming when he wished to be. He failed to display this characteristic since the days he chased after Lucy.

"You're all dirty and your suit is torn," informed Hannah. Hollis attempted to dust himself off and inspected the ripped shoulder of his jacket. He frowned at Hannah's comment, "You look like a vagrant."

* * *

Hollis' destination was the El Paseo restaurant. As he looked around and smelled the food, he wanted nothing more than to satisfy his appetite—almost nothing. His goal was to be turned away, believing Hannah would be embarrassed if her casual attire wasn't tolerated in the upscale restaurant. His plan went immediately awry.

"Miss Granville, so good to see you."

"So nice to be here!" she replied. "Although Mr. Rowland isn't accompanying us this evening, might his table be available?"

"For you, of course!" came the eager reply.

Hannah's attire wasn't the problem Hollis hoped. It was him who barely passed muster as Alberto eyed his ruined suit. Nonetheless, they were soon seated in a booth on the far side of the restaurant.

"I take it you come here frequently."

"I've been here a few times as Mr. Rowland's

guest. Since he usually comes alone, there was a great fuss made over me. I'm surprised you have such excellent taste, Hollis. This is a charming and delectable eatery."

"So, there's something going on between you and your boss?"

Hannah's first inclination was to torment Hollis for his ridiculous assertion but she decided on a different tactic. "What if there is? Is that any business of yours?"

"I thought you never went on a date before?"

"I guess I don't think of Silas as a date, exactly." Hannah didn't understand what she said to cause Hollis' evil glare but tormenting him was the first fun she had all evening.

"That old coot could be your grandfather."

"He certainly could not. I don't think he's over 50." Hannah casually glanced at the menu although she planned to order her favorite item. "Remember that girl, what was her name? I believe it was Beulah, Beulah Thompson. She married a banker back home. He must have been 20 or even 30 years older. There are advantages for a girl who finds an older husband— financial security, an established home. I imagine there are fewer physical demands from a husband of that age, if you get my drift."

Hollis chuckled, "Your inexperience hardly qualifies you as an expert on the amorous intentions of males. I'm certain a groom's eagerness is undaunted by the number of his birthdays. I also find it rather funny— your ideas seem an exact replica of Lucy's. Have you taken her strategies to heart?"

It was strange, the way Hollis managed to vex her. Hannah kept her temper in check. "I wasn't talking about me. I was simply making small talk."

The waiter returned and took their orders. He was

as eager to please Hannah as Alberto.

"Is this what you order when Mr. Rowland brings you here?"

"As a matter of fact, it is. I adore Mexican cuisine, but enchiladas are my favorite."

"You better watch out for Mr. Rowland. It sounds as if he might want something in return for his favors."

"What favors?"

"Your lunches, the deed to your house. I know you don't appreciate my opinions but I wouldn't be at all surprised to find he has designs on you."

Hannah laughed. "You are such a fool, Hollis. Just because your mind is always in the gutter, doesn't mean every other man's is. I believe he considers me the daughter he never had."

"He doesn't show up to help the way a father might. He knew the house he gave you was in poor shape. Did he ever spend a dime on that house? Did he come when the roof leaked? No, no. That was all me."

"I thanked you for your help, Hollis, I admit sometimes begrudgingly. What is this about? Are you jealous? Are you trying to prove yourself a better friend than Mr. Rowland? I can assure you, I like him a hundred percent more than I will ever like you."

"I think we should go home. I've had enough of you."

"Oh, now you want to go home. Well, you go right ahead. I plan to stay and eat."

The natural silence occurring when hungry people are presented with a meal accompanied the feast. Hollis motioned for the waiter and asked for the bill, eager to check on his car, as if it were some sick patient in need of attention.

"Shit!"

"What happened now?"

"My wallet is missing." Hollis stood, frantically searching every pocket. "The man who knocked me over at the carnival must have picked my pocket!"

"Is there some problem, sir?" asked the waiter.

Hannah struggled not to laugh at Hollis' perplexed expression. She could not resist the urge to humiliate him. "It seems Mr. Rumsford cannot pay," she helpfully replied.

"Sir, is this true? Management frowns on people trying to eat for free. These may be unfortunate times, but we don't tolerate freeloaders."

"I'm not trying to freeload. I brought money. My wallet is gone. My pocket was picked. Surely, the manager would understand my dilemma."

"I'll have to call him over. The last time this happened, the man worked off his debt washing dishes."

Hannah's eyes grew wide at Hollis' look of despair. The evening certainly took an entertaining turn. Hollis peered helplessly at her.

"I notice you didn't bring a purse. You wouldn't happen to have money tucked away, would you?"

"I left my purse at home. A person can get robbed at a carnival. Whatever are you going to do?" Hannah eyed the approaching manager, who was probably intent on pressing forced labor on her escort.

She listened intently as the two men exchanged explanations—Hollis of his sudden poverty and Alberto of the restaurant policies. People at other tables were staring, much to her delight. In the end, it seemed a good idea to rescue Hollis. He would be beholden to her for a change.

"Alberto, Mr. Rowland will vouch for Mr. Rumsford. If you give me a copy of the dinner bill, I'll see the money is sent over first thing Monday. There's no need for alarm." She aimed what Hollis considered the most stunning smile he ever saw in poor Alberto's direction. The man was completely disarmed. Hollis would have to admit, Hannah might disarm him with that smile. He stood impotently by while Hannah arranged payment of the dinner bill.

"Shall we go then? I don't think we ought to push our luck by ordering dessert," Hannah suggested.

"No, we should definitely go." The pair was soon on their way to the car.

Hannah smirked as Hollis explained, "I'll go to the restaurant before work on Monday and take care of the bill. There's no reason Mr. Rowland need know about this problem."

"You mean your problem. This certainly wasn't my problem, even though I fixed it for you. I think you owe me."

Hannah stepped on the curb, catching the heel of her shoe. As she awkwardly stepped forward, the heel snapped off and flew toward the street.

"Watch out!" she yelled as Hollis took a step toward the curb. The heel of her shoe landed in front of his foot and he inadvertently kicked it into the storm drain. "You have to get my heel out of there! I need these shoes. I can't get them fixed if I don't have the heel."

"I'm not crawling into a sewer for you."

"It's not a sewer. There must be a way to go down."

Hollis shook his head, "Don't look at me."

"I saved your bacon. This is how you repay me?"

"Now you know how it feels."

Shocked at his reply, Hannah climbed into the car as Hollis paused to wipe his handkerchief across the damaged fender. "I sure wish the sun was out so I could see the damage. Now I can't afford to fix it." Helping

Hannah had taken a toll on his savings.

"Yes, that's a real tragedy," Hannah sarcastically replied. "Can we go home now?"

Not another word was spoken until they parked in front of Hannah's house.

"Don't get out, Hollis. Your date is over and I imagine you found what you always believed to be true. I despise you. There is nothing between us."

Nonetheless Hollis got out and held the door.

"What do you think you're doing?"

"I want you to get your flashlight so I can take a better look at my car."

"You are surely joking," Hannah mocked as she hobbled toward the front porch on her broken shoe.

"This has been the worst date in history," commented Hollis. "The least you can do is get your flashlight."

Hollis suddenly erupted in laughter. Hannah believed the circumstances of the evening might have caused his fragile mind to become completely unhinged but couldn't help laughing with him.

"It was horrible, wasn't it? Everything went wrong. I wish you could have seen your face at the restaurant."

"I wish you could have seen yours on the Ferris wheel."

Hollis grasped Hannah's shoulders. He stared into her face, then impetuously kissed her. As he drew away, Hannah lifted her arm.

"Don't slap me!" he warned and was amazed as she put her arms around his neck and drew his lips toward hers. He pulled her close for a more ardent kiss. Hollis finally ended the embrace.

The pair gazed into each other's eyes. Both wore a look of complete confusion. Without a word, Hannah walked into her house and shut the door.

Chapter Eleven

"Is Hollis coming for dinner?" Jonah asked.

"I don't know," replied Hannah as she peeled carrots at the sink. She was a better listener—a result of Hollis' comments. Often, she found her brothers' conversations to be the highlight of her day. "He didn't say anything about it last night."

"Oh, you went on your date. Was it fun?"

"It certainly was not."

"Are you going to marry Hollis?"

"Wherever did you get the idea I was interested in marriage?"

"That's what happens. You go for a date and then you get married."

"No, you're missing a few steps, Jonah. Hollis simply wanted me to go to the carnival."

"It would be good if you got married."

"It surely would not. What would make you say such a thing?"

"Well, he's here all the time. Hollis is my friend. He shows me how to do stuff and he listens to me. He thinks I have good ideas. He brings food. I like him a lot and I wish he could live here."

"Maybe you should marry him."

"Don't be silly, Hannah. I'm going to marry Charlotte."

"Who is Charlotte?"

"She lived next door in Pennsylvania. She is a killer-diller. She promised she would wait for me, until I come back."

"This sounds serious."

"You bet. You should get married too, Hannah. I don't want you to be an old maid."

"Well, thank you so much but if I chose to be an old maid, won't you love me just as well?"

"I would like it better if you married Hollis. Then he wouldn't have to go home no more. He could sleep in the living room. We could throw another mattress on the floor for him."

"You'll have to tell him about your plans. But I have a feeling he's not ready to marry anybody."

"He asked you out."

"So he did. Our evening was not enjoyable. I think he better look for someone else with space in their living room for a mattress."

It was at this precise moment, Hollis made an entrance.

"Have you given up knocking?" asked a grim Hannah.

"I did knock. Didn't you hear me?"

"No, I did not. I think it's probably best if you wait until we answer the door. That's only proper."

"Hey, Jonah, why don't you get the paper airplane you were telling me about. I'd like to see it."

"Sure, Hollis." The eager little boy made a beeline out of the kitchen.

"I want to talk to you, Hannah." Hollis walked beside the sink.

"I don't want to talk to you."

"I think we should go out again."

"We made a bargain, Hollis. I kept my end. Please keep yours."

"But something happened last night. I need to figure this out. We'll never do that sitting at the dinner table with all your brothers."

"There is nothing to figure out."

"What about that kiss—your kiss?"

"I believe that was a case of mutual hysteria caused by the unfortunate disasters of the evening. I think nothing of it."

"Yes, you do. I bet you stayed awake half the night thinking about our kiss. I know I did."

"I assure you, I have not thought about it since. You might as well forget, as well. There will be no repeat."

Hollis grabbed Hannah's shoulders and spun her around. She first looked into his eyes and then, pointedly, turned her gaze out the kitchen window. "Find some other girl to kiss," she warned. "I never found you amusing, even less so now. You can stay for dinner. I know the boys enjoy your company. I don't want to ruin anything for them. But you are not welcome for dinner again. You'll have to make arrangements to see the boys outside of my house." Hannah turned back to her carrots as Jonah came running through the kitchen door.

Hollis stared at her back, recalling odd moments: the way Hannah's black dress clung to her body in the rain, her smile for Alberto at the restaurant and the way she gripped his arm when the Ferris wheel car swung. He admired her devotion to family and the overwhelming sacrifices she made on their behalf. There was more to Hannah than Hollis ever took time to notice. Had he realized his attraction too late?

Dinner seemed normal. Hollis and the boys carried on a lively conversation. Hannah did not take part. After dessert, Hollis bid the boys a Merry Christmas, indicating he wouldn't be by until after the holiday. He turned to Hannah before he headed out.

"Merry Christmas, Hannah."

"I have something for you." She reached into her apron pocket. "It's not much, but I've been saving up to repay you. I have five dollars so far." She handed him the money. "It may not go far toward getting your car fixed, but I thought it might help. I'm earning more now so I'll be making regular payments. Have a safe trip."

Hollis stared at Hannah's mouth and wanted to reach down and kiss her. Confused by her coldness, he left without another word. He needed time to think. Hours of driving might prove just the thing.

* * *

Hannah was concerned about Christmas, even before Hollis left. It was not so much David or Samuel who caused her worry. Their holidays were bleak in the years since Father died. She imagined they would be appreciative if all she managed was a turkey dinner and all the fixings. Jonah was another matter. He lived a fine life in Pennsylvania with cousin Aubrey's family and did not hesitate to recall Christmases past, when Santa brought toys and games. Last year at Christmas, the family made plans to attend the circus when it came to town, another happy memory Hannah could not replicate.

To be honest, Hannah could not afford Christmas. She purchased new underwear and socks for the boys and stashed away some candy for their stockings. In the end, she took five dollars from money she saved for Hollis and headed for Woolworth's, where she splurged on gifts—at least it seemed like splurging to her. Hannah briefly regretted having spent so freely on her home before the boys turned up.

An immigrant from the Philippines by the name of Pedro Flores opened the Yo-yo Manufacturing Company in Santa Barbara in 1928. His improvements on the toy allowed a sophistication of movement previously unknown. His immediate success led to factories, not only in Santa Barbara, but in Los Angeles and Hollywood. Although a Mr. Duncan purchased the Flores Yo-yo Corporation, Mr. Flores' entertaining toys remained a fixture in their city of origin. Hannah bought each of the boys a yo-yo, then spent $2.75 on a Big Performing Circus set for Jonah. The boxed toy included wooden circus animals with moveable parts, a clown, a cage, ladder, teeter totter, barrel and ball for the circus performance. As excited as Hannah was to provide a memorable Christmas for her brothers, there was a hollow feeling in her stomach as she paid for the gifts.

Life was not at all what Hannah envisioned when she started her business and accepted the house. She knew it would take all her resources to make a go of it on her own. She hoped there would be time and money to improve her home.

Her brothers turned all her ambitions on end. An immense portion of each day was now spent cooking, cleaning, washing dishes and doing laundry. Although the boys were able to help now they were healthy, Hannah knew she took on a mother's role while trying to pack a father's 12-hour workday into each 24 hours. This left little time for sleep, even less for Mollie's friendship, reduced now to only an occasional letter. Hannah was reluctant to limit game nights, which served to improve her relationship with the boys.

Thoughts of Hollis and his kiss came to mind, more frequently than Hannah cared to admit. She remembered the thrill of being wrapped in Hollis' strong arms and gazing at those warm brown eyes in his handsome face. It was her girlhood dream come true. Hannah was putty in Hollis Rumsford's hands, even though she knew he was a scoundrel and seducer of women. He proved himself extraordinarily helpful and asked for little in return but she could never allow herself to become involved. Hannah decided it was best to discourage him. Someday, she hoped a decent and moral gentleman might come into her life. For now, her hands were full.

When the clock struck 11 on Christmas night, Hannah sat alone at the kitchen table. Only her ledger books provided company. Apprehension about the holiday proved unwarranted. Her brothers obviously enjoyed the day from morning church services right up to bedtime. The food was good, spirits were high and even Jonah seemed thrilled. Mollie's mother invited them all for dessert, which made for an opulent ending to the day and afforded an opportunity for Mollie and Hannah to visit.

Their small table-top tree sported homemade decorations and proved an adequate focal point. Hollis managed to hide a gift for each boy before his departure.

"This feels like a piece of wood," noted David as he fingered the present.

Each gift actually contained a small block of wood. A note was enclosed promising Hollis would supply wood and foreman skills. The boys would supply the brawn. It seemed the mattresses in the bedroom would soon be removed from the floor. Hollis left directions for the boys to cut wood he left in the shed for bunkbeds. When he returned, he would help the boys construct one built-in bunk bed and one elevated bed with room for a dresser underneath. Since the boys eagerly helped build the staircase in the kitchen, they felt competent to cut the wood according to Hollis' directions.

Hannah was overcome at her brothers' thoughtful gift. She opened a small box to find an assortment of seed packets.

"What is this?"

"It's for you, Hannah. It's a front and backyard for the house," offered an eager Jonah.

"We're farmers after all," added Samuel. "We'll make short work of planting those for you. We just need you to tell us where everything goes. We'll do the rest!"

"We'll pull out the weeds and bramble. We figured you'd wanna keep the rose bushes beside the house and the honeysuckle on the fence. Once spring comes, we'll be ready to sow the seeds," continued David.

"I don't know what to say!" replied an emotional Hannah. "This is such a thoughtful gift!"

"It was Hollis' idea," continued Jonah. "He thought it up, but we're the ones gonna do it."

Hannah squelched her sudden desire to frown. Jonah's grammar had gone the way of his older brothers.

"And so you are. Thank you." Why did it seem every conversation circled around to Hollis Rumsford?

Next afternoon, the boys began measuring and sawing. Turkey pie made an easy supper, so Hannah decided to take on her own improvement project that afternoon. She hung wallpaper purchased for her bedroom. Once her brothers took up residence in the downstairs room, the paper lay unused in a corner of the attic. In short order, Hannah sprawled on the attic floor and gazed up at the oddly angled walls ablaze in pink and yellow cabbage roses. She believed the wallpaper looked better in her attic than it would have looked downstairs.

Every member of the Granville family was worn out and barely spoke as they devoured dinner. It was Samuel's turn to wash and Jonah's to dry, which left Hannah and David at the kitchen table.

"I need to talk to you," began a nervous David.

Hannah peered over the rim of her teacup. "Is this some serious matter?"

"Yes, it is. I know you won't approve, but I'm not going back to school after Christmas vacation."

"This is a serious decision. What prompted it?"

"I don't like school. I gave it a go because it was important to you and Hollis told me to try. I'm not going back."

"What do you intend to do?"

"Hollis can get me a job, the same kind he got when he started. I'll be a worm on the oil rigs. I can work my way up, the same as Hollis. I'm a hard worker, Hannah. I want to make my own way in life, just like you. I'm the same age you were when you took work at the Rumsford's boarding house. I can help you out. I know it's hard to provide for all of us. I want to do my share."

"You present a well thought out argument. Did Hollis help you?" She could see by the sheepish look on David's face her comment hit the mark.

"He might have helped me put things together but this is my idea."

"But he's the one getting you the job. How will you make it all the way to Goleta and back every day?"

"I can walk down the hill. Hollis'll pick me up. He said he'd drive me home, but he can leave me off at the same place if he's not coming for dinner." A poorly masked look of defiance met Hannah's gaze.

"What if Hollis can't manage to get you a job?"

"I'll find a job someplace. I'm not going back to school."

"I think you might regret losing the opportunity to have an education. You're right, I'm not pleased. Will you at least go to school until you find a job?"

If that were Hannah's only condition, David was relieved, certain Hollis would get him a job when he returned from Placerville.

"I'll agree."

Hannah offered her hand and gave her brother a firm handshake.

"We have a deal then. You'll stay in school until you find a job and I will not forbid you to find one." As she took another sip of tea, Hannah contemplated ringing Hollis' neck, if he ever dared show up again.

* * *

"I thought I'd find you here," noted Hollis as he approached the workbench where his father was cleaning tools.

"Your ma always liked a houseful of family. She's living high on the hog these days. Would you believe, when I married her, I never intended to be a father? That was downright stupid of me. I knew how crazy she was about babies and children. She never once brought up the subject of how many children she wanted. Women are pretty tricky. They find ways to get what they want."

"She must have wanted you," noted Hollis.

"That she did. She got me, too."

"There hasn't been much chance to talk with everybody here." Hollis quickly became the favored uncle, available for horsey-back rides and mock battle. One small nephew named Nelson could not say Hollis and anointed him Uncle Hollie. The name stuck. Now everyone in the family referred to him as Uncle Hollie.

"This sounds serious. How can I help? Is there a lady in this conversation?"

"How did you know?"

"All your brothers came to me at some time or other for a talk about a lady. I figured either you or Dock would be next. How's Dock doing?"

"Same as always. He spends all his money on the fairer sex. He seems to be taking his work more seriously, though."

"That's a good thing. I bet you had a hand in that."

"I don't know."

"Who is this lady you wish to discuss? Oh, lord, it's not that Lucy Granville, is it?"

"No. What's wrong with her?"

"That girl is nothing but trouble and I know both you and Dock admired the swish of her skirt when we were in Fresno."

"True enough but I never took a serious interest in her. There is someone though. You know her."

"Lucy is the only girl I know in Santa Barbara, besides your Aunt Bitsy."

"You know her sister, Hannah."

"Little Hannah, yes. She is rather a mousy girl. I wouldn't think she could hold your interest."

"Once she got out from under Lucy's shadow, there's a lot more to Hannah than you might think."

"Truly?"

"She's quite a little spitfire. She and I have been at each other's throats this past year. But I think there's something I never took notice of. Now, it might be too late to convince her I could be a suitor."

"Are you certain you want to be her suitor? If what you say is true, maybe you just don't like each other."

"She always seemed to have a bad impression of me right from the get go. Maybe it's because I competed with Dock for her sister's attention. I haven't seen Lucy in a long time. She moved on once she got to Santa Barbara, eager to cut all ties."

"Girls is kind of funny that way. Did I ever tell you how your ma took a dislike to me?"

"No. I can't believe she ever did."

"We went to school together. I was a typical boy and I could be a bit ornery from time-to-time. I don't even remember but I pushed your ma in the mud one rainy day. She wore a new dress so she harbored a grudge against me for years. When we got older and I took a likin' to her, she wanted nothing to do with me because of that dress. I had a terrible time trying to figure out why she was so mad. Once she told me, I had an even worse time convincing her to go courtin'."

"Then how did you convince her?"

"Persistence. And then I finally got kind of mad and told her I wasn't going away 'til she gave me a try. I told her I'd prove I was a gentleman and I did. There was a long courtship. I didn't win her over right away.

"Our lives didn't turn out anything like I thought they would. There's been a lot of hard times. I never thought I'd take a job where I was gone from home so much. She never complained about being here alone but I know it was hard on her. I wouldn't trade a minute with your ma, though. She is the glory of my life. Times being what they are, I can't make much of a living on the road. I'm thinking of quitting."

"It's a rough life, being gone all the time."

"That ain't the half of it. I see how bad life is for the farm workers. I feel real sorry for those folks, living in filth, not enough to eat, no money for clothes, no place to live. It ain't no wonder they're mad and getting madder. It's all about to explode.

"I've seen the pickets. I've seen the way the police

and the vigilantes work against those poor folks. I know there's the communists in the middle of all of it but they're just an excuse for the big farmers to do as they please. There's even a pretty, young girl mixed up in this. She's a communist too. Name's Caroline Decker. Watch for her name in the papers.

"They use those new-fangled mimeograph machines to spread word about the unions. It's like a bomb ticking away, waiting to explode. I don't want to be around when it does."

"What will you do, then?"

"Your ma has made a going concern here. I'm thinking of staying home and helping out at the boarding house."

"Will you be happy here all the time? You're so used to being gone."

"I'm tired, Hollis. I think we need some time together, Ma and me. We're not getting any younger. How about you? How are you going to win over your Miss Hannah?"

"Persistence, I guess. I want a family, Pop, my own family. Hannah is smart and resourceful. She's good and trustworthy."

"Sounds like you're describing man's best friend."

Hollis laughed. "She can kiss too, and she's fair of face and figure. Now I just have to get her to kiss me again."

* * *

Hollis crawled off the makeshift bed on his parent's parlor sofa and crossed the room to look out the front window, if only to reassure himself he was able to stand. He had the dream again, at least he thought of it as a dream now instead of a nightmare. It started years ago.

Originally, he struggled to awaken from the realistic nightmare. It was always the same. He woke up knowing he could not get out of bed. He was disabled and alone. Intense anxiety washed over him as he lay helpless in the dark, a prisoner in his own body. The dream ended this way for years. Hollis would manage to wake up, soaked in his own sweat, disoriented and distraught.

The dream grew longer over time. First, Hollis heard the sound of a baby crying. Eventually, he could make out a woman's voice, first soothing the crying infant, then reading a story. He could never hear the words she read. Then would come the sound of children's laughter.

The longer the dream lasted, the calmer Hollis felt. He somehow knew the woman would come and help him. Hollis abandoned his struggle for consciousness, curious to find out what happened next. To date, he never managed to sleep long enough to satisfy his curiosity. Of one thing, he was certain. The woman's voice was Hannah's.

They knew how to fight and they knew how to kiss. How could Hollis possibly make a marriage out of that?

* * *

The new year came and went, and there was no sign of Hollis. The boys sawed the wood to their mentor's specifications and were eager to begin their project.

They also managed to clear the weeds and dead vegetation from both the front and back yards in anticipation of warmer weather. Hannah was not fond of the bare dirt so easily tracked into their small home. But the pristine earth, ready for planting, held a certain appeal.

On New Year's Day, Hannah directed her brothers out to the little cemetery. The family took on the project of cutting grass and amending years of neglect. All three boys were unhappy at being forced into community service but it was a lovely day. Their camaraderie and the promise of freshly baked cookies made the work bearable.

"When will Hollis help us build the bunks?" asked Jonah as he stomped on a tumbleweed.

"I think he'll be back soon. I'm certain he'll come by as soon as he can." But Hannah realized she was harsh with him. She might have driven him away for good. If anything happened to Hollis on his journey, they would likely never find out. Despite her anger over his meddlesome ways, concern for Hollis' welfare invaded her thoughts.

A miserable and reluctant David accompanied his brothers to school. No sooner had the boys left than Hannah walked out her front door and spied a smiling Hollis bounding up the walkway like some eager puppy. Relieved, she briefly contemplated apologizing for her harsh words before Christmas but having planned a brawl over David's schooling, she considered the apology a moot point. Before she could say a word, Hannah found herself flabbergasted at the first declaration out of Hollis' mouth.

"I've decided to marry you, Hannah." Observing his bride-to-be, Hollis imagined the term "struck dumb" seemed fitting. "Let me explain. I am unhappy with the entire courtship process. I have tired of pretending to be someone I am not in order to attract a palatable female who is likely playing the same game. In short, I want to be myself and know the woman beside me is not putting on some show to ensnare me.

"I've always been completely honest with you. I can say anything I like, assured you will come crawling back to me. Don't look so shocked. History proves me entirely correct in this assumption. You can say anything you like to me, knowing it will be quickly forgotten once I sit down to dinner at your table.

"Men only desire two things from marriage. The first is a woman to warm his bed. The second is a good cook. I certainly have no doubts about your abilities on the second score. Your reaction to my kiss last month assures I will enjoy having you in my bed. Further, I know you'll enjoy being there.

"I know what you're thinking. No man in his right mind would want you. I commented on that fact numerous times. But, you meet my requirements for marriage as listed and I make the ideal husband. You see, I've been offered an office job. Although not appreciated by the fairer sex, my obsession for automobiles, carburetors, axles and such makes for fascinating discussion at an oil company. Management has come to believe my assets are being squandered on an oil rig. I am evidently more suited to a suit. My sturdy body and ample good looks are to be put to use representing my company." Hollis paused only long enough to come up for air.

"Not only do I have the wherewithal to support you financially, I am used to your eccentricities. I have a favorable history solving your constant crises. I eagerly anticipate the day we live under the same roof so as to avoid your pounding on my door for help in the middle of the night.

"I have vast experience battling over your wardrobe, driving, housekeeping and poor life choices. I have no delusions about your desire to keep your business and your little hovel, although I can't imagine how you will stuff our ten children in this tiny abode with all your relatives. Nor can I guess how you will lug them around in a single automobile while you work. At least nothing you try to accomplish will be particularly stunning in light of past escapades. So, you see, I am your ideal mate."

"Hollis Rumsford, if you think for a minute I or any other woman on the face of this earth would consider your proposal, you are out of your mind. Perhaps some piece of equipment hit you in the head and you are no longer rational—not that you were ever very rational. You are vulgar, vain, immoral and just, just, full of yourself!"

"You see, you are only proving my point. How can I possibly take offense at anything you say, when I have only to kiss you and sit down to your chicken dinner and all will be immediately forgiven? Further, I know you can't live without me, no matter how cross you might seem at the moment. You have proven repeatedly you need a keeper. Really, Hannah, no man I know would take you on with all those brothers of yours. I am your one and only option. Even you must realize that.

"I am the only thing standing between you and the title of old maid and I know exactly what you're thinking. You are fully embracing the notion of spinsterhood but you've already proven to me and yourself that you really can't do without a man's help. You have demonstrated this on so many occasions, I can't begin to count them. Just because I am too much of a gentleman to throw them all in your face doesn't mean I haven't noticed how much you need and desire me. So, what's it to be?"

"No! Go away!"

"I am more than willing to give you time to accept the inevitable but I am coming for you on Saturday, rain or shine. We will have our next date. I will hunt you down if you are not ready. You *will* wear a dress. The black frock you wore to Lucy's party should be adequate. If you dare to wear trousers again, I will dress you myself."

"What makes you think you can boss me around?" Hannah spluttered. She was much too angry to imagine a brilliant reply.

"I can't seem to picture my life without you and have come to believe the unlikely possibility I love you, Hannah. Furthermore, I am completely certain you love me. You missed me while I was gone, didn't you? I can honestly admit I missed you. You are about to be entirely impressed."

"Why, because you'll attempt to fool me into believing you are some kind of gentleman?"

"No, because we are meant for each other and I'm going to prove it."

At this, Hollis grabbed his beloved and planted a kiss on her resistant lips. He smiled down at her, kissed her forehead and turned to leave. Hannah hurled her purse toward his back. Hollis leapt into his automobile and waved as he passed her house.

"I'll be by tonight," he yelled.

Taking a deep, calming breath after retrieving her purse, Hannah was disgusted at the surge of relief she felt. Hollis was as maddening as ever but he was home safe. Soon a smile formed. Hollis was a good-looking man. He was right about that, if nothing else.

* * *

Hollis shamelessly hid behind Hannah's brothers when he appeared that night after supper. The four fellows took Hannah's flashlight and spent an hour in the shed while Hollis demonstrated the assembly of the bunk framework.

As Hannah concentrated on her bookwork at the kitchen table, an excited Jonah came bounding through the back door.

"Hollis is gonna come back to help us put up the bunks on Sunday afternoon. Can we invite him for supper?"

It was never Hannah's intention to keep Hollis from her brothers. She would be first to admit the man was a good influence on the three boys even if it was hard to stomach the fact her brothers idolized him. The possibility her siblings could become egotistical, vain and immoral miniature versions of Hollis Rumsford briefly crossed her mind. Hannah was certain her own influence was not lost on the boys.

She successfully avoided Hollis before, she undoubtedly could manage again. Once she had her say during their "date" on Saturday, perhaps Hollis would be equally eager to avoid her.

The week flew by for everyone but David. No job materialized since Hollis took extra time in Placerville. David kept his word to his sister but was loathe to make the trip to school each morning. He began to regret the bargain he made and fantasized about cutting class.

Never an enthusiastic student, a belligerence developed. David was kept after school twice that week for smart-aleck remarks. At the end of the school day on Friday, David was handed a note to his parents, cataloguing recent shortcomings. The note was to be signed and returned on Monday.

Samuel thought the situation extremely funny. Although he enjoyed going to school and having friends his age, he would never admit such a thing to his older brother or even to Hannah.

"What are you gonna do? Hannah will be fit to be tied," Samuel inquired as the boys walked home.

"I'm not going back to school. There's no reason to do anything."

"Hannah will figure you out. What if she throws your ass out of the house? You made a deal," goaded Samuel.

This comment proved distressing to young Jonah, whose grasp on family and home was extremely tentative. "Don't say that, Samuel. We're all there is. We need to stay together." Tears welled in the boy's eyes.

Samuel pulled his little brother's cap over his face as they stepped off the curb. "Don't worry, squirt. Hannah ain't a real parent anyways. She won't throw nobody out. She acts tough but she's just a girl, barely older than Davy, here. You go on being perfect little Jonah, teacher's pet. You got nothin' to worry about. Nobody would ever throw you out."

"But I don't want Davy to go away!" Jonah clasped his oldest brother's hand as they continued down the sidewalk.

"You need to grow up, Jonah. You're a big sissy," taunted Samuel.

"Aw, leave him alone, Sam. He's just a kid. At least we was older once nobody wanted us," offered David, although in truth, Jonah was not much younger than Samuel was when they were shipped off to Montana. "I bet he doesn't even remember our dad or the house in Placerville."

"Yes, I do. I wasn't a baby. Father used to let me ride on his back and we went for walks on the boardwalk in town. He was always dressed fine and everybody said hello to him. He took me to school on the first day but then he died. I never went back to that school ever again."

"Well, you lived fine in Pennsylvania, though, didn't you?" goaded Samuel. "You was the lucky one there. Things didn't go so well for Davy and me. Being here is the best life we've known since Father passed. I don't see why Davy wants to throw it all away."

"Don't throw it away, Davy. Hannah might get

mad but you should be honest," urged Jonah. "Everything will be all right, then. You'll see. Maybe Hollis could help."

"Yeah, listen to your perfect little brother," mocked Samuel.

"Maybe I will," replied David. "He's a lot smarter than you'll ever be."

But David's life would change in unexpected ways before Monday, his day of reckoning.

Chapter Twelve

Hollis knocked on the Granville family's front door. He was probably more excited than nervous. There was a lot riding on this date. It might chart the course for the rest of his life. Hollis knew he could charm Hannah. She loved him. She simply didn't understand quite yet. It was his duty to help her sort out her true feelings.

Hannah opened her door to find Hollis standing straight and tall, a silly grin on his face. She appraised him carefully. He wore a pale gray suit and vest; she never saw him dressed so immaculately. He held a small nosegay of white irises, baby's breath, and lavender sweet peas in one hand and a small box of chocolates in the other. Without a word, Hannah held the door wide and waved him inside.

Hollis took note of his date's apparel. As he commanded, Hannah wore the black dress, although he appreciated it more when it was wet and clung seductively to her body.

"You look lovely," he commented honestly. "These are for you."

"Thank you. How sweet of you," Hannah sarcastically replied. At least her words of dating advice finally sunk into Hollis' thick head. "I'll put these in water before we go."

As Hannah turned toward the kitchen, she noted her brothers were all agog at the uncharacteristically civil and proper behavior occurring in their living room.

"I brought something for you boys, as well," Hollis continued as he reached inside his coat pocket. Hannah turned her head and caught sight of some sort of magazines. "I've been told by experts a gentleman should buy off his date's parents. You are the only relatives here, so you three boys are the beneficiaries of my collection of *The Funnies.* They're like magazines full of Sunday funny papers. I actually hate to part with them but it's high time I gave up boyish pursuits." He grinned arrogantly in Hannah's direction.

"Gee, thanks Hollis. These are swell," commented Samuel. All three boys seemed pleased at Hollis' thoughtful gesture.

"Assuming I have your permission, I'll take your sister out on the town. You'll take good care of Jonah, now, correct?"

"Sure, Hollis. Don't worry about us," assured David.

"We won't be late," promised Hannah as she attempted to put on her coat before Hollis could help, but failed. Her plan was to end the farcical date and return in moments.

Hollis properly held the car door and helped Hannah in, then took the driver's seat and started the engine.

"It will save time if I say what I have to say. Why don't you turn off the engine?"

"We're having our date, Hannah. I thought I was

perfectly clear."

"You got your turn to talk when you came back from Placerville. I simply want a chance to reply to your comments. Isn't that only fair?"

Hollis stopped the engine and turned in his seat. "Nothing you say will make a difference."

"I find that difficult to believe."

"Fine. Go ahead."

"You made several untrue comments. I wish to set the record straight."

"I have done everything you consider proper tonight. I am being the model boyfriend by your exact specifications. Isn't that true?"

"It seems you finally paid attention to my advice, but those suggestions were for other girls, not me. If you will kindly shut up for a moment, I will proceed."

Hollis waved his hand in reply, shutting up completely, per her request.

"First of all, my house is not a hovel. I resent you referring to it in such a derogatory manner. It's true, the living room is not what it could be, but it is clean and nothing about my house suggests the description you offered."

"The roof on your house is the best part and it belongs to me," commented Hollis.

"It certainly does not. I am paying you back."

"At the rate you're going, that house will need a new roof before your debt is paid."

Hannah chose to ignore the remark, intent on her practiced list of grievances. "Secondly, I have never gone crawling to you for anything. I may have asked for help from time-to-time. You were my neighbor in Placerville. I was only requesting what a good neighbor would offer of his own free will."

"Are you suggesting I was not a good neighbor? I

should have made a pest of myself to determine any possible need? I might remind you, my parents took you in when no one else would have you."

"Those were your parents. You can't take credit for their generosity."

"And so, I get no credit for helping when you begged for assistance?"

"I didn't say that, Hollis. I simply want to make a point. Any neighborly person would have helped."

Hollis was not willing to concede this point but he attempted to keep his eye on his goals for the night. "Anything else?"

"Certainly. Despite your delusions, I have no interest in you whatsoever. Not only is there no love between us, I do not and have not ever liked you. I have no desire to share your bed or cook for you. I would never have asked you for dinner of my own free will. You exacted that service in return for what should have been neighborly good will.

"There are plenty of men who would like to take me out. I am not a scary woman. If it were my desire to find a husband, men would be lined up to date me."

At this Hollis actually guffawed. He received a blistering stare in return. "Go on. I assume you aren't finished."

"I resent your interference with my brothers. I understand they look up to you, and I would even admit there are positive aspects to the relationship you've made. But you should never have promised David a job nor supported his desire to quit school."

"I'm the one who got David to try school. If not for me, he would have quit months ago. Do I get any credit for this? No. Only criticism. He tried it and he doesn't like it. He is more a man than a boy. He needs to find work. Lord knows you need help. He could bring in extra money. It never ceases to amaze me how rapidly you dismiss perfectly obvious solutions."

"I would give anything to still be in school."

"As I said before, David is not you. He is a different person. Furthermore, I find your allegation without merit. Would you be willing to give up your house, or your business or your brothers to go to school? I don't think you would give up any of that, not one of those things."

Hannah couldn't think up an honest retort. Fuming, she continued. "There is nothing wrong with my trousers. Movie stars wear them. They are all the rage."

"Are you done?"

"I believe so." Hannah expected their date would meet a quick demise and she reached for the handle of the door.

"Then we'll be off now," commented Hollis as he started the car and stepped on the gas, a little more forcefully than needed.

Hannah could see she managed to anger Hollis but was amazed when he slammed on his brakes and stopped in the middle of the street. She braced herself for another rear-end collision, which would undoubtedly have occurred if anyone was behind them.

"Why did you come tonight?" demanded Hollis.

"You had your say the other day, I wanted mine."

"And that's the only reason?"

"It is. I'll get out here and walk home."

Hollis grasped Hannah's forearm before she could open her door.

"It is apparent we got off on the wrong foot. I'm not certain how or when this occurred, but I have gone to some expense and trouble to arrange our date tonight and I intend to see it through. I would like to start over—pretend we never met before. I promise you if, at the end of the evening, you honestly tell me you failed to enjoy yourself, I will consider this experiment a failure without any hope of winning your favor." Hollis extended his right hand. "Do we have a deal?"

Hannah grasped his hand and applied a firm handshake. "This can't possibly be worse than our first date. All right, Hollis. I will pretend I never laid eyes on you, only for tonight."

"Say something nice."

"What?"

"I want you to say something nice, as if you didn't know a thing about me."

"You look handsome tonight in your suit. Is it new?"

"It is. I need proper clothes for my new position."

"Well, your suit is quite—becoming. And you cleaned up so nicely."

"What do you mean by that? I'm always cleaned up. That's no easy feat when you work on an oil rig all day."

"Yes, I noticed the day I saw you after work. Your nails were caked in dirt; your clothes were filthy."

"That's right. I've always cleaned up to come to your house."

"So, you have," agreed Hannah hastily. Perhaps she pushed him too hard. Her assertion he was deranged might be truer than she ever imagined. Hannah decided to add another kind comment.

"Thank you again for the flowers. They are lovely. Did you know sweet peas are my favorite flower? And the baby's breath always makes a bouquet look so airy." She was relieved when Hollis started the car. It seemed odd such a simple remark served to calm the man. As they rode in silence, Hannah realized her only goal was to survive the evening intact. Then she could tell him there was no hope and that would be the end of that.

They proceeded to the Saint Barbara Hotel for dinner. The elegant restaurant had a reputation for ignoring current prohibition laws. Hannah was shocked when Hollis ordered red wine and the waiter produced it as if this were the most common occurrence on earth. She looked at Hollis curiously when he proposed a toast.

"To us, the newest of total strangers, the oldest of adversaries." Hollis tipped her glass and sipped the wine, watching to see if Hannah would follow. She was out of her element, unsure how to proceed. "Don't worry, you're not in imminent danger of being dragged off to the hoosegow."

"You would know this because—"

"I wouldn't bring you here if it wasn't safe. Have a sip. You'll like it better than the beer I gave you."

"I don't know what you're talking about, Mr. Rumsford."

"Oh, right."

The pair made polite conversation throughout their excellent dinner. It was invariably Hollis who slipped up and mentioned topics too familiar for their "game." As when he referred to the beer they shared in the cemetery, Hannah did not hesitate to call him on his errors. She was content to treat him as a polite stranger and be treated so herself.

After dinner, they walked down State Street to the Carrillo Ballroom, one of the few buildings in the center city to survive the earthquake of 1925. The maple floor was spring loaded, meant to provide the ultimate in dancing comfort.

"What a large band," commented Hannah.

"This is the best place to dance in Santa Barbara," noted Hollis.

"You come here often?"

"I do."

The idea of Hollis dancing the night away seemed foreign to Hannah. She tended to think of him wielding a hammer or wrench more than enjoying life. He failed miserably to show her a good time on their first date.

"Can you do the Balboa?"

"I never even heard of it," admitted Hannah.

"But you can waltz, surely?"

"Of course."

"Well, the Balboa is waltz steps with a brush step on both ends." Hollis collected Hannah's coat and placed it on a chair before leading her onto the dance floor. The band was playing *Life is Just a Bowl of Cherries*, as Hollis took up dance position. "Here we go. One, brush, step, two, three, brush, step, four. It's a good dance for a crowded floor since it doesn't take up much space. You can dance to a slow song like this or to a faster beat. Pretty simple, huh?"

"I think I get the hang of it."

"All but one thing. Don't dance with your head, Hannah."

"What are you talking about?"

"Dance with your legs. You're bouncing up and down too much. It's smooth. Use your lower legs. That's better. Girls can do a kick to the rear instead of the brush step."

Hollis pulled Hannah into a close hold. Before admonishing him for his boldness, she took a look at other couples on the dance floor, who appeared plastered against each other in a similar fashion. The intimate dance position made Hannah uncomfortable. She was relieved when the song ended and they parted to applaud. The next song had a slightly quicker beat, *Embraceable You*.

"This is a good one," Hollis noted as he again

pulled Hannah against his right side. "It's not too quick. If we practice a bit, you'll be ready to fly when they play a fast song."

Hannah felt self-conscious, never having given so much control of her body to any person in her life. Hollis was strong enough to move her anyway he pleased. She felt entirely at his mercy with little choice but to react when he led her in a simple turn. Her shocked expression as Hollis pulled her back into his embrace caused him to laugh.

"What's so funny?"

"You look a little like a lamb being taken to slaughter. Relax, Hannah, this is for fun. I told you before, I'm not going to bite."

"I'm not so sure about that."

The tempo of the next song was quicker, *It Don't Mean a Thing if it Ain't Got That Swing*. Before Hannah knew what happened, Hollis was leading her in intricate patterns she could not comprehend. Barely able to keep pace with the tempo, she believed Hollis would not let her fall. She could barely manage to move her feet and stay upright. If they looked competent as a couple, it was entirely Hollis' doing.

Somewhere in the middle of the song, Hannah abandoned any idea of self-control and allowed Hollis to have his way. By the time they stepped apart—Hollis leaving his hand at her elbow to assure she was steady on her feet—Hannah sported a big smile.

"See, that's fun," urged Hollis.

"I guess it is. I wish I knew what I was doing."

"You're doing great!" he complimented. "Let's get a soda and sit down so you can catch your breath."

Hannah bit her tongue, about to comment she was young and able. If Hollis needed to sit one out, he didn't need to blame it on her. She struggled for a kinder thought. Perhaps he was simply being considerate.

Hollis led Hannah to their little table and hurried off to obtain refreshments. The band began to play *Until the Real Thing Comes Along*. Hannah listened intently to the words, sung by a crooner on the stage. He catalogued everything he would do to prove his love, including crying, working, begging and even dying, at least until he actually fell in love. Hannah wondered if Hollis was doing that. He admitted he wanted a family and was tired of looking for a suitable wife. Was she simply filling some temporary need? What would he do once he really fell in love? Unhappy at the direction of her thoughts, Hannah was relieved when Hollis returned carrying two beverages.

As they sat and watched other dancers, Hollis admitted, "A man really only needs to know two dances, the waltz and the Balboa."

"Is that all you know?"

"Just about. But as in all my other accomplishments, I am good at what I do."

Hannah smiled at his boldness and uncharacteristically refrained from criticism. She danced the evening away and was disappointed when the band played their last tune of the night. By this time, she considered herself a Balboa expert. As the couple made their way onto the sidewalk, Hollis noted Hannah's reluctance to leave and suggested another activity.

"We could park at the beach and walk on the shore if you're not in any hurry. It's a mild night, unless you want to go home now. I'll understand if you do."

Hannah bit her lip. "No, a walk in the sand sounds therapeutic. I have a feeling my feet are going to be the worse for wear by morning."

It was a short drive down State Street to Cabrillo and the shore. Hollis opened the passenger door and waited while Hannah removed her shoes and stockings, intent on letting the sand massage her tired feet.

"Aren't you going to take your shoes off?"

"I guess I could." Hollis quickly untied the laces and threw his shoes and socks behind the seat. Offering his arm, he guided Hannah toward the wet sand near the water's edge, admiring the moon shining on the ocean as they walked. "Where did you get your dress?"

"It was Mollie's dress, a graduation gift from her aunt. It never fit so when I needed it, she generously gave it to me."

"It's lovely. I felt proud to escort you all night. You're beautiful, Hannah."

"I don't think there's any need to be deceitful, is there?"

"I'm not being deceitful. I'm being honest," but Hollis could see Hannah might never view herself objectively and changed the subject. "You wore that dress the night your roof leaked. You told me you sold your soul for 30 pieces of silver. I always remembered your comment because I hadn't any idea what you meant."

"Now Mr. Rumsford, whatever are you talking about?"

"No, Hannah. Our game is over. I think we can manage one conversation without resorting to subterfuge."

Hannah rather doubted that. "I told you what I did. I made Lucy pay me to attend her engagement party."

Hollis laughed. "You surely did not."

"But I did. I was certain God ruined my house because of my sin."

"I don't know. I like the fact you made her pay. Money is all that really matters to your sister, I'm afraid. She must have admired your boldness. You spoke to her in the only language she understands, dollars and cents."

"If you knew that about her, why did you chase after her all those years? Tell me honestly."

"Your sister has a pretty face. I liked competing for her attention. It was a game, really." Hollis could see Hannah's face in the moonlight. She was glaring up at him. If he said something wrong, he didn't understand what it could be. "I'm being honest, Hannah."

"Skip it," she replied, sincerely intending to enjoy the last of their lovely evening.

"When is Lucy's wedding?"

"It's in June. My mother is coming."

This proved an interesting piece of information. It meant Hollis had over four months to implement his plan.

"How did you get your car fixed?" Hannah inquired, understanding Hollis' Model A was his true love.

"My dad knows a mechanic in Placerville. I got it fixed while I was there. It was less than I thought it would be. Maybe the garage needed work so they gave me a low bid."

"Did you have a good time back home?"

"I did. I wish you came too."

"I don't know how I could have left my business, even if there was a place to stay."

"You know Ma would have found a place for you. Did you ever think about hiring someone to work for you? You might be able to expand and focus on getting new clients."

"I don't even make enough to support us all, how could I afford an employee?"

"It might be difficult at first but you have to look at your business in the long run. Did you know Mr. Oddgood was a bookkeeper for the studios when they were here? Aunt Bitsy made it clear her in-laws are in difficult straights financially. Mr. Oddgood might be willing to work on an hourly basis to make a little extra money. After all, you don't have any backup plan for when you might need a day off. Even you can't manage to work every day, all year long, year after year. Like I say, you could grow your business. You've taken on an awful lot, Hannah. I know that better than anyone."

"You need to understand, Hollis. Aside from finances, it's important for me to succeed."

"Why? What are you trying to prove?" Hollis offered a seat on a piece of driftwood so they could sit and talk.

"I think a lot about my father. I have ever since he—he died. He was a failure."

"That's not true. Everyone in Placerville respected him."

"But that was foolish of them. Father always meant the world to me. I think a lot about what he did, how he made me feel. He listened intently to my every childish concern and made me feel important. But he never solved any of my problems. Father asked questions until I figured out my own solutions. He treated everyone like that, simply validating their ideas. Father never made his own plan so he never made a success of himself. That was why, when my grandfather's money ran out, he couldn't think of a single way to go forward and ended it all. I never want to be like him."

Hollis studied Hannah's serious expression as she gazed toward the ocean. It was as if he weren't sitting beside her. He was almost afraid to intrude on her reverie.

"He ruined everything. My family was disbanded. My home was sold to strangers. My mother gave up and let her aunt dictate all our futures. I need to show my brothers not everyone is like that. I need to prove somebody loves them enough to take care of them. I need to show them they can be successful and I need to give them every opportunity possible."

Hannah turned toward Hollis and pled, "I'm begging you, Hollis. Couldn't you please wait until school is out to help David find a job? Give him these few months to see if he can adjust. He will learn that much more and maybe he'll see how important school is. I will manage to support them all until then. I promise you, I won't stand in the way of a summer job but I need more time to convince David this is what's best for his future. Promise you'll do this for me?"

"I gave him my word, Hannah."

"You can keep your word. Explain there may not be any jobs for a few months. If you encourage him to stay in school, I know he'd listen to you. Please, Hollis. It would mean the world to me."

"All right, Hannah. I don't think this is the best thing for you or David but I'll try, for you."

"Thank you." Hannah grabbed Hollis' hand as she looked back toward the shore. "Why don't you come early tomorrow. I know the boys are anxious to build the bunk beds. I'll make fried chicken."

"How can I possibly resist?" asked Hollis. "Tonight was fun. I had a good time."

"I did too."

"Does this mean you'll go on another date?"

"I'm not making promises about the future, but yes. I will go out with you."

Hollis managed, barely, to contain his glee. "I guess I better take you home then, Short Stuff. I don't want you to be too tired to fry my chicken."

"What do you mean, Short Stuff? I kept up while we were dancing. My legs are as long as yours."

Knowing the top of Hannah's head barely reached his shoulder when she wore high-heeled shoes, Hollis rebuked, "They certainly are not."

Hannah got up and pulled Hollis' hand so they stood hip-to-hip. Hannah put her arm around his waist to demonstrate their waists were almost even.

Gazing down into her eyes, Hollis pulled her close and stole a kiss, which Hannah fervently returned. Soon, the pair strolled hand-in-hand to the car.

Reluctantly, Hollis drove his date home. Once parked, he attempted to keep her all to himself a few minutes longer.

"I thought about what you said. Hannah, I don't think you need to prove yourself to anyone. You're just a girl. You don't need to be a captain of industry to separate yourself from your father. Do your brothers know about your ambition?"

"I don't even know if they were told how Father died. I can't talk to them about any of this. I can't talk to anyone about what my father did. You know already. I would not discuss this otherwise. And what do you mean, I'm 'only a girl?'" she added disgustedly. Hannah wondered if they could ever be cordial. "I need to go inside."

"I don't mean anything, don't take offense." Hollis rounded his car and opened Hannah's door. "Traditionally, women care about their husbands, and children and household, not whether or not they inherited business sense. You're young and much too serious. Why can't you enjoy life a little and respect tradition?"

"If tradition is all you're interested in, you're barking up the wrong tree." Before Hannah could get another word out, Hollis pulled her close to kiss her goodnight. The kiss became impassioned. Hollis boldly ran his hands along Hannah's sides, then wrapped his arms around her slight frame. When he ended the embrace, Hannah ceased her complaints.

"I'll see you tomorrow. Thank you, this was a lovely evening." She slipped silently through the doorway, leaving a frustrated Hollis, who was only beginning to comprehend his longing.

Chapter Thirteen

When no one answered his knock on Sunday afternoon, Hollis tried the door, which he knew would be unlocked.

"Hello?" The house seemed empty. As he entered the kitchen, a frantic Jonah came tearing through the back door, nearly running into Hollis, who grabbed him by the shoulders.

"Hold on there, buddy. What's the emergency?"

"It's Hannah," panted Jonah. "In the backyard!"

In his mind, Hollis wondered what mess that girl had gotten herself into now but it was his heart that sent him running out the door. He came upon a strange sight. Hannah lay in the dirt, her arm across her forehead. Samuel knelt by her side as David ran from the shed carrying a shovel. The Granville brothers all appeared relieved to see their hero.

"What's going on here? Hannah, are you all right?"

"No, it hurts," was all she could manage.

"What hurts?" Hollis tried to give the perception of calm.

"Hannah tried to help us pull out a root," explained

David. "She backed into an old gopher hole and twisted her foot. I got the shovel to dig her out."

Hollis knelt to examine the trapped foot. "Get a trowel out of the shed," he commanded. "Can't you pull your foot out, Hannah?"

"No, it's stuck and it hurts! Be careful."

Hollis used the trowel to dig a hole beside the trapped foot, then pulled the dirt away, carefully lifting Hannah's leg. The ankle appeared swollen and bruised. Her face was pale.

"It might be broken. Run on in the house, Jonah. Call for the doctor." Hollis effortlessly scooped Hannah into his arms and made for the back door.

At first, Hannah thought to protest. After all, there was no need for melodrama. But she put her arms around Hollis' neck and laid her head against his shoulder. It felt good to be taken care of for a change. Perhaps the part of damsel in distress was not completely abhorrent. She was actually sorry when Hollis gently sat her at the kitchen table. He propped her foot on a nearby chair. All three brothers sported worried expressions.

"I'm certain it's fine," Hannah explained.

Once the doctor arrived, it became apparent she was not fine at all.

"I don't think it's broken but this is a bad sprain. Bones heal but sprains can last a long time," Dr. Chasen explained as he wrapped the injured ankle. "I'm afraid you have to stay off the foot for at least a week. That means bedrest or keeping the foot propped up. No walking. This wrapping must be left on. It will decrease the swelling and provide support. Do you understand, Miss Granville?"

Hollis surmised the doctor already pegged Hannah as an overachiever.

"You must follow my orders explicitly. I'll be back to check on you next Saturday. If it appears the ankle is broken, you'll have to incur the cost of an x-ray. If you fail to follow my instructions, there is a possibility you will never have full use of that limb. This is serious. Do you understand?"

A disgusted Hannah gave a nod. Hollis imagined her mind was struggling to solve the problems caused by her injury.

Dr. Chasen continued, "You boys will have to pitch in and help this week. I expect you to have a sense of pride in the way you care for your sister. After all, she has done so much for you."

"Let me see you out," offered Hollis, who fished some cash out of his pocket to pay the doctor for his house call.

"Are you a relative of Miss Granville?"

"No, I'm an old neighbor."

"I hope you're prepared to help that girl. I kept an eye on this family since treating young Samuel when he first arrived. Miss Granville is awfully young to take on so much responsibility. I don't imagine she's been taking care of herself. Perhaps her injury is a blessing in disguise. She lost weight and appears exhausted. I think she needs rest. I would hate to see her turn into a consumptive."

No comment could have proven more stunning to Hollis. "I assure you, doctor, I will do everything in my power to make Hannah rest and take care of her ankle. I give you my word."

Dr. Chasen inspected the tall, young gentleman. There was a man in love if ever he saw one. "I believe you will."

No sooner did Hollis return to the kitchen than Hannah began to voice her fears.

"What am I going to do? I can't drive, I can't pick up deposits or bills. I could lose my business over this." Alarm was clearly written on the Granville brothers' young faces.

Hollis suggested, "Boys, why don't you go put the tools away? We'll figure out what to do about dinner." Once the boys left, he continued, "Calm down, Hannah. There must be a way around this. Let's think this through. You're upsetting your brothers and you don't need them to go off half-cocked trying to help you."

A queer expression crossed Hannah's features. "That's it! My brother is the solution."

"What are you talking about?"

"David. He is the solution. I need you to do something for me, Hollis."

"Now what?"

"Don't look so apprehensive. This isn't hard. If you teach David to drive my car, he could make the rounds, picking up receipts and invoices. He could bring them here so I can work and prepare the deposits. Then, David could go to the bank. I'll have to call my clients to let them know what happened. Hopefully, I won't lose any business—not for only a week. I'm certain Mr. Barney will be difficult. What do you think? Could you teach David to drive?"

"To be honest, I already let him drive my car a few times. He would be your employee though. You'd have to pay him."

"Yes, I will. He didn't want to go back to school, I'm sure he'll be delighted. I wouldn't choose this solution but I don't see any other option."

Hollis heaved a sigh of relief. He dreaded informing David there would be no job at the oil company until summer. Now that wouldn't be necessary. "I know you want something different for him, but maybe this will all work out for the best. Now, tell me what we have to do about dinner."

Hannah sat at the table, directing Hollis and her brothers. For a time, it seemed dinner was hopeless. In the end, the men served reasonably cooked chicken, lumpy mashed potatoes, watery gravy and over-seasoned green beans. Dessert—a custard pie Hannah already prepared—burnt up in the midst of kitchen chaos. By the time the dishes were washed and put away, all four cooks were completely done in, too tired to play cards.

As the week wore on, it became apparent David was adept at filling in for his sister. He enjoyed driving and was a gregarious representative for what he now referred to as "the family business." He took Hannah's advice to heart, watching his grammar and appearing an intelligent and responsible young man.

Her parting comment on Monday was, "Remember, ain't is not a word."

At first, Mr. Barney proved difficult. He had no intention of turning his money over to a young, unknown boy. Hannah was accustomed to charming the old character in person. She soon discovered her ability extended to the telephone. The endless practice with Mr. Rowland over lunch served her well. Hannah assured Mr. Barney he could call her at home any time. When the deposit and bookwork went smoothly that first day, Mr. Barney calmed down but telephoned frequently. Hannah didn't know if this was because he was ill at ease or simply because he missed their daily chat.

For her part, Hannah spent mornings and early afternoons on bookwork, surprised how quickly she finished when she wasn't doing errands or making her own rounds. She found herself nodding off constantly and took to her bed for large portions of the day. She navigated the stairs on her fanny, using her good foot for leverage, and crawled when she needed to go anywhere in the house. The doctor's assertion she could be lame or have a limp frightened her into compliance. Her foot hurt incredibly each morning when she swung it off the bed but tended not to bother her much during the day. She could tell the swelling was subsiding, which she took to be a sure sign the ankle was not broken. Hannah began to fantasize about accompanying Hollis on the dance floor.

Housework proved a serious problem, especially cooking. Hollis came each night after work to help and confirm Hannah was taking care of herself. He resorted to taking the dirty clothes to a laundry. Hannah assured general housekeeping could wait for a week. But, no matter how carefully Hannah planned a simple meal, this seemed beyond her helpers' ability. Hannah took the deplorable meals in stride, happy to nap while the men cleaned up the kitchen.

She was amused at the overheard comment, "There's a lot more dishes since Hannah ain't cooking." The fact most of the pots and pans sported some degree of burnt food made the evening chore that much more odious.

Since Hollis spent so much time at the Granville house, he helped the boys build their bunks. For the first time since the brothers' arrival, their room was tidy.

It was Hollis who stumbled upon the ideal dinner—hot dogs. He believed any male occupant of the Granville household could boil water. This plan worked remarkably well but after several dinners of hot dogs, his solution lost its luster.

An eager Hannah stayed in bed on Saturday, wishing to impress the doctor with her adherence to his restrictions. Dr. Chasen and Hollis arrived at the same time.

"How has our young patient been doing this week?"

"I think you scared her thoroughly. She's been getting a lot of rest and staying off her foot. We can go on in." Hollis opened the front door and directed the doctor down the hall to the kitchen. "Hannah, are you upstairs?" he shouted.

"Yes."

"I've got Dr. Chasen here. I'll send him up."

Seeing Hollis' reluctance to visit Miss Granville's bedroom, the doctor encouraged, "I think it would be all right if you accompanied me. I'd like you to hear my findings when I examine Miss Granville. It's only her foot, after all."

"All right," replied Hollis. After the men climbed the narrow staircase, Hollis asked, "Where are the boys?"

Hannah replied, "David hasn't come back from his rounds. Samuel is supposed to be in the front yard planting seeds. If he's not there, perhaps he needed something from the shed. Jonah went to play at a school friend's home." She could see Hollis appeared mesmerized by her attic, which was improved from the time he built the staircase.

"Let's see what we have here, young lady," noted Dr. Chasen as he unwrapped the injured foot. He poked and prodded as Hannah and Hollis looked on.

"I believe my diagnosis is correct. This is a bad sprain. I would like for you to stay off the foot one more week. You can remove the wrapping while you sleep. The bruising seems better. Even though it spread, the green areas indicate healing. You look well-rested."

"I slept more in the last week than I thought possible."

"That's nothing to be embarrassed about. Rest is good when your body is healing, even better if you are worn out. I'll stop by next week to confirm you're ready for more activity."

"Another whole week?" Hannah whined.

Dr. Chasen patted Hannah's hand.

"Don't worry, my dear. This is simply a little bump in the road. A month from now, you'll forget this entire experience." The doctor shook Hollis' hand and descended the stairs. "Don't bother, I'll let myself out. Good day."

"Thank you, doctor," added Hollis as he walked toward Hannah's bed, staring at the wallpaper. "What the hell happened in here?"

"What are you talking about?"

"When did you put this paper up?"

"After Christmas. I bought it for my bedroom and then the boys showed up. Since this is my room now, I decided to put it here. It's like waking up in a garden every morning." Noticing the frown on Hollis' face, she asked, "Don't you like it?"

"I think I'd feel like I was waking up in a funeral parlor if I slept in this room."

"What a dreadful thing to say!"

"You asked. I'm being honest."

"I suppose you'd like looking at bare walls?"

"I suppose I would. This is too feminine for me."

"It's a good thing you don't live here, then."

"But I will, one day. We'll have to negotiate about the wallpaper when that time comes."

"I will never understand your conceit. This is my bedroom and I like the way it looks."

"I'll admit you did a fine job painting the furniture and sewing linens. I have nothing but admiration for those skills. And as I noted before, I don't expect I will ever budge you from this house. But when you are mine, this will be my bedroom. I intend to have some say in how it looks. It's bad enough we have a cemetery in the backyard. I don't intend to sleep in a mortuary."

Hannah was aghast. She was careful not to find fault this week. To be honest, she did little but sleep, which seemed to have a tranquilizing effect. Although she still needed Hollis' help, his comments were unpalatable.

Before Hannah could articulate her displeasure, Hollis continued, "We'll have our date after dinner."

"What date? I never agreed to any date and I can't leave the house until my foot improves."

"But you did agree to our date last week, before you so clumsily fell in the backyard."

"I never agreed to go out this week."

"Nonetheless, you did agree to a date and I've decided exactly what needs to be done."

"Have you now? What makes you think—"

Hollis bent over the bed and applied a kiss, much to Hannah's displeasure.

"What are you doing? This is highly improper. You best leave," Hannah commanded as she pushed against Hollis' chest.

"I will reluctantly leave your side, and eagerly leave your wallpaper but I'm only going downstairs. You can get some rest and I'll see you at dinnertime. We're having hot dogs with a twist. I bought a can of sauerkraut."

"I'm certain that will make all the difference." She glared at the back of Hollis' head as he tramped down the stairs. That man was the epitome of arrogance. She simply could not understand the enchantment of his kiss, the longing she experienced at his touch. As she buried her face in the pillow, Hannah remembered all too well their kiss on the porch last Saturday night—the way Hollis touched her body, her desolation when he let her go. If only that man could manage to shut up, he might be tolerable—for some other woman.

* * *

Hannah was quiet since joining the men when the hot dogs came to a boil. This did nothing to dampen Hollis' enthusiasm. Hollis put the boys to work washing dishes after their meal.

The brothers were disappointed when he announced, "Then we'll be off for our date."

"Aw, Hollis, can't we play cards tonight?"

"No, maybe tomorrow. I plan on giving your sister my undivided attention." He scooped a surprised Hannah out of her chair and headed toward the back door. "You could be helpful and turn the knob, Hannah. You might be a mere slip of a girl but even a fit young man such as me has trouble balancing your carcass while operating machinery."

Hannah turned the doorknob but could not refrain from mockery. "If you consider a doorknob some sort of heavy machinery, I'm amazed you ever advanced from your job as a worm. Or is that the problem? You handled equipment so poorly, they were forced to find you a different position? What exactly are you doing?" she asked as Hollis headed for the gate in the back of the yard.

"I told you, we're having our date."

"We're having a date in the cemetery?"

"It is one of your favorite places and we have such fond memories there. Why, Halloween night was the first time we had fun. Besides, this is the one place I know your brothers won't disturb us."

Once Hollis got to the far back corner of the little graveyard, he carefully deposited his lady love on a pile of cushions.

"What have you done? When did you make this?"

"I am a man of mystery," Hollis teased, but he could see Hannah was not amused. "The cushions are from the sofa at my house." Hollis propped Hannah's injured foot on a pillow. "Dock will not be happy when he gets home tonight. He often sleeps on the sofa."

"But the cushions will get dirty," Hannah commented as she looked behind the cushion to find it rested against a headstone.

"No, I put a tarp underneath. Here, have a beer." Hannah accepted the bottle Hollis pulled from behind a tombstone.

"This is some date. What will we do for entertainment?"

"I think we should talk."

"I think that's the worst idea I ever heard. We seem to get in a fight every time we exchange words."

"Well, that's not our only entertainment. You can't dance tonight but we can have music."

"Really? Is a band going to pop out from behind the fence?"

"Nothing quite so dramatic. I will perform my impersonation of Maurice Chevalier singing *You Brought a New Kind of Love to Me*," and Hollis proceeded to do just that. He emphasized the line about the woman being a queen while he was only her slave, then slathered on the French accent so heavily, Hannah could not understand the words at all. She began to laugh.

"I don't know why you're laughing," Hollis commented as he took a bow from his seated position. "I sound exactly like Monsieur Chevalier."

"Well, you don't have a bad voice, that's true enough."

"Now it's your turn."

"No, no. I didn't volunteer to provide entertainment."

"I've never heard you sing. I have a request."

"You can request anything you like, I'm not going to sing," commented Hannah as she downed her beer at a good clip.

"I think you can do this. Be Marlene Dietrich. Sing me *Falling in Love Again.* I won't stop pestering you until you give it a try. I sang for you, after all."

Hannah took one more swig of beer and started on the song.

"No, Hannah, give me your best, throaty, German accent," Hollis interrupted.

Hannah's rendition proved every bit as entertaining as Hollis' impersonation. She hung heavily on the last word, "eeeeet," then burst into laughter.

"Oh, bravo!" approved Hollis when the song was done. "We don't need a band at all. Want another beer?"

"Sure. How many of those do you have in your stash?"

"Well, at the rate you're drinking, probably not enough. I thought you didn't like beer?"

"It's all right. That sure is a beautiful moon."

"The full moon in January is called the Wolf Moon."

"I never heard of such a thing."

"It's true. The Indians have a name for all the full moons."

"Well, that's appropriate enough. Here you are, the biggest wolf I ever met."

"Who, me?"

"Yes, you—with all your sweethearts coming and going. For as long as I can remember, you've been chasing after some poor, foolish girl."

"I told you, Hannah, I don't want to live that way anymore. You are the one I want."

"No, I've been 'liminated."

"Have you now?" Hollis noted the beer was having an immediate effect on his unworldly companion. "Why is that?"

"Cause you don't like my wallpaper."

"I see. If you recall, you were upset about your foot when the doctor left. By the time I left, I don't think you gave a fig about that foot."

"You're telling me you were mean to take my mind off my ankle? You really do like my wallpaper?"

"No, I despise your wallpaper."

"See, it's those comments that make me sorry your mother ever taught you to talk. Do you know, there was a time I would have given anything, anything to sit alone with you in the dark? You with your handsome face and fit body."

Hollis was shocked at her admission. "I think you've had enough to drink, Hannah. Give me the rest of your beer."

"No! You get your own. I'm serious. When we lived in Placerville, I thought you my ideal man."

"Then what happened?"

Hannah glared in response.

"It was Lucy, wasn't it? I took an interest in Lucy."

"No, it wasn't because of Lucy. It was because of what happened. That night when you took her to the hospital—it changed everything."

"I was only being neighborly. Wasn't that enough for you?"

"It was the least you could have done."

"Hannah, your ideas of neighborliness are extreme. How much do you think the world owes your sister? Lucy told me once you would have kept her baby. I thought it noble of you to even suggest that. No one would believe the baby wasn't yours. You would never have kept your job at the hotel. You'd be penniless, living in some Hooverville. I doubted Lucy when she told me but I am certain now you would have done exactly as she claimed. I've seen how important your brothers are to you, how much you sacrifice for them. It makes me love you all the more." But he could see there was something else, something Hannah wouldn't admit.

"I didn't know about the baby until it was too late. If Lucy confided in me, maybe her baby would be alive now," Hannah proclaimed.

"So, you're suddenly able to control your sister? When did she ever listen to a word you said?" Hollis knew this topic would only inflame Hannah. Taking a deep breath, he tried a different tactic.

"While I was home for Christmas, my dad told me a story. When he was first interested in my mother, she couldn't stand the sight of him. He could never figure out why. It turned out, when they were children, he pushed her in the mud one day when she wore a new dress to school. She never forgot that and held it against him for years. A silly boyish prank almost kept them from falling in love and marrying. I wouldn't be here today serenading you in a graveyard if she never forgave him.

"I'm asking you to tell me what it is you hold against me. I want to apologize. Our ten children are counting on it," Hollis joked but he could see Hannah was having none of it.

"You don't owe me an apology."

"Then tell me what I did to upset you. I'm serious, Hannah. I want you. I need you. I want to get past whatever bothers you, what it is that holds you back."

"Why do you think I'm holding back? Don't I

return your kiss in kind? Don't I become weak-kneed at your touch?"

"But why does that happen? Don't you wonder? Is it the same when I touch you as it was when that man sought your favor at the engagement party?"

"No, it's not the same at all."

"Why? What is different? Do you ever stop and think you might love me?"

"I don't love you, Hollis. I am as certain as I can be."

Hollis considered this a challenge. He pulled Hannah into his embrace and kissed her. As before, she did not resist. All too soon, he found himself taking liberties he only dreamed of. He cupped her breasts, kissed her throat, and explored her figure. He covered her body with his own, kissing her more passionately than he ever dared before.

Realizing the situation could rapidly get out of hand, Hollis groaned as he rolled to the side and threw his arm over his eyes, knowing he was almost at the point where he would not be able to stop.

Hannah struggled to catch her breath, certain she wanted more. Her body told her there was more, although she couldn't imagine what that might be. Was there a kiss so fulfilling it would make her longing go away? An embrace so titillating it would relieve the undeniable tension? Was this some childish desire for Hollis' handsome face and body? Or was this simply biology—her body yearning for a baby? It was probably a similar feeling that led Lucy to shame. She would be no better than Lucy if she gave in to her desire. Hannah reached out and touched Hollis' arm.

"This is wrong. We shouldn't be doing this here."

"These people were lovers and spouses. I don't think they'd disapprove," Hollis replied.

"Hold me, Hollis."

Having gained a modicum of control, Hollis swept Hannah into his arms but refrained from anything more.

"Is this what it was like for Lucy?"

Hollis chuckled at that idea. "Hannah, you are nothing like your sister. She went to bed with any man who would give her a trinket. She didn't love them—I don't think she even wanted them. Lucy sold herself to the highest bidder, yet somehow, she is getting what she always wanted, a rich husband. I doubt he understands what he's getting."

"So, these men, none of them would feel responsibility for what happened?"

"Somebody is responsible, but how would she know who? How could any man feel responsible, never knowing if they were the father? Everyone knew what she was, Hannah, maybe not you or your parents. It was no secret among the young men of Placerville. I suppose some smitten boy would have married her and tolerated a child who likely was not his. Your sister is a beautiful woman and a lot of men would overlook almost anything to have her."

"Would you overlook anything?"

"No, Hannah. I love you because you are decent and true. You're strong, and beautiful, and you fight and kiss better than any woman I ever knew. Our life together would be my greatest adventure and I know I could make you happy. I won't ask you to marry me again until I'm certain of your answer. I promise when I do, it won't be some facetious commentary on our past. It will be as proper, and romantic and fitting as you can imagine. All I'm asking is for you to keep an open mind."

"I can't imagine living with you."

"How can you say that? I live here now. I simply

want the right to sleep in your bed."

"But you don't like my wallpaper."

"If I can wake up every morning and see your face, I promise not to look at the wallpaper again." Hollis pulled a quilt from behind a cushion and spread it over them. "It's getting cold and I don't want to take you inside. I want you all to myself."

"Kiss me again, Hollis."

Hoping he could manage to control himself, Hollis replied, "Whatever you say, my queen."

Chapter Fourteen

David sat at the kitchen table reconsidering his options. It never crossed his mind he would need to protect his sister from his idol, Hollis Rumsford. Yet, that was exactly what he planned to do.

When Jonah asked if he could stay up late to play checkers, David thought he would run it past Hannah. Gathering all the bravery he could muster, David set out for the back fence, intending to shout over the gate at his sister. Briefly mesmerized by the intense moonlight outlining the grave markers, he soon understood his sister was in a compromising position. Hollis' body covered hers near the far corner of the cemetery. It seemed obvious his sister's honor was destroyed.

David made a quick decision, telling both Samuel and Jonah it was bedtime. He promptly collapsed onto the living room floor, his legs too unsteady to support him.

Hannah took control from the moment he and Samuel appeared in Santa Barbara. She was only three years older than him, yet Hannah accepted the role of parent and provider from that first day. It never crossed David's mind to step up and be the man of the house. Hollis somehow filled that role, yet David never dreamed there was more going on between Hannah and Hollis than met the eye.

Hollis was a strong influence, an example upon which David modeled himself. He respected and loved Hollis, almost like a father, but he owed his allegiance to his sister. Even though he was nearly as tall as Hollis, David was slight of frame and no match for the older man. But his sister's honor was at stake and it was up to him to defend her.

It was late when Hollis carried Hannah through the kitchen all the way to her bedroom. He didn't linger and found an angry and bewildered David seated at the kitchen table when he came downstairs.

"I'm surprised you're still up," commented Hollis, smiling broadly as David stood and punched him square on the jaw. David shook his hand up and down in obvious pain. Hollis grabbed David by the neck of his shirt, held him at arm's length and made for the back door.

David was prepared to be beaten within an inch of his life.

"Is something wrong?" came Hannah's voice.

"No, nothing," yelled Hollis as he opened the door. "I'm just talking to David."

"Go ahead, beat me up," taunted David once the pair stood in the glow of light shining through the kitchen window.

"What's got into you?" Hollis was afraid to loosen his hold, intent to avoid playing the part of punching bag.

"I saw what you did to my sister. That's not right! It's my duty to defend her. You need to marry her."

David was surprised when Hollis laughed. "It's not funny!"

"Yes, it is. I love your sister. I want to marry her. She, unfortunately, is not ready to say yes. Besides, I didn't really do anything but kiss her. I assure you, nothing untoward is going on. But I admire you for defending her honor. It shows what a decent young man you are." Hollis could see David was still angry. "Rest assured, I have your sister's best interests at heart. In fact, anything you can do to further my cause would be appreciated. I would whisk her to the altar tomorrow, if she would only consent. Will you put in a good word for me if you get the chance? Can I count on your help?"

"I guess so. I'm sorry I hit you, Hollis."

"Me too. Next time you decide to come after me, perhaps we could have a talk first. It might save my jaw and your knuckles."

* * *

Sunday dinner was generously provided by Mollie's mother, an act of kindness Hollis appreciated. Although the hot dogs were his grand solution, he didn't care if he ever saw one again.

There was to be a final training session in Hannah's car. David was a good driver but knew virtually nothing about servicing the Model A. A sheepish David seemed relieved when Hollis said nothing about their altercation, explaining away the bruise on his chin with his own clumsiness.

David noticed a difference in his sister's demeanor. He was privy to information previously unavailable that probably contributed to this new awareness. There was an undercurrent of aloofness on Hannah's part contrasted by unbridled enthusiasm from Hollis. As David agreed, he planned to further Hollis' matrimonial ambitions but could see this was not the time nor place.

No matter how assuredly Hannah promised David he could work for her, he remembered her hopes for him hinged on educational, not occupational experience. He also knew the past week was the most incredible of his short life. Driving Hannah's car was undeniably entertaining. David enjoyed visiting his sister's clients. He even hungered to learn the accounting end of the business and enthusiastically inquired about deposit slips and ledger entries. He doubted she took his questions seriously but intended to impress his sister, knowing there was one more week to make his case.

Hollis had an appointment in Santa Barbara on Monday morning. Instead of heading back to Goleta, he stopped at Hannah's to grab lunch. A leftover roast beef sandwich would hit the spot and was something he could accomplish unaided. He could make Hannah's lunch at the same time.

As he entered the front door of the Granville home, Hollis yelled, "It's me!" Heading for the kitchen, he imagined Hannah was still abed. The scene that met his eyes was not at all what he expected.

Hannah was ensconced at the kitchen table, using a small can of mint green paint to refurbish one of the wooden chairs her brothers found at rummage sales. Over time, the mismatched chairs served to replace the kegs around the table in the living room. Always eager to make use of every possible asset, Hannah had David and Samuel cut the kegs in half and drill holes in the ends for use as planters on the front porch.

"What are you doing? Shouldn't you be in bed?"

"I'm tired of lying in bed. Besides, Dr. Chasen told me to stay off my foot, not stay in bed. I have it propped on a chair." Hannah's domestic pursuit clearly had her interest. "I'm going to paint every chair a different color. I considered having the boys spread a tarp on the floor and painting them all at once but Boots would have gotten into the paint."

Hollis spied the kitten curled up with a ball of yarn under Hannah's chair, soundly asleep.

"See all these pretty colors? There's peach, and yellow, and pink and aqua. I have fabric for a tablecloth. I'm glad you came. Could you please set this chair on the back porch and put my sewing machine on the table? Be careful to hold the chair on the bottom of the seat."

Hollis cooperatively moved the chair and lifted the sewing machine onto the table.

"Thanks. What are you doing here?"

"I thought I'd come by and make us roast beef sandwiches for lunch."

"That would be lovely!"

As Hollis prepared the sandwiches, he made small talk about work. Hannah seemed friendly if a bit standoffish.

"They gave you filling stations in the area to visit?"

"For now, since I'm training. Once I'm an expert, I'm sure they'll send me further afield."

"Doesn't that mean you'll be on the road just like your father?"

"Well, Pop was successful selling farm equipment back in the day—before the crash. Fortunately for me, people need gasoline. Serving as a liaison between the oil company and filling stations is a paid position, no commission involved. I like it, getting away from the office, driving around and visiting managers. I think it's much the way David feels about the opportunity you gave him. What happens after this week?"

Hannah knew Hollis replied to her question from a financial aspect when it was his absence from Santa Barbara that concerned her. She let the issue drop.

"David can do my rounds. He wants to learn

bookwork. I'm going to buy an adding machine. I find those tedious and slow but I think it will help David check his work. I thought about your idea to seek out more clients. Actually, David may have made some inroads for me. It seems a florist in the same block as one of my other clients asked David to provide information. I think he did a wonderful job. I'm supposed to go next Monday to give them a quote and explain the nuts and bolts of the services I provide—we provide. To be honest, I like being home. I need time to cook, and sew and care for everybody. Bless his heart, David spent his first week's wages on new clothes to impress our clients." Hannah looked across the table as Hollis served lunch.

"I feel confused, Hollis. Much more confused than I have in a long time. All my rest last week was refreshing but it also gave me time to think about things—about what I want."

"Do I figure in the things you want?"

"I don't know but I'm keeping an open mind. Are you coming back for dinner?"

"Wild horses couldn't keep me away," returned Hollis.

He was dumbfounded when he returned that night to find Hannah standing at the stove. The boys attached a box to the platform of a scooter they made for Jonah from scrap wood. Hannah's knee was propped on a pillow on the box.

"What have we here?" Hollis inquired as he walked up behind Hannah and put his arms around her waist. He hoped for a warm greeting but should have known better.

Hannah turned her head and warned, "Don't rush me, Hollis." She waved a wooden spoon in his face to punctuate her threat.

Hollis considered Hannah's youthful face, highlighted by her homebound hairdo—what would have been a ponytail on most girls. Instead, her wild curls formed a bun near the top of her head. Stray locks framed the delicate features of her face. She sought a mature look since starting her business but Hannah appeared every bit the 19-year-old she was. Hollis' heart melted at sight of her, a decided disadvantage. Suddenly, his ornery nature overcame him—the perfect antidote to passion.

"Just think, Short Stuff. Soon I'll come home to find you cooking my meal with my baby in your belly." Hollis moved his hands below Hannah's waist. She did not hesitate to respond, using the spoon to whack his knuckles.

"Oww! That hurt!"

"It was supposed to. I imagine your knuckles got hit plenty when you were in school. Accost me again and I'll be happy to further demonstrate my defensive prowess. The last man who touched me inappropriately ended up rolled in a ball of pain on the ground."

Stepping away in self-defense, Hollis eyed his lady love anxiously. "You don't have to be so mean."

"You don't need to be so forward."

"You like it when I'm forward. You long for me when you lie in bed at night, don't you? Admit it."

"Hollis Rumsford, you need to shut up. My brothers might hear you. You will get yourself uninvited for dinner real quick if you don't watch it."

Hollis sat down at the kitchen table, rubbing his sore knuckles and nursing his bruised ego. How was he ever going to convince this slip of a girl to devote her life to him?

Dinner was a tremendous success. The boys, thrilled at the return of their cook, eagerly took care of the dishes. Hollis kept a safe distance for the balance of the evening. He needed a clear plan to quell his inappropriate outbursts.

As the week went on, Hannah's commitment to keeping David as an employee became apparent. Hollis felt tremendous pride watching the two pouring over Hannah's figures each night. He felt irrationally responsible for the course Hannah set and delighted at her newfound enthusiasm for housekeeping.

She seemed in no hurry to return to her pre-injury activities. David relaxed into his work, becoming ever more confident he would not be banished to the classroom.

Hannah finished painting the chairs. After the flowered tablecloth was complete, Hannah commenced various sewing projects, including scrap quilts for her brothers' bunk beds.

Dr. Chasen pronounced Hannah fit enough to walk. Her foot was stiff; her leg quite weak. She knew it would take time to fully recover. The doctor encouraged her to proceed cautiously.

* * *

Hannah heaved a sigh as she sipped her tea at the kitchen table. Hollis made it clear he was taking her for a date on Friday evening. What was she to do about Hollis? She agreed to keep an open mind but wasn't she wasting his time? Certain it was best if Hollis got on with his life, Hannah didn't want to hurt him. The memory of his strong arms gently holding her, his kiss and her reaction to his touch thrilled her in ways she couldn't comprehend. Her reverie was broken by someone at the door.

"Good day, Madam," began an elegantly dressed chauffeur as Hannah peered from her doorway. "I work for Mrs. Durnam. She's waiting in the car." He pointed.

"Although she is elderly, she has a quick mind and a good sense of direction."

"I'm certain you're looking for my neighbors," interrupted Hannah. "They're about 500 feet in either direction." She started to close the door.

"No, wait! We're not looking for houses. Mrs. Durnam's relations were buried in a graveyard somewhere near here. Do you know if they moved the graves when they developed this area? Can you point me in the right direction? Any information at all would prove invaluable," the chauffeur continued.

"A little cemetery is behind my house."

"Do you know where the gate might be?"

"Mrs. Durnam is more than welcome to come through my backyard."

"Thank you, Miss. I'll get her."

Hannah watched the chauffeur help a diminutive and elegantly dressed white-haired lady from the back of the limousine. He offered his arm and made friendly conversation as he escorted the woman toward Hannah's house.

"Thank you for your generous offer, young lady," began Mrs. Durnam. "I appreciate your kindness." She stopped abruptly and looked up at her chauffeur. "You can pick me up in an hour, Wilson."

"I'm not certain this kind lady is able to usher you into the cemetery. Perhaps I should stay and help."

"Nonsense," offered Mrs. Durnam, an unmistakable sparkle in her eye. "I will be fine if she will show me the way. What is your name, young lady?"

"Hannah. Hannah Granville."

"My eldest sister's name was Hannah. You see, Wilson? I have a new friend."

Wilson looked less than convinced. Hannah descended the porch stairs to take Mrs. Durnam's arm.

"I'll be delighted to show you the way. I might even be able to help you find the site you're looking for."

Mrs. Durnam smiled over her shoulder. "It will be an hour then, Wilson." The elderly lady turned her full attention to Hannah. "It is unfortunate when one reaches a certain age, there are always spies. My children are convinced I am too addle-brained to be left to my own devices for even the shortest time. If it's not Wilson watching my every move, it's a maid, or a cook or a nurse. This is the true curse of being old. One is never alone. I miss my solitude more than anything. Do you like to be alone, dear?"

Hannah walked slowly down the side of her house, feeling this was the most direct and easy route since it did not include stairs. "Actually, I always enjoy time to myself. I happen to be alone here today, at least for a while."

"Do you have a husband and children at your young age?"

"No, but three of my younger brothers live here."

"And no parents?"

"No. Our father died. Our mother was overcome at his death. She resides in Chicago. Her aunt took her in."

"This seems a heavy burden for one so young. How old are you?"

If Mrs. Durnam were not so charming, Hannah might have balked at her personal questions. It was a beautiful day, she was able to walk and it seemed fitting to befriend the elderly lady, who she would likely never see again.

"Nineteen."

"I was 19 when I married. I didn't feel young at 19. Perhaps I was too serious-minded at that age, too busy trying to prove I was all grown up. Looking at you, I imagine you are all grown up."

Hannah smiled. "Your chauffeur mentioned you wished to visit some family members' graves?"

"Yes. My grandparents were early settlers in Santa Barbara. My sisters and I were sent here when our own parents passed on. I was 12. I can tell you, this was a much different place than it appears today. My grandfather was a shopkeeper. My grandmother was tied to the land, having been brought up on a farm. They had a lovely home. I tried to find it today. I'm certain it's been torn down.

"When my grandniece asked me to come for a holiday, I could not resist the opportunity to visit the past. Unfortunately, not much of my past is still here."

"A lot of Victorian-era buildings were ruined in the 1925 earthquake," offered Hannah. "What was their last name? I like to wander through the cemetery. I might know where to look." The ladies slipped through the back gate.

"My, this is much better kept than I imagined," commented Mrs. Durnam. "Their last name was Engelside."

"My brothers help me keep this up. We did a major weeding and trimming right after Christmas. You're the first person who's come to visit since I moved in. I think those graves might be over here."

"Oh, my yes. Here they are. Old memories certainly come flooding back. They are much sharper than recent memories for some reason."

"Why don't you stay here and I'll go get a chair."

"Oh, get one for yourself. We can chat. My grandmother loved to chat."

Hannah, as quickly as possible, returned carrying two kitchen chairs.

"You seem to be having trouble walking, my dear.

Have you injured your foot?"

"I'm on the mend. That's why I'm home but the doctor gave me the all clear. My ankle will be completely healed soon. I believe a cup of tea would be in order. I just made a pot. I'll be right back," Hannah assured as Mrs. Durnam took her seat.

Hannah brought a folding tray, tea and cookies. Mrs. Durnam reminisced about her long-dead relations but her curiosity frequently seeped into their conversation.

For some reason Hannah could not fathom, she eagerly offered up her story. She explained her life in Placerville before her father's self-inflicted demise: the shame of his death, the loss of her family, her relocation to Santa Barbara, her business ventures and her sister's upcoming wedding. She even offered vague testimony about Hollis' constant help.

"So, this young man has proven himself indispensable?"

"I imagine he has," admitted Hannah, sheepishly.

"How lovely! I sense a romance."

"No. I don't think that's what you sense."

"I'm rather good at this sort of thing. I can see there is more than gratitude when you speak of him."

"Well, he is quite handsome."

"Tall? Fit?"

"Yes, those too."

"And he desires you, doesn't he?"

"He says he does. He wants to marry me."

"Then what's the problem?"

"There is a shortcoming, a serious shortcoming."

"Don't tell me—he is a murderer?"

"No, certainly not."

"A thief then?"

"Of course not."

"Well, what is this shortcoming? We're running out of time, Hannah. Wilson will be back soon. You simply must tell me."

"I can't tell you, it would be indiscreet of me. I can say it is a moral issue. You see, if Hollis admitted what he did was wrong, I think I could get past his deficiency of character. But he believes what he did was no worse than what others did so he takes no responsibility."

"I see," commented Mrs. Durnam, although she did not. "It's like when your mother asks, 'Would you jump off the bridge because your friends did?' and he says, 'yes.'"

"That's exactly right! He did, in fact, jump off the bridge. People were hurt, but because he wasn't the only one jumping off, he doesn't see his part in this."

"Oh, dear Hannah. Don't let a good man get away because he made a foolish, childish error, especially if you love him. I can see on your face you do, even if you can't see it yourself. Have you never wondered what it would be like to be his wife? Have you never written out your married name? What would it be? Mrs.—"

"Rumsford. And yes, when I was a girl, I used most of the pages of my journal writing out Mrs. Hollis Rumsford. But that was before."

"My husband was several years older than me. As I told you, I was married at 19. Archie was 27, one of the reasons I was drawn to him. I thought there was nothing of the boy left in him. He seemed so mature and steady. That was well before I realized men never do grow up. You'll see for yourself one day. At any rate, Archie had several, let's call them indiscretions before he met me.

"Shortly before we were married, he made a complete confession in an effort to wipe the slate clean. I tell you, Hannah, I was furious beyond belief. I threatened to cancel our wedding. I understood it was childish of me to believe a man like Archie would sit on his hands and wait for me to grow up, even if he recognized early on I was the one for him. I knew in my heart he would always be true to me. I trusted him and I have to say, my trust was well-placed.

"It's not as if our life was perfect but Archie was devoted to me until the day he died. We enjoyed a good marriage; we made a good team. Men are beyond aggravating but they are what fulfills us as women." Mrs. Durnam sipped the last of her tea.

"Take some advice from an old lady. Give your Hollis a fair chance. Start fresh and try not to dwell on the past. Be as unbiased as you can manage."

"What happens when the time for true confessions comes?"

"Then listen objectively. Only you can decide if your Hollis is trustworthy. It does seem, from past history, he is terribly devoted to you. I would be surprised if you find his past unforgiveable.

"Love is a terrible thing to waste. Some people never find it at all. You are a smart girl who knows how to make the most of her opportunities. Hollis seems like the best of opportunities, to me." Mrs. Durnam reached over and patted Hannah's hand as Wilson appeared at the gate. "Life is incredibly short. Don't be so serious, Hannah. I know it's difficult to be light of heart considering all your tribulations. A good marriage might be your reward. Don't waste a moment of the time you could have together."

Other doubts came bubbling out of Hannah's mouth, almost unbidden. "How did you know your husband would be a good provider? What if I give up my house or my business for Hollis and he does not provide for our family? Perhaps his weak character would make him a failure."

Mrs. Durnam, realizing Wilson would soon come within earshot, advised, "There are no guarantees in life, Hannah. Anything can happen. If you and your Hollis are as well-suited as I think, doesn't it make sense to share your life with a loving and caring partner instead of trying to make your way alone?"

As the ladies strolled toward the street, Hannah promised to put flowers on Mrs. Durnam's family graves. Before she climbed into the back seat of the limousine, Mrs. Durnam handed Hannah her beautifully engraved calling card.

"Let me know how everything turns out."

* * *

Hollis was certain—something was different. Hannah appeared for their date in a feminine, salmon-color dress. She wore flats, which were easier on her foot than heels. This made her seem smaller than usual. Hannah was agreeable, friendly and calm, not at all herself. This put Hollis quite ill at ease. He nervously attempted conversation in the car on the way to the movies.

"Does this venue indicate we are past the talking part of our relationship?" inquired Hannah, eyeing the theater when Hollis parked.

"No. It indicates you can't go dancing, or walking on the beach or do anything but sit. This was the most entertaining place I could think up."

Hollis guided his date to the end seat in the last row of the theater to ensure a bit of privacy. Hannah was surprised when he leaned over and kissed her as the lights went dim. He proved a model of decorum during the rest of the movie as they shared a box of popcorn, now for sale right in the theater lobby instead of on the sidewalk outside.

The feature film was *She Done Him Wrong*, starring Mae West and an all-star cast, except for a handsome newcomer by the name of Cary Grant. The movie was set in the 1890s and was a tale of intrigue, murder, vice and people of generally low moral standards, except for the Cary Grant character. He managed to redeem the tarnished Mae West character by proposing marriage in the last scene.

Once the double-feature ended, Hollis didn't want to take Hannah home. He suggested a drive that ended at the beach. It proved to be a quiet trip and quiet evening, culminating in considerable kissing.

Tired of the awkward angle of her body in the front seat, Hannah thoughtlessly swung her leg across Hollis' lap, which put them eye to eye. This caused an intensity in Hollis' passion, which Hannah much enjoyed. He paused to look at her eyes then fumbled with the buttons on the front of her dress. He pushed the sleeves down her arms and sat transfixed, staring at her camisole.

Hannah felt a thrill she could not deny. She closed her eyes and tipped her head back to invite Hollis' exploration, only to be shaken by the shoulders.

Hannah was amazed as Hollis tugged her dress up almost violently and attempted to pull the two sides together. He seemed incredibly irritated. His hands shook too much to attempt the buttons.

"You're supposed to say no, Hannah. Do I have to do everything for you?"

A confused Hannah found herself plopped back in the passenger seat as Hollis started the car and hit the gas. She was further amazed when Hollis stopped the car in front of her house and waited for her to get out.

"What? No goodnight kiss?"

"I think there was enough of that tonight."

Hannah stepped out of the car.

"Will we see you tomorrow for card night then?" she asked hesitantly.

"Of course."

Hollis sped off as Hannah watched from the sidewalk. Somewhat bewildered, she was certain men made absolutely no sense but tonight was fun. She enjoyed Hollis' companionship, even though they hardly spoke. Maybe things would be better if they didn't speak at all.

* * *

Hannah was always quiet at the supper table when Hollis was there. Her brothers did not think this odd, although they knew their sister was being courted persistently by Hollis.

For his part, Hollis gave up trying to engage his intended in conversation outside their dates. His efforts to converse were met with resistance, even hostility. The four male members of the current dinner party stared curiously at Hannah when she began to converse over pork chops, string beans and au gratin potatoes.

"The church is having a social on Saturday. I think we should go, Hollis. My foot seems healed."

A bite of potatoes wavered in mid-air on Hollis' fork. Not only was Hannah speaking, she suggested an outing. Looking around the table, it was apparent he was not the only one stunned into silence.

"What's wrong? Don't you want to go?"

"It's not that." Hollis appeared unusually tongue-tied.

"I know the caliber of music won't be what you're used to but it might be fun. We could all go," Hannah added enthusiastically. "I'll bring a dish for the potluck, maybe a big pot of stew, and we can stay for the dancing. You boys need to learn to dance. I'm certain you'll be expected to at Lucy's wedding. What's wrong? Does the cat have your tongues?"

"No, not at all," added a clearly perplexed Hollis.

"You don't normally plan outings. We're a bit surprised," and confused, added Hollis to himself.

"Why have we gotta dance?" chimed in Samuel.

"Now boys, your sister has never suggested an activity before. We need to honor her proposal. It's a good idea."

"It's only proper you learn," continued Hannah. "We can't be neglecting all social instruction. Hollis can show you how to waltz after dinner. I will be your partner. Dancing is a great deal of fun, isn't it Hollis?" Hannah smiled warmly across the table.

"It certainly can be," agreed a wary Hollis. "I learned in school and I must admit, I wasn't an eager pupil. But my dancing prowess served me well through the years. Girls love to dance, don't they Hannah?" Hollis felt certain some sarcastic retort would be flung his way so he was amazed when Hannah's smile only widened.

"I would say a strong and knowledgeable dance partner is much sought after. Dancing is how Hollis won me over. I never thought I could have so much fun as when we went dancing the first time."

Hollis was speechless. He didn't know what part of Hannah's commentary was the more incredible: her admission he won her over or her compliments about his dancing. Surely there was something wrong with his beloved.

It was no surprise when Jonah turned out to be the most enthusiastic and accomplished dancer of the Granville brothers. They practiced several times before the Saturday night social.

At the dance, Hannah seemed eager to befriend new acquaintances. Having only ever witnessed the shy Hannah in social situations, Hollis considered this newfound cordiality could be a ploy to attract new customers. Then, Hannah suggested church might be a place to find nice couples their own age.

For the first time, Hollis dared to imagine a married life full of family, friends and children. He believed something or someone influenced Hannah in a positive way. As he watched a nervous David invite a girl to dance, Hollis smiled, wondering to whom he owed this pleasant turn of events.

Chapter Fifteen

As spring unfolded, Franklin Roosevelt was sworn in as President. The seeds the boys planted began to take off. Not a single Granville understood the climate or growing principles of Santa Barbara, where it was always a good time to plant. No one would suspect their ignorance upon observation of the greenery taking hold in both the front and back yards.

A modest vegetable garden showed signs of promise near the back door. Hannah often helped her mother in their garden in Placerville but had forgotten the joy of puttering outside every day. Boots frolicked in the garden and was a source of endless entertainment as she pounced and pawed at every bug she found.

David proved invaluable as the front man for Hannah's accounting business. He not only attracted two new clients, including a soda fountain on State Street, but studied the figures in Hannah's ledger books and provided valuable insights to their customers. He told Mr. Johnson his receipts were always higher on Wednesdays because he ran a special. David suggested specials for slow weekdays to draw more customers. Mr. Johnson was thrilled at the results.

Card nights continued to be a favorite activity. All the men mocked Hannah's colorful tablecloth and chairs. No male would be caught dead sitting in the pink chair, save for Hollis, who never seemed to mind. Despite his dislike of her wallpaper, Hannah surmised he was so cocky, the pink chair posed no threat to his masculinity.

The couple went out, sometimes for dinner and dancing, more often to the movies, but seldom watched one. Their corner of the theater was isolated so Hollis freely cuddled his beloved, applying ample kisses and hugs. In actuality, he felt safely in control in the theater, where he could not get carried away.

Necking in the car or on Hannah's front porch proved more difficult. The fact Hannah seemed uninterested in restraint made their romance rather dicey as far as Hollis was concerned. He was determined to be a protective and proper beau but realized he had his limits. If Hannah did not show signs of consent to marriage in the near future, the day might come when Hollis would be unable to curb his amorous activities. Hannah was no help at all in this regard.

Hannah continued to be uncharacteristically easygoing. Hollis kept waiting for this pleasant interlude to evaporate. But as the weeks went by, he was lulled into an unprecedented security, certain Hannah would agree to marry once he asked Mrs. Granville for her daughter's hand in marriage.

While Hannah successfully refrained from baiting him into an argument, Hollis learned to bite his tongue when a rude remark occurred to him. Although this seemed somewhat superficial, it provided a basis for a more cordial relationship. Hollis knew over time, they would undoubtedly fight. He hoped the camaraderie they shared would provide a better bridge when one or both of them launched a verbal tirade.

Hollis took his role as prospective husband to heart. He wrote to his father for advice. The elder Mr. Rumsford provided Bible verses for Hollis to study. He was particularly impressed with 1 Corinthians 13:4-7:

"Love suffers long and is kind; love does not envy; love does not parade itself, is not puffed up; does not behave rudely, does not seek its own, is not provoked, thinks no evil; does not rejoice in iniquity; but rejoices in the truth; bears all things; believes all things; hopes all things; endures all things."

He was working on the rude part, realizing he needed to put Hannah first, even above his own wants and needs. But knowing what he wanted to be and becoming that man proved challenging.

Easter was late in the year, April 16. Hollis was thrilled when Hannah invited him not only for dinner, but also to church for the first time. He did not stop to evaluate his emotions but was inordinately proud when he escorted Hannah into church and took his seat beside her. Her family had become his own.

Little Jonah was parked on his sister's other side. Young Samuel sat next to Hollis. Samuel appeared quite the handsome young man despite constantly being thumped in the head by his sister for his poor English. David sat at the end of the pew, next to Samuel. On observation, Hollis believed David, though three years younger, actually appeared older than his sister. No doubt the harsh years in Montana aged him.

The holiday served as a turning point in Hollis and Hannah's relationship. It was now obvious, both to

Hannah's brothers and the world in general, the pair was a couple and courtship would soon lead to marriage.

On the business front, Hannah conceded customers were more comfortable seeing David every day, except, predictably, for Mr. Barney. She was often accused of taking jobs from men with families to support. A woman of business was still an anomaly. This fact did not upset her. She rarely made daily rounds to clients but appeared regularly at the hotel. She seemed content, ever more appreciative of David's help.

The invitation to Lucy's wedding arrived addressed to Hannah Granville and guest. Hannah wasted no time in returning the reply, writing in the names of all her brothers and Hollis as her escort. Maybe Lucy would never be forthcoming in helping their brothers but Hannah was determined they would all have a meal at her expense.

Since business was good, Hannah splurged on new suits for the younger boys. David, who spent most of his earnings on business clothes, was prepared. Hannah determined to buy an extravagant dress but need for a new dress was about to dissolve.

* * *

Hannah sat at the kitchen table, mulling over the newspaper. Her work was caught up. She already picked the ripe produce of the day on the foggy morning. Contemplating her next activity, an ad caught her eye.

An RCA radio was on sale. The boys were eager to have a radio, which was now a common household device. It seemed an extravagance in a home where almost everything came from rummage or bring-and-buy sales. She could certainly afford the sale price listed. If she rushed a bit, she would be ready to use the car when David returned. There might be enough time to do her errand and have the deposits ready before the banks closed. No sooner did Hannah arrive at this plan than there was a knock on the door.

"Who would be visiting us today, Boots?" she asked aloud. Opening the door, she found Lucy, an unwelcome visitor if ever there was one. Not knowing what to say, Hannah only stared.

"Well, can't I come in?"

"I suppose. I was on my way out."

Although Lucy moved inside the door and shut it, there was no place to sit except at the card table so the conversation continued on foot.

"This won't take long. You received my invitation?"

"Yes."

"Are you planning on coming?"

"I sent back my response."

"I don't look at those things. Other people do that. Can't you just answer my question?"

"I am coming. So are our brothers. You remember them? The ones who live here. The ones you never bothered to visit."

"Yes. Mother wrote to me and said they were here. But honestly, Hannah. It's not as if they want to see me."

"I'm certain they would have liked to see you. They certainly could use your help."

"I don't have time to go over your grievances. I need to ask something. And I'm not going to pay you so don't get any ideas."

"What is it you want? I'm aware you wouldn't show up unless you wanted something."

"My husband-to-be's family is close-knit and assumes all families are like theirs. Gregory's brother is standing up for him at the wedding and he thinks it would be grand if you stood up for me."

"Does he now? Because you and I are so close?"

"Don't be snippy. Mother assured me you would be cooperative if I came here, hat in hand, and asked you to do this one thing."

"I don't recall appointing Mother as my decision-maker. Isn't she the one unable to make her own decisions? How did she come to realize she's capable of making mine?"

"You have really become impossible of late, Hannah. No one will like you if you are rude."

"Well, that solves my problem. I am too rude to stand up for you."

"You don't have to do anything but show up and stand there. I will buy your dress." At this, Lucy handed her younger sister a card. "Meet me here on Tuesday morning at 10. We'll agree on a dress. I will pay."

"What about shoes? A hat and gloves?"

"Everything will be at my expense. I'm asking for very little here, Hannah."

"I wrote the boys' names on my response. They can come?"

"Of course. They're my brothers too. But this is not really for children so they'll need to behave."

"They're not children any longer. They don't look the way they did when Father died."

"I suppose not. Perhaps I won't recognize them. I'm certain Mother will, though. She'll sort them out if I am in need. I'm counting on you, Hannah. You will come to the fitting?"

Hannah nodded. "I'm certain I will choose a very, very expensive gown."

Frowning, Lucy agreed. "Money is no object." She turned on her heel, walked out the door and toward the street where a driver waited.

"Yes, I'm certain it's not," commented Hannah as

she scooped Boots into her arms, wondering what made her so agreeable. She didn't want to be.

* * *

The amenable Hannah Granville met her sister at the appointed time and place on Tuesday. The pink satin dress Hannah chose was ankle length with a wide sash, elbow-length, loose sleeves, pointed collar and gathered bodice and skirt. It was simple, form hugging, but extremely elegant and tremendously expensive.

"Honestly Hannah, your dress cost almost as much as mine."

"You said money was no object. I'd like to see if they have a pink shoe to match. Otherwise, I'll have to use white."

It was at this moment, the soon-to-be bridegroom made an impromptu appearance.

"Gregory, darling, whatever brings you here?" Lucy licked her lips and nervously forced a smile.

"You have been keeping little Hannah all to yourself these past weeks. I wanted to drop by and express my thanks for all your help, Hannah. That is a beautiful dress. Is this to be the one?"

Hannah stood dumbfounded. Evidently Gregory believed his fiancé's family was indeed, close-knit. The idea she held the power to spoil Lucy's ruse proved impossible to resist. "I don't know what you're talking about, Gregory," Hannah replied innocently. She smiled as all color drained from her sister's face. "I haven't done a thing."

"Oh, Hannah, don't be so modest," interrupted Lucy. "She has been such a help these last weeks. But we are right in the middle of something here, darling. Won't you leave us girls to our shopping adventure? That's a dear," she added as she pushed Gregory's shoulder to head him toward the door.

"I've heard all the stories about your organizational abilities—your help addressing invitations, your advice about the flowers and cake. I would like to do something for you in return," commented Gregory over his shoulder.

"Well, there is something." Hannah's smile welled from somewhere deep in her soul, a reaction to Lucy's stunned expression. "I wasn't able to get to the store because of all the time I spent on your wedding. Our brothers were unhappy when I didn't manage to purchase the new RCA radio when it was on sale."

"It's the least I can do. Lucy explained your unnecessarily thrifty lifestyle, which I commend," replied Gregory as he resisted being pushed out the door of the dress shop. "I'll have one delivered immediately!"

Hannah happily continued to taunt her sister. "Thank you! What a lovely gift. Nice to see you, Gregory. We'll talk soon, I'm certain."

"Was that necessary?" asked a grim-faced Lucy once her fiancé safely departed.

As Hannah headed for the dressing room, she replied, "I can't understand you, Lucy. Is your entire marriage to be based on lies? Does your betrothed know anything about you other than the fact you have a beautiful face?"

"Honesty is overrated. I've never gotten a thing I wanted by being honest."

"Maybe you were never meant to obtain the things you have. This will all come back to haunt you."

"Of course, Hannah. I'll take all the advice I can get from my ignorant, unworldly, little sister," Lucy derided. "As if you know anything. You have no idea what I've been through, what I've done for this opportunity. And I'm not about to let you ruin it."

"It's not too late. You can get someone else to

stand up for you. It's not as if you can control my every comment."

"I think I have you figured out. I'm not worried. Good little Hannah would never mention my past indiscretions. It would cast a bad light on our family. What little standing Father has not managed to destroy would soon be completely lost. No matter how much you might enjoy hurting me, you would never adversely impact your brothers or your business."

"I think you put much too much importance on your little corner of the world. Your society contacts do not matter to me," Hannah replied over the dressing room door.

"They matter to Mother. Why else do you think she would come all the way back to California? I don't think you want to upset her." At least, the Hannah Lucy always knew wouldn't be caught dead disappointing her family. This new Hannah seemed difficult to manipulate.

"You have threatened me with Mother about as much as you can. I simply haven't the time to care about such things." Hannah threw the pink dress at Lucy. "Pay for it or not, I could care less. You can have it delivered if you want me to wear it." Hannah turned and strode purposefully from the dress shop.

* * *

"See what the boys found when they cleared all the brush from this side of the house. What is it?"

Hollis, dressed for a date, was in no mood to rummage around Hannah's side yard.

"It looks to be the entrance to a basement."

"I didn't think there was a basement. I thought there was only a crawl space."

"Well, you thought wrong. Let's go. There's a western tonight."

Knowing Hollis had no intention of actually watching the movie, Hannah continued with purposeful helplessness, "But how do I get in? There's a padlock."

"There's a bolt cutter in your shed. Let's go."

"But I can't use a bolt cutter. I don't even know what it is. And I need you to go in the basement to be sure it's safe." Hannah innocently looked up at her boyfriend, trying her best to encourage gentlemanly behavior, doing everything short of fluttering her eyelashes to elicit the desired response.

Hollis closely observed his beloved. She wore a white dress with tiny blue flowers and lacy trim. So demure and defenseless did Hannah appear, Hollis imagined no one would guess she was a hardened businesswoman with a cruel wit who rode roughshod over brothers who towered over her.

"Why wouldn't it be safe?"

"There could be snakes," Hannah admitted seriously.

"Snakes?" Hollis chuckled. "Have you ever seen a snake in your yard?"

"No, but—"

"Then why would you think they were lurking in your basement?"

"They could be. Can't you do this one thing for me? I haven't asked you for help in ever so long."

"I don't want to get dirty." Hollis turned to leave.

"You come back here this instant, Hollis Rumsford. All you have to do is cut the lock and make sure it's safe down there. I'll go too if you go first. *I'm* not worried about getting dirty."

Shaking his head in disgust, Hollis walked toward the shed to obtain the bolt cutter as Hannah tagged behind. Hannah was awestruck as she stuck her head through the door to see where the bolt cutter was stored.

It appeared every tool, now cleaned and oiled, had a home somewhere in the shed. Every nut, bolt and nail was carefully stored and labeled. It seemed Hollis was an excellent steward of her tools and taught the boys to do the same.

Hollis made quick work of the lock. The cellar door gave an angry creak as he pulled it open.

"It's dark in there," he muttered.

"But now the snakes can get out. I'll go get the flashlight. You keep an eye on the door."

When Hannah returned, there was no sign of Hollis. She peered into the darkness and switched on the flashlight.

"Are you down there?"

"You better come down."

"Why?"

"You need to take a look at this."

A seriously frightened Hannah took a first tentative step on the narrow and rickety staircase. As she reached the bottom, she shone the light around an empty space.

"Where are you?"

"Gotcha!" yelled Hollis as he jumped from the side of the stairway. "There's a whole nest of snakes!"

Hannah gave a shrill scream and promptly dropped the flashlight. "Hollis Rumsford, I'm going to kill you." But then she sought his embrace. "Are there really snakes?"

"Of course not. There was enough light from the cellar door to see. The only thing down here is a trunk in the corner. Let's go to the movies."

"The least you can do is pick up the flashlight and open the trunk. I want to see what's inside. Maybe it's a pirate's treasure chest. Didn't Spanish pirates ply these waters back in the day?"

"I don't know about pirates but I'm pretty sure they

never visited a house built in this century. Watch out for that rat!" Hollis yelled. The comment drew the reaction he sought as Hannah grabbed him for dear life.

Laughing, Hollis walked toward the trunk dragging Hannah alongside. He opened the trunk and shone the light. "Looks like a bunch of junk to me."

"No, look. There's a beautifully knitted blanket here on top." Sadly, the textile was badly deteriorated. Hannah rummaged through the trunk to find odd bits of someone's life. There was a family Bible and an intricately embroidered baby dress. Near the bottom were a few dresses, including an old-fashioned lace tea gown. "Look at this, isn't it exquisite?"

"Ah! Something from the days when women were women. How I long for times like those." Hollis noted Hannah's disdain for his comment.

"Yes, and men were men. How I long for the strong, silent type."

"Watch it, Hannah, or I'll leave you down here with your snakes and rats."

"Are there really snakes and rats?"

"Not a one. Come on. Let's go."

Hannah closed the lid of the trunk but took the white dress to have a better look. She stopped in the kitchen to examine the garment, then held it up to her shoulders. "Look, Hollis, I think it would fit. It's perfect."

"It will probably fall apart when you wash it. Is that the kind of dress you're wearing for your sister's wedding?"

"Hardly. My dress, since Lucy actually sent it, is the height of fashion, very modern, just like me. Let's go to the movies. *You* have dawdled long enough. We'll miss the beginning," and the middle and the end, if Hollis has any say in it, Hannah thought to herself.

"Maybe you can wear the tea gown when we get married," Hollis suggested. "It will save me some money."

"Hollis Rumsford, if you should ever dare to ask for my hand in marriage again, be assured I have every intention of wearing trousers to our wedding. Besides, the groom doesn't pay."

Surprised Hannah didn't spurn the idea of marriage, Hollis continued, "Well, you certainly aren't going to pay for it. And you will wear trousers over my dead body."

"Whatever you say, dearest. But you can't say your vows if you're dead." Good natured bickering continued all the way to the theater. Hannah briefly wondered how long Hollis would wait to propose again. Surely, he felt secure she would accept him now.

* * *

As Hollis returned to their corner of the theater before the second part of the double feature commenced, he offered Hannah some popcorn and took a seat beside her.

"Tell me why you think snakes would be in your basement."

"No."

"Fine. You can't have any popcorn."

"I don't need your popcorn," pouted Hannah. "I'll make my own when I go home."

"You do that," replied Hollis as he moved the popcorn toward the empty seat beside him and gloated as he shoved a handful in his mouth.

"Is my 3 Musketeers bar still in your pocket?"

"It is."

"Can I have it?"

"No." Hollis glanced at his date out of the corner of his eye. She pressed her lips firmly together; a sure sign of anger.

The new, relaxed, and girlie Hannah was something of an enigma. Their relationship had been cordial for so long, Hollis welcomed a little controversy. "Tell me about the snakes and I'll give you the candy bar." He turned to look Hannah square in the face. "You better hurry up. The cartoon and the newsreel will start up in a minute. If your 3 Musketeers stays in my pocket, it will melt."

"It would serve you right."

Hollis only shrugged in response.

"You'll think I'm childish."

"What leads you to believe I don't already think you're childish? Didn't you use every feminine wile in your repertoire to get me in your basement? Wasn't that rather childish? Don't pout, Hannah. It doesn't become you."

"You are not a gentleman," began Hannah.

"All right. I agree. Now what?"

Hannah turned her attention to the blank theater screen and began her recitation. "When I was little, maybe four, there must have been money because I remember there were several servants. It wasn't difficult for Mother to keep up appearances. I recall a nanny, a cook and a maid. The nice part was, there was usually someone around so it wasn't easy for Lucy to be mean, at least without getting caught.

"One day, the nanny made a tea party for Lucy, and me and our dolls. It was memorable. I still recall the little desserts and milk tea, the lumps of sugar in the tiny sugar bowl and the elegantly decorated cookies. We were both excited to play, but Lucy must have decided she would rather have the tea party to herself so she told me a lie to get rid of me. She explained the nanny put new dresses for the dolls in the cellar and I was to go down the basement stairs and retrieve them. I knew I wasn't allowed in the basement but Lucy assured me it was all right this one time.

"As soon as I walked into the landing at the top of the stairs, she shut the door behind me and turned the lock. To keep me quiet, she told me not to make any noise or the snakes would crawl up the stairs and bite me. I stood stock still for hours, not responding when the nanny and Mother yelled my name for fear a snake was lurking inches away, waiting for me to make a noise. Father finally rescued me.

"I believed for years there were snakes in the basement. I drew a picture at school for some assignment about animals. You were supposed to show where each animal made its home. I drew a picture of a basement for the snake. Everyone at school thought this quite hilarious. I was deeply embarrassed."

Hannah turned to look at Hollis. "It's not funny, don't laugh," she warned. "I can't think of any basement without memories of being trapped in one, fearful for my young life. I was ashamed at being so gullible to believe Lucy's lie."

"What if I told you I pulled similar pranks on Dock?"

"I would think you incredibly cruel and vicious."

At this, Hollis reached in his pocket and retrieved the 3 Musketeers, handing it to Hannah. "Help yourself," he commented, then offered popcorn.

Chapter Sixteen

"You can drive," Hannah informed David as she herded her brothers into the car. She took the front passenger seat. The family was on its way downtown.

"Why do we have to go to the barber? Why can't you cut our hair?" whined Jonah.

"A wedding is a special event, like Easter when we went to the barber."

"But why do we have to go to the wedding, anyway?" Jonah continued.

"That's what families do," reminded Hannah.

"We aren't much of a family," added David, driving much slower than was his habit.

"We most certainly are. The Granvilles of Santa Barbara are a tight-knit bunch," replied Hannah.

"I'm not talking about us, Hannah. I'm talking about Mother and Lucy. Why are we going to this wedding? They don't want anything to do with us. Why can't we stay home and live our own lives?"

"I told you, David, this is what families do. Besides, you boys have been practicing your dancing.

As your dedicated partner, I know how accomplished you've become. It will be fun. Our radio has certainly come in handy. We wouldn't have it if not for Gregory."

"Aw, Hannah, you tol' us you was gonna buy one anyways."

"I'm going to thump your head when we get out of the car. You need to practice your English, Samuel. Say that correctly."

"You told us you would buy a radio anyway."

"Much better. That comment deserves an answer. Free is better in this instance." But if she were to be honest, Hannah would admit she felt tremendous guilt, having pried the radio out of the innocent Gregory. She could not imagine what came over her that day, even though Lucy did ruin her shopping plans.

When the boys went to explore the recently discovered basement, Hannah relayed the events of the day to Hollis over the kitchen table.

"Why do you want to go to the wedding, Hannah? I don't understand, either."

"Hollis, even if your least favorite sibling got married and you were available to attend, wouldn't you go?"

"No one in my family compares to your sister."

Hannah frankly did not understand this comment. Was he talking about her sister's looks? Before she could frame a question, she became appalled at his next comment.

"The boys don't want to see your mother, you understand, don't you?"

"Why would you say such a thing?"

"They never mentioned this to you? Are you certain? You sometimes only hear what you want to hear."

"They asked why we were going and I explained

that's what families do. They didn't say much more about it."

"So, you laid down the law and they were afraid to inquire further."

"You make me sound like some stubborn old battleax."

"I don't mean that. But you somehow have complete control of those boys. This is probably my doing." Hollis thought of the Halloween prank and how it changed the dynamic in the household. "You are almost the smallest person in this house but you rule with an iron fist. Don't you have hard feelings toward your mother? She virtually dumped those boys on you."

"She did not dump them on me. I want them."

Hollis rolled his eyes. "Maybe you don't dwell on the past, that's actually a wonderful quality but your brothers have not forgotten your mother didn't want them, twice. I don't blame them for wanting to avoid her. I think I have this figured out, though."

"You have figured out exactly what?"

"You are proud of those boys. You want to show them off. And you probably want to show your mother how capable you are."

"I think that's offensive."

"Well, feel free to prove me wrong."

"How?"

"Don't go to the wedding. Send the dress back." Hollis could see Hannah was speechless. This was the rarest of occasions and he meant to savor it. Hollis waited patiently to see how she would respond.

"I can't," Hannah finally managed. "I gave Lucy my word. I suppose you're not going to come to the wedding now?"

"Oh, I wouldn't miss this for the world. Just keep in mind, your brothers are like my own family. I don't want to see them hurt. I won't stand by and let anyone hurt you either, Hannah."

"Nobody's going to hurt me, Hollis. It's just a garden wedding and reception. You're making a mountain out of a molehill." But Lucy's wedding day would prove devastating to Hannah and the younger Granvilles.

* * *

Hannah's men felt abandoned when she was bustled away by a wedding helper named Irma. After all, Hannah was the one who orchestrated this excursion, now she left her brood rudderless.

"We don't want to sit up front, Hollis," explained David.

"But you're family. I'm no expert on wedding etiquette but I know you're supposed to sit up there. Your mother will be waiting for you."

"We want to sit with you," chimed in Jonah.

"We ain't stupid, Hollis," offered Samuel. "Our mother's been in Santa Barbara, prob'ly for days, and she never called or come by. She don't want to see us any more'n we want to see her."

"I understand how you feel but this is important to your sister for some reason. She thinks we will have fun here." Hollis could see the less-than-eager expressions on his young companions. He allowed Jonah to take his hand and lead them to the last row of chairs.

* * *

Hannah sat at a dressing table, quietly submitting to the irritating Irma's ministrations.

"Your sister told me your hair would be a problem. She was certainly right. Thankfully for you, she put me in charge."

Having never seen the small pink woven hat that fit

close to her head, Hannah pulled her hair straight back and allowed her curls to explode across the nape of her neck. The only difference Irma made in her coiffure was to allow Hannah's hair to curl at the bottom of the hat, a correction Hannah would have made herself.

She made no comment as Irma applied a dark rouge and garish red lipstick, additions Hannah felt too bold for her complexion and the pale pink dress. Shortly before the ceremony began, Hannah excused herself to use the powder room where she quickly removed Irma's handiwork and reapplied her own paler shade of lipstick, hidden in the pocket of her dress. She pulled on the white gloves Irma supplied and took up the bouquet of pastel roses. Taking a last look in the mirror, Hannah knew she would never be the beauty Lucy was. But her reflection proved sufficient and she was ready to take on the world.

* * *

Lydia Granville sipped champagne as she watched couples take the floor after Lucy and Gregory's first dance as a wedded couple.

Today was perfectly satisfactory. She was prepared for disappointment in this backwater town but had been treated with respect as mother of the bride. Although lacking in true culture, Santa Barbara was not disappointing.

Lucy managed to make a good match, considering the locale. After all, the depression turned the world on end. Eligible bachelors of earlier years were now vagabonds and gigolos.

Lydia looked around the opulently decorated garden of her daughter's new in-laws. This was an exquisite setting for a wedding. Every flower seemed perfectly placed. Not a twig or leaf littered any bed. The weather was ideal. She even found the house above her minimum standards. Aloysius always claimed there was sophistication in California, although he never provided it. At least Lucy found a modicum of refinement. That girl always did have a head on her shoulders.

Lucy's siblings were another challenge, one Lydia would have to confront sooner than later. She caught only the briefest glimpse of the boys. Thanks to Lucy's efforts, Hannah managed to give the impression of a proper young lady during the ceremony. Uncomfortable at the idea an unsupervised Hannah might prove embarrassing to Lucy's sophisticated guests, Lydia tried to locate her in the crowd.

As the music ended, she spied Hannah standing next to a tall and handsome young man dressed in a light gray suit. Her diminutive and dainty pink-clad figure contrasted sharply with the man's strength and fine features.

At first, Lydia imagined Lucy provided this escort, a clever move to keep Hannah in line. As Lydia looked more closely, she could see this man clearly adored her daughter. The feeling appeared to be mutual as Hannah lovingly touched the man's arm. He leaned down as if spellbound by her every word. As the couple began the next dance, recognition dawned. Lydia hurried over to Lucy and Gregory's table, intent on confirming her suspicions.

"Lucy, isn't the man dancing with Hannah one of those Rumsford boys? Is that Dock?"

"No, mother. It appears to be Hollis, the older of the two."

"Did you know he was coming?"

"I frankly never looked at the guest list. Some servant took care of those details. I did see him once at Hannah's house. I never dreamed she would take up with him."

"They appear to be quite friendly," noted Lydia.

"I noticed. More than friendly, I would say."

"Yes, it looks as if they've danced together before."

A flair of jealousy welled in Lucy. This was her day, yet everyone remarked on Hannah. Curious comments about the lovely girl in pink were unwelcome. Lucy was the bride. All eyes were supposed to be on her. And even though Gregory was the catch she always desired, Hollis easily bested him in strength, looks and stature, if not wealth. After all, Lucy consoled herself, affluence was the true asset. Damn that stupid Hannah, she was ruining the day.

"Have you seen the boys?" remarked Lucy in an effort to turn her mother's attention to her own difficulties.

"No, but I believe I see an opportunity." Hannah was shepherding one of the boys to the dance floor. Only one remained seated at their table. Lydia had no desire to take them all on at once but one by himself seemed promising. She managed to cover half the distance to the table when the Rumsford boy stopped her progress.

"Mrs. Granville?"

"Yes."

"You may not remember me but I used to live next door."

"But I do remember. It's Hollis, isn't it?"

The man delivered an engaging smile. "Very good. I thought I blended into the vast array of Rumsfords."

"Don't be coy, Hollis. No one could forget a face as handsome as yours."

Hollis was taken off guard. Was the woman actually flirting? Perhaps he should proceed as quickly as possible, before Hannah sought him out or before he got into some other trouble. "Mrs. Granville, I have a question. Since your husband passed on, I need to ask you. I love your daughter and she loves me. I intend to marry her and I would appreciate your consent and blessing."

"My, that is proper and correct. You seem quite earnest." This was a development Lydia could not have anticipated. She would try her best to put a quick end to this particular problem. "Does Hannah know of your request?"

"No. When I found out you were coming to Santa Barbara, I decided to ask you first. I proposed to Hannah some time ago as something of a joke. I intend to do a proper job of it once we have your consent."

"I see. I'm sorry, Hollis, but I cannot give you my consent." The young Mr. Rumsford's crestfallen features seemed so gratifying, Lydia believed she might have a difficult time weaving her web. Pulling herself together, she continued, "You see, my children are accompanying me to New York. Their grandmother passed away a few months ago. My father is in ill health and requires help. He wishes to see his family and I promised to bring them. I longed for an opportunity to have my children with me again. We are to be reunited for good. This is the answer to my prayers. Perhaps Hannah hasn't mentioned this to you? It might be best if you wait until she explains. Perhaps she has not told the boys."

"I'm certain they don't know."

"Yes, well, we'd best keep this our little secret for now. It was a delight seeing you again, Hollis." Lydia extended her hand and watched delightedly as the devastated young man politely took her fingers. He turned and walked away, his shoulders slumped in dejection.

"One obstacle overcome," whispered Lydia aloud.

This was an unforeseen obstacle. Others awaited.

* * *

"See, all it took was one dance and Samuel is as popular a dance partner as can be. Both the boys seem to be enjoying themselves, don't you think, Hollis?" Hannah looked up at Hollis' handsome face. "What's wrong? I thought you were having fun?"

"I was, I am," commented Hollis, trying to make sense of Mrs. Granville's declaration. Could she be right? Was Hannah leaving Santa Barbara? Her family was tremendously important to her, of that Hollis was certain. "I don't think Jonah is having any fun. There are no other children here."

Hannah glanced her brother's way. "I'll dance with him soon but I want you all to myself for a moment."

Hollis pulled his partner close against his body. He never wanted to let her go. Was this to be their last dance, ever? All these months, he planned their future. He felt certain it was a future Hannah welcomed. Was he a complete fool? Was this the reason Hannah was anxious to attend her sister's wedding? He pressed his lips against her neck and gave her a tentative kiss.

"Hollis! People will see," hissed Hannah.

"I don't care. I want you, Hannah. I love you." He looked into her face to find the truth. Her gaze spoke only of love and commitment. Alarms went off in his head. Something was wrong, very, very wrong. Realizing there was little choice but to wait and see how this played out, Hollis intended to spend every possible moment with Hannah. If ignorance was bliss, he would wallow in it as long as he could.

"I love you too but this is Lucy's day. You best behave or we'll get kicked out. This isn't the back corner of the theater."

Hollis smiled weakly and pulled Hannah close

again. He couldn't let her go; he could not believe she would go. Yet, he had never been a good forecaster of Hannah Granville's whims or actions.

* * *

"Samuel?"

"No, ma'am. I'm Jonah."

"Yes, of course you are. You've grown so big, I didn't believe it could be you." Lydia received a blank stare in return. "Give your mother a hug," she commanded.

A stiff-legged Jonah obliged, then quickly regained his seat. His critical glare put his mother off her game.

Lydia took the seat beside him. "It has been a long time. I'm sorry I did not get by to see you before Lucy's wedding. The mother of the bride has so many obligations." Lydia could see her apology meant nothing to the sullen little boy. "Perhaps you could tell me what you've been up to. Are you in school?" Lydia tried to determine how old the boy was, but she was flustered and unable to remember birthdates. It seemed odd how quickly she distanced herself from motherhood, once she had the chance.

"Yes, ma'am, but it's summer vacation."

"How old are you now?"

"I just turned 10. It's been a long time since you sent me away."

"Yes, it is, and I'm going to do my best to right things for you."

Jonah didn't understand. "Are you going to give Hannah money so she don't have to work so hard?"

"Well, no, no dear. That's not at all what I meant. I was talking about providing a better home for you."

"I have a home at Hannah's. She takes care of me. I love her."

"I'm sure you do."

"Hannah wants me. Nobody else does."

Alarmed at the way the conversation was progressing, Lydia rose from her chair.

"That's not true, Jonah. You are too little to understand." Lydia displayed a patronizing smile. "We'll talk more later." She patted Jonah's knee and retreated. How was she going to conduct a conversation with the older boys if she could not manage to charm a 10-year-old? Perhaps the direct approach she first envisioned was her best course.

* * *

Hollis' Model A was filled to capacity with Granvilles. He danced almost every dance and was distraught when the small band played their last tune. He feared the end of this day as none other of his life. If Hannah did not discuss her plans tonight, Hollis knew he would have no choice but to ask, or possibly sweep Hannah off her feet and carry her to the justice of the peace for a hasty wedding. He never wished to control another person the way he did Hannah.

"Don't be so moody, squirt," urged Samuel as he ruffled his younger brother's hair. "None of us had any fun."

"Speak for yourself," added Hannah. "Besides, I saw you smiling at those girls you asked to dance. You saw him too, didn't you, Jonah?"

Jonah could not be coaxed from his sorrowful state. "I guess so."

"Leave him alone," offered David, protectively. "He got stuck talking to Mother."

"What a terrible thing to say!" Hannah retorted.

"No, it's not," continued David. "Every time she looked to be coming my way, I took off."

"You did not!" his sister replied.

"Yes, I did. Samuel too. Why, did you two have a

- 257 -

warm chat?"

"Well, no. Hollis and I were dancing. I didn't see her when we left. I'm certain she'll come by and visit now the wedding is over. We can have a good talk then."

"She won't come to visit, Hannah." David seemed sure of himself.

"Aw, you just don't want her to come. None of us do but that don't make it so." Samuel put in his two-cent's worth.

Glancing in the rear-view mirror, Hollis observed tears glistening in Jonah's eyes. "You boys best change the subject. You're upsetting your brother."

This caused Hannah to turn in her seat. "What's wrong, Jonah?"

"I don't want to live nowhere else!"

"Nobody said you have to," answered Hannah, flabbergasted by Jonah's lapse of verbal skills.

The conversation suddenly became interesting to Hollis. "Why would you say that, Jonah?" he asked.

"Mother said some stuff about how she wanted to help us now, about our house."

"She don't have no money, how could she help us?" inquired Samuel.

"She told me I'm too little to understand. I'm 10, I can understand. I don't like her!" At this, tears rolled down Jonah's face.

"Here, Jonah, climb over the seat and come to me."

Hollis could not get used to the sight of Jonah's tall frame cuddled on his sister's lap, still a common occurrence. The boy needed all the comfort he could get but Hannah seemed dwarfed as the boy laid his head on her shoulder.

"I'm sure you misunderstood. Of course, you love her, she's your mother. You're tired. This will all seem unimportant in the morning," Hannah assured.

Jonah fell asleep before they reached home. Hollis woke him up and helped him into the house. As they approached the bedroom, there was a knock on the door. Hannah answered to find her mother on the porch.

"I didn't anticipate you'd come tonight," she began. "Come in."

Lydia walked through the door, expecting to be offered a seat. There were none in evidence. She looked around the living room of the tiny house critically.

"Where exactly does one sit?"

"Oh, I'm sorry. We play cards in this room." Hannah pulled a chair from the table. "Won't you sit here?"

"I think I'll stand," replied Lydia. "I've been busy with the wedding. You'll have to accept my apologies but you see, we will now be spending a great deal of time together." She paused and smiled, taking in the less-than-eager faces around her.

"Why would we do that?" inquired a belligerent David.

"First, I need to explain a tragedy. Your grandmother passed away several months ago. Probably only Hannah remembers her. We visited New York when you were small, you may have been too young to recall. Your grandfather is in ill health. He wants to see all of you. The best news of all is he has invited us to come and live in New York. Isn't this grand? Even little Turner and Jessica will be coming. I have so longed for a way to keep us together ever since your poor father passed."

"What if we don't go?" asked Jonah, surprising everyone in the room.

"I insist we all go. I am your mother and legal guardian. Our train leaves tonight. You have time to pack up your things. My driver is bringing some valises you can use. There will be many new things once we reach New York. Hannah, have the boys gather their belongings, then you can get yours."

Hannah seemed rooted to the floor. "No," came her simple reply. "You can't do this."

"I can and will. I am your mother. Get your things. You have no choice."

"You might make the boys go but I'm an adult. You can't make me go."

"Don't be ridiculous, Hannah. This is the opportunity you always wanted. Grandfather will be happy to pay your way through college. These boys have come to count on you."

The boys could see they had no choice in this situation. Jonah cried out, "Come with us, Hannah! You have to come, too!" He ran to the only grownup he trusted completely. Hannah enfolded him in her arms.

"I can't go, Jonah. My life is here. I'm not a little girl." The boy became hysterical, sobbing loudly and clinging to Hannah's neck.

"Come too, come with us! I need you Hannah, please come!"

Lydia motioned the older boys to go pack. She noted the angry look on Hollis' face. She was caught in a lie but that would not deter her now.

"You must come, Hannah. The boy needs you."

Hollis had seen Hannah angry on more occasions than he could count but never witnessed the look of sheer hatred she shot at her mother.

"What right have you to do this? The boys and I made a home together. We're happy here. Why would you take them away? You haven't cared in all these years, why now?"

"I am a mother. You don't understand."

"I understand this is cruel." Hannah caught herself. She didn't want to make this more difficult for the boys than it already was. She took Jonah by his arms and looked into his face. "Jonah, maybe you can come and visit me, maybe I can come and visit you."

"You won't come and she won't let me come back. I need you, Hannah. Don't stay here!"

Having obtained the suitcases from the porch, David and Samuel had quickly packed their belongings and Jonah's.

"Look, Jo. I've got your circus set here. You can take it along," offered Samuel helplessly as he handed Jonah the tiger, his favorite piece.

"David, take your brother," ordered Lydia. "We have to go now."

David first shook Hollis' hand.

"Thank you for all you've done." Then he turned to Hannah. "I'm almost 17. I'll be back as soon as I can. I love you, Sis." He then pried a frantic Jonah from his sister's arms.

Samuel followed suit, shaking Hollis' hand and hugging his sister, but he was unable to speak a word.

"Wait, wait!" screamed Jonah. "Put me down," he said more calmly. David set him on his feet. Jonah walked back to his sister. "You keep my tiger. Bring it to me when you come to visit." At this, he hugged her one last time and walked out the front door under his own power.

Lydia looked toward her daughter. "If you change your mind, I will send you train fare. But you have to come within the month. Any longer and it will be too late." She turned and walked out the door, closing it behind her.

Hollis, amazed Hannah still stood in her house, watched as she began to tremble. He met her shocked expression and crossed the room to take her in his arms. The only sound was the car taking her family into the night. He knew, to Hannah, there was nothing crueler than her mother's actions.

Hannah looked at him in obvious shock.

"They're gone. She took them away. How could she do that, Hollis? Not care for years and then take them all away?" Tears spilled down her cheeks. She wept loudly, her entire body shuddered with pain.

Hollis was uncharacteristically unable to speak. He couldn't think of one comforting thing to say. He held her tightly as sobs racked Hannah's small frame. "Maybe you should lie down," he offered, having no idea what else to suggest.

"Will—will you hold me?"

Hollis nodded and tenderly guided Hannah down the hall, into the kitchen and up the little staircase the boys helped him build. He felt he lost his own family but there was no place for his feelings right now. His only concern was Hannah—Hannah, who stayed for reasons he could only imagine.

Once they reached Hannah's attic room, she fell on the bed in despair. Clinging to Hollis' hand, she pulled him beside her. He held her and stroked her back, quietly waiting for her misery to pour out, which he understood might take a long while.

He thought about their time together at the wedding. She was right, he did have a wonderful time. The day was beautiful, the food good. The music was great. His fears about Hannah's eminent departure were now laid to rest. He was proud of Hannah and the boys. This house would never be the same without them. His reverie was broken when he looked down to find Hannah unbuttoning his shirt.

"What are you doing?"

"I want to touch you Hollis, not through layers of clothing." Once the buttons were unfastened, Hannah pushed the shirt off his shoulders and urged him to remove it. His undershirt quickly followed. Hollis delighted in the sensuousness of Hannah's hands on his chest. She moved her hands over his shoulders and offered her lips, wanting to be kissed.

No sooner did Hollis oblige than Hannah jumped off the bed. He watched in awe as Hannah, standing in the moonlight spilling through the dormer window, made quick work of the buttons on the back of her dress, only pausing to wipe tears from her cheeks. Soon the pink satin dress lay in a pool at her feet.

"Hannah, you don't have to do this. I won't leave you alone."

"I know." She sat on the side of the bed and stared at Hollis' bare chest. Then came the words she dreaded.

"I need to explain something," Hollis admitted.

"Oh, no you don't. I can't take any more tonight, Hollis. Explain later." Hannah turned her face toward the window. It appeared the moment for true confessions had arrived, just as Mrs. Durnam warned.

"I do, Hannah," Hollis continued as he captured her delicate wrist in his hand. "Look at me."

Hannah turned her tear-stained face to find Hollis' earnest expression.

"I need to tell you, I have never been with a woman before. This will be a new experience for me. I don't know how to say this. You mustn't have high expectations. I don't want you to be disappointed."

No comment could have surprised Hannah more. It took a moment for her to respond, an uncomfortable moment for Hollis.

"We'll learn together then," she replied as she fell into Hollis' embrace.

Chapter Seventeen

Hollis awoke to find sunshine streaming through the window, filling the room in ethereal yellow and pink light. A surreal warmth spread through Hollis, who would never complain about wallpaper again. He felt as if he awoke in heaven. Still asleep, Hannah lay beside him.

He took a deep breath, happy he proposed to Hannah in January, before her brothers left. She might otherwise think he only proposed now because they were gone and that was not the case.

Another thought caused greater concern. What if Hannah accused him of taking advantage? Admittedly, he had. Hollis was unable to control himself from the moment Hannah unbuttoned his shirt. She was in no frame of mind to think clearly. He considered the advantage he held over her. Unable to conjure any appropriate words to seem sincerely apologetic, Hollis ran out of time as Hannah stirred from slumber. He hoped she would not think less of him.

"Good morning, Short Stuff." Her smile relieved

his anxiety.

"Good morning," she responded as she put her arms around his neck.

Nothing in Hollis' life came close to the love he felt at that moment. "Are you all right, Hannah?"

"I am. Thank you, Hollis."

Hollis was dumbfounded. If anyone deserved thanks, it was Hannah. "For what?"

"For staying here, for—being with me."

"Hannah, I love you. You realize, biblically speaking, I have taken you for my wife. I want to make it legal. Can we go on Monday to get a marriage license?"

"Is this the proper, elegant proposal you promised?" she teased. "This seems a bit more intimate than I imagined."

"You are a temptress, woman. Are you disappointed? We could go to the Justice of the Peace after we get the license. I could propose properly today."

"Well, I accept your proposal, this proposal. But Hollis," she added more seriously, "I don't want to be sad on our wedding day. I want it to be the happiest, best day of my life. Can we decide on a date later in the week?"

"I don't know why not. But I'll be hoping for the earliest possible day, Hannah. I will stay so you don't have to be alone but I think we need to wait for our official wedding before we indulge ourselves again."

"Why?"

"That is proper. I don't want to do anything to hurt you or your reputation. I should have thought more about this last night."

"Really?" Hannah taunted as she pressed her body against his. "Are you quite certain? It would be a shame to waste our morning."

Hollis' willpower dissolved without another thought but after this morning, he was determined to stay out of Hannah's bed until they married.

* * *

As Hollis contemplated the days since Lucy's wedding, he knew he was happier than he ever imagined he could be. He also knew this came at a cost. It was difficult to hide his euphoria in light of Hannah's struggles to adjust to life without her brothers. Just as Hollis believed Hannah's enthusiasm for their upcoming marriage matched his own, he would find her distraught over some reminder of her recently overpopulated home.

She stood in front of the stove one morning, tears streaming down her face because she began to scramble eggs for a houseful of boys who were no longer there. She flinched when Hollis discovered her near the mantle in the living room staring at the wooden tiger Jonah left in her care. She refused to go in the boys' bedroom, even to open the window so the ocean breeze could cross-ventilate the house on a warm afternoon.

Hannah was frantic trying to accomplish her work. David managed to expand their business, now it seemed impossible for any single person to complete the daily tasks. Hollis imagined the heavy workload served to keep Hannah's mind from darker thoughts. He understood, even if she did not, she would never manage to keep up.

It was the nights that proved Hollis' complete undoing. He dragged a mattress from one of the bunkbeds onto the living room floor, having found the bunks too confining. Intent to stay in the house while sleeping at a safe distance, he awoke to find Hannah beside him on the mattress. She was sound asleep, curled against him. When he attempted to inch toward the opposite edge, Hannah awoke. One thing quickly led to another and Hollis found himself unable to resist Hannah's wiles.

Breathing heavily, Hollis groaned as he rolled on his side. "I'm sorry, Hannah. I could resist any other woman on earth but I can't seem to mind my manners with you."

"There's a declaration of love if I ever heard it. Who says I want an apology? Really, Hollis, it's not as if we can put this genie back in the bottle."

"Then we need to get married. We have our license. Let's go tomorrow."

"It won't hurt to wait a few more days, will it? I don't think it would make a good start to our marriage if I am melancholy at our wedding. Then there's the fact I'm falling behind more each day at work."

"If you recall, I told you Mr. Oddgood used to do accounting. I think the Oddgoods are on the verge of losing their house. You could hire him to work for you. And you have to admit, it's as if we're married now. We're living under the same roof, you cook for me as if we were already married."

"Yes, and then there's bedtime," she teased, knowing this made Hollis uneasy.

"If you'd stay in your own bed, this wouldn't happen."

"But I want to be with you. Do you know, once Jonah recommended I marry you so you'd never leave? His solution for where to put you was right here on the living room floor. I guess he was prophetic, more than he'll ever know."

This marked the first time Hannah spoke of one of the boys without a tinge of sorrow. Hollis was hopeful a few extra days might serve to lighten her spirits so he decided to bide his time.

Since Hannah continued to sneak into the makeshift

bed, Hollis abandoned the living room mattress in favor of Hannah's bedroom. To him, they were a newlywed couple. Hannah was his wife in every way but legally and he intended to prove himself the best possible husband.

One evening after work, Hollis took his beloved to Woolworth's to buy her a bathing suit. Hannah never accompanied Hollis and the boys on their waterfront excursions. He decided the beach could be their place as well, not only for walks. Ignoring Hannah's desire to work, he urged her to pack a picnic supper.

They arrived at the store right before closing. She chose a red suit of the latest fashion but concealed it under her trousers and shirt before emerging from the dressing room. Hollis took the tag to a cashier, all the while reflecting on his gratitude for current fashion. Women's suits were touted as practical for swimming but covered relatively little of the female body; bare arms and legs and low necklines were no longer taboo.

Once they got to the beach, Hollis suggested they swim first. He was hungry but anticipated the feast for his eyes more than his meal. He was not disappointed when Hannah removed her blouse and trousers. The bright red bathing suit hugged Hannah's curves and stood in stark contrast to her pale skin. Amazed how modesty in swimming attire vanished since he was a boy, a mesmerized Hollis held his breath.

"Aren't you going to strip down to your suit?" Hannah asked, apparently unaware of her effect on him.

"Sure. Give me a minute." But as Hollis removed his shirt and slacks, an unpleasant realization took hold. Although he dreamed up this excursion to see Hannah in a bathing suit, he quickly realized he wasn't the only one looking. A surge of jealousy welled inside him. He possessively held Hannah's waist and escorted her to the water, attempting to shield as much of her body from bystanders as possible.

"What are you doing, Hollis? I can hardly walk," Hannah complained. "I can't say I mind being close to you but we're both going to fall in the sand if you don't lighten your grip. Or maybe that is your wicked plan," she whispered. "Are you going to ravish me right here on the beach?" She laughed as Hollis blushed. "So, it is your plan!"

"Why do you say such things?" Hollis complained. "Nice girls don't even think such things."

"Well, I am obviously not a nice girl anymore," taunted Hannah. "You made me a worldly woman."

"What I'm trying to make you is my wife. Wives don't say such things either."

"How do you know? Did you ever have a wife before?"

"You know very well I have not."

"I know a lot more than I used to, thanks to you. If you are going to be a proper boyfriend, I assume you will keep a safe distance once we go farther out," Hannah suggested as they stepped into the water. "After all, it might be improper if you were to say, hug me where no one can see what we're doing. I think my bathing suit strap is actually a little loose. I might need you to adjust it for me," she hinted as she pushed her fingernail under the strap and slid it down her shoulder.

Hollis stopped suddenly. Incredulous at her implication, he stared in disbelief.

Hannah walked deeper into the surf, tugging at the shoulder strap of Hollis' bathing suit as she went.

"Hurry up, Hollis, or I may find some other man waiting in the waves."

Hollis considered the idea no one could appreciate Hannah's attire if she were neck deep in the Pacific

Ocean. "I'll race you!" he shouted as he dove in and swam for the delights that awaited.

* * *

Once the swimmers emerged from the surf, the beach was almost empty. If Hollis was hungry before their "swim," he was ravenous now. As he devoured his sandwich of cold sliced chicken, cheese, lettuce, tomato and Hannah's homemade mayonnaise, he was stunned at her next comment.

"I have a question about sex."

Hollis choked, all the while looking around to see if anyone was close enough to hear.

"Don't worry, there's no one nearby. Are you all right?" Hollis nodded, unable to speak. "Have some lemonade," Hannah urged as she handed him the jar.

Hollis sipped the drink as his breathing returned to normal.

"If you're quite recovered, may I continue?"

"Go ahead," Hollis croaked.

"Well, you said you were never with a woman before me."

"Correct."

"I find that difficult to believe. It seems to me you know exactly what you're doing."

No comment could have stroked Hollis' male pride any better. "I suppose men have a drive women may not have. Men talk. It's not as if I felt unprepared, only inexperienced. I'm glad I meet your expectations," Hollis grinned awkwardly as he considered the wet curls covering Hannah's head. He thought it odd. He considered her a grown woman but at the moment, she seemed more a playful little girl. The tenor of their conversation switched suddenly as Hannah became serious.

"It's just that, I assumed—" She struggled for

words, then stated her question directly. "I thought you slept with Lucy."

Hollis mulled her comment and all its implications. "You thought I was the father of Lucy's child?"

"I thought you a likely candidate—you and Dock."

"I understand why you think so, but no. I never slept with Lucy or anyone else. You have my word."

"But you know who did?"

"I know possibilities. Boys talk about their conquests but there's usually a lot of exaggeration."

"Was it Dock?"

Hollis stared toward the surf, unsure how to answer. "Yes, Hannah. I didn't find out until after Lucy went to the hospital. I was furious. We fought, probably the worst one ever. Dock took off." Hollis turned to look into Hannah's eyes. "You thought I might be the father and so you never liked me."

"Not because of that." Hannah looked down at the sand. "Well, because of that and the cavalier manner in which you dismissed her problem. I thought you cold-hearted, if you were the father and took no responsibility. In retrospect, knowing you couldn't be the one, you actually were kind to her and helpful to me when you didn't have to be."

"I'm glad you asked about this. You believe me?"

"Hollis, I don't think you've ever lied to me, maybe teasing, but not a real lie. I believe you."

"Good, I'm glad this is out in the open. I always wondered what you held against me. I have a question too. Will you answer it?"

"Certainly."

"Why did you stay in Santa Barbara?"

Knowing what Hollis wanted her to say, Hannah thought carefully about the truth and turned her own gaze toward the ocean as she formed her answer.

"I want to be honest, Hollis. It was shocking when my mother revealed her plans. I wasn't prepared for that, not remotely prepared. My first thought was about my life in Santa Barbara. I'm a grown woman. I have my own business, a car and a home. Why would I revert to being a child again, dependent on family? I worked hard for what I have but it was agony to let the boys go, especially Jonah.

"Not a day goes by that I don't wonder if I made the right decision. But then I look at you and I think about the way you make me feel. I love you, Hollis. I know I haven't told you that enough." At this, Hannah turned her gaze from the shore and looked into Hollis' brown eyes, so like her father's. "I know in my heart, I made the right decision. I want to marry you. I need a little more time."

Hollis looked around. Two small children began constructing a sand castle not far from their blanket.

"I shouldn't kiss you here but I want to." Hollis took Hannah's small hand in his. "We will wait until you're ready but I hope it won't be long. I want us to be official. I want to show the world my wife. I want to share our good news with my family."

"I think—can we choose a date this weekend? Maybe for next week?"

"Perfect. We can go on Saturday to get a ring. You can pick. After all, you'll be stuck with it and me until death do us part." At this, Hollis planted a kiss, not caring who could see.

* * *

Friday was always a busy day for Hannah, the last banking day of the week. She was eager to return home and make an elaborate dinner for Hollis. No sooner did she drop her things in the living room and start down the hall than there was a knock on the door. She opened it to find a radiant Mollie, who burst through the door and gave her friend a hug.

"What are you doing here?" queried Hannah.

"I took an extra day to come home and see my parents."

"Come back to the kitchen and tell me all about your new job. How long are you going to rent a room? Will you have any time off this summer?"

"Whoa! Let me answer some of your questions before you think up any more. My job is fantastic. When the school district superintendent became ill, this job fell into my lap. I have hope it might be permanent! If so, I'll look for less temporary accommodations and I'll certainly be able to afford it.

"I don't have the summer off as I would if I were teaching but I plan to take a long weekend here and there. It's a small district, after all. I'm not exactly overwhelmed. I thought I'd come by and see you and the boys." Mollie watched her friend's eager expression disappear. "What's wrong? Where are the boys? Don't you have card night anymore?"

"Oh, Mollie, so much has happened since I wrote you last. The boys aren't here. Card night is a thing of the past."

"Where are the boys?"

"My mother came to Lucy's wedding and she took the boys back East. She wanted me to come too but I have a life here now."

"You didn't want to leave your work and your house?"

"That's true enough. But I didn't want to leave Hollis, either."

"Have things gotten serious?"

"Very serious. We're going to be married. I'm not sure when but soon." Concern was clearly etched in

Mollie's expression. "What's wrong?"

"I don't understand, Hannah. You never liked him before."

"There were circumstances I didn't understand. And then, Hollis is not as egotistical as I used to think. He's always helped me when I needed help."

"Yes, and he complained about it for all the world to hear. I don't think he's right for you, Hannah. I know he helped you. Don't mistake gratitude for love. Lord knows, I never got along with him."

"Why don't you stay for dinner? Hollis will be here soon. You can see for yourself how happy we are."

"I can't stay for dinner. My mother would be disappointed. Are you free at all this weekend?"

"I don't know. I have to pick up my work in the morning. Then Hollis and I are going to look at rings. Can I call you tomorrow and let you know my plans for Sunday?"

Mollie could see how excited her friend was. Maybe she needed to be more supportive. "Sure. You can leave a message if I'm not around when you call. My parents are always there.

"Hannah, remember the hankie I let Jonah use? You don't happen to know where it is, do you? It was a gift."

"I washed and ironed it. I think it's on the dresser in the boys' room. Jonah wanted to give it back to you himself, next time you came."

Mollie noticed tears well in Hannah's eyes. "It must be hard for you, now they're gone. I know how close you were."

"It is hard," Hannah admitted, "but Hollis is helping."

"Here, I'll get the hankie while you work on dinner. I'll be right back."

Mollie bit her lip as she walked down the hall and through the living room, the site of so many fun-filled evenings. She did not consider Hollis an adequate partner for Hannah. It was true, she made peace with him, but considered him lacking in proper respect for ladies in general and Hannah in particular.

She entered the bedroom and found her hankie on the dresser, as Hannah suggested. Turning to leave, she noticed the closet door was ajar. Clothes hung inside, a man's clothes. Curiosity got the best of Mollie as she continued toward the kitchen.

"I need to use the bathroom," she shouted through the door. "I'll just be a minute."

Mollie locked the bathroom door and opened the medicine cabinet over the sink. Even though she suspected she would find a man's toilet articles, the shock of Hannah's living arrangement was no less diminished. She stared at Hollis' razor and other belongings on the shelf inside. Mollie took a moment to wash her hands before returning to the kitchen.

"Hannah, as a friend I have to ask you, are you and Hollis shacking up?"

Hannah stopped her meal preparation and stood still, then turned to face her friend. "He's been staying here since Mother took the boys so I wouldn't be alone."

"That's not proper. How long is he staying?"

"We're going to be married. There's no reason for him to leave," Hannah replied defensively.

"I see. I suppose he sleeps in one of the boy's bunks." Mollie watched as Hannah's cheeks turned a bright red. "Don't make up some lie to appease me, Hannah. I can see the answer written clearly on your face. I'm worried about you. This isn't right. You could be hurt. Send Hollis home. Let me stay here this weekend. You need some help and probably a different perspective. This is dangerous—what you're doing."

"It's not dangerous. I love Hollis and he loves me. This will all be fine. The only reason we're not already married is because I've been sad since the boys left."

"So you say. It seems to me, Hollis is taking advantage of you in the worst way possible. Leave him a note and come to my parents' house, then. I want to help you, Hannah."

"Thank you for the offer, Mollie," Hannah replied formally. "You will see, I'm right about this. But I think you should leave before Hollis comes home."

"Because you know I will speak my mind to him?"

Hannah did not move or reply.

"I'll go then, but you haven't heard the last of this. You could be in trouble, Hannah. This is nothing to joke about. Please call. Promise me you will?"

Hannah nodded and offered a weak smile. "I know you want the best for me, Mollie, but this is what's best."

Mollie crossed the kitchen and gave her friend a hug. "You are my dearest friend. I think the world of you. I only want you to keep safe."

"I know. I'll call you," added Hannah as she walked Mollie to the front door.

Hannah waved as Mollie drove away. She looked down to find Boots at her feet.

Scooping the cat into her arms, Hannah commented, "What do you think, Boots? Isn't Hollis the most handsome, wonderful man you ever met? Oh, that's right, you don't like him any more than he likes you." Hannah returned to the kitchen with a heavy heart. The recent promise of a lovely evening seemed suddenly impossible.

* * *

Laughing as Hollis applied kisses to her cheeks, neck

and forehead, Hannah hugged him tightly and looked carefully into his eyes.

"I missed you today, Short Stuff," Hollis confessed, unwilling to let her go.

"I missed you, too. I made you a special dinner."

"It smells good. What is it?"

"Steak and onions. See, I made a tomato sauce. You put the whole mess over mashed potatoes."

"I don't think the word mess should be used by a cook to describe her handiwork."

"Well, it's not exactly elegant but I think you'll like it."

"And what have we here? You spent extra time on the table. The flowers are beautiful. This is better than going to a fine restaurant."

"If you can manage to let me go, I'll dish up your plate."

"Well, let me see. What makes me happier, my dinner or my Short Stuff? I think I'll take you." Hollis kissed his betrothed vigorously.

"Hollis! Dinner will be ruined if we don't eat."

"Are you hungry?"

"I am. Have a seat."

Hollis soon became enthralled with the tender steak. "I guess I was hungrier than I thought," he admitted. He noticed, despite her declarations of hunger, Hannah was picking at her food. "This is good. Why aren't you eating?"

"Mollie was here today. She came into town to visit her parents."

"You should have asked her for dinner."

"I asked her to but then I asked her to leave."

"Why?"

"I don't think she approves of you, of us."

"Did she actually say so?"

"In so many words. I don't know how but she got the idea you were staying here. She thinks this is bad for me. Maybe she never put her hard feelings for you aside. She accused us of shacking up. I told her we would be married if not for my desire to wait. She thinks you should take your things and go home. I hoped she would be happy for us."

Hollis laid his fork on his plate and reached across the table to take Hannah's hand. "I would never hurt you, Hannah, but Mollie is right in one thing. We should already be married."

"We will be. Soon. After all, we're going to the jeweler tomorrow and—"

"Wait, Hannah. I have to tell you something. We can't go to the jeweler tomorrow." Hollis thoughtfully chewed on his bottom lip before continuing, "I have to go away for work. I'll be gone a week. They're sending me down to the Los Angeles area. I knew I'd have to go further afield at some point but didn't think it would be this soon. We can't get the ring until I return." He tried to read Hannah's expression. "Come along to Los Angeles, Hannah. Quit work and come with me. A week apart seems like an eternity."

"Hollis, I can't walk away from my obligations. You know that. I haven't asked Mr. Oddgood about taking a job. I can't leave my customers. And if living here is dangerous, I don't imagine tagging along while you work is any less so."

"But we could get married first. We could find someone to marry us in the morning. I would have to work but it would be something of a honeymoon adventure—you and I on a trip together, exploring new places. Come along, Hannah."

Hannah pulled her hand from Hollis' embrace. "I can't. There's too much against your plan. You could get fired for bringing me along and I'm not ready."

"I wouldn't get fired. Besides, no one would know you came."

"I'll bet other men don't take their wives much less their girlfriends to work, do they?"

"Well—"

"I need my work, Hollis. I need to support myself."

"No, you don't. I can support us. You don't need your job. Besides, I prefer you stay home."

"You told me before you understood if I kept my business."

"That's a poor choice of words. I don't understand why any married woman wouldn't want to devote herself to her husband and family. I know you're proud of your accomplishments and I even understand the satisfaction you get from supporting yourself and being independent. But we belong together, Hannah. It's time we both settle into the roles of man and wife."

Looking at her hands as she placed them in her lap, Hannah asked, "When are you leaving?"

"I don't have to leave until Monday morning, but I thought I'd get a head start and go tomorrow. I'll be done sooner if I make some stops, go as far as possible, then work my way back. I should be home sometime on Friday, maybe earlier. We can get the ring next Saturday. There must be a way we could get married the same day. I don't want to leave you alone. Maybe you could ask Mollie to come and stay while I'm gone. Will she still be here next week?"

"I think you should leave, Hollis."

"What?"

"I need to stay alone tonight. I need to think about this, all of this."

"You're upset about what Mollie said, aren't you? Or are you upset about the ring?"

"No. Too much has happened. I need time to think."

"Don't push me away, Hannah."

"You need to go."

Hollis' anger flared, but rather than engage in an argument and say things he might regret, he threw his napkin on the table and stormed out.

Hannah sat grim-faced at the table, listening to the sound of Hollis' car speeding away. She felt unable to think clearly. What had she done and why did she kick Hollis out?

She was completely alone. Words flooded her thoughts—Mother's words, Mollie's words. Too much happened in too short a time. Did she throw herself at Hollis? Did he take advantage of her? Why did she put him off? Did she feel obligated to marry or did she truly love him? Worst of all, could it be her long ago fanciful dream of Hollis she loved? Tears fell silently down her cheeks but all too soon, violent sobs racked her body.

Chapter Eighteen

Hollis slammed on his brakes as he pulled to the side of the road. He didn't sleep well. Thoughts of Hannah pounded through his brain.

Almost to Ventura when he stopped his car, Hollis looked out at the Pacific as the sun crept above the mountains. How could he leave town this way? What would he come back to next week? Angrily, he turned the car around and headed back for Santa Barbara and Hannah, realizing this might be the most stupid thing he ever did.

"What good are women, anyway?" he mumbled to himself. "Well, there's the obvious, like I spelled out to Hannah. Maybe we would be better off if we lived completely separate lives. I could come home, eat dinner and take Hannah to bed in complete silence. That is the ideal life, a real man's life. No repairs, no family difficulties, no nosy friends, just the basics. Hannah's problems would remain her own. I wouldn't even know what they were. Then, I would have no problems at all."

Hollis frowned. Last night was the longest of his

life. He tossed and turned. Visions of Hannah played through his mind as if he watched a movie: wet ringlets of hair at the beach and the way the red bathing suit clung to her curves. Hannah was fascinated with the stubble on his face. How he missed the way she rubbed her thumb along his jawline as they lay in bed every morning. He thought about her love for the stupid cat, how he enjoyed fitting his fingers in her curls and how well they danced together.

Hannah was not the timid, introverted girl she appeared to be. She was feisty and wild. Hollis felt he was the only one who truly knew her. She was his.

It was only a short while since they began playing man and wife but it seemed as if Hannah was part of his life forever. Why was it so difficult to corner that woman into marriage? It was supposed to be the other way around.

Continuing to document his tribulations, sometimes in silence, sometimes loudly, Hollis found himself parked in front of Hannah's house as she walked out her front door. He bounded out of the car and flew toward the porch, intent on having his say before Hannah could rebuff him.

His fears of rejection were dispelled as he looked into Hannah's haggard face. It was obvious her night was as unpleasant as his.

"Hannah, I couldn't leave without seeing you. I want you to listen to me." She stood stock still, staring into his face, her lips pressed tightly together.

"I love you. I don't know what I can do to convince you. A man needs a job. If I have to quit in order to have you, I'm prepared to resign."

Surprised when Hannah reached up to put her fingers on his lips, Hollis waited to see what she would say. She dropped her bag on the porch and put her hands on his shoulders.

"A man does need a job, you're right. I don't want to take your opportunities away. It would be unwise to start our marriage that way." Hollis caught a twinkle in her eye as Hannah continued, "I would have to support you while you stayed home and cared for the ten children you promised. I always did think Hannah Rumsford sounded like a dowdy woman in a gingham dress and apron laboring endlessly in her kitchen. Now, Hollis Granville sounds like a man who *owns* an oil company, not only works there."

"Hannah, if you are suggesting I would ever let you support me or I would ever take your name—"

"Well, if I'm going to be the breadwinner, it's only right you take my name." Hannah flashed a wicked grin before Hollis scooped her in his arms and kissed her soundly.

"Go on, Hollis. Do your work and we'll make our plans when you come home."

"I have your word?"

"I give you my word. I will wait patiently for you." Hollis stole one last kiss before hurrying back to his car.

He stopped short and hollered, "You've been working too hard. Get some rest while I'm gone."

"I will. I'm going to talk to Mr. Oddgood first thing Monday."

Hollis grinned, scrambled into his car, honked and waved. Hannah stood on the porch, watching the dramatic departure before grabbing her bag and walking to her own car. She had no way of knowing how many promises to Hollis Rumsford she was about to break.

* * *

After another bad night, Hannah woke up smiling, eager to find Hollis lying beside her in the attic bedroom. Opening her eyes, she remembered. Hollis was gone.

It was late. Another cool, foggy morning after her restless night made sleeping in all too easy. She bounded out of bed, intent on implementing plans made in darkness.

Hannah put a kettle on for morning tea and sat down at the kitchen table, wondering why sharing her bed with Hollis was already a way of life. She set goals for the week and didn't want to forget a single one.

She used a tablet to jot down the first item on her list—avoid Mollie. Tapping her pencil on her bottom lip, Hannah was temporarily unable to recall why this seemed important as she lay in bed last night.

Mollie was her first real friend since school. But Hannah didn't want to hear disparaging remarks about Hollis. She was filled with doubts and fears and wasn't up to defending recent decisions. Despite assurances before Hollis left, Hannah's misgivings about their relationship were undiminished.

An unpleasant idea crossed Hannah's mind. Was she like Lucy? She considered Lucy a loose woman and knew Hollis did, as well. Realizing she never should have judged her sister, by some twist of fate, was she in an identical situation?

Hannah's mouth flew open. There could be a baby. How did she manage to complicate her life so thoroughly? How could she be so stupid? If Hollis gave her his baby, she would have little choice as far as marriage was concerned. The enormity of her actions cloaked her in doom. It wasn't as if she didn't want to marry Hollis but she didn't want to be forced into it. Her mind was clearly in a fog these last days. She sought Hollis' touch to soothe her sorrow. Now she might have to pay the price for this foolishness.

Of one thing, she was certain. Hannah needed to reclaim her house. She concentrated on the list. Her intention was to clean every last inch, wash every dish and linen, scrub every wall and floor.

She scribbled the words "shelf paper" on the bottom of the page so she would remember to go to the hardware store on Monday. The last household task listed was "boys room." She planned to summon the courage to clean and clear out that room, although she wouldn't be able to do much about the bunk beds until Hollis returned. Hannah's goal was to face her demons, for better or worse. She couldn't go on pretending the bedroom didn't exist.

But her list was not complete until she added Mr. Oddgood's name. She planned to visit on Monday and offer him a job. Hopefully, activity would serve to clear her mind. Hannah knew, by the time Hollis returned, she would understand exactly what she wanted.

When the telephone rang after noon, Hannah instinctively walked toward it, then stood and watched until the ringing ceased. She was certain it was Mollie who called. Not even the thought it might be Hollis tempted her to answer. Best to keep to her work and so, she did.

* * *

The days unwound more comfortably than Hannah anticipated. She made headway on her cleaning projects while spending time in her garden each day. She attempted to duplicate her initial attitude toward the house. It was the first time she had her own bedroom, much less an entire house to herself.

Enjoying the solitude, Hannah failed miserably at putting Hollis out of her thoughts. If it were possible, she actually ached for him. These feelings were so intense, they overwhelmed her desolation since the boys' departure.

Fortunately, Mr. Oddgood eagerly accepted the job.

Since he was an experienced accountant, it took little effort on Hannah's part to get him working independently. She maintained her duties at the hotel and let Mr. Oddgood pick up receipts, keep the books and make deposits for her other accounts. Her plan was to let him have at it, then do a thorough review of his work at the end of the week.

But her productive rhythm broke down when Hannah collected her mail on Wednesday. She was unable to write her brothers until she heard from them, having lost touch with her grandparents when her father died. She both anticipated and dreaded a letter from the boys. Hesitant to hear how they were faring, she imagined anything they wrote—good or bad—would contribute to her unhappiness.

Taking a deep breath, Hannah opened the envelope David addressed to find both David and Jonah's letters. She tackled David's missive first.

After a factual accounting of their trip East, David described their grandfather's opulent house, the array of servants, the humid weather and Samuel's reluctance to write at all, much less an entire letter. In a mature manner, David assured they were fine.

He and Samuel were allowed to get jobs. Reading between the lines, it seemed the boys were intent on stockpiling enough money to return to California at their first opportunity. Hannah made a mental note to advise the boys any trip to the West Coast would undoubtedly be annulled and a waste of resources until they came of age.

Jonah's letter proved more troubling. The boy vented his unhappiness in no uncertain terms. His entire message was fraught with frantic pleas. She imagined his tears as he expressed longing for their home in Santa Barbara and his intense anger at their mother. In a childish manner, Jonah asked after his tiger, then abruptly closed his letter with love.

Hannah's cheeks were wet by the time she reread both letters. She felt the need to write immediately. It took several hours to compose a caring response.

When it came to her own life, there was little to convey. If she had no idea what she was doing, how could she help the boys understand? She expressed delight because Mr. Oddgood agreed to work for her, if only temporarily—so as not to discourage David's hopes of returning to his job. She explained Hollis' trip to Los Angeles for work and attempted to cast her daily routine in a pleasant light.

Having struggled through the last days, full of work and little sleep, the letters cast a pall on Hannah's plan to clear her mind. A gloom hung over the little house that intensified as the hours until Hollis' return dragged on.

* * *

Thursday proved another foggy, cool day. Intent on finishing housework, Hannah took a deep breath and entered the bedroom. It seemed eerily haunted. After touring the perimeter of the room, Hannah filled her scrub bucket and went to work, stripping beds, washing curtains and putting her own brand on the room. She cleaned the closet and carefully hung Hollis' clothing back inside. Only a few tears fell as she worked.

If she married Hollis, Hannah planned for them to move to this room, knowing Hollis never liked the wallpapered attic space. Once he dismantled the bunkbeds, a new coat of paint might serve to erase recent memories.

Hannah heaved a sigh as she backed out of the room on her knees, pulling the scrub bucket behind her. The clean floor marked the end of her efforts, not only in the bedroom but in the entire house. She sat back to consider her handiwork, only to have her reverie interrupted by a knock on the door.

"I was afraid I might have missed you. You do still work, don't you?" queried Lucy as she stood, immaculately attired, on Hannah's front porch.

"Yes, I do." Hannah nervously pulled at her apron, then removed her head scarf. She knew she appeared every bit a scrubwoman.

"Might I come in for a moment? I wanted to thank you."

"For what?" replied a suspicious Hannah.

"Honestly, you do need to be a better hostess," complained Lucy as she entered the house. "I returned from my honeymoon and decided to visit you first. You might be friendlier."

"I'm sorry. There's tea in the kitchen. Why don't we go back there?" Had Hannah's back not been turned, she would have been offended at her sister's careful scrutiny as she followed along to the kitchen. "Have a seat," Hannah offered as she gathered the teapot, wrapped in its cozy, and two cups and saucers.

"Isn't this civilized? You and I sharing a cup of tea."

"What brings you here?" Hannah inquired as she poured.

"As I told you, I wanted to thank you. I'm grateful you kept my secrets. You might have given me up. I appreciate your discretion."

Hannah was surprised at Lucy's newfound maturity and thoughtfulness. "You're welcome."

"I understand we'll never be close as many sisters are but we're surely adults. I wanted to return the favor, since you have evidently taken up with Hollis Rumsford."

"I don't think that's any of your business, Lucy."

"But I'm right, aren't I? It was obvious at the wedding, when you were dancing. It seemed to me, and Mother as well, you and Hollis were hardly strangers."

"We'd been dancing before."

"That's not all there is to it, though."

"What do you mean?" Hannah asked defensively, then turned her attention to her tea.

"Hollis asked Mother for your hand in marriage. Didn't he tell you?"

"No, I had no idea. Are you certain?"

"Quite certain. She was protective of you. Mother pulled Hollis aside to ask about his intentions. Then he asked for her blessing. She told him no. That's probably why he didn't mention it. Has he asked you to marry him?"

"Not in so many words."

"Well, you better think about it carefully if he does."

"Of course."

"Good. You're a smart girl. I'm certain you can figure him out. I assured Mother you would."

"Figure him out how?"

"Oh, you know what I mean. I bet he used that line on you. 'I've never been with a woman. I'm saving myself for my wife.' That line. I bet he could get a hundred women with those words. Maybe he already has."

Hannah's face grew pale. "How do you know it's a line?"

"Seriously, Hannah? Perhaps I gave you too much credit. Hollis used his line on me. I found out he said it to quite a few girls in Placerville. Far as I know, it worked every time. It was clear to me, Hollis knew what he was doing but it was too late by then.

"Hollis stuck around for months after my—after I was sick. Don't get me wrong, he can be a nice guy. He left me alone when it became obvious I could do better than him, much better. There is a certain irony. He took up with you when it became clear I was out of his league.

"He must have told you about the boys before Mother came to pick them up, surely?"

"What about the boys?"

"Why, Mother told Hollis at the wedding she was taking the boys to New York. She assumed he would break the ice so you could prepare them and it wouldn't be a shock for you. He didn't tell you, did he? I can see by your expression."

"No, no he didn't," mumbled Hannah. She thought about the way Hollis stood in the corner, not commenting on the situation as it unfolded. To think, this was right after he promised to protect the boys because they were so dear to him. He stood silently by while Mother dragged them off. Could this be true? Was Lucy being honest? As she looked across the table, she saw no deceit in Lucy's expression. If anyone was a shrewd judge of Lucy's antics, it was her younger sister.

"I haven't much time, Hannah. I'm just back in town. I have my own household to put in order. Thank you again, and for tea. If you should decide to join Mother and the boys, I'm certain they'd love to have you. Maybe there isn't so much to stay in Santa Barbara for now?" At this, Lucy rose from her chair and headed for the front door. A numb Hannah trailed behind.

"This is my new address," Lucy handed Hannah an elegantly printed card. "Call sometime. Maybe we could go shopping if you decide to stay. We're all the family west of the Mississippi now. It would be a shame to lose touch." Lucy gave Hannah a peck on the cheek before she turned and headed for her limousine. "Take care!" she added over her shoulder.

Hannah stood at the door until long after her sister's limousine was out of sight. Her head spun as she attempted to assimilate Lucy's startling conversation. Hannah's life had turned upside down in the course of a few minutes.

Closing the front door, Hannah leaned against it. She felt sick, alone and more confused than ever. Everything Lucy said made perfect sense. She had fallen for Hollis' line and was simply one in a string of conquests. How could he have lied to her? All the while they danced, he knew the boys would leave after the wedding. Was it simply his plan to use her as long as possible? He certainly invented an excuse as soon as they set a date to buy a ring.

Hannah found it impossible to sort fact from fiction. Her stomach gave a lurch and she hurried to the bathroom. Usually vomiting relieved an upset stomach but as Hannah leaned against the bathroom wall, she felt worse. Her hands shook; her head hurt. One thing was certain. She needed to cut all ties to Hollis Rumsford.

* * *

Hannah focused on driving as she headed for State Street. She had already been to the hotel and completed her work for the day. A phone call before she left home prompted one additional stop. Her client at Sam's Ice Cream Parlor asked her to come by. There was some problem requiring her attention.

After parking, Hannah walked inside and asked the young man behind the counter for the owner.

"My dad had to leave. Are you Miss Granville?"

"Yes, I am."

"He wanted to talk to you, something about how Mr. Oddgood is a fine man and wonderful representative for your business. He asked me to give you this." The young man opened the register and handed Hannah an envelope. "I guess these bills got left under the drawer when Mr. Oddgood picked up the deposit. I imagine he won't be able to balance the receipts from yesterday. I'm sorry if this caused any inconvenience."

"Not at all. I'll phone Mr. Oddgood, and we'll do an extra deposit. It's really no trouble. Please give your father my thanks for his consideration." Hannah smiled as she stashed the envelope in her purse.

"Say, it's dinnertime. I'm done here for the day. How about I get you some dinner for your trouble? You look like you could use a square meal."

"What do you mean?"

"I didn't mean anything bad. It's just—you look a little peaked. Did you eat lunch today?"

"Oh, I think I forgot. I was working, you see—"

"Well, have a seat back there in the corner and I'll bring you something. It's the least we can do for dragging you over here. What would you like? Between you and me, you can't go wrong with a chocolate malted and a hamburger." The owner's son provided the first kind words Hannah heard all week.

"That sounds wonderful."

"Great! I hope you don't think it forward of me but I haven't eaten either. Would you mind if I joined you, Miss Granville?"

"It's Hannah and I would be happy to share a meal."

"Call me Bud. That's what my friends call me."

The boy bounded toward the kitchen as Hannah removed her jacket and took the corner seat. She didn't want to think anymore. Maybe dinner would occupy her mind for a while. It seemed only moments before Bud returned balancing burgers and a chocolate malted for two on a tray.

"It's a big drink," he offered sheepishly.

Hannah smiled then took a sip. "My brother is the one who convinced your father to use our services. I should have tasted your food. I didn't know what I was missing."

Bud beamed. "We are proud of our ice cream and hamburgers. That's what we're known for."

"You work here with your father, then?"

"I'm just an employee. I'm lucky my dad made a go of this. I lived in Los Angeles for a while but it was hard to find work. My dad offered me this job hoping I would take over for him one day. He's not ready for retirement or anything. But it's good work. I make enough to have my own place."

"Really? Where do you live?"

"Behind my parent's garage," Bud offered affably, then blushed. "I guess I didn't move very far."

"It's a start," Hannah offered.

The pair made polite conversation as they enjoyed dinner. Hannah avoided Bud's personal questions with queries of her own. Bud didn't seem to notice. Hannah stayed after finishing her meal, listening to Bud describe his high school football accomplishments.

"Can I ask a question?"

"Sure, Hannah. Anything."

"How old are you?"

"The same age as your brother. I'm 21. How old are you?" Bud blushed again. He appeared born to live at the beach, close to six feet tall, he had sandy blond hair and blue eyes. "I'm sorry. You're not supposed to ask ladies that question. You look so young but you have your own business."

Amused David passed himself off as 21, Hannah replied, "It's all right. I'm 19. I fell into my business by accident. People assume I'm older than I am. It's nice to know I look young. Thank you."

Bud was clearly enamored of the delightful and modern Miss Granville. Hannah enjoyed the attention after her difficult week.

"I need to go home. I must call Mr. Oddgood before it gets too late. Thank you for the delightful dinner and conversation. This was a bright spot in what has been a trying day," Hannah managed.

Even the inexperienced Bud could see his dinner companion had turned morose.

"I'm sorry you had a tough day. Will you come in again?"

"Most likely. I won't be able to resist another hamburger and malted." She almost laughed at Bud's huge grin.

Hannah considered her dinner companion while she drove. It was nice to have someone friendly to think about. But as she parked at home, Hannah could see today's unpleasantness was only beginning. The lights were on in the waning daylight and Hollis' car was parked in front.

* * *

"You're home," Hannah stated matter-of-factly as she removed her hat and dropped her purse on the table in the living room.

"That's not the greeting I expected," noted Hollis as he approached his bride-to-be, gripping her arms to administer a kiss.

"Wait, Hollis. We have to talk."

"Fine by me, but can't I have a kiss first?" Hollis could see his beloved was in no kissing mood. "What's wrong?"

"I've had time to think. There are issues, things I need to make clear."

"Well, I can only wait so long for my kiss. Can we sit at the kitchen table? I'm hungry."

"That's too bad. I already ate. I think we should talk here."

"You already ate? You weren't even here."

"A client bought me dinner downtown."

"What client?"

"Bud. His dad owns the ice cream parlor."

"He doesn't sound like a client to me."

"I was there on business."

"Since when did your business include dining out?"

"I didn't dine out. He served me a hamburger and we shared a malted. He was just being nice."

"I'm sure he was." Hollis' sarcasm was hard to miss. "I don't like this, Hannah. Not one bit. Engaged women don't do such things."

"That's what I want to talk to you about."

Hollis blinked his eyes and stared at Hannah. "What do you want to talk about?"

"I've had time to think this week. There are obstacles."

"What kind of obstacles?"

"You know some of them. One is your habit of expecting certain behavior but there are many others. I won't sit at home raising a family while your job takes you away six months of the year."

"I thought we had this out already. I thought we agreed I would continue at the oil company a while and see what happens. I'll find another job if need be."

"I won't move, Hollis. I have too much at stake here. I won't give up my business."

"I thought that might be the case. I'm not asking you to."

"But you expect it."

"I think there will come a time when it will be

impractical."

"For who?"

"For both of us and our family. But we can work this out when the time comes. I don't see why this needs to be an issue now. We can marry and see what life brings us."

"That's another problem. This house is too small for a family. I know it is. But I can't leave. I gave Mr. Rowland my word I would live in this house."

"I imagine he'll understand once it's full of children. But we might be able to remodel as the years go by. Why does this bother you?"

"I'm reluctant to sacrifice all my accomplishments and allow you to support me. You could be a poor provider. I'm certain my mother never imagined the difficulties my father's unreliability would cause."

Hollis was dumbfounded at this comment. "I always helped you. I had money when you didn't. Maybe I should be the one to wonder if you are fiscally responsible!"

"When did you fall in love?"

"What? What does that have to do with anything?"

"You didn't love me when we came to Santa Barbara. You didn't care for me when I asked for your help. When did you fall in love?"

"I don't know exactly. It kind of dawned on me."

"When?"

"Before Christmas. Before I went home."

"After my brothers were here. After there was a ready-made family waiting for you."

"What are you talking about?"

"You said you wanted a family. When my brothers came, you fit right in, all of a sudden. Maybe you never wanted me. Maybe it was the idea of a family you loved."

"That's ridiculous."

"Is it?"

"Hannah, I was relieved I already asked you to marry me when your brothers left. I was afraid you might think I only wanted to marry because they were gone."

"Or so you say now. Hollis, did you know my mother planned to take the boys?"

"She told me her plan at the wedding."

"Why didn't you tell me?"

"From what she said, I thought you planned to leave. You didn't tell me anything. I was afraid to bring it up. I thought you would choose your brothers over me and was surprised you decided to stay."

"I would have appreciated knowing what you knew. My mother's visit wouldn't have proven so shocking. Didn't you trust me enough to ask?"

"I guess I didn't."

"There seems to be a lack of trust on both sides. Did you tell Lucy you were never with a woman and you were waiting for marriage?"

"Yes, I did. How did you know?"

"She came to thank me for something. She said you used that line on all the girls in Placerville."

"That's not true."

"But you did tell Lucy?"

"Yes, but—"

"How could you, Hollis? I believed you when you said I was the only one. Now I find out I am just another notch on your bedpost. I gave myself to you. I trusted you," Hannah began to lose control.

"I never lied to you. I told Lucy because she wanted me to—to make love. I didn't want to so I explained why. It's not the same as when I told you." But Hollis could tell he wasn't convincing Hannah of anything. "You don't believe me?"

"The point is, too much is against us. I thought carefully about this, about us. This isn't going to work, Hollis."

"What are you saying?"

"I won't marry you. I don't trust you; you don't trust me. We never got along. Our marriage would be a disaster, from start to finish."

"No, Hannah. You have to listen to me—"

"I'm done, Hollis. You need to go."

"Is it this man who bought you dinner tonight?" Hollis' anger flared.

"Certainly not."

"Then how could everything change in a week? You were ready to marry me when I left."

"I had doubts. I wondered if I even loved you or only the idea of you. You promised to protect me, to protect the boys. Yet you stood there while my mother took them away. You didn't say a word. That's another lie."

"It wasn't a lie. She's their mother. What could I possibly have done?"

"We will face nothing but problems."

"But we would face our problems together." Hollis was yelling now.

"I didn't want to be cruel but you're not leaving me much choice. I don't want you, Hollis. This has been a terrific mistake. I was vulnerable and confused. You took advantage. You lied to me. I can't ever trust you. I don't understand you. I will never marry you. I don't know how I can be any clearer. Leave."

Breathing heavily, Hollis turned and walked out the front door, slamming it loudly behind him. The little house shook from the impact. Jonah's tiger fell from its perch on the mantle as Hannah dissolved into tears.

Chapter Nineteen

"The truth is, Mr. Oddgood, I need to work right now. I was making other plans when I asked if you wanted a job," explained Hannah.

"I'm disappointed. I enjoyed working last week. I can't tell you how pleasurable it was to get out in the world. Then there is the unfortunate fact, I need the money."

Hannah felt immense guilt as she listened to Mr. Oddgood's laments. This was clearly her fault. "I'm sorry, Mr. Oddgood. But if I ever need an employee again, I won't hesitate to hire you."

"Before you give up on this, I have a suggestion. I have a lot of contacts in the city and believe I could increase your business. It doesn't hurt to have a mature presence. You are young. Although you've clearly gained the trust of your clients, I think I lend experience, or at least the illusion of experience, to your business.

"I'd like to partner with you, Hannah. I assure I can have at least five new accounts before the week is out. Your services are unique. There's the likelihood FDR will broaden taxes as never before. Your bookkeeping expertise will be much in demand. We would share the profits from our business 50/50. I concede your work at the Vista Mar Monte will remain in your hands, for your profit alone. I'm only talking about the businesses you service downtown. How does the title Granville and Oddgood Accounting Services sound to you?"

Hannah bit her lip. The offer was tempting. She needed to make a life outside of work. "You will guarantee five new accounts?"

"How about this? You don't owe me a dime until the day the fifth account is firm."

"Then you have a deal, Mr. Oddgood," Hannah agreed as she shook hands.

"It's Dewie. Partners should be on a first-name basis. There's one more thing, Hannah. You underestimate the value of your work. You need to raise your prices."

"But I might lose customers."

"I assure, you won't lose a single one."

Hannah paused to consider Mr. Oddgood's ideas. She put on a brave front, fought the urge to break down, burst into tears, and confess how lost and alone she felt. Instead, Hannah mustered a smile and asked Mr. Oddgood how high he thought their rates could go.

* * *

"Get up, Hollis. It's noon. You're late for work." Bitsy shook her nephew's arm to no avail. Harsher tactics seemed in order. She threw open the shade, allowing sunlight to pour through the window, and left to fill a pot with cold water. After trying once more to waken Hollis, she poured the water over his head, attaining instant results.

Hollis sprang from his bed, sputtering. Although his instant reaction appeared violent in nature, he pulled himself together, shocked at the sight of his aunt in his bedroom, pot in hand.

"What the h—what are you doing here?"

"Dock told me you are near death from a broken heart," jabbed Aunt Bitsy, who was no less shocked at her nephew's appearance. Hollis was always careful about his grooming and attire. Bitsy was not prepared for this unshaven, unkempt version of her sister's son. "Get up and get ready for work or you're going to lose your job."

Hollis expected at least a modicum of sympathy, "I called and told them I was sick."

"Well, you aren't sick. Having a hangover is no excuse to avoid work. Being heartsick is not an illness. I'm disappointed in you, Hollis. I thought you had more sense."

"I'm going back to Placerville. There's nothing for me here," Hollis complained as he gathered the corner of the bedsheet to wipe his face. He was in no state of mind to endure further cruel treatment.

"How do you expect to make intelligent decisions if you are only drunk or asleep?" Bitsy asked as she pulled up the blind of the corner window. She almost laughed at the incredulous look on Hollis' face. "Your mother isn't here to straighten you out. I'm only telling you what she would say. She never liked a slacker. I never dreamed you were one. Dock always seemed a lay about, but never you."

"I loved her, Aunt Bitsy. I can't seem to face a future without her. I thought we were of one mind. I can't think of a way to undo her current opinions of me. All I did was go away for work and everything changed. She cares more for her stupid little house than me. Somehow, I always knew she would never leave Santa Barbara if my work took me away."

"Well, I think you might regret telling me the nature of your disagreement so keep that to yourself. I always liked Hannah, despite the fact she was so timid and quiet."

"She is anything but timid and quiet these days."

Noting her nephew's hostility, Bitsy explained, "When love is new, we tend to forget the object of our desire has a past."

"What is that supposed to mean?"

"It was always clear to me, from what little Hannah discussed, her father was the most important person in her young life. She never mentioned her mother or seemed to miss her. Would you agree?"

"I suppose. Why should it matter?"

"It would be one thing if her father left or died in some accident. He chose the most permanent and unalterable form of desertion he could manage. Perhaps he felt abandoned himself, but Aloysius Granville rejected his family completely and added no small amount of stigma in the process.

"Hannah trusted him but his suicide meant the end of her world. He left her without resources, without love and without a home. It's no wonder she might have trouble trusting the next man who came along. You left her for work and asked her to choose between you and the home she made for herself. Hannah probably thinks she is in for the same kind of treatment she got from her father."

No comment could have proven more sobering to Hollis. "What am I supposed to do?"

"Maybe there's nothing you can do. You have no course of action at all? No apology on your part would bring her around?"

Hollis shook his head. "She believes lies about me. I doubt anything I say will make a difference."

"Your grandmother always said if you don't know what to do, it's not the right time to act. Sober up, Hollis. Go to work and get your mind off Hannah Granville. All things have a purpose, no matter how cruel or horrific they may seem at the moment.

"There is the possibility you and Hannah are not meant to be. Better to find out now. Your experiences today might prepare you for something even better in your future. Or perhaps, Hannah might need a little time to figure out her feelings.

"Drinking and sleeping your life away are not going to help you, in any case. Get cleaned up and I'll make you a sandwich before I go check on the baby. Mother Oddgood hasn't the stamina she used to have."

Although Hollis managed to pull himself together enough to get to work the next morning, much of Aunt Bitsy's advice fell on deaf ears. One thing was clear. Hollis felt as devastated as ever.

* * *

Staring out the window at the foot traffic on State Street, Hannah considered her options. Dewie Oddgood had been a fountain of information and ideas. Hannah might have felt bulldozed by the man's enthusiasm and zealous devotion to work if she weren't in a fog these last weeks. His idea they needed a presence in the heart of downtown Santa Barbara was what brought her to this location.

Granville and Oddgood Accounting Services was growing by leaps and bounds. True to his word, Dewie managed five new accounts by the end of his first week. When word got out he was in business, they continued to pick up new accounts.

Dewie was not only gracious but extremely grateful for the opportunity Hannah provided. He believed this was the time to expand. The office was the first step;

hiring a receptionist and accountants would be the second. His plan was to make the office function independently of both his and Hannah's presence, enabling them to provide customer service and investigate new business opportunities.

Hannah would undoubtedly have been offended at Dewie's take-charge work habits at any other time. Now, she was happy to be the cooperative founder of the accounting firm and grateful someone else was managing most of the business.

A mother pushing a baby carriage down the sidewalk caused Hannah to recall recent concerns. She was regular since her cycle began at 13. Panic set in as the days crawled by after their final argument. Worried she must be carrying Hollis' child, Hannah attempted rational solutions. She did not want to marry Hollis Rumsford. She would never choose Lucy's way out. Hannah considered moving to New York to live with her family. She could claim a hasty marriage and widowhood. The possibility Hollis could find out about the baby made that plan dubious at best.

Her baby was incredibly precious. She would protect him at all costs. This thought circled around to the undeniable fact her baby deserved a father, even one as shallow as Hollis.

She contemplated scenarios where she would tell Hollis about their baby. Her mind turned endlessly on what she would say and how he would react. Perhaps he would not agree to marry her or provide the child a proper name. Did she drive Hollis away only to return on bended knee to request further help?

But her worries were for naught. She awoke two weeks ago to find her time of the month was finally upon her. Her reaction proved dumbfounding. Instead of the relief she imagined, Hannah dissolved into tears of disappointment and regret.

It was that afternoon the letter arrived. Hannah found herself referring to the missive so frequently, she began to carry it in her pocket. Every nuance, every word seemed more important each time she read it. She opened the envelope to find a cashier's check in the amount of $20,000 and hand-written correspondence:

My dearest Hannah,

I was so happy to acquire your address when your brothers arrived. I can't tell you how your grandmother longed to write after your father's death. Her own health was failing. I'm afraid, I did not do all I could to obtain the information she requested. Please forgive my carelessness. When a man reaches a certain age and business interests are a thing of the past, often there is a period of adjustment. You are not the only person I ignored when I should have been engaged.

Did you know you were your grandmother's favorite? I don't imagine you remember much of your visit here. She was always taken with you, fascinated by your dainty mannerisms, your grace and loving disposition. I believe she saw herself in you. I hoped you would come to New York so I might be able to make a comparison in person.

I feel the need to explain. I was not pleased when your mother decided to marry. It was not as if I disliked your father or wished them ill. Perhaps your father was simply too much in love. His most fervent desire was to make your mother happy, an impossible aspiration if ever there was one. You see, your mother was never a happy person. She badgered your father to succeed so he would provide the life she wanted. Before he could make a man of himself, she deemed him a failure, a stigma he likely never overcame. He was all too ready to take money he did not earn, money I should never have surrendered.

This monetary relationship became impossible to continue. It made your father a weak man. As your grandmother predicted, it gave me more power and control in their marriage than I should ever have had. I regret the tragic situation that tore your family apart. I apologize for any part I played.

Your family would never have been divided amongst relatives if your grandmother had not been ill. She would have moved heaven and earth to bring you all here but it was not meant to be. It is my fondest desire to see you once more and help as much as I am able. This desire is what led to current unfortunate circumstances.

I first learned your mother misconstrued my wishes when I received a telephone call from my youngest daughter, your Aunt Rose. She took in little Turner and baby Jessica upon your father's death and raised the children as her own. Imagine her dismay when your mother showed up to take them. The little ones didn't understand Rose was not their real mother. Rose, quite frantic, begged me to intervene.

I explained to your mother, it was never my intent to tear my grandchildren from happy homes. I assured her I would reward her for the two little ones if she would simply come ahead to New York and leave them behind. Quite naturally, she agreed. I don't believe it was ever her intention to take up mothering at this late stage.

You are probably wondering what reward I offered and well you should. I hoped your mother would come to run my household and I promised her a monthly stipend in return. She was anxious to climb from the ranks of impoverished widow and so, accepted. My offer to provide an increased stipend for every child she managed to bring was meant to unite your family, if only for a visit. I'm afraid she took my proposal much too literally and proceeded to gather you all without any thought for your welfare.

The enclosed check is from your grandmother's estate. My Nelda managed her own funds, and her wish was to give you a good start in life. Even though I understand her love for you, I must admit I do not understand why you were singled out for this inheritance. I am, nonetheless, committed to fulfilling her wishes and hope you might use a portion of the funds to visit me in New York.

I am thrilled to provide a home for your brothers, however temporary. Their devotion to you is commendable, something I have only rarely witnessed in my long life. David assures me he intends to find a way back to Santa Barbara on his 18th birthday. Samuel, though less vocal, seems similarly committed. I explained they would need money to complete this journey so I pulled a few strings to see they both were given business opportunities. David, especially, seems well-suited to business, a characteristic none of my own children possess. I hope you will encourage the boys to stay in New York. I can provide far-reaching opportunities you might only imagine. Because their dedication to you is so complete, I will not hold them back if they wish to return. Your mother is, curiously, something of an obstacle in that regard but one I'm certain could be overcome.

However, it is young Jonah who most needs your attention. The boy is unhappy here. He talks about you incessantly, suffers from nightmares and begs to be returned to your care. I'm certain your visit would be welcomed. Perhaps, as a family, we could sit down and decide our best course of action.

I am ashamed to admit, I always left family responsibilities to your grandmother. Since I was happy to live the life of a businessman, domestic matters were her exclusive domain. Since her death, I have been a lonely old man. I wish only to make amends. This has somehow backfired to an alarming degree but most of your mother's undertakings have failed in the past. Perhaps she was born under an unlucky star.

I have also written to Lucy. I understand she is a newlywed but hope she will find it in her heart to visit her old grandfather in the not-too-distant future. I would like nothing so much as for you girls to come together. We could all be reunited if only for a few days. I'm certain your Aunt Rose would agree to bring the little ones so you could see them again.

I have rambled on long enough but allow me to repeat, it is my sincere desire to see you once more. I learned late in life how important family is. To my credit, I always understood the value of my loving wife. A good marriage to a trustworthy and supportive spouse is a true blessing, one I have always cherished.

Enjoy your grandmother's gift. I know you will put it to good use. I feel as if I know you. Your brothers talk the ears off anyone who will listen, eager to extol your virtues. God bless you.

Your devoted Grandfather Sherman

Hannah stuffed the letter back in her pocket. She now had the wherewithal to live any way she liked. Mr. Oddgood would doubtless buy her half of the business if she chose to sell. Suddenly, there were more options in life than Hannah ever dreamed of.

Evidently, her mother's devotion to family was purely financial, possibly a problem easily solved. Determined to take no action until she felt secure in her decisions, Hannah took one last look around the future home of Granville and Oddgood as she composed a response to her grandfather's letter in her head.

* * *

Bitsy paused in front of her father-in-law's new offices. Father Oddgood was thrilled to find a business relationship in time to save his house from foreclosure. It further served to give him a new outlook on life. Although her excuse for visiting was familial, her true reason was to speak to Hannah Granville.

Bitsy received regular and uninvited reports from Dock on Hollis' state of mind. Really, she was a married woman with a baby. How much time did she have to play matchmaker?

Yet, that was her intention as she breezed through the entrance and inquired of the receptionist, "Is Mr. Oddgood in?" Bitsy knew he was not.

"No ma'am. He won't be in today. Miss Granville is available. Did you have an appointment?"

"I'm Mr. Oddgood's daughter-in-law. I found myself downtown and thought I'd pay a visit. I'm sorry I missed him."

"Is this Mr. Oddgood's grandchild? He'll be disappointed he missed you."

As if on cue, Hannah stepped through a doorway, apparently ready to leave the office. A polka dot band accented her fashionable black tilt hat. Her gray pinstripe suit had a white collar and buttoned near the shoulder. Bitsy remembered the girl was fashionably attired at her wedding but her clothing today was truly stunning. Hannah exuded confidence and wealth. She looked every bit the successful businesswoman. Bitsy felt overwhelmed. Perhaps her plan was ill-advised.

"Aunt Bitsy?"

"Hello, Hannah. I stopped by to see the new office. I hoped to catch my father-in-law and invite myself to lunch."

"He's not in."

"So I've been given to understand."

"Is this your son? What a little doll he is," gushed Hannah, unable to take her eyes off the baby.

"Thank you." Bringing Alex was an afterthought. Perhaps he was the ice-breaker Bitsy needed. "Would you like to hold him? Oh, I'm sorry. Were you on your way out?"

"I'm actually done here. I was on my way home. I would like to hold him."

"I'm starving. Would you join me for lunch? We could go across the street and eat at the Woolworth's counter. You could hold the baby there." Bitsy saw Hannah's reluctance to share conversation but the lure of holding Alex won out.

"I'd love to."

Bitsy kept the conversation light, hoping Hannah

would inquire after Hollis' wellbeing. Hannah charmed little Alex, who seemed fascinated by the strange, lovely lady. Hannah was clearly smitten. Bitsy surmised, despite Hannah's fine clothes and success, this was a woman in need of a family.

"I can't get over how wonderful you look," admitted Bitsy.

"Thank you. I don't think I look much different than I ever did."

"No, there's a definite change in you. You are hardly the shy girl who traveled here in Hollis' automobile. You're confident and successful. You're very beautiful."

"You're kind to say so."

"Hollis bought a new car."

"Did he?" Hannah turned her full attention on little Alex.

"I think it was meant to appease his unhappiness." Bitsy waited for commentary, which was not forthcoming. She decided to plunge ahead. "It didn't work. I've been worried about Hollis. He cares deeply for you. Hollis and I were close growing up. I would do anything for him. I was hoping I could persuade you to talk to him."

Hannah gave a weak smile as she handed Alex back to his mother.

"It's been a delightful lunch. I'll get the check. Lovely seeing you."

Hannah beat a path to the cash register. She waved before she turned and walked determinedly toward the front of the store.

Bitsy took a last sip of coffee and looked down at Alex.

"Well, we are failures as matchmakers, you and I," she admitted. "We probably should have gone a little slower. Clothes make the man, that's what they say. Maybe Hannah's attire makes her appear so capable and mature." The more she considered this idea, the more Bitsy imagined she read Hannah's shyness as sophisticated disdain. "Did you hear her call me Aunt Bitsy? There is more of the girl in that particular parcel than meets the eye."

Bitsy might be grasping at straws but it seemed Hannah Granville's feelings for Hollis were undiminished. Why else would she leave at the mention of his name?

* * *

"Come on, Hollis. You can't back out now," urged Dock. "You'll like this girl. It's been months since you went on a date. This is like riding a horse. You get bucked off, you gotta get right back on."

Hollis did not appreciate the analogy and scowled at his brother. "I was drunk when I agreed to this."

"Well, hell, go ahead and get drunk now if it helps. I set this up 'cause you agreed. It's just a dance. You ain't forgot how to dance have you?"

"It hasn't been months."

"Nit-picking at me ain't gonna change the facts. You ain't seen that girl since June and September is fading fast."

"No. I saw her in July."

"Hollis, get your ass in gear and come on, now. You know I'll pester you till you do. We'll have a fine time. I'm the best judge of women you'll ever meet and Susan is a humdinger."

"Then why didn't you take her out?"

"Even I can only manage one date at a time." Dock slapped his brother on the back and steered him toward the front door.

As the evening progressed, Hollis began to think

his brother might know what he was talking about. It was true, Hollis' heart gave a lurch when they entered the Carrillo Ballroom. After all, he and Hannah spent many pleasant evenings there. Dock had no way of knowing when he planned the date.

It didn't take much to impress the attractive Susan. She was tall with red wavy hair and bright blue eyes. Her fresh freckled face, red lips and buxom figure were probably most men's idea of a model girlfriend. She wore a simple blue cotton dress and appeared the embodiment of chaste womanhood. Hollis suddenly comprehended the reason Dock was not interested.

The two couples enjoyed a fountain drink and conversation before the band began to play. Hollis struggled to pay attention, smiling when he failed to keep up, too intent on his own thoughts to do justice to the friendly banter.

Once Dock took his date to the dance floor, an awkward silence ensued. It was clear to Hollis, as he admired the sociable Susan, she was keen on him. She hung on every word he managed to utter and gushed encouragement when he replied to her banal attempts at conversation.

Hollis had little choice when he inquired, "Would you like to dance?"

"Oh, I would, I would."

Hollis held her chair and offered his arm to lead Susan onto the dance floor. He took up dance position as the band played the sultry *When Your Lover Has Gone*.

Closing his eyes, Hollis recalled the last time he heard the song. He held Hannah in his arms, swaying almost imperceptibly to the rhythm. Hannah leaned into his chest. She always surrendered so completely when they danced, and when they kissed and when they—

Hollis jumped back, holding a stunned Susan at

arm's length.

"I don't want you."

"Excuse me?" uttered the surprised Susan, looking around to see if anyone was watching.

"I don't want you." Hollis was unprepared for the devastated expression on the girl's features. "I'm sorry. I didn't mean it that way."

"I think you made yourself quite clear."

"No. I'm in love with someone, someone else. She doesn't love me. It's too soon. I can't do this." Hollis turned and marched out the door. He didn't mean to be cruel but he needed out. He needed air.

Chapter Twenty

At first, Hannah could not decide if she liked her living room. She stood in the doorway to the hall, trying to determine if the funds she spent were worth the result.

Hannah took Hollis' long-ago advice and hired a fixer upper. The man built book cases with glass doors on either side of the fireplace and applied crown molding, wainscoting and a chair rail. He built a closet in the attic for Hannah's new and impressive wardrobe. He gave her a quote to build a wider, safer staircase, but Hannah knew she would never replace the one Hollis and her brothers built.

She purchased a new dresser and headboard, which were inserted into the attic through the window by a pulley and rope.

Her sudden good fortune meant hours spent shopping for dresses, suits, shoes, hats, purses and gloves, blouses and trousers, all of the highest quality. A new Magic Chef stove trimmed in jade green and the latest model Kelvinator refrigerator were now ensconced in her kitchen.

Hannah took on a substantial share of the work. She was the one to paint the wainscoting, shelves and fireplace a pure white. The walls of her living room were now a soft fern green. She sewed drapes from pink gingham fabric for the front windows and sanded and varnished the wood floors.

Then came more shopping. Hannah decided against a sofa, instead purchasing four overstuffed easy chairs, which now encircled a round mahogany coffee table. The chairs were covered in soft pink floral fabric on a white background. She hung a mirror over the fireplace. Two small round tables sat on opposite sides of the coffee table between the two pair of chairs. Each table held a white lamp and shade. Hannah purchased a pale area rug to cozy up the seating area. A crystal chandelier hung above the coffee table. Always filled with flowers from Hannah's garden, a large white vase took center stage beneath the chandelier.

She used books and knickknacks to fill the new cupboards on the sides of the fireplace. A mismatched collection of plates purchased at rummage sales hung on the wall outside the boys' bedroom. There was enough room for a small writing desk beside the front door.

As she studied her handiwork, Hannah knew she created an incredibly feminine room, one no man would approve. But that was just as well. She did not intend to share her house again, unless her brothers somehow managed to return. Hannah kept the door to their bedroom closed.

A sudden feeling of dread came over her. Hannah worked relentlessly to improve her wardrobe, and her house and gardened daily. She made barely a dent in her windfall and was making more money from her business while working less than ever before. Nothing needed doing in the bathroom or kitchen. She was at the end of home improvements. The distractions that kept her mind off Hollis Rumsford were no longer viable.

Hannah's desperation to find new activities ebbed for the moment as she decided her living room was exactly as she envisioned. Her house was pretty, well-kept and completely repaired, inside and out. Though still developing, her gardens were coming along nicely. Deciding to visit the graveyard and put some flowers on Mrs. Durnam's family graves, Hannah began a market list in her head. She could spend the afternoon cooking but needed groceries. She would continue to take refuge in activity for as long as possible. Perhaps it was time to do something to the porch.

Grabbing a pair of garden shears from her kitchen drawer, Hannah remembered there were red roses in bloom at the side of the front porch. She used the opportunity to take a look around. Her usual porch activity consisted of kissing Hollis.

There was more space than she ever considered. She regretted having not utilized the porch when the boys were there.

As Hannah turned her attention to the rose bush, it seemed to shudder. Curious what caused the unnatural movement, Hannah crept to the edge of the porch and looked down to find a small boy picking her roses.

"Excuse me. What do you think you're doing?"

No sooner were those words out of her mouth than the boy dropped the roses and ran toward the front gate. This gave Hannah the opportunity to catch him. The latch was in need of oil. The gate tended to stick.

Hannah grabbed the boy's arm and spun him around to face her. The child was rail thin. His shirt and overalls were mended in several places. Before she could admonish him for his thievery, the larcenous child began a frantic explanation.

"I didn't mean nothin' by it, lady. It's just, the roses were real purty and my ma don't have anything nice. I thought she might like a few flowers. They was just growin' there all by theirselves. I didn't think anybody would care if I picked 'em. Please let me go! I swear, I won't try an' take your flowers again. You have my word. And the word of James John Caulfield is good anyplace at all. Please, lady. Don't vex my ma."

"Well, it so happens I was preparing to cut some roses myself so you saved me the trouble."

Hannah surveyed the youngster carefully. He was an Okie if ever there was one, from his bowl-shaped haircut to his bare feet. She remembered her brothers' tales about the kindness of strangers they encountered on their trip to Santa Barbara.

"Perhaps we could strike a bargain," began Hannah. "Since I need some roses, do you think you might help me out?"

"How?"

"I will let you use my shears and I'll go get a bucket so you can cut the rest. If you manage to do a good job, I have some cookies and milk for you and I'll let you take some roses to your mother. Do we have a deal?"

The boy's immense relief was apparent. "Sure. I'll shake on it."

Hannah offered her hand. "How old are you, James John Caulfield?"

"I'm seven years old."

Hannah retrieved a bucket, handed over the shears and allowed James John to do his best. If he cut the stems on the short side, at least he was thorough. Not a rose remained. Hannah brought a plate of cookies and glass of milk to her newfound gardening companion and sat on the porch steps beside him while he ate.

"Do you live around here, James John?"

A guilty look met her question. "Not ezactly."

"What does that mean?"

"My pa works on a farm not far away. He don't like my ma to work in the fields but a lot of families do. I'm big enough what I could. I got a little sister, Teddie. My ma has to look after her."

"But where do you live?"

"It ain't nice livin' on the farms. It stinks there. The food is bad. There ain't much of a outhouse. So, we live in a tent."

Hannah saw tent cities full of indigents on her way to Santa Barbara but never imagined one was nearby.

"I wish you would do me a favor, James John. You see, my brother lived here until recently. He outgrew a whole box full of clothes while he was here. I need to get rid of them. You could sure help me out if you took them home to your ma. I'd like to send the rest of those cookies, too. If they stay here, they'll go to waste. I could never eat all those cookies. Could you do that for me?"

"I guess."

Hannah packed up a basket with Jonah's old clothes, the cookies, some cans of food from her pantry and a bunch of roses. She slipped a five-dollar bill in the bottom and handed the basket to James John.

"Take this to your mother. And, thank you for your help today. Tell her you did a lot of work for me."

Hannah watched as a jubilant James John managed to open the front gate, lugging the basket as he walked down the street. Nothing Hannah did in the last months made her feel as satisfied as she did this minute. She was lucky. She had so much. Perhaps there was an outlet for her pent-up energy. Desperate to provide for her own family, she never considered the plight of the poor.

* * *

June Caulfield marched behind her son, carrying baby Teddie in her arms. It was a warm day and James John certainly walked a long distance to get himself in trouble. Why couldn't the boy position his tribulations closer to home? The problem was, the Caulfields were proud people. Charity was not required nor welcome.

"You understand what we're doing, don't you, James John?"

"Yes, ma'am."

"We are Caulfields. We don't need help. We are a strong and able people. Is this the house?"

"Yes, ma'am."

"Good. I'll come along but I want you to return the food, flowers and clothing to this lady."

"But Ma, I earned that. The lady said."

"I don't think you could have possibly earned anything close to this. There was money in the basket."

"I don't know nothin' about no money. I just know I did the lady a favor by taking the clothes so she didn't have to get rid of them. I helped her pick the flowers. I guess she put the money in so Teddie could have somethin' new."

"It sounds to me like you were stealing, James John. Can you explain?"

"Well, mebbe I was in the beginning, just a little. But it didn't turn out that way at all. I only took the flowers anyhow. Nobody was using 'em."

"Go up and ring the bell." Expecting an elderly woman to answer, someone too frail to pick flowers, June was surprised when a young girl came to the door.

Smiling, Hannah began, "Hello James John. May I help you?"

"My ma says I gotta' return the basket and them goods to you. Here you go."

"You must be Mrs. Caulfield."

"I am. We don't take charity. Thank you for your kindness, but you best pass this along to folks that need it."

June gave a wary look at her son as the girl put her hand over her eyes. Her shoulders seemed to shudder. It was difficult to determine if she was laughing or crying but it soon became evident the girl was in the throes of considerable despair.

"Miss?" inquired June.

"The lady's all upset," James John surmised as he sat the basket on the porch and walked down the steps to his mother.

June may not have needed charity herself but she was not a cold person. It was her Christian duty to see if she could help.

"Miss?" she began again as she stepped onto the porch and touched Hannah's arm. "Are you all right?"

"No, no, I'm not all right," a tearful Hannah sobbed. "Helping you was the highlight of the last few months. I finally felt useful. Now you don't even want it!"

"It's not that," explained a flustered Mrs. Caulfield. "We are proud people. We don't take charity. Why, my husband would throw a fit if he knew James John was out soliciting favors from total strangers."

"He didn't. He wanted to give you something lovely. There was a time I wouldn't have understood, but my brothers were here and Hollis showed me it was more important to love them than to punish them when they were just being boys." Once Hannah started, the words poured out. All illusions of maturity quickly vanished. She did not even register Mrs. Caulfield's shocked expression nor James John's curious one. Even the baby stared at her.

"Now everyone is gone. My brothers are gone, Hollis is gone. I've lost my family for the second time. I'm all alone. I only wanted to pass on Jonah's old clothes; it pains me so to see them. And when James John expressed a sincere interest in brightening your day, how could I be mad at him? He's a sweet little boy and so caring. I thought you could use the food and I can certainly spare five dollars.

"When I came to Santa Barbara, I had nothing. My brothers are gone and I have money. I wanted to help *somebody*. Now you're offended, and I can't help you and I'm all alone. I didn't know it would matter so much. All I wanted was a place to call my own and a good job. I thought I would be happy then. Nothing has gone right, nothing! I can't turn Hollis into something he's not. I lost everything that matters to me, everything really important! And I didn't even understand how good things were when my house was full of people."

June could see this girl needed more help than the Caulfield family.

"There, there," she declared as she put her arm around the girl and guided her through her front door. "Things can't be all that bad, can they?"

"Well, things can always get worse. One can imagine horrible things: a fire, or sickness or death. I suppose I'll have to take comfort in that. Helping you made me feel good. I wanted to do more and now you've returned my gesture of good will."

"Would it help if we accepted the basket?"

Nodding vigorously, the girl agreed, "It would."

June wondered how her intention to return the charity basket came full circle so quickly. "Where is your kitchen? Perhaps we could sit down and have a cup of tea and a good conversation."

"All right," agreed Hannah, still sobbing, as she

allowed herself to be led inside. "The kitchen is back here."

"You play on the porch, James John," June commanded as she entered the cozy little home. She could not recall the last time she was inside a house. Curiously, the girl removed an object from the mantle and returned to her front door.

"Here, James John. I'm keeping this for my brother but I'm certain he wouldn't mind if you played with his tiger."

Hannah gave a timid smile to Mrs. Caulfield, who appeared a model of serene self-assurance, when in fact she was completely befuddled by Hannah's confusing litany of difficulties.

Tears streaming down her cheeks, Hannah managed to put a kettle of water on her new stove. Then, she produced a quilt from a basket near the door and spread it on the floor so Teddie could inspect her recently discovered toes.

All sense of etiquette and decorum evaporated in the frank discussion that followed. The two women were strangers, bound by difficult circumstances, sharing intimate details of their lives. Hannah inadvertently set the parameters for the candid nature of their conversation.

"James John told me you lived in a tent. I thought about what it would be like after he left. What would I most desire if I lived in a tent? Don't you long to take a bath? Just soak in a tub at your leisure?" Hannah took in her guest's shocked expression. "Oh, don't take this the wrong way. You look entirely clean, surprisingly so. James John does not but boys are boys. I understand completely. You don't even know my name." Hannah offered her hand and introduced herself. "I'm Hannah Granville. Please call me Hannah."

June shook the offered hand. "You can call me June."

Hannah launched a series of questions, barely giving June a chance to respond. Before their first cup of tea was consumed, June, normally a discreet person, found herself openly discussing her current circumstances: what it was like living in a tent in a Hooverville and how her small family came to this low point.

"Let me get this straight. You have a tent, bedding and a cook stove. Your husband comes home on Sunday and provides funds for food. It does sound remarkably like camping out but on a permanent basis."

"My husband has been working steady picking hops but that work is about done for this year."

"It's too bad you invested so heavily in farm equipment right before the depression began. Do you feel safe, where you're living now?" inquired Hannah.

"I feel pretty safe. There are other families. We ladies stick together. There's only a small group of us so far. But we've been in places before where the sheriff or vigilantes came and threw us out. Then we have to start all over somewhere else. I'm about fed up. The next time they come to kick us out, I'm not going anywhere until I pack my things. Lord knows there are few enough of those," June complained then stopped short, realizing how much of her private life she was revealing to a stranger.

But June soon became both enthralled and appalled as Hannah confessed her own tribulations. She started, inappropriately, with her father's suicide.

Hannah finished her recital by explaining her business success and gave a tour of the recent improvements in her home.

"You see, there's really nothing to keep me here

except my house."

"What about your friends?"

"My only real friend is living down the coast, in Carpinteria. To be honest, she doesn't know the things I told you. Hollis is the only one who knows everything and I have to keep him out of my life. Surely, you can see that?" inquired Hannah, seeking validation for her current circumstances.

June could see the disappointment in her new friend's expression. Hannah was eight years her junior, and suffered through the years since her father died, but there was a refreshing innocence to her or perhaps it was some naïve hope in an uncertain future. June believed the girl was still in love.

"I suppose so. From what you say, your Hollis would make a terrible husband, if he even intended to marry you. Maybe you should go and visit your grandfather and see your brothers. Maybe you could better envision your future. I have to tell you, I envy the choices you have."

Hannah stared across the table. "I never had choices before. I realize how incredibly lucky I was when I came to Santa Barbara. I need to concentrate on being thankful for what I have instead of dwelling on what was never meant to be. You helped me today."

"Hannah, I didn't do anything but listen. I must admit, it felt good to do my own complaining. Some days, I feel ready to explode. I'm impatient and tired. I never dreamed my life would be like this. My husband has always been responsible and a hard worker. Now, he is as lost and confused a man as you could possibly imagine."

"This is why you have to let me help you."

Before the hour was out, Hannah stood at the kitchen sink, giving Teddie a bath. A complete stranger was lounging in the bathtub across the hall. Her guest's clean clothes flapped on the clothesline. James John, wearing a pair of Jonah's pajama bottoms secured by a clothespin, was helping himself to cookies at the kitchen table. Hannah regretted her clothes were too small to donate to June.

After Hannah served a hearty dinner, the Caulfield family, dressed in their clean clothing, prepared to make the journey home.

"You could stay here," offered Hannah. "There are unused beds in my brothers' bedroom and—"

"No, Hannah. I appreciate your generosity today but my husband is a proud man. I can't belittle him by taking your charity." Hannah's crestfallen expression spoke volumes. "I envy you. You really made something of yourself. You have a lovely home, an automobile and a successful business. I see you envy me, as well. But you'll have a family of your own, I'm certain. Probably sooner than you think. And I like to believe I will have a home again before long. Today has been a wonderful day—a vacation for me."

"I enjoyed having you here. It seems so clear—how much I miss having family around. I like to think I was good at running a household and caring for my brothers." June noticed Hannah did not mention Hollis. "Could I drive you home?"

"Why not?"

As Hannah drove toward the canyon where the Caulfields lived, June pulled a magazine out of her purse.

"I want to give you something in return."

"Oh, that's not necessary."

"I know but there's a quilt pattern inside I think you'd enjoy. It's an old copy of *Farm Wife* I picked up at a bring-and-buy. Read the article, too."

Before the Caulfields walked toward the canyon and their tent, Hannah extracted a promise they would come to visit soon.

When Hannah reentered her empty home, it seemed like hours rather than minutes since children's laughter filled the house. Never realizing how purposeless her life was, Hannah glanced at the magazine.

Thumbing through the pages, she located an illustration of a quilt block and read the accompanying article, submitted by the woman who designed the block. She lived in Missouri and wrote not of her difficulties caused by the depression but of two birds she watched out the window.

The birds huddled together to weather a storm. The farm wife recognized she pulled away from her husband during their difficulties. The birds helped her understand the way forward was to pull together. Hannah thought the message inappropriate to her own circumstances and wondered why June thought the article so apt.

* * *

Glancing in the mirror before leaving for work, Hannah tipped her hat slightly to the left and was surprised by the sound of someone walking across her porch. Although she rarely had company, it seemed something unpleasant was always showing up on her doorstep. Hannah contemplated not answering but relented to find Mr. Rowland, his own hat in hand.

"Come in," Hannah offered. "What are you doing here?"

"No, I can't come in. I need to explain something. You come outside. The photographer will be here soon."

Hannah obligingly stepped through the front door onto her newly decorated porch. She couldn't help but smile every time she walked across that porch. A small table and chairs occupied one end, two rocking chairs were located near the door and a porch swing filled the far end. Potted flowers and cheery floral fabrics made the outdoor area seem like an additional room of the house. The mild beach nights ensured Hannah could take advantage of the new space each evening until darkness made it impossible to see. Mr. Rowland's obvious admiration confirmed Hannah's belief she did a masterful job improving the front of her house. Then, her thoughts returned to his comments.

"What photographer?"

"I knew I gave this house to you in terrible condition. I was getting telephone calls on an almost daily basis from your neighbors and my brother. Although they tried every conceivable idea to get me to sell, I knew they stopped short of involving officials." This drew a curious frown from Hannah. "You see, if they tried to have the property condemned, I wouldn't have hesitated to tear down the house and clear the property. The graveyard would have been perfectly obvious, something your neighbors wished to avoid. I hoped everyone would settle down and leave you in peace. I underestimated my brother. You see, your two neighbors put forward a petition to have your house condemned."

"No!"

"Don't be alarmed. I have friends in high places who tipped me off, knowing the property once belonged to me. The unfortunate fact is, photographs of this house from the time it was mine, inside and out, have been submitted. They make a compelling case against you.

"All that's necessary to rectify the situation is documentation of the work you've done. Your house obviously does not need to be condemned. I got you in the middle of this little war and I want to apologize. I'll take care of the details. There's no need for you to worry."

"I can't lose this house, Mr. Rowland. I will do anything to help. Do you need pictures of the interior?"

"I think exterior photos are all we need. The paint, the new roof, and the garden make it obvious the home is being cared for and is in good repair."

"I'm proud of the inside of my house," offered Hannah.

"I'll take the pictures to my friend. I'm sure there won't be any further problems. Even Mr. Barney put in a good word for you."

"Mr. Barney?"

"Yes, he has influence with the Chamber of Commerce, the city and even county officials. He's been a member of the Santa Barbara Historical Society and before that, the Plans and Planting Committee, probably the most important organizations in this city. You see, Hannah, it pays to have good customers. I assure you, no harm will come to your little house."

"Thank you does not seem enough to say." Mr. Rowland was stunned to see tears well in young Hannah's eyes. "My home means the world to me. I can't lose it."

Avery suddenly felt a cad. He believed the house would motivate Hannah to make the most of her business and settle down. He never understood how important the home was to her. This property was a game to him, a way to irritate his brother and little else. Even the showdown over saving the property from being condemned was more a lark than a serious defense of Hannah's home.

Now, he saw she poured her heart and soul into this venture. It was her only interest since her brothers moved 3,000 miles away. Although not privy to most of Hannah's personal difficulties, he understood some suitor was recently put out to pasture.

"I think I need to apologize," he offered. "I embroiled you in a rich man's game. It seems cruel."

Hannah took a moment to decipher Mr. Rowland's apology. She never thought of him as rich but knew he bought and sold property. She suddenly understood his position at the Vista Mar Monte was never his primary source of income.

"If this is your game, I only profited from it. I don't think your apology is necessary."

"Why don't you help the photographer? I'm certain you can explain your improvements far better than I." Mr. Rowland instructed the photographer to take a few shots of Hannah's living room and kitchen, still doubting any other photos were necessary.

Before the photographer left, Hannah pointed out every enhancement she accomplished. The transformation from hovel to comfortable bungalow was documented carefully. Even a contented Boots was photographed asleep on the hearth.

As the photographer left, Mr. Rowland paused at Hannah's front door. "There's something else I want to tell you."

Hannah's mentor seemed rather nervous. She wondered what other difficulty she might be in.

"I met someone."

"Someone like who?"

"A lady. I'm serious about her, I think. I'd like you to meet her. She's a widow with three grown children and a daughter still at home. I believe the daughter is about your age. Aside from my sister, you are the person who means the most to me. I don't know why I've been so dense about this. Something about this morning made it quite clear. I would like your opinion of this lady friend of mine and I'm hoping you might join us for dinner sometime this week."

Smiling, Hannah consented, "I would be delighted."

Hannah waved as Mr. Rowland drove away. She folded her arms and considered the fact Mr. Barney had come to her aid. What a strange world it was. Hollis would be amazed at this turn of events. So much happened. Hannah frowned. Hollis would never know.

Chapter Twenty-One

Grinning, Bitsy closed her front door and looked toward her husband.

"I think that went well."

"What dinner were you at? I can't imagine it going worse."

"How can you say that, Silas?"

Silas was incredulous. "I never imagined in my wildest dreams you would enjoy the role of matchmaker. I suppose, realistically, I have been a fool. Women are matchmakers, that's just what they are."

"Nonsense. I'm not playing matchmaker. I tried my best to get Hannah to talk to Hollis, to no avail. He deserves to be happy. It's been months. Judith is a lovely girl and not at all like Hannah. It was obvious she's interested."

"And he did everything in his power to discourage her. He was embarrassed the entire evening. It was the most awkward dinner I ever sat through in my life. You shamelessly threw that girl at your nephew from the moment he walked in the door. He is a handsome fellow. Any girl would be interested. And what do you mean, *you* tried your best to get Hannah to talk to him?"

"Oh," Bitsy didn't mean to let that slip out. She bit her lip and contemplated how she might explain to Silas' satisfaction. "Well, I happened to run into Hannah downtown." This was true enough. "She was thrilled about the baby so I asked her to lunch at Woolworth's. I happened to mention Hollis' name in passing and she just up and left the counter. Even though I believed she must have feelings for him, I doubted Hollis would ever win her over. I coaxed him to move on."

"And he told you he wasn't ready, isn't that what you said? Then you decided to force his hand."

"Exactly. Things went much better than I expected."

"Why? Because Hollis didn't walk out on you, too? I assure you, he wanted to. Hell, I wanted to walk out."

"There's no need to be vulgar."

"Bitsy, you must stay out of Hollis' affairs. He doesn't like what you did tonight. I didn't like what you did. Once Judith understands this was all for naught, she isn't going to like it either."

"Who says nothing will come of it?"

"I would bet my life on it. Stop meddling, Bitsy."

The baby started to cry. Silas watched his wife's lip quiver. A tear trailed down her cheek. "You don't have to be rude. You don't understand. Men are so thick-headed. I simply want Hollis to be happy, the way we are!" Bitsy shouted as she turned toward the nursery.

"Women," mumbled Silas as his wife left the room. Prohibition couldn't end soon enough for him.

* * *

Hannah made her way down Chapala Street, pausing when someone called her name. Looking around, she was surprised to find Mrs. Durnam leaning out the window of a limousine, trying to get her attention. Grinning, Hannah walked toward the car and put her hand out to catch Mrs. Durnam's.

"What are you doing here?" asked Hannah.

"Don't go yet, Wilson," commanded Mrs. Durnam.

"The sign says go, Madam. I have no choice."

"If you move forward, it will cost my arm!" yelled Mrs. Durnam, so loudly pedestrians on the sidewalk paused to see what was happening.

"Have Wilson pull to the curb, I'll meet you there," offered Hannah as she attempted to extricate her hand from Mrs. Durnam's surprisingly strong grip.

"Promise me, you'll follow?"

"Certainly. Go ahead Wilson, I'll catch up."

It took Wilson a block to find a spot by the curb. When Hannah approached the vehicle, she noted Mrs. Durnam's relieved expression.

"Climb in, dear," urged Mrs. Durnam. "I want to take you to tea. I insist. You were such a charming hostess. You must allow me to return the favor."

"Very well," responded Hannah. "I was on my way to the bank but it can wait."

"Oh, yes, your business. How are things going?"

"My business is going well."

"I would say so by the looks of your wardrobe." Mrs. Durnam took a careful look at Hannah's immaculately tailored aqua, Swiss dot, short-sleeved suit with white collar, sleeve bands and buttons. A pert aqua bow tie added a proper amount of business to the ensemble.

"When did you come back to Santa Barbara?" inquired Hannah, surprised as Mrs. Durnam raised a gloved finger to her lips.

"The walls have ears," she whispered, mysteriously. Once Mrs. Durnam bid Wilson continue to their destination, the two ladies chatted amiably about the beautiful weather and delightful scenery.

Before Hannah could assimilate her exciting ride in Mrs. Durnam's limousine, she found herself seated at a discreet window table at the tea room in the Biltmore Hotel in Montecito, the most luxurious resort in the entire Santa Barbara area.

"I feel like a character in an Agatha Christie novel," commented Hannah, "whisked away in broad daylight and taken by limousine to an extraordinary locale. You must tell me what this is about. When did you return to Santa Barbara?"

"I have lost my home."

"Oh, how terrible. Have you nowhere to stay? You can stay with me." But Hannah quickly realized if Mrs. Durnam were destitute, she would not be riding around in a limousine and having tea at the most expensive venue in a city devoted to entertaining the rich.

"You are such a dear girl. I simply mean, I have an unwelcome guest and when my grandniece offered to put me up, I jumped at the chance. I hope I don't wear out my welcome. She has come to appreciate what a lot of fun I am! I have no idea if Wilson's loyalties lie with my daughter so I don't like to talk in front of him. It was my intention to come and visit you at my first opportunity.

"This is my first outing since I arrived," Mrs. Durnam confessed. "I know the summer events are designed to draw visitors during the off-season. But the crush of people for the Old Spanish Days Fiesta, the costume parades, pageants and concerts were too much for me. I don't even understand the fascination of Rancheros Vistadores. Why do tourists want to watch ranchers and their families ride on horseback from Mission Santa Barbara to Mission Santa Ynes in the heat of summer? At least the Semana Nautica is picturesque. I enjoyed watching yachts going out to greet the Navy ships anchored offshore—from my grandniece's balcony. Since the tourists are gone for a few weeks before the winter season starts in earnest, I felt it safe to venture out. I can't abide the tourists, you see."

Smiling, Hannah imagined Mrs. Durnam would likely be considered a tourist, visiting to enjoy the fine winter weather. "Who is your unwelcome guest?"

"My son-in-law passed away about five years ago. My daughter came to visit and never left. She is quite a tedious, boring girl. You would think by 60, she might have learned to be a bit more entertaining."

"Perhaps she misses her husband. It is a terrible thing to lose the person you love most in all the world."

Mrs. Durnam took a careful look at her young companion, who displayed a sorrow not apparent the last time the ladies chatted. "True, but I don't think my daughter lost anyone of particular importance. In all my life, I never saw two people more mismatched. They lived apart almost their entire marriage. But you sound as if you're speaking from experience. What happened to your Mr. Rumsford?"

"Oh, I never loved Hollis."

"Things did not work out, then?"

"No. I gave it my best. It looked for a while as if we might make a match."

"What happened?"

"He lied to me. I believed the lie at first and then it became clear he was simply stringing me along."

"I'm so sorry. Try the currant scone. It's delicious. What have you been doing since Mr. Rumsford proved untrustworthy? Working on your business, I'm sure."

"Yes. I took on a partner, an older gentleman, very

experienced. We hired staff to do the actual accounting. I visit customers and follow leads for new business. I spend a few hours in the office every day, mostly to confirm work is being done properly."

"You must have more time for your brothers." This comment served to deepen Hannah's mournful expression.

"My mother came and took the boys last June."

"I see. How are you spending your time?"

"I work on my house—gardening, painting, and remodeling a bit. I finally decorated the living room, and purchased new appliances and a swing for the porch. I never knew how pleasant it could be to swing on the porch and read or do needlework. I have my cat to keep me company."

"Hannah, you sound more like an old lady than I do. Don't you see friends? What about boys?"

"I do have a dear friend, Mollie. We had something of a falling out over Hollis. She didn't believe he was good enough for me. I can't muster the courage to confess she was right. I met a lovely family." Hannah bit her lip, not knowing how much she wished to reveal about the Caulfield family's difficult circumstances. She felt Mrs. Durnam might not approve.

"But you are young. You should be enjoying the company of gentlemen, going to dances or movies. An accomplished girl your age should be relishing every moment of your youth."

Hannah bit the other side of her lip in response.

"Oh, my dear girl, it's a good thing I am here. You need to have some fun!" Although Mrs. Durnam managed an engaging smile, she wanted nothing so much as to ring Hollis Rumsford's neck. What a fool that boy was to let this lovely girl get away.

"I'm glad to know you're not destitute," remarked

Hannah as she tried one of the tiny desserts. Observing Mrs. Durnam across the table, Hannah recalled how fortunate she'd been to fall into the company of affluent people. She doubted this would have been possible if not for her mother's relentless insistence on good grammar and manners. Hannah unconsciously fell into the same habit of promoting proper behavior in her brothers. This idea sparked Hannah's curiosity.

"Could I ask a question of a personal nature?"

"Anything."

"I know Santa Barbara is a destination for the wealthy. It always astounds me how many people here don't seem effected by the depression. You are a widow, on your own, but you weren't wiped out in the stock market crash, or you don't appear to have been. Now I'm saving money and need to know how to preserve it for the future. Do you have any advice?"

Mrs. Durnam chuckled. "My Archie always told me never to react impetuously, especially where money is concerned. I simply did not sell my stocks when the market crashed. Most of them have come back. My advice when it comes to money is never be spontaneous.

"That is not my advice regarding love, however. I may appear too old to know anything about romance, but my fondest memories are of youthful impetuous flirtations and my more meaningful romantic interest in dear Archie. You simply must get out in the world, Hannah. Surely there is some boy eager to take you out on the town?"

"I do know of one."

* * *

As Hollis drove on East Carrillo Street, he spotted Hannah's car parked in front of a soda shop. Pulling to the side of the road opposite her car, he parked his red, incredibly flashy LaSalle convertible coupe. Hollis did not understand what possessed him to purchase this new toy, aside from the fact he could.

Turning slightly in his seat, he settled in to get a glimpse of Hannah. If she saw him, so much the better. He could not recall how many times he wanted to park near her house, always talking himself out of it. He was certain the sight of her would be more than he could bear.

But she was near and he was determined to see her face, watch her walk. If he were lucky, he might find he was over her. Hollis was eager to get on with his life and make decisions about his future. This could be his day of catharsis or one of unabated pain.

Hollis did not have to wait long. Before he could change his mind, Hannah emerged from the soda fountain, accompanied by a young man—a soda jerk, dressed in apron and paper hat. The boy was tall, and lean, and sported a ridiculous grin as he looked down at Hannah. He walked her to the driver's side of her car and opened the door. There was too much traffic noise for Hollis to catch any of their conversation. Hannah waved as she drove away, leaving the young man standing in the street, watching after her.

Quickly deciding on a course of action, Hollis bounded from his vehicle and crossed the street.

"Pretty girl," Hollis began as he walked beside the smitten boy.

"She sure is."

"Your girl?"

"No, not yet. But I would like her to be. I've been after her to go on a date for months. She finally agreed. I think I might die of anticipation before Saturday rolls around."

"When you see her, tell her Hollis said hello."

"You know Hannah?"

"Much better than you can imagine," replied Hollis as he turned back to his LaSalle.

Hollis' heart pounded in his chest at sight of his former love, if she ever really was. Now he felt only bitterness. He needed to start over, somewhere he could never run into Hannah again. Somewhere he could make a new life. Somewhere he could stop hurting.

As he started his car and sped away, Hollis wondered why he stayed. What was he waiting for? To open his newspaper and find Hannah married the soda jerk or some other foolish boy? To catch a glimpse of her as she made her way through life without him?

He was pathetic. Finding a new job in a new city might be challenging so Hollis decided to ask for a transfer. Although most genteel and aristocratic Santa Barbarans snubbed the sprawling metropolis of Los Angeles, Hollis enjoyed the excitement and glamour of the city to the south.

If a transfer were out of the question, he would quit and return to Placerville. But that could wait until Monday. There was an icebox full of beer at home, albeit the low-alcohol beer now legal under the Cullen–Harrison Act. The illegal beer he used to buy was more potent. It would take a lot of the legal stuff to drown his sorrow appropriately.

Hollis was more passed out than asleep on the sofa in his living room when he had the dream. He awoke, his pulse rapid, his brow full of sweat. His heart ached. For the first time, Hannah's sweet face appeared out of the darkness to help him.

* * *

The morning already proved disappointing. June, baby in arms, appeared at the front door, exuding excitement, just as Hannah was leaving.

"I can't stay," she cautioned, interrupting Hannah's

greeting. "Mr. Caulfield found a job. A real job."

"Oh, how wonderful!"

"It is. He tried to find work at a place where they raise Palominos and the owner noticed his way with horses. Palominos are important to Santa Barbara. They were virtually extinct when a rancher here was able to breed them again." Pride emanated from the excited Mrs. Caulfield. "My husband has a job exercising horses and there is a house. We're going now. I'm sure it needs a lot of work but it's a house, Hannah!

"I wanted to come and let you know. I'll send you our address as soon as we're settled in."

It was not as if Hannah begrudged her friend the new home but once June bounded off the porch, loneliness settled there again.

After a short drive, Hannah took a deep breath and glanced at Lucy's card to assure she found the correct address. The home was lovely, though smaller than Hannah imagined.

It was a beautiful fall morning. Hannah meant to put this unpleasant chore behind her before she went to the office.

A man carrying a satchel emerged from the front door and proceeded toward an automobile parked in front of Hannah's. She exited her vehicle, smoothed her light blue, short-sleeved, sweater dress and proceeded to the front door.

A diminutive Chinese woman answered.

"Is Mrs. Edison at home?"

Jiao Lan eyed the stranger on the porch. In truth, Mrs. Edison, always a handful, was particularly irritating since her accident. Jiao Lan long considered herself to possess infinite patience. As the irritating little bell from Mrs. Edison's table rang again, Jiao Lan believed she deserved a brief respite. This girl might prove to be the distraction required. She never hesitated to use lack of understanding when an instruction was ignored. If she were lucky today, Mrs. Edison might not ascertain who broke her rules and admitted a guest.

"Have you an appointment, Madam?" inquired Jiao Lan.

"No. Mrs. Edison is my sister. I hoped to speak to her."

"Certainly, Madam," Jiao replied as she led the girl down the hallway.

Hannah gawked at the richly decorated home. Surely, Lucy could not have managed this in the few months since she married. It reminded Hannah of their home in Placerville. No one would have suspected the Granvilles suffered abject poverty from the looks of their home. Appearances were everything to Mother.

Hannah timidly entered a room near the end of the hallway and flinched when the maid closed the door behind her. Curious as she looked about, it took a moment for Hannah to notice a prone figure on the fainting couch near the window. A lacy sleeve fell nonchalantly over Lucy's face. Since she hadn't been announced, Hannah approached the couch as her sister rang the bell she held in her right hand.

"I think she left," offered Hannah.

A shocked Lucy lifted her arm to see who entered the room just long enough for Hannah to catch a glimpse.

Hannah quickly closed the distance between them and pulled Lucy's arm from her forehead.

"Merciful heavens! What happened to you?"

It was apparent Lucy was not prepared to answer. Hannah watched her sister struggle to concoct some believable story. "It's not as bad as it looks."

"I doubt that. It looks bad. How did this happen?"

"I fell. It was clumsy of me. There's no need to worry. The doctor was here. He said I'm healing nicely but I had a bad night. He gave me some medicine so I'm feeling sleepy. You should probably go."

"I will not go until you explain this." Hannah was appalled as she stared at Lucy's bruised and swollen face. No one would suspect she was a true beauty.

"Let go of my arm. You're hurting me."

Hannah complied but thought she saw bruises through the lacy fabric of Lucy's sleeve. She waited for further explanation.

"I fell down the stairs," Lucy finally admitted.

"Really? You fell down the stairs and bruised your entire face? I think you better imagine up some better explanation."

Lucy stalled for time, realizing she would simply doze off—the usual effect of the doctor's wonderful potions. "What are you doing here?"

"Grandfather has written me another letter."

"Another?"

"Yes. He first sent one after Mother took the boys. He said he wrote to you, as well."

"He did."

"You never wrote back?"

"I'm newly married, Hannah. It takes time to set up housekeeping."

"This house looks like it's been set up for some time." Hannah noted the house appeared settled, nothing like her own living room. There was something fresh about a newly furnished room.

It was difficult to read Lucy's expression due to her damaged and puffy face. Her angry tone of voice was easier to interpret.

"I'll admit, I had some help." The fact her new husband lived in the house for years and paid a professional to decorate were not facts Lucy cared to share. "I need sleep. What do you want?"

"I'm planning on going to New York. It's Grandfather's wish we all be together. I came to see if you and Gregory decided to visit."

"Because you're afraid to go alone?"

"I'll be truthful. I've never traveled by myself, much less across the entire country. I would be willing to make my plans to accommodate yours, if you decide to go."

"Gregory felt badly when he—when I fell. So badly, he decided to take me to Europe for a tour once I am healed. I expressed my desire to stop and see Mother before we cruise across the Atlantic. Since our honeymoon was brief, you would not be welcome to join us."

"I see."

"I assume Hollis might accompany you."

It would be impossible to discern slyness in one whose face was so distorted but Hannah believed Lucy was up to something.

"I broke off my relationship. I haven't seen Hollis in months." Hannah caught a twinkle dancing merrily in her sister's eyes.

"Too bad." Lucy gave a mighty yawn and continued, "I always enjoyed being seen with Hollis. He is such a good-looking man. You two stole the show at my wedding. I was incensed." Lucy's eyes fluttered as she struggled to stay awake. "I managed to get you back," she mumbled.

"How?" asked Hannah.

"Oh, I mean, you should go, Hannah. I can't stay awake. We'll talk some other time." No sooner were the words out of her mouth than Lucy dozed off.

Hannah decided to bide her time and see what

enlightening remarks might tumble out of her sister's mouth.

"You said something clever to me, didn't you?" she continued.

Lucy smiled but then grimaced. "I did it for Mother. She wanted as much of Grandfather's money as she could get. If you showed up in New York a bit late, she was certain it would still count in her favor. I didn't hesitate to tell her you would go along when she took the boys. I thought you would, Hannah. If it was Hollis who held you here, I found a way to—"

"To what, Lucy? Wake up and tell me." Hannah grabbed her sister by the shoulder and shook her gingerly. "What did you do?"

Lucy made an effort to prop her eyes open, to no avail. "I got Hollis out of the way," Lucy yawned again. "I thought for sure you would dump him if you thought he slept with me. I was right, wasn't I? I'm always right. Besides, why should you get Hollis Rumsford and a houseful of his little brats when I can't have a baby at all? Gregory was truly enraged—"

No sooner were those words out of Lucy's mouth than she fell into a deep sleep. Hannah was unable to rouse her further. She sat in the chair beside the fainting couch staring at her sister.

Hollis told her the truth all along and she didn't believe him. Why did she ever believe Lucy, who she knew to be deceitful?

Hannah raised her hand to cover her mouth. At minimum, she owed Hollis an apology. As she considered some way to accomplish this, a question turned in her mind. What future did she want?

* * *

Having been on dates before, Bud was surprised how unsure he felt. He stood on Miss Granville's porch and pulled nervously at his collar before knocking on the door.

Hannah answered, looking radiant in her raspberry-colored dress. Bud eyed her from her wide-brimmed, brown hat to her brown-and-white, buckled, spectator heels, which probably added three inches to her height. The belt of her dress wrapped around her low-cut cross-over bodice. The short, puffed sleeves were gathered in white lace bands. His date was fashionably attired for him and him alone. He was speechless.

"Good evening," offered Hannah.

"Yes, good evening," stammered Bud, who seemed rooted in place, unable to speak further.

"Should we go then?" helped Hannah as she draped a sweater over her arm.

"Certainly." Bud blushed but remembered to offer his arm as he escorted the lovely Hannah Granville to his father's 1931 Chevrolet coupe.

"What a beautiful car." Hannah started to think she would have to provide all conversation.

"Yes, it is. It's just swell," replied Bud. This was not exactly a lie. Normally not tongue-tied, Bud climbed into the driver's seat and managed to find a topic. "Before I forget, I ran into a man the other day. He told me to tell you Hollis says hello."

"Oh. Where did you run into him?"

"In the street, the day I saw you to your car. I think it was Thursday."

"What else did he have to say?"

"Nothing. He has a fine car. My dad's is pretty plain."

Hannah took note of the fact Bud was not driving his own car, not that it mattered. She decided against taking issue.

"How do you know him?" inquired Bud.

"He's an old neighbor of mine, from before I moved to Santa Barbara."

"Do you see him often?"

"When I first came here. Not much lately." Hannah was curious. How did Hollis look? Was he angry? Why would he stop Bud but not speak to her? There was only so much she could ask without arousing suspicion.

The pair rode in silence: Bud, because he lacked common ground with his glamorous date; Hannah mulled over ways to get more information about Hollis.

Remembering how important this date was to her, Hannah tried to refocus. Work seemed their only common interest. She decided to start there.

"Do you like working at your father's ice cream parlor?"

This was enough to loosen Bud's tongue. In fact, he barely came up for air until he parked at a little café near the beach.

"I thought I'd bring you to my favorite restaurant. The food here is great." Bud's nervous banter continued through dinner. Nothing Hannah said or did seemed to calm the young man. She was relieved when they drove to the movies after dinner. Although it was her longstanding desire to avoid theaters on dates, she hoped Bud might relax if he was off the hook conversationally for an hour or so.

The feature film was *I'm No Angel*, ironically starring Mae West and Cary Grant—their second pairing. Hannah sat perplexed throughout the film. First, it was a long time since she actually watched a movie. Second, Miss West seemed to be playing the same part. There were so many similarities to the original West/Grant movie she saw with Hollis, Hannah began to wonder what became of originality. Was this to be the way of the future? Endless repetition of any character that managed to make a dollar?

The audience seemed more appreciative than Hannah as the theater lights came up. No doubt, the poor girl netting a rich husband proved appealing to a depression-ravaged public.

"That was swell," commented Bud. "Did you like it?"

Afraid to utter her true opinion, Hannah nodded. "It was good."

She found it difficult to pay attention as Bud drove her home. Fortunately, all she needed to do was smile, and nod and he seemed pleased. Bud offered his arm after opening her car door, intent on escorting Hannah to the front door.

"Aren't you afraid, living here all alone?"

"No. I'm used to it."

"But your neighbors are so far down the street. What if you needed help?"

"Well, there's always the telephone." Hannah wondered what Bud would think of the graveyard behind her little house or the fact her neighbors recently tried to have her property condemned. As Bud offered an awkward good night, Hannah made a request.

"I know this seems forward but would you kiss me goodnight?" She found it difficult to keep from laughing. Bud's eyes about popped out of his head. He shyly bent down and gave her a timid but tender kiss on the lips. In the dim light from the porch lamp, she could see Bud's face turn a bright red.

"Good night and thank you for a lovely evening." Hannah turned the knob on her front door and left a clearly smitten Bud standing on the porch, too worked up to utter a parting word.

Chapter Twenty-Two

"It's for you, Hollis. Get your sorry ass out of bed," yelled Dock as he climbed back into his own.

"What? It's the middle of the night. Who is it?"

"Go see for yourself."

Hollis reluctantly climbed from his bed, pulled on a pair of slacks and padded to the front door, scratching his belly absent-mindedly through his t-shirt. He found the landing empty and was about to turn off the porch light when he spied a slight figure seated at the bottom of the staircase. He would recognize the back of that curly head anywhere. What could she be doing here in the middle of the night?

A thrill of hope quickly replaced Hollis' initial flare of anger. Contemplating ways to keep Hannah engaged long enough to plead his case, Hollis retrieved two beers from his fridge and hesitantly descended the staircase. As it turned out, Hannah would be the one doing most of the talking.

"You want a beer?"

"Yes, thank you," replied a calm and rational

Hannah. She accepted the offered beverage and took a sip. She seemed relaxed as she gazed across the garden toward the Oddgood's darkened home.

"What do you want?"

"Here," she handed Hollis an envelope.

"What's this?"

"It's the money I owe you."

Hollis searched for words but only managed, "It's about time. You must be doing well," he added as he thumbed through the bills.

"I assure you, it's all there. I also came to tell you, you were right."

"Say that again," he urged as he took a seat on the step beside Hannah.

"I said you were right."

"Glory be. Have I died and gone to heaven? This can't be happening here on earth. How could I possibly be right about anything?"

"You were right when you advised me to hire Mr. Oddgood. I suppose you know we are partners. I surrendered many of my responsibilities and found real success. There is something else."

"Really? I was right about two things?"

"You were right when you told me dating was a waste of time. You see, I have decided to settle."

"Your evening didn't go as planned?"

"Actually, it was a delight from beginning to end."

"You came here in the middle of the night to gloat?"

"No. You're not listening. This has been an extraordinary and enlightening day. Very bad things happened lately and some good things—besides my date. The fact is, the boy from the soda fountain and I have nothing in common. He is really a boy, not a man.

"I realized I wanted to share my day with you. I

want to tell you all about the good things and the bad things. I can't tell anyone else. Besides, why should I spend time trying to get to know someone when I already know you? You already know me. You know all about me. I am ready to settle."

"I don't understand."

"I think I'm being clear. You once told me you were my ideal husband; that you would never hold anything against me as long as I would share your bed and cook. You promised nothing I did would prove particularly shocking.

"I am here to tell you, I want to share your bed. I want to cook for you and be your wife. I know you will be an amazing father to my children. I want you for my husband. I love you, Hollis." Hannah turned to stare into his eyes, to see if there was any love left in him. Hollis did not appear to have shaved in several days. Hannah never saw him so unkempt. He had a gaunt look. She apparently tested him to his limits. "I know I'm late for the dance but am I too late?"

"Is there a baby? Is that why you came?" Hollis contemplated this possibility over recent months. At best, it would give him a path into Hannah's life. At worst, it would be a source of contention between them forever.

"There is no baby. I'm here because I want you and only you, that is, if you still want me. If you tell me to leave, I give you my word, I will never bother you again. I know you are the one who hears what I say."

"I don't have much choice if I'm going to be able to defend myself. But wanting to tell someone about your day is not a reason to spend your life with them."

"True. But I want to talk to you. I want to share my life with you. I want to be with you and only you. I am, after all, your ideal wife. To be honest, all a woman really wants in a man is someone who can fix the plumbing and the roof; someone who appreciates her cooking and knows how to repair an automobile; someone who can adjust a swimsuit in the middle of an ocean and always has a few dollars stashed away for emergencies.

"I can't promise I won't be difficult on occasion. I'm equally certain you will be difficult quite often. I am prepared to stand toe-to-toe and give you my honest opinion, whether you want it or not. I expect no less from you."

Never would Hollis be able to accurately describe his feelings when he looked back on this moment. Words would never do justice to the ecstasy and relief flooding over him. Yet, he chose to proceed cautiously.

"You have a daunting list of requirements."

"I don't think you have anything to worry about. I'm fairly certain you already demonstrated your ability regarding my prerequisites."

"What about all our problems? What will happen when I have to move away because of work? You don't trust me to tell you the truth. What will happen when we outgrow your house? I might demand you quit working. What happens then?"

"I do trust you, Hollis. I was a fool to believe Lucy over you. I honestly don't understand why I did. She managed to confirm my deepest fears and I fell for it. It was almost as if I was looking for an excuse to call it quits, afraid of the power you have over me, to make me happy or sad. Lucy's lies gave me the excuse I thought I needed. I am truly sorry." She placed her hand under his chin and stroked his jawline with her thumb.

"I can't imagine my future without you. You are the one I want to share my life, be my partner. As for the rest, I am willing to tackle today's problems and leave the rest for tomorrow. Today's troubles are enough to bear. I'm tired of trying to solve difficulties that might never materialize."

"Well then, I have to tell you there has been a bevy of women after me. I don't know what will happen if I break so many hearts at once. Before I begin burning bridges, I need to know if this is a formal proposal."

"It's not the real one. I assure you, when the time comes, I will get down on my knee and make a formal request. Very proper and romantic. Just like yours. Oh, wait. I believe we were naked in my bed when you proposed, despite your similar assurances."

"I think I might be able to find our marriage license. It has been wadded in a ball and thrown in the trash several times. Maybe we can iron it."

"Yes, maybe so. What about Boots?"

"What about her?"

"Do you mind if I keep her?"

"Hannah, I'm hardly going to insist you give up your cat."

"And my wallpaper. I know that's a sticking point."

"In all honesty, I grew fond of your wallpaper."

"Good. Then maybe you won't be bothered by what I did to the living room."

"What did you do?"

"You never minded sitting in the pink chair. I expanded on that theme."

Hollis covered her hand with his. "Will you meet me at the courthouse on Monday morning? Nine o'clock at the Anacapa Street entrance?"

"I will be there, Hollis, if you still love me."

"I never stopped loving you, Short Stuff. I never will."

"Then I have one request."

"What do you need now?"

"I was hoping we might honeymoon briefly on the East Coast, when you are ready."

"Where we would, no doubt, be visiting relatives?"

"Correct."

"And bringing some or all of them home?"

"Possibly. But we will have babies too, Hollis. Lots of babies. As many as God will give us. You have my promise."

"Then we should seal the deal with a kiss, don't you think?"

"I most certainly do." Hannah tipped her head back and closed her eyes, anticipating Hollis' kiss. Instead, he held her chin and watched her eyes come open.

"I don't want you to feel guilty," Hollis declared.

"Why would I?"

"You always have regrets about your actions and feel guilty later. If it took this long for you to be sure about us, then this has been time well spent. No regrets, no guilt."

"No regrets. No guilt. Now kiss me."

* * *

A nervous Hollis spent Sunday trying to find some substitute for the wedding ring he never bought. Even though he didn't expect to find Hannah at the courthouse on Monday and was braced for disappointment, Hollis felt the need to be prepared. He was afraid to delay the wedding for want of a ring.

As he climbed from his car near the courthouse, Hollis patted his vest pocket containing the only thing he managed to find—the toy ring from the Cracker Jacks box Hannah shoved in his pocket on the Ferris wheel. He discovered it in the little dish on his bureau where he kept his cuff links and tie clips. If he managed to coax Miss Granville's vows from her lovely lips, he would buy the ring of her choice.

Hollis was incredulous to find the soon-to-be Mrs. Rumsford waiting patiently. She wore the white lace tea dress they found in the basement of her house, no doubt a nod to her desire to appear a traditional and old-fashioned bride. He realized she would be anything but.

Offering his arm, Hollis, dressed in his best gray suit, escorted Hannah through the courthouse entrance and into their future.

Epilogue

No one had to tell Hollis that Shirley Temple was all the rage. Four-year-old Mazie's dearest possession was her Shirley Temple doll, delivered by Santa last Christmas and purchased by a reluctant Hollis, who was truly appalled at the price tag.

As he sat in the small school auditorium watching what seemed an endless stream of little girls with dreams of movie stardom dancing in their heads, he leaned over and whispered in his wife's ear, "No good can come of this."

"We have been through this, Hollis. There is no reason why our daughter should not have dance lessons," Hannah hissed. "She enjoys the classes and I intend to give our children every advantage, even if you do not. Look, it's her class now."

Hollis clapped politely and spotted his daughter on the far left of the line of tiny hoofers. The girls all sported the curly-headed coiffure of their idol. Only Mazie's brown curls were natural, inherited from her mother. The little girls were all dressed alike: white leotards and tights from dance class, blue satin shorts and red ribbon suspenders. Appropriately, a record player blared *On the Good Ship Lollipop.*

Although the older girls gave amazingly good performances, this troop of young ladies was too immature to remember even a simple series of steps. Hollis was amused when Mazie attempted a turn, became dizzy and wandered toward the side of the improvised stage. As he chuckled, he was sternly admonished by a pinch on his hand.

"Ow! Why did you do that?"

"Don't laugh. You'll hurt her feelings."

"I'm not laughing *at* her. Listen, their class is getting the warmest applause of the afternoon. Mazie was the hit of the whole program. It's not as if this is serious. She's not going to be a movie star or a world-class dancer."

"You don't know what she will be, but I agree, she should not be a movie star."

Hollis' heart leapt with joy as his girl blew kisses at her parents before exiting the stage. He smiled and waved at her. Looking down at Hannah, Hollis could see his wife was fighting back tears, a common enough occurrence. In her condition, emotional outbursts were the order of the day.

"You look uncomfortable. Hand Charlie over here." Hollis held out his arms and urged his two-year-old son onto his lap. "Us men have to stick together," he whispered in the boy's ear, realizing the active Charles Rumsford must be at the end of his ability to sit still. Hollis was surprised when Charlie collapsed against his shoulder.

"Look, all this dancing has done him in," observed Hollis as he put his other arm around his wife, who seemed intent to watch the next performance.

"Hush, Hollis. You're supposed to be a responsible and interested parent. You make more noise than Charlie. I don't know how I put up with you."

Smiling, Hollis indulged in a moment of reflection. However Hannah managed to put up with him, she did it well. As Hannah reached up to touch the hand her husband draped over her shoulder, Hollis spun her wedding ring around her finger, a habit he developed since their marriage. The ring sported small diamonds set into an ornate leaf-patterned design that decorated the circumference of the ring. Hannah claimed since they were never really engaged, she wanted only a wedding band. Hollis considered her choice of the dainty but elegant ring a wise decision, a true symbol of their love and commitment.

Once Hannah finally committed to marriage, she was as true as any wife could possibly be. It was not as if they never fought, far from it, though never in front of their children. But, they belonged to each other in ways he never imagined. They shared their lives completely; they were best friends, confidants, and partners.

Mr. and Mrs. Rumsford started off happily enough when they were alone together in Hannah's little house. Being married in public proved a challenge. First came the difficult Thanksgiving spent in Placerville. Hollis' parents and an array of siblings, spouses, nieces and nephews were in attendance.

Hannah immediately reverted to her persona of mousy attic-dweller, much to Hollis' dismay. He finally coaxed her out of her shell before their return to Santa Barbara by picking a fight while they lunched with his parents.

But that was nothing compared to their "honeymoon" trip to New York for Christmas. They argued interminably about the timing and expense of their trip. Hollis would not be paid for the time they vacationed and was lucky to secure permission to be away from work. Hannah's solution to every financial discussion was her grandmother's money. Yet, they somehow managed to make the trip a success, the first time Mr. Rumsford traveled outside the state of California.

Hollis always smiled when he recalled that particular Christmas morning. Unable to find Hannah, Hollis seated himself at the breakfast table. Even Lucy and her husband were in attendance, having recently returned from their trip to the continent.

Hollis found Lucy's continuous gloating difficult to stomach. He would never forget the look on her face when Hannah appeared at the breakfast table, too excited to be discreet.

She stood behind his chair, put her hand on his shoulder and blurted out, "We're going to have a baby!"

This news proved alarming on many levels. Hollis rose quickly from his chair, almost knocking Hannah over. He grabbed and kissed her inappropriately, then asked her how she came to this sudden realization.

"I threw up!" she replied elatedly, which caused a definite reluctance on Hollis' part to apply further kisses.

"Maybe you should lie down," urged Hollis.

"No! I'm famished!" replied Hannah as she took her seat and eagerly filled her plate.

At this point, Lucy burst into tears; her new husband looked completely disgusted. Mrs. Granville hurried to soothe her eldest daughter's wounded pride. David and Samuel looked uncomfortable, and Jonah, who wanted more than anything to return to California, appeared confused and unhappy. Hannah's grandfather seemed only fascinated with the commotion at his dining table.

Hannah's aunt, who brought Turner and Jessica to the family reunion, was the only member of the family to offer warm congratulations. This definitely served to put her in good stead after having introduced her children to their sister as "cousin Hannah," much to the young Mrs. Rumsford's dissatisfaction.

It was not as if life ran smoothly after this initial rough water. Hollis would admit, he was gone for work more than he liked. Although Hannah's priorities were for their family, she refused to sell her share of the accounting business to Dewie Oddgood, using the excuse Hollis would not spend her money anyway. Hollis often loudly complained all she wanted was to wallow in Dewie's admiration. Hannah saved his finances, not his life, but you would never know it for the praise and veneration Dewie heaped upon her. Hollis was openly jealous of the time his wife spent on her business and the various charitable activities she supported.

Hollis no longer commented on the fact their house was too small for their growing family, even in the rare instances when none of his brothers-in-law resided there. He knew Hannah was cognizant of the problem and imagined she would have to relinquish her stubborn resistance when the new baby came. He planned to patiently bide his time and fantasized about the moment Hannah admitted he was right.

But all-in-all, Hollis' life was everything he ever wanted. He was the head of his household, loving father of the best and most beautiful children on the face of the earth and married to the most fascinating and passionate woman he ever met. Problems seemed to iron themselves out. He was content to enjoy the ride.

As the recital ended, Hollis stood, balancing the

sleeping Charlie on his shoulder, and helped his wife rise from her seat with a modicum of grace.

"Let's get Mazie and go home. Didn't you say we were having fried chicken tonight?"

"That's what your daughter ordered for her special night. I do believe there's a chocolate cake sitting in the back porch."

Hollis smiled delightedly, wondering at his own brilliance in finding the ideal wife.

About the Author

Author Jean Jegel lives with her husband, Carl, in Santa Clarita, a suburb of Los Angeles County. A lifelong Californian dedicated to marriage, raising three children, and working for the Man, Jean now enjoys quilting, gardening, sewing, reading and, of course, writing.

California as it used to be serves as Jean's inspiration and the background for her vintage romantic novels. Love of research is the catalyst for the rich details of historical eras she portrays. Visit jeanjegel.com for book excerpts, giveaway information, Jean's blog and the latest news. Come home to a simpler time and fall in love.

Works by Jean Jegel

Truer Beauty

By Light of Day

A Keepsake Love

Catching Nettie Gordon

A Home on Carroll Avenue

What Money Can't Buy
    Book One—The New Saleslady
    Book Two—Family Ties
    Book Three—Character
    Book Four—Brotherhood
    Book Five—Trust
    Book Six—Love